"STUNNING."

"Like other masters of crime fiction, MacDonald learned his trade by grinding out work for the pulps. . . . MacDonald's early stories can be great fun. They are boldly written, with bright, vivid lines, and move as fast as Tommy gun fire. . . . Each involves an ingenious idea, often with a stunning plot twist at the end."

USA Today

"FASCINATING."

"Like a magician who can do hundreds of fascinating tricks with a single pack of cards, MacDonald has always been a master at fashioning an infinite variety of workable plots from a few basic components. . . . He's an excellent observer, especially in the longer stories, and is able to pass that gift along to his readers. . . . After a few pages you're almost always hooked."

The Washington Post

"EXCELLENT, ENTERTAINING."

"MacDonald's stories transcend the genre because of his psychological depth, knowledge of people and keen perceptions of character. All of these stories are excellent, entertaining."

The Miami Herald

MORE GOOD OLD STUFF

John D. MacDonald

FAWCETT GOLD MEDAL • NEW YORK

A Fawcett Gold Medal Book
Published by Ballantine Books
Copyright © 1984 by John D. MacDonald Publishing, Inc.

Library of Congress Catalog Card Number: 84-47643

ISBN 0-449-12765-6

This edition published by arrangement with Alfred A. Knopf,
Inc.

These stories have been previously published in the following periodicals: *Black Mask, Crack Detective, Doc Savage,
Detective Story Magazine, Detective Tales, Dime Detective, Mystery Book Magazine, The Shadow,* and *New
Detective.*

Manufactured in the United States of America

First Ballantine Books Edition: August 1985

Contents

Author's Foreword

IN THE FOREWORD to *The Good Old Stuff* I explained how Martin H. Greenberg and Francis M. Nevins, aficionados of the pulp mystery story, had proposed a collection be made of my old pulp stories, how I had reacted—flattered, hesitant and dubious—and how they, with the invaluable aid of Jean and Walter Shine, had gone through the hundreds of my stories published during the nineteen forties and fifties, and weeded the list down to thirty.

When I reread the thirty I was pleasantly surprised to find that twenty-seven of the thirty seemed to merit revival. A book with all twenty-seven would have been too long and hefty, so I divided them into two groups, trying to keep the quality of both groups in balance.

The Good Old Stuff was published by Harper & Row in 1982, and the paperback edition was published by Fawcett in November 1983. It has done far better in the market-place than any of us expected. In September 1983, Collins, Ltd., purchased the rights to publish in Britain, and possibly Pan Books will bring out a paperback edition as well.

In my foreword to *The Good Old Stuff* I explained that I had resisted the temptation to edit the florid patches of prose, but had taken the liberty of updating such mechanical matters as taxi fares, pay scales, phone procedures and the price of a drink in those stories which did not depend upon the particular year in which they were placed to achieve their effect. Also, I took the liberty of changing those words in common usage which over the years have acquired a flavor I did not intend. "Gay" is an example of one of these unfortunate changes.

I received a few score letters of objection, saying that I should have left these period pieces alone. I still do not think so. I want my stories to entertain. If a story captures and entertains a reader, one certain way of breaking the spell is to make him conscious of the fact that he is reading a story. If the hero rushes into a candy store and puts a nickel in a pay phone, it jars. If he buys a quart of milk for twenty cents, the spell is broken.

Had these stories been written a hundred years ago it would perhaps be a sin against history to update them in this fashion. But the events of these stories are in a past so recent they could just as well have been written today. And that is a portion of my intent, to show how little the world really changes.

Some of the stories—for example, "Death for Sale" —could not be pulled forward into the present time, and so it was left relatively unaltered, though I must confess I was tempted to clean up some of the very stilted dialogue, and I wanted to invent a more plausible gimmick than the cigarette lighter in the purse. Also, the relationship between the hero and the woman is too cute-trite at the end. I would handle it very differently today. But it would be unfair to excise the warts to make myself look better than I was.

"Secret Stain" is another period piece that could not be reasonably updated, as it dealt with the numbers racket the way it used to be set up, with the stitched, tear-off tickets, the candy store outlets.

I decided it would be best to leave "The Night Is Over" back in 1947, when it was written, because the chronology gives an almost adequate reason for the protagonist's bleakness and despair. This is one of the two longest, and perhaps one of the clumsiest, because in my early innocence I handicapped myself by making the motivations unreal.

"Neighborly Interest" is an example of how I updated the stories which could have taken place today or tomorrow. I turned a 1938 Plymouth into a 1968 Plymouth. I increased a $150,000 ransom to $400,000. But while I was at it, I changed the name of one of the three lead characters. In the original 1949 story they were Stan, Steve and Art. In those days I was careless about unnecessarily confusing the reader. So they have become Stan, Howie and Art.

I have used the same device with the titles as was used in *The Good Old Stuff*. My original title is the one used on each story. The table of contents gives the magazine editor's title in parentheses whenever my title was changed, along with the name of the magazine and the date of publication.

I am grateful to the four editors who presented me with this project, Greenberg, Nevins and the Shines, and I wish to assure them and you, kindly reader, that there will be no additional versions of *More Good Old Stuff*. This is the end of the mother lode.

Deadly Damsel

WHEN SHE HAD awakened that morning, she had looked at her husband in the other bed. Howard's slack mouth was open, there was a stubble of beard on his chin and he was puffy under the eyes. It was at that moment she realized how bored she was.

Howard Goodkin bored her and so did the little city of Wanderloo, Ohio. As had happened so many times before, the plot and lines and scenery failed to wear well.

When he came down to breakfast she kissed him warmly, smiled up into his eyes—and wondered if he should be buried in the blue suit or the gray one.

The gray would go with his eyes, she decided. The gray suit and one of the new white shirts and the blue silk tie with the tiny pattern of white triangles. While she talked casually with him about the weather, the state of the flower garden and the leaking faucet in the upstairs bathroom, she mentally decided on the Gortzen Funeral Home. They seemed to do the best job. Mrs. Hall had looked so lifelike. She thought of it all, and she could almost hear the soft music, the sonorous words of the service. She wanted to hug herself with excitement.

Finally Howard stood up, patted his mouth with the napkin, leaned over to kiss her good-by and left. She stood at the window and waved to him, wondering how much she would get for the year-old car. She decided that she'd try to get seventeen hundred.

She hummed to herself as she finished up the breakfast dishes. The house was pleasantly warm. She kicked off her slippers and walked through the dim rooms of the pleasant house.

When she passed the full-length mirror in the hall, she jumped. Then she smiled at her own foolishness.

She stood near the mirror and looked at herself. She thought it was odd how young her figure remained. Absurd the way it was still the figure of a young girl. She frowned as she tried to remember her true age. Forty? No. Born in 1908 in Wilmington. That would make it forty-one. Howard thought she was thirty-two. She was a small woman with an erect carriage, shapely legs, a tiny waist. There was no trace of gray in her rich brown hair, and her large eyes were a pleasant deep blue, almost a lavender.

She assumed the exaggerated pose of a model, then laughed at herself with her voice of throaty silver and tripped prettily up the stairs. She took the heavy suitcase from the back of the closet, lugged it out into the room.

With a needle, she picked the stitches out of a place where the lining had been ripped and mended. Reaching through the rent, she pulled out the heavy packet, took it over to the bed and opened it with excited fingers. The packet contained three envelopes. That was the secret. To be systematic.

The first envelope contained small pictures of varied sizes. Five of them. Five pictures of five men. On the back of each picture, in neat, dainty printing, were a few facts. The name of the man. The city or town where they had lived. The name she had used each time. A guarded phrase to indicate the manner of death. A tiny figure to indicate the net gain, in thousands, by his death.

Humming once more, she went to her bureau drawer, took out the small picture of Howard Goodkin, took it back to the bed along with her silver fountain pen. Resting the picture face down, she printed certain facts neatly on the back of it.

2

She put it in the envelope with the other pictures. In the second envelope was a listing of several Chicago banks. Following the name of each bank was the name she had used to open the safety-deposit box, and a statement of the amount of cash in each box.

The third envelope contained the keys to the boxes, each one carefully tagged. On the back of each tag was the date when the box rent would be due. In the beginning she had paid ten years' rent in advance, and each box had been renewed through the payment of a second ten years' rental.

She sat on the bed and thought of the wonderful massive vaults, the tightly locked boxes, the neat bundles of cash in each box. A great deal of cash. An enormous amount, she thought, considering the ease with which it had been obtained.

She replaced the packet in the suitcase under the lining, repaired the rent with clean, tiny stitches.

Already there was great delight in thinking ahead to the wreath on the door, the neighbors bringing baked things, the quiet words of comfort. It was so easy to cry when they spoke to her—so easy to play the part of the stricken widow.

Then, after several months of wearing black had gone by and she had begun to tire of her practiced role of widow, she would go to a few selected friends, the ones who would talk, and she would explain how she could no longer remain there where her memories of Howard were so clear and so sharp. She would sell everything and go away. Some letters, a few postcards—and then silence.

They would forget. They always did. Then she would be ready for a new little city, a new man, a new background, carefully memorized so that there would be no slip-up. The eternal delightful gambit of courtship, marriage, setting up a home and making friends. Then, in a year or two—death. It always ended in death.

To be such a friend of death gave her a feeling of power that she bore with her wherever she went. She looked on the dull, tidy little lives of the women in the

3

small cities in which she lived, and she felt like a goddess. She could write all manner of things on the black slate of life, and then, with one gesture, wipe the slate clean and begin all over again. New words, new love, new tenderness and a new manner of death.

She had read of stupid women who poisoned one husband after another. That was the most spectacular stupidity. Through such methods the police were enabled to establish pattern. No, murder, to be successful, must be done with infinite variety—and in ways that could not be connected with the heartbroken little woman who sobbed out her grief to the coroner and to the police.

Whenever she read articles which proclaimed that there was no such thing as a perfect murder, she laughed inside. She sat and laughed without any change of facial expression. And inside of her she felt a glow of triumph.

It was good to kill men. Only one thing sometimes bothered her. To get such joy out of killing men must indicate some psychotic condition. She was a well-read woman, but it was not until after the fourth death that she managed to connect her joy with that half-forgotten incident in the woods near her home when she had been fourteen.

The man had caught her by the wrist, reaching out from beyond a patch of brush as she walked slowly by. He was ragged and he stank of liquor and his filthy hand had muffled her screams.

Sometimes she would wake up in the night and once again feel the hand pressing on her lips.

They had sent him to jail. Shortly after that both of her parents died. As she had looked on their faces she had thought that they were dead and yet that horrible man still lived.

It bothered her that her hatred of men had to be based on a particular incident. She would rather it had been hatred without apparent cause, because it would have seemed cleaner that way.

She married at seventeen. A boy named Albert Gordon. After the first week with him, she knew that one day she

would kill him. In killing him she would somehow be
exacting her just vengeance.

She married him under her own name—Alicia Bowie.
For two years she planned. For two years she endured
him, and got delight out of being able to successfully
play the part of the happy bride.

Two days after her nineteenth birthday, the papers
announced that tragic death of Albert Gordon while on a
swimming picnic with his young wife at Lake Hobart.
According to the newspaper accounts, Albert Gordon
had dived from the high limb of a tree and had mis-
judged the depth of the water.

She could still remember exactly how it was. The
late-afternoon sun slanting across the water. Albert was
near her, waist deep in water, looking out across the
lake. The tree was above them. She had fumbled on the
rocky bottom, found a loose boulder of about ten pounds'
weight. She had held it poised. The shore dropped steeply,
and the water, while up to his waist, lapped gently
around her legs. She had brought it down on the top of
his head. Some of Albert's blond hair adhered to the
rock. She had carefully placed the rock in three feet of
water under the limb of the tree, bloody side up. That's
where they had found it.

With Albert's insurance, she had moved eight hundred miles away. She had changed her name. She had
established the pattern.

Now she got up from the bed, showered, put on a
crisp cotton dress and raised the shades, filling the house
with sunshine. As she listened with part of her mind to a
morning radio program, another part, a cold mechanical
part, was weighing, discarding, considering alternate methods of accomplishing the sudden death of Howard
Goodkin, successful manager of a chain of grocery stores
in and around Wanderloo, Ohio.

By lunchtime she had cut the feasible methods down
to two. Neither of them duplicated any of the previous
murder methods. Both of them were carefully selected
to fit the habits of Howard Goodkin.

Howard came in for lunch, smiling. He kissed her,

patted her affectionately and said, "Anything exciting happen this morning?"

I decided to kill you, Howard. "Not a thing, darling. That dog across the street chased the Robinsons' cat up into our maple tree and Betty was standing around wringing her hands. When she was about to call the firemen, the dog went away and the cat came down. When she picked it up, it scratched her wrist."

Howard grinned, his eyes crinkling pleasantly. "Big morning, huh?"

It won't be hard to weep for you, Howard. In many ways you're quite nice. "A nice, quiet morning, darling. Is the salad all right?"

"Wonderful, honey! I love it with onion."

Cristofer, Florida, was a small, inland town, sleepy in the hot sun. Because it was not near the sea, the prices at the tourist courts, shabby hotels and cabins were low. Many old people came to Cristofer to live out what remained of their lives. The men, their work-gnarled hands resting on their thin thighs, dozed in the sun. The buxom and indestructible old ladies lifted shrill voices throughout the endless days and the monotony of the sun.

Ben Lawton, wearing ragged khaki shorts, his bronzed back knotted with muscle, trudged with the wheelbarrow down to where the truck had dumped the load of small, gleaming white shells, filled the wheelbarrow and pushed it back up the slope to the Komfort Court— Cabins by the Season—Reasonable Rates.

There had been a time, just before the war, when Ben Lawton had sat behind a blond streamlined desk in a New York office. His novel sales promotion ideas had caught on, and he was looking forward to a great deal of money.

In the middle of 1947 Benjamin G. Lawton had been released from the Veterans Hospital. The parting words from the resident psychiatrist had been: "Emotionally, Lawton, you're not able to resume your prewar activities. We recommend some quiet and isolated spot—manual labor—no worries. Any sort of tension will tie you in knots that we may not be able to untie. Maybe, some-day . . .''

And so Ben Lawton had ended up doing manual labor for Jonas Bright, proprietor of the Komfort Court. After more than a year, Ben thought of the outside world with a fear that chilled him through.

The Komfort Court consisted of sixteen two-room cabins. Jonas Bright, a semi-paralytic, was a blunt, gruff but fair employer. Ben took care of maintenance and the odd jobs that came up. Serena Bright cleaned the cabins, replaced the sheets, towels, pillowcases. She was the nineteen-year-old motherless daughter of Jonas.

Ben jammed the shovel into the barrowload of white shells, spread them along the path to Cabin 8. He straightened up for a moment, watched Serena carrying fresh sheets over to Cabin 11. It was only while watching Serena that Ben felt as though he were coming alive once more. Whenever he thought of Serena, whenever he watched her tall, slim, young figure, her proud walk, her warm strength, he thought of how wonderful it would be to take her to the New York shops he knew so well, to have the clever clerks transform her back-country charm into a city splendor that would halt the casual male in his tracks.

In spite of Serena's lack of advantages, lack of breeding and education, there was a fine sensitivity about her, an alert awareness of her surroundings.

He watched her, saw how the thin cotton dress clung to the lines of her body. When the screen door of the cabin slammed behind her, he sighed, returned to his work.

He knew that he had no chance with Serena. She had looked too long and too often on the gilded faces on the Bijou screen, and on the sleek automobiles, the shining clubs and bars. A subdued, solemn psycho case, a man fresh out of a PN hospital, held no charms for her. Sure, she would laugh and joke with him, but always he saw that faint withdrawal in her eyes, and sensed that she was saving herself for someone who could give her the things she read about and saw in the movies.

Jonas Bright was pathetically proud of his daughter.

By the time Ben had worked his way down to the walk that led up to Cabin 11, Serena came out, perspiration beaded on her upper lip.

"Don't hit me, Ben," she said, "if I ask you if it's hot enough for you."

"If you were standing closer, I'd hit you, honey," he said, grinning.

"Phoo!" she said, sticking her underlip out, blowing a wisp of silverblond hair away from her forehead. Every visible area of her was honey brown.

"Tonight," he said, "would seem to be a good night for you to walk a half mile with me and drink beer which I can barely afford. Okay?"

There had been many evenings like that. Gay and happy evenings, with lots of laughter and no hint of emotional entanglements.

There was a hint of amusement in her soft brown eyes. "Laddie," she said, "you are talking to a girl who has better plans. Mr. Kelso is taking this kid to the Palm Club."

Ben was surprised at the amount of annoyance he felt. "Works fast, doesn't he?"

"He's a perfect gentleman!" she snapped.

"He's a perfect phony!" Ben said angrily.

She lifted her chin, gave him a cool stare and said, "And how would you know, Lawton? You've never traveled in his league."

She pushed by him, carrying the laundry down to the main building to be picked up by the truck. He watched her go, saw the indignation that she managed to express with each step.

For a moment he was tempted to call her, to tell her that Jay Kelso could never have made the league that he once traveled in. But he had never talked of his past to the Brights, and this was no time to start. Probably she wouldn't believe him anyway.

He wheeled the barrow down toward the pile of shells.

He frowned as he thought of Jay Kelso. The man had arrived in a flashy convertible some three days before, had rented Cabin 3 for an indefinite period.

It was impossible to guess what his business was. To Ben Lawton, Kelso looked like a racetrack tout who had cut himself a piece of a killing. He wore loose-weave sports shirts in pearl gray, lemon yellow and powder blue. His neckties were knotted into great bulky triangular knots. His luggage was of shining aluminum. His faun and pearl slacks were knife-edged, and his sports shoes were obviously elevators.

His face was thin, with a deep tan over the sallowness, dark hair pompadoured with a greasy fixative, his facial expression a carefully trained imitation of a movie tough guy.

He carried his wad of bills in a gold money clip, and he went out of his way to adopt an air of patronizing friendliness with Jonas, Serena and Ben. He ignored the other tenants, and his every action said, "I'm one hell of a smart and pleasant guy. I know all the angles and I'm giving you people a break just by being around. See?"

Ben had seen Jay Kelso practically lick his lips the first afternoon when Serena had walked by. The program was clear. With Kelso's motives and Serena's ambition to be a city girl, the end result seemed more than obvious.

Ben wondered how much longer Jonas Bright would be able to be proud of his daughter. . . .

The sun was low by the time Ben Lawton had finished his work. He took the barrow and shovel to the toolhouse, walked slowly down to his room in the west wing of the main building. Business was slow. He saw that Tommy, the boy, was pumping gas into a big car covered with road dust. The tourists from the car were in at the counter, and Beth Bronson, the fat high school girl, was serving them Cokes.

He took a long shower to clean off the dust and sweat. When he turned his shower off he heard the roar of the shower on the other side of the thin partition, in the portion where Jonas and Serena lived. He guessed that

Serena was getting ready for her date. He changed to white slacks and a T-shirt and went to his front door, sat on the concrete step and lighted a cigarette.

Within ten minutes Jay Kelso came wheeling down in his canary convertible, parked near the pumps and bleated the horn. Serena came hurrying out in a matter of seconds. Her linen suit was a bit too short and a shade tight across the shoulders. She climbed into the car and Kelso reached across her, pulled the door shut. He roared it out onto the highway in a cloud of dust. Ben saw the setting sun brighten her fair head, Kelso's dark one—and the two heads were close together.

He sighed and stood up.

Jonas was beside him. Jonas spat, the brown tobacco juice slapping into the dusk. He said softly, "She's too old to give orders to, Ben."

Not believing his own words, Ben said, "She's smart enough to find out for herself."

Jonas sighed. "I hope so. I surely hope so." He turned and limped dejectedly away.

The investigator looked so much like a depressed bloodhound that she wanted to laugh at him. But of course that would be a silly thing to do. The room was darkened and he sat across from her, obviously ill at ease. The tiny wadded handkerchief was damp in her palm. She inhaled, a long, shuddering sound, and mopped at her eyes with the handkerchief.

"I know how tough this is for you, Mrs. Goodkin, but we just have to ask these questions so that our reports'll be complete. You understand, don't you?"

"I understand," she said in a small, weak voice.

"It was Howard's practice to do minor repairs on the car?"

"Yes, it was. He was always doing something or other to it. He loved to—to get all greasy, and he said that he was saving money by doing things himself. He always said he—he should have been a mechanic."

"And then yesterday afternoon, after he finished work, he went right to the garage?"

"Yes. I remember he said something about repacking the rear wheels and adjusting the rear shocks, whatever that means, Mr. Brown."

Mr. Brown sighed. "Well, it's a pretty clear case. He jacked the car up and took off both rear wheels and blocked the axle with bricks. It was a damn fool thing to do. Probably when he was tightening a nut or something, he moved it enough off balance so that it—"

She suddenly covered her face with her hands and sobbed hoarsely. In a matter of seconds, she felt his heavy hand on her shoulder, patting her gently.

"There, there, Mrs. Goodkin," he said. "Sorry I had to upset you this way. Howard wasn't in any pain. He never felt a thing. That differential came right down and killed him instantly."

As she sobbed, as she felt his comforting arms around her, she relived those few moments in the garage. She had bent over, looked under the car, said, "How are you doing, honey?"

His face was smeared with grease. "Just about another twenty minutes ought to do it."

He was in the right position, his face under the bulge of the differential. She had straightened up, walked to the side of the car, picked up a dust rag, used it to shield her hands as she pushed the car with all her strength.

It had swayed and the bricks had cracked in warning. Howard had given one startled gasp as the car had come down heavily.

Screaming wildly, she had run out into the street. As soon as she was certain that neighbors were running toward her, she had slowly and gracefully collapsed in a mock faint.

Yes, this one had been smoother than most of them. Less questioning. She could leave sooner, cover her tracks, go to some quiet resort place and start over again.

Seventeen hundred for the car and at least twelve thousand for the house. Counting incidentals and insurance, you could figure on twenty-six thousand after all expenses.

11

Through her sobs she said, "Mr. Brown, I—I can't stay here. The—the memories. I won't be able—to stand it."

"I understand," he whispered. "We'll all understand."

Mr. Davis, the vice-president of the Wanderloo National Bank, coughed a few times and said, "This is—well, it's rather a large sum of money for a woman to take away in cash, you know. We could establish a trust for you and send you the income every—"

She lifted her chin bravely. "Mr. Davis, I'm sorry, but I want to cut all strings tying me to Wanderloo. If you'd authorize the cashier to give me the cash balance—"

"Possibly traveler's checks, Mrs. Goodkin?"

"No one but you and the cashier and myself will know I'm taking that amount of cash with me. And I certainly don't plan to advertise it. If you must know, Mr. Davis, I plan to pin the major share of it inside my girdle. I rather imagine it will be safe there until I decide where I want to settle."

Mr. Davis blushed, scratched his chin and sighed. "How do you want it, Mrs. Goodkin?" he said, standing up.

"Twenty one-thousand-dollar bills and the balance in fifties, hundreds and twenties."

"I may have to contact the other two banks."

She glanced at her watch. "Please hurry. My train leaves in an hour and fifteen minutes."

With the money on her person, she bought her ticket to Detroit. She carried one suitcase containing her best clothes and the all-important packet. In Detroit she could shake off any possible pursuit and then take a train to Chicago. The large bills would go into one of the four boxes. The remaining four thousand and something would give her a new start with a new name in a new place. Resort places were best.

She decided that this time she would look for a younger man. They felt so flattered when an older woman became interested.

The trip from Chicago to whatever resort she decided

on could be used in devising a new name and new background. A new identity was the easiest thing in the world to establish. It was merely a case of arranging to take out a driver's license, opening a checking account and a few charge accounts.

She would be forgotten in Wanderloo. "I wonder what happened to that sweet little Mrs. Goodkin. She left town, you know, after her husband died. Tragic affair. They had a perfect marriage. A good thing there were no children, you know."

As she waited for her train to be announced, she looked at herself in the oval mirror in her compact. The off-lavender eyes stared back at her with clarity—innocence—and an uncanny youthfulness. It was good to be free again. Free for adventure . . .

Jay Kelso sat like a scrawny Buddha in his bed, clad only in blue silk shorts that were too big for him. The afternoon was hot and he was bored and troubled. A pair of faun slacks were slung over the back of a straight chair not far from the bed. He knew without looking that there was but forty-two dollars in the gold money clip in the pocket of the slacks.

He had intended to stay a week in this hole called Komfort Court, but the week had turned into six weeks. That was bad.

By now the finance company in New Jersey would have turned the license number over to the skip tracers and they would be hunting the yellow wagon. He knew from experience that his equity was just large enough so that they would enjoy repossessing the wagon.

And maybe that Myra dish in Camden had hired lawyers. That would be bad, because they could make trouble and he didn't have the money to buy the legal talent to squeak out of it. He had always felt wonderfully independent of the female sex.

And here he was stuck in inland Florida just because a hick babe was keeping him on the hook.

He wondered if he should run out, make some dough and come back this way for a second attempt. No, that tan bruiser, Lawton, had too eager a look in his eye when Serena—what a hell of a name—walked by. It would be a sad thing to come back and find that Lawton had nailed her on the rebound.

He knew that the longer he stayed, the worse shape he would be in. He knew that already his stake was too small.

He smacked his fist into his palm and glared at the far wall. Suddenly a startling thought entered his mind. Maybe he wanted to marry the girl.

Maybe that was the right deal. Unload the car. Sell it for cash. Then ease that Lawton punk out of his job and settle down right here. After the old man kicked off, which shouldn't be long, he and Serena would own the business. Then if he got sick of her, he could sell and shove off.

But he remembered how the muscles stood out on Lawton's back while he worked. No, better keep Lawton around for the heavy stuff. Besides, it might be too tough to ease him out. He and the old man seemed to get along pretty good.

He grinned. Jay Kelso—thinking of marriage. That was a hot one!

Slowly he got off the bed. He put on a sand-pink sports shirt, carefully knotted the white and crimson tie, belted the high-waisted faun slacks around his trim, flat middle and slipped into a pair of brown-and-white moccasins.

At that moment there was a knock on his door. A gentle knock. Eagerly he opened the door, hoping that it was Serena Bright. Instead he saw Lawton's bronzed broad chest, impassive face.

"After the trash," Lawton said.

"Hell, you knock like a woman," Jay Kelso said, turning away in disgust.

"Thought you might open quicker if I did," Lawton said gently.

Kelso wheeled on him. "Are you being wise?"

Lawton smiled tightly. "I wonder exactly what you'd do if I said yes."

14

Kelso straightened his shoulders. "I might take a poke at you. I was Golden Gloves, guy. Remember that."

Lawton grinned lazily and said, "Yes, sir. Anything you say, sir." The contempt was obvious.

At that moment a small woman stepped to the doorway. Jay Kelso gave her a quick appraisal. Not too bad for a biddy in her middle thirties. Nicely stacked. Wearing a dress that spells dough. No gray in the brown hair. Funny color of blue for eyes. Not bad at all, at all.

She smiled at Kelso, turned to Lawton and said, in a voice of throaty silver, "You are the man that works here, aren't you?"

"Yes, Mrs. Oliver."

"I just moved into Cabin 11 an hour ago, and I can't seem to get any hot water. I wonder if you'd—"

"Right away, Mrs. Oliver."

Jay Kelso noted the "Mrs." But there had been more than casual politeness in those odd blue eyes. Maybe a chance to chisel a little money. Badger game in reverse. A "loan," please. You can lend it to me, or I can ask Mr. Oliver for it.

With his best smile, he stepped forward, extending his hand, and said, "As long as we're almost neighbors, Mrs. Oliver, we might as well know each other. I'm Jay Kelso."

"How do you do, Jay Kelso," she said, dimpling. "I'm Betty Oliver."

Her hand was very soft in his, and lay passive, warm, giving him an oddly protective feeling. Also, it was nice that she was short. He liked short women. Even with the trick shoes, he was only about a half inch taller than Serena.

Lawton carried out the trash and went up toward Cabin 11.

Jay Kelso sauntered out, said to Mrs. Oliver, "How do you and your husband like it here?"

"Oh, there's just me, Mr. Kelso. George died over a year ago." She laughed softly. "I guess I'm just a footloose, lonesome woman."

He beamed at her. "Footloose, yes. Lonesome, never."

15

"And I thought courtliness was dead!" She laughed. "We must get better acquainted."

"We certainly shall," he said warmly.

"Is your wife with you, Mr. Kelso?" she asked.

"I'm the footloose, lonesome type too." he said, "Yes, I'm on a little vacation all by myself. I'm in the—real estate business in Camden, New Jersey. I got pretty tensed up over a few fair deals I pulled lately and decided I needed a rest."

He laughed. "I told my employees when I left that they'd better make all decisions themselves because they wouldn't be in touch with me at all. At first I thought I'd go to my usual hotel at Miami Beach, but then I realized that I'd run into friends and there'd be parties and all that sort of thing. So you might say I'm hiding here."

He strolled casually over to the canary convertible, leaned on the door.

"Is this your car?" Mrs. Betty Oliver asked. "It's pretty."

Jay coughed. "This is the one I brought along."

"I've never learned to drive," she said wistfully. "I'm really a helpless woman."

"If you're staying long enough, I could teach you."

She looked up into his face, swayed so that for a moment she brushed against him. "Oh, would you?"

Jay Kelso was suddenly faintly dizzy and very exultant. This was pie in the sky. This was coin in the pocket. It wouldn't be too tough to fix it with Serena. Milk this doll for a few hundred or a few thousand, and then grab Serena and kite off to a license bureau. From there he and Serena could hit the tracks. By the time they came back the Oliver woman would be gone. Perfect!

When the last sobs were finished, Serena waited, the damp pillow against her face. It was dark outside. On the highway an occasional car roared by at high speed. The headlights made patterns that flashed across the ceiling of her darkened room.

After a time she stood up, padded into the bathroom, stepped into the shower stall. The chill water felt fresh

16

and good. She made up carefully to conceal the signs of tears, put on a cool white dress, walked out into the warm night. The sound of laughter from some of the cabins accentuated her loneliness.

In Cabin 2 four old people were engaged in their nightly bridge game. A radio was playing a sweet, sad tune from a distant cabin. Far off, near the marshes, the frogs croaked dolorously.

The cool breeze stirred her pale hair. She tried not to look up the slope toward Cabin 11. Of course, that woman, that Oliver woman, wasn't there. No, she was out with Jay. Out with Serena's Jay. Probably at their spot—at the Palm Club.

She wondered bitterly if Jay would park with her, would try to kiss her. How could he? Why, that Oliver woman was old, old, old. A hag. A simpering, silly hag with a lot of money.

She wondered how many hours Jay had spent with the Oliver woman since she had arrived four days before.

Jay had acted so funny. He had taken her out for the last time the same evening that Betty Oliver had arrived. He had been quiet at the Palm Club. Later on, in the parked car, he had made no attempt to kiss her—had merely said, "Serena, honey, there are a lot of things about this world that you don't understand."

"What do you mean?"

"Look, baby. I love you. That's the first time I've said those words since I was fourteen."

"Oh, Jay."

"Now don't go soft on me. Understand? Love means trust. Look, baby. Look into my eyes. I trust you. See? Now, the sixty-four-buck question is, does Serena trust Jay?"

"You know I do."

"Now, here's the kicker. I got my own angles, see? I can't talk about them. And I don't want you to talk to anybody about what is going to happen."

"But what is going to happen, Jay?"

"You and I are having a fight. We don't talk anymore. We don't go out anymore for maybe a long time. You are going to see me running around with that Mrs. Oliver that checked in today. But you don't ask any questions. You trust me. Remember?"

"But, Jay, I—why do you—"

He had touched one finger to her lips. "No questions, baby. Then after maybe a week, maybe two, maybe longer, we move fast. I ask you the ring question and you say yes and off we go. Right?"

"But I—"

She had seen the gleam of his teeth as he smiled in the darkness. "Look, baby, it's a wonderful night. Come here."

Yes, it had been easy right then not to ask questions. But the next day it wasn't so easy. Not when she had seen the yellow car head out with Betty Oliver's brown head next to Jay's shining dark one. It hadn't been easy to see Betty wriggling kittenishly, smiling up into Jay's shining smug face. Nor had it been easy to hear their merged laughter, their warm friendliness.

And on the third day she had walked by the two of them, had heard Betty Oliver giggle and whisper to Jay. Jay had laughed also. Serena Bright knew that they had talked about her.

She strolled aimlessly down the narrow street between the cabins, avoided the glare of the floodlights that lit the front of the main building. She circled the left wing of the building, saw the pale gleam of Ben Lawton's white shirt in the darkness. He was sitting on the concrete step at his doorway.

"Hi, lady," he said softly. "Sit down and smoke up one of my hard-earned cigarettes."

"Thanks, Ben," she said gratefully. He moved over to make room. She glanced at his face as he held the match to her cigarette, and she detected no expression that she could identify.

"Nice night," he said.

"I guess so."

"Little bit blue, gal?" he asked.

It was too much. She buried her head in his shoulder. "Oh, Ben!" Then great, hoarse sobs shook her.

But they didn't last long. Finally she moved back to her side of the step, dabbed at her eyes with a handkerchief. She laughed thinly. "Sorry to use you for a crying towel, Benjamin."

"The guy isn't worth it, you know. Not by half," he said flatly.

In cold rage she stood up. "I'll be the judge of that," she snapped.

She walked off into the night. But the night was lonesome. The sky was an immeasurable distance away and she felt small, futile, purposeless. Everything seemed to be going wrong. If only Jay could send her a note, or glance at her, or arrange to speak to her. But every time he looked in her direction his face was cold and his eyes were hard.

She wandered into the part where the tables and soda fountain were. Jonas Bright sat in a wooden rocker, his shoulders slumped.

He smiled up at her and said, "I'm sure glad, honey, that you aren't running around with that fancy-clothes fella anymore."

She glared at him for several seconds and then walked aimlessly out into the night. Ben and her dad were fools, both of them. In some funny way they were jealous of Jay Kelso. Jealous because his clothes were nice and he had nice manners and was a perfect gentleman. And his dark eyelashes were long. And his lips were hard and demanding. She felt a deep warm tumult inside her as she thought of his lips and his arms.

Then like an angry child, she bent over, picked up a stone and hurled it out across the highway. She remembered all the bad words she had ever overheard, and she said them under her breath. She went back to her room and stretched out across her bed, her chin propped in her palms. What could he be thinking of, going out with that hag? That silly, simpering hag!

The feeling of excitement had been growing for a full week, and this time there was something completely different about it. She had fallen so completely into her

19

assumed part that she really thought she was Betty Oliver.

She looked at Jay. He was cupping his hands around the flame from his lighter, and the orange-red light threw his cheekbones into sharp relief, deepened the hollows in his cheeks.

Yes, Jay Kelso had created a puzzle. Not in himself, because she knew all too well exactly what Jay Kelso was. She had seen many of them. Flagrant little men strutting around in gay plumage, hard and selfish, unbelievably greedy and cruel. A most despicable little man. Yet there was something so pathetic about his swaggering and his strutting, something so forlornly second-rate about his tin-plate veneer, that he oddly touched her heart, as no man ever had.

A plucked little chicken of a man trying to be masterful, sophisticated. His clothes were in horrid taste, she knew. His manners were frightfully obvious. And he was full of a deadly seriousness as far as using proper English was concerned.

All in all, a very amusing little man. And obvious. She guessed from the way he licked his lips when he had to pay a check that he was close to the end of his small hoard of money. And pretending to be such a big shot.

Such a second-rate little person should have revolted her, she knew. And yet she wanted to cradle his head in her arms, hold him close and soothe him—tell him that she knew the wide world and he could cease his frantic struggling that got him nowhere.

She wondered if it could be some misshapen form of love.

He must be at least thirteen years younger than I, she thought. At least. Maybe more.

She smiled in the darkness. Jay Kelso had been quiet for a long time. She knew that he was going over in his mind the words he had planned.

Abruptly he laughed. "A pretty funny thing has happened to me, Betty," he said, a nervous note in his voice.

"Yes, Jay, dear?"

20

"You remember I told you how I was having my employees make their own decisions while I was gone? Well, I got a letter yesterday from the man I left in charge. He has my power of attorney. He got a line on a big deal and sunk all the working capital into it. I didn't bring along as much as I should. I was wondering if you'd trust me with a little until I got word that the deal has gone through and the bank account is back to where it should be."

"Why, of course, Jay! How much do you need?"

"Oh, a few hundred ought to carry me over all right."

"Will five hundred do?" She grinned inwardly as she saw him suck hungrily on his cigarette.

"Fine. That is, if it won't put you out."

She knew how it would work. He would take the five hundred and be very attentive and spend quite a bit of it on her—and then he would come to her, very excited and yelling about the big deal that his man in charge was pulling off, only they needed just a few more thousand to grab the property options necessary. Just a few thousand. And then she'd never see Jay Kelso again.

She said, laughing, "Goodness, Jay. You've kept me so busy that I haven't gotten around to opening up a bank account down here. I'm carrying far too much cash on me. You might as well take the five hundred right now. Hold your lighter over here so I can see into my purse."

It was sort of a nasty little trick to play on him, she thought. She unsnapped the white leather purse, held it so that Jay couldn't help seeing it. She held open the red leather wallet, fingered off four hundreds and two fifties, crumpled them and handed them to him. "Here you are, Jay, dear," she said casually.

His hand shook as he snapped off the lighter. Hoarsely he said, "You certainly carry the cabbage—er—carry a great deal of money around with you."

The same small demon that had inspired her to show him the large wad of cash made her say, "Oh, money is the least of my worries. I could just as easily have loaned you five thousand—or fifty thousand."

When she said the last figure, he started as though a pin had been jabbed into him. Quickly he recovered control. "I don't need quite that much," he said, laughing. But his laugh was hollow.

She was filled with secret amusement. The smell of money was to him like sunshine and rain to a growth of weeds. It expanded him, made him luxuriant.

And she noted, as he pulled her roughly into his arms, that it gave him a new sense of mastery. She tilted her piquant face up and prepared herself to give a timeworn imitation of interest.

It was as though a tiny fire, a strange fire never before experienced, burned deep inside her; growing, finally bursting through the cold artifice, shattering the layer of indifference.

Never before had she experienced such a feeling.

She pulled herself away from him, suddenly frightened of herself more than of him. Her cheeks were hot—partly with anger, because up until that moment she had been the dominant party, the superior being, amused at this tiresome little man. And suddenly he was dominant, his teeth glowing whitely in the darkness as he smiled at her, as he sensed her confusion.

It was with shame that she heard her own disordered breathing, and she stilled it with enormous effort. Her voice sounded rusty and old as she said, "Don't you think we ought to head back?"

"Sure thing." He started the motor, turned out into the road, and she heard him humming under his breath as he drove rapidly back toward the Court . . .

Long after she was alone in her cabin she still walked restlessly back and forth, from the bureau to the bed, her hands clenched in fury. She fought to regain her feeling of power, of amused condescension. At this late date was she to fall into a sticky emotional trap like any schoolgirl?

At last she lay exhausted on the bed, defeated, abject. She knew that this emotion which had struck her down was stronger than her will. She wanted nothing more than to be with Jay Kelso for every hour of every day.

And it was impossible to think of his dying, to think of a world where he did not exist. After weeping, she laughed —softly and without humor.

Jay Kelso felt that he was rapidly approaching the biggest opportunity of his life. He stood outside his cabin in the darkness, and fingered the crisp texture of the bills in his pokets. The taste of the liquor he had just drunk from the opened bottle was raw on the back of his tongue.

Life had suddenly become very complicated. He had been almost completely discouraged about the Oliver woman. She had seemed so—so remote. And he had caught her looking at him from time to time as though he was some sort of a bug she found when she tipped up a flat rock. She had made him feel stupid and young.

When he had given her the yarn about needing a few hundred, he had done so with the idea that she would brush him off, maybe laugh at him. She had an odd way of hurting his confidence. The willingness with which she had handed it over—in cash—had taken his breath away. And then, when she had said that about five thousand or fifty thousand, he had felt as though somebody had hit him in the pit of the stomach with a hammer.

Yes, he had figured it wrong. The old biddy was a hell of a lot better heeled than he had suspected. And she had no reason to lie.

Then, when he had kissed her, she had fallen apart— come all to pieces like a young kid. That was funny. His lips curled in slight distaste as he thought of the sagging looseness of the flesh under her chin. But to give her the benefit of the doubt, that was the only place she showed her age. Yes, she was all right. But compared to Serena— hell, it was like comparing a cube of sugar to a hundred gallons of honey. And he had all that dough on the hook, but good!

He arched his chest and beat his clenched fist against his thigh. More dough than he had ever had a smell of before!

The deal was to get hold of as much of it as possible. He knew that if he chiseled five thousand, he'd always think of the much larger amount he had left behind. What was five thousand? You couldn't even live a year on that. No, there had to be a better way.

In the morning he would send a hundred to the finance company and a hundred to Myra. That would shut both of them up. Give him time to think.

Betty and Serena. Serena and Betty. What a mess! Now if Serena only had Betty's money—or if Betty had Serena's looks. The deal was to find some way of grabbing all of Betty Oliver's money, and then marrying Serena.

There was that marriage idea again! Must be getting soft in the head. But no getting around it. He wanted to marry Serena. The trouble was, the only sure way to get all of Betty's money was to marry her. From the way the old biddy had reacted, she would be a pushover for marriage. Yeah. She'd grab the hook like a starving bass. Then where would he be? Tied to her apron strings for a couple of thousand years while Serena went off with somebody else. Maybe even with that Lawton punk. What'll you have, Kelso—money or the gal? But why not both?

Suddenly he stood very still and almost stopped breathing. The idea was vivid, startling and full of cold fear. Marry both of them! Marry Betty and fix her up with an—an unfortunate accident. Husband inherits. Widower, loaded with dough, marries young gal.

For a moment a vision flashed across his mind. A neat little chair with straps on the arms, electrodes and a black cap to fit over his head.

No, that would have to be avoided at all costs . . .

Maybe his marrying Betty would put Serena off him for keeps? But then he'd have dough to help him forget. Forgetting was easy with money in the kick. And if he moved fast enough, talked fast enough after Betty was—was dead, he could probably rope Serena back into the fold. "Darling, I made a horrible mistake. It was you all along." Something like that.

Probably be a good idea to lay the groundwork before Betty died. But how would she die? Fall guys were better than accidents. How many fall guys were there around this dump? Just one. That Lawton guy.

Kelso frowned in the darkness. With sudden resolution he strolled down toward the main building. It was so late that the floodlights were off. He knew that Jonas Bright, unable to sleep, often sat out there after the place was closed, thinking old-man thoughts, remembering, tasting the night.

Jonas was in his usual chair. Kelso went up behind him, said softly, "Nice night."

The old man's head jerked around. "Yep. Can't you sleep either?"

Kelso laughed. "Usually I can. Tonight, no." He let a long period of silence go by. Then he said, "You know, pop, that Lawton is a funny guy."

"How do you mean?"

"I saw the son of a gun talking to himself, yesterday. Is he a little bit nuts?"

Jonas was quiet for so long that Jay thought he wasn't going to answer. Finally the old man said, "Guess he had a bad time in the war. From a couple of little things he said, about prison camps and stuff like that, I shouldn't wonder if he was in one of those head hospitals."

Kelso fought to keep the delight out of his voice. He said, "Yeah, that makes it a rough deal. They wouldn't take me, you know. Bad teeth. I got a full set of choppers top and bottom. The rule says you got to have eight of your own teeth."

Jonas Bright grunted. Kelso turned the conversation onto the weather and then walked slowly away. When he was out of earshot of the old man, he quickened his steps.

What a break! A psycho right on stage. His mind began sifting through the possible clues he could leave. That Lawton was a powerful guy. It would have to look as though a powerful guy had done it. Snatch a couple of hairs out of her head and sneak them into Lawton's quarters. Those torn knaki shorts of Lawton's would be a good deal. Rip off a small hunk and wedge it into her dead hand like she had torn it off in a struggle.

That ought to be enough. Too many clues would be bad, would make even the hick cops wonder about a frame.

He reached toward the doorknob of his own cabin, then paused. Hell, this was too good to hang back on. Better use the speeding hours to talk the Oliver dish into that quick ceremony that would make Jay Kelso the legal heir.

With quiet steps he went up the slope toward her cabin. All the cabins were dark. He glanced at the luminous dial of his wristwatch. A little after two. He knocked lightly.

"Who is it?" she said softly.

He made his voice hoarse. "Me, Betty. Jay. I want to talk to you."

"Can't it wait until morning?"

"Please, Betty. It's important. Don't show a light when you open the door."

There was a long period of silence. Then her latch clicked softly and the door opened. He slipped through, reached for her, pulled her gently against him.

"Oh, Betty," he said.

"You shouldn't have come here," she whispered.

Ben Lawton was putting new washers in the faucets of Cabin 5 when Serena Bright walked dully in with clean sheets, pillowcases and towels. He looked up, saw her face, desolated and ravaged by tears, and his heart went out to her.

She had been badly fooled by Kelso, but that didn't make it any less bitter for her. He had a sudden appreciation of the agonies she must have to go through when she took fresh linens to Cabin 11, now shared for these past ten days by Jay Kelso and his bride.

But it was time that Serena snapped out of it, he thought. The girl couldn't go on this way forever. And that marriage escapade certainly must have given Serena some idea of the sort of man she had been dealing with.

Ben grinned up at her, straightened up and said, "Well, maybe she'll be a mother to him."

Deadly Damsel

A weak, sad smile touched Serena's lips. "I thought so at first, Ben. But have you looked at the darn woman? She's dropped fifteen years. Now I know what they mean by the 'radiant bride.' Ben, I can't understand how it happened so—so quickly."

"He probably got a look at her financial statement."

"But he really isn't that way, Ben. That woman must have some hold over him."

He put the wrench down, wiped his hands on the sides of his shorts, went over to her and took her by the wrists.

"Honey," he said, "I've never talked this way to you before. I've kept my past to myself. I'm working here to get back some measure of mental stability. But before the war, I was successful in a rough, tough business in New York City. Kelso comes from around that area. I cased him the minute I saw him. His type are a dime a dozen up there. Amateur sharpies. Hangers-on.

"But you can't condemn them. They come up out of the city slums, and they get their training battling for nickels when they're six years old. Life makes them unscrupulous, selfish—and the smarter ones pick up a sugar coating of the mannerisms and dress they see in the movies. Kelso is one of the smarter ones, but that doesn't make him a more noble human being. His life and his instincts are on an animal level.

"You are a nice gal, Rena. It would be a shame if, this early in your life, you threw away everything you have to offer on a citizen with the sweet instincts of a rooting hog."

"But, he told me—"

"Serena, he told you the things he thought you wanted to hear. And if I don't miss my bet, he wants to have his cake and eat it, too. He married the Oliver woman because he was running short of money. Now you watch him. When he gets a chance, he'll feed you some more sweet talk just to keep you around. Maybe he'll milk her of as much money as he can and try to talk you into running off with him."

27

Her eyes were suddenly angry. "He won't get any-where, not after this!"

"That's what I wanted you to say, Rena. I think you got through this without being hurt too bad. And it probably taught you something. You're a sweet gal, believe me."

Still holding her wrists, he leaned forward, and kissed her lightly. He let go of her wrists, and she came into his arms, young, fresh, eager.

He held her away, his hands on her shoulders. "Hey," he said, "don't you understand about rebound?"

In a wondering tone she said, "And you've been around all the time! Right under my nose."

"Hey, hold it! I don't help anybody do their forgetting. Once you get rid of the weeping look, then we'll see if I hold the same attractions."

"I'm not doing any more weeping, Benjamin," she said.

"Good. Will you go out with me sometime?"

"Of course, Ben. When?"

"Exactly one month from today. Okay?"

She frowned. "Hard to get, huh? I can wait. One month from today."

After Jay Kelso had heard Serena's and Ben's voices, and had looked in at the open door of Cabin 5 without being observed, he had walked in anger up to Cabin 11, wondering if he had waited too long.

Before entering Cabin 11, he put on the mechanical smile that had become a habit with him. It was hard to conceal the distaste when he stepped in and Betty came prancing kittenishly toward him, put her arms tightly around his neck and whispered, "Ooo was gone so long, lover man."

"Yeah. Sure," he said absently, untangling her arms, trying not to see the hurt look in her eyes. He dug back into an uncertain education to find the word he wanted. Oppressive—yes, that was it. This was an oppressive woman. No wonder that Oliver guy had kicked off. She had drowned the poor guy in melted sugar.

28

If only she wouldn't try to be twelve years old. It made her ridiculous. All this prancing and posturing and baby talk was turning his stomach. He felt as though he were being sucked down into a sticky pool.

And those kid clothes she was buying. Bright halters and shorts and sandals. He was forced to admit that from the rear she looked like a slim young girl. But when you saw the face, it didn't go with the getup. There were too many fine lines around her lavender eyes, too much fullness at her throat.

Yes, it would have to be quick before he was smothered. It was like being married to a combination chorus line, Girl Scout troop and kindergarten. But at least she was liberal with her dough. She had said that pretty soon she'd have to make a trip to get more, that it was tied up in a trust that she could cancel and take in cash. He had hinted around about how much cash, and she had said that it was enough for the two of them to have everything they wanted for the rest of their lives. Cars, clothes, fun, nice places, cruises.

The silk gabardine suit she had bought him was the nicest piece of goods he had ever owned. As though by mutual consent, they had never mentioned his mythical business in Jersey. It was as though she had known all along that he had been lying.

Yes, it was time to have a quiet few words with Serena, and then to put the plan in motion. He suddenly realized that he would be deathly afraid to kill Betty. But he would get a great deal of satisfaction out of it just the same.

Her heart sang her new name. Betty Kelso! Betty Kelso! She thought of herself as having been a barren winter landscape. And now the warm sun of spring had melted the frost.

Never before was it like this. She had not known that she was capable of such feelings. How had she ever thought Jay was a cheap and amusing little man? No, Jay was the finest man she had ever known. He was sweet and dear and kind and wonderful. She wanted to

29

dance and sing whenever she thought of him. She was upset when he was away from her, wonderfully happy when he was with her.

Her past was a strange, horrible dream, full of things done by an entirely different person. That part of her life was definitely finished. She wondered if fate had saved her for this delectable happiness.

And yet, with that thought came a superstitious awe. She knew that she had sinned against society—against the laws of the church, against the moral laws of civilization—and she was afraid. Afraid that, in retribution, this new happiness would be taken from her.

No, that was impossible. She and Jay were the two happiest persons in the world. Her tracks had been so carefully covered that there was no chance of the authorities catching up with her, even if they did suspect any of the deaths.

No, nothing could happen to spoil it. She felt warm, alive, vibrant—beyond anything she had ever felt before. She was sorry that she hadn't met Jay first instead of Albert Gordon. Then she smiled. That was silly. At the time she had married Albert Gordon, Jay Kelso had been, at the very most, four years old. But the difference in ages was unimportant. She felt younger than Jay. And she knew that this new love would keep her young.

She walked to the door of Cabin 11 and looked down the narrow sloping street. There was that Serena girl. She smiled as she remembered how Jay had been going out with Serena before she, Betty, had come along. Now Jay knew how silly he had been.

That old couple had moved out of Cabin 7 the day before. The girl went into the cabin laden with linens. Jay had gone down to buy cigarettes from the girl behind the counter. She saw him turning into the road, walking slowly, and her heart gave a great leap as it always did when she saw him again after a short absence.

She stepped back out of the doorway, as she wanted to watch him without his knowing that she was doing so. She wanted to try to look at him as a third person, to see how wonderful he was. She looked through the venetian blinds. He was coming near, nearer.

Soon his arms would be around her.

He paused, glanced toward her, though he could not see her of course, and then turned into Cabin 7. She frowned, then realized that he probably wanted to give that girl some instructions.

But a deep jealousy stirred inside her. As the seconds passed she grew restless. Quickly, and with unconscious animal stealth, she went down the street, avoiding the line of vision of anyone inside Cabin 7. The door was ajar.

Unconscious of who might be observing her, she flattened herself, shoulders against the outside wall of the cabin, her ear near the crack of the door.

"Let me go!" Serena Bright said, her voice muffled and irregular, as though she struggled.

"Don't! You've got to listen to me. Serena, darling, listen to me!"

"What do you want to say?" Her tone was sullen.

"I made a mistake, Serena. I don't know what was the matter with me. She's a horrible woman. I hate her. I love you, Serena. Only you. I should have known that. Please don't condemn me for a mistake. Please."

"Is that all?" Serena said in a flat tone.

"Don't do this to me, darling. I'll be free of her soon. Believe me. I'll find a way. You're the only one, Serena. The only one I love. When I'm free, will you marry me? Will you?"

Betty Kelso walked away from the cabin, walked mechanically back to Cabin 11 and shut the door behind her.

It was as though in the back of her mind there was a gleaming and accurate machine which had, a few weeks before, ground to a stop. And while it was stopped she had gone through antics that were ridiculous and absurd. She had made a complete fool of herself and, in the bargain, had lost that deep sense of power, that power of death that had made her feel like a goddess.

31

Now the machine had started again, slowly at first, then faster, until it was running as before.

How had she thought that Kelso, the absurd man-child, was charming and attractive? She flushed when she thought of the things she had said, the way she had behaved. That was over. Her mind was clear and firm again. She thought of death. She was not known in this place. They had no address for her. Their description would fit any of ten million women.

Kelso had taught her to drive. Obviously the best thing to do would be to kill him quickly, take the car, drive a good distance, abandon it, cover her tracks, reestablish herself. Some other state. Idaho. She had never lived in Idaho.

Yes, this could be done quickly. But in this case it would be worth it.

Yes, this time she could be brutal, and this time she could let the man know, as he died, just why he died. Suddenly it seemed very good. Very, very good.

Jay Kelso reached into his pocket, and his fingertips touched the little torn fragment of khaki cloth. It would fit the ragged edge of Lawton's work shorts as perfectly as a piece of a jigsaw puzzle.

Serena had been difficult. She had been cold and distant and contemptuous. But he thought that after Betty had died and Lawton had been taken away, it would not be too difficult to bring her back to his side like a well-trained puppy. He thought of how well Serena would look in clothes from the Miami branches of the better New York shops. A girl to be proud of.

He went into the cabin, and Betty came tripping across to him, her arms reaching up, tightening around his neck. He held her close and she murmured, "Betty missed you."

"I missed you, too," he said softly.

But when a few minutes later he looked into her eyes, he wondered if something was wrong. Her odd lavender eyes didn't have that depth of warmth they had before. They seemed—brittle.

Deadly Damsel

He shrugged away the impression. Probably it was his imagination. Probably it was because he had thought of her dead body so many times. When he thought of killing her, his hands began to sweat and the hair on the back of his neck prickled oddly.

It would have to be tonight. Everything was set. The plan looked perfect. He would kill her, as quietly as possible, then run down the hill yelling for the old man. He would say that he couldn't sleep, had gone for a walk, had come back just in time to see Lawton sneaking away from the cabin. Inside he had found the body of his wife.

The police would do the rest.

It was eight o'clock. Four hours to wait. Betty sat at the dressing table and he stood behind her, his hands on her shoulders, looking at her face reflected in the glass. She was filing her nails, using a long heavy file with a plastic handle.

He felt her eyes on him and glanced into the mirror. Odd. She seemed to be staring in a fixed way at the base of his throat. She was smiling. It was a warm, contented, wifely smile. The nail file made a raw buzzing noise as she used it deftly. He took his right hand from her shoulder, touched his fingertips to the base of his throat.

"After we eat, we'll come back here and have a long evening alone, just the two of us," he said quietly.

"Big lover man understands his little Betty," she cooed.

He concealed his irritation at the liquid baby talk and managed to smile at her. He glanced at her face and throat. Her features were delicate. They would have to be spoiled a little. It would have to look like a killing by a powerful man . . .

He moved his arm with great stealth until he could see the luminous dial of his wristwatch. Just midnight. Faint light drifted into the room, and he could make out the shape of the chair where his clothes were. Beside him, Betty was breathing softly and regularly.

His nerves were bad. The room seemed very cold, and he shivered. But it had to be done. To give himself courage, he thought of Serena walking in the sunlight.

He looked at Betty, lifting himself up on one elbow. He imagined that there was a gleam of the dim light against her eyeballs. That was silly. She was sleeping. Her breathing was soft and regular.

He reached gently until his fingers hovered inches from her slim throat. Then, tensing his muscles, he drove his hand down onto her throat, fingers biting into the soft flesh.

She exploded into motion with such sudden, horrid strength that it frightened him. One hand slipped but he managed to replace it, his lean thumbs on either side of her throat. She writhed, and together they tumbled off the side of the bed. A stinging, burning pain ripped across his shoulder.

They were in the patch of light that shone in the window. He was underneath, panting with strain, his arms straightened and rigid, holding her high above him. The pain struck again, this time across the muscles of his arm. When her flailing hand paused for a moment in the moonlight, he saw that she clenched the nail file.

Sudden fear gave him strength. The moonlight struck her darkening face, her eyes that widened and bulged, her lips that seemed to snarl.

Her struggles slowly weakened and something gave under the pressure of his thumbs. The nail file clattered to the wooden floor. Her arms hung limply, and he lowered her so that she rested beside him.

He took his right hand from her throat. With bitter, sodden strength born of fear, he drove his fist into her face, again and again and again. He was dimly glad that her face was in the shadows. The sound of his fist was wet and heavy.

Shivering, he stood up. Her legs sprawled loosely in the patch of moonlight. Sweat ran down his body. And something else. Blood from the two shallow rips.

That was dangerous. Quickly he closed the blinds, took the flashlight and shone it on the floor. He didn't shine it on Betty. He went to the bathroom, got a scrap of tissue, moistened it and cleaned up the drops of blood. He hurried into the bathroom, washed the nail file, dried it and put it on her dresser.

Time was flying by. He dressed hurriedly, and felt sudden nausea when he forced the scrap of knaki into her hand, because already her hand had lost warmth and life.

He paused for a moment, checking back to see if anything had been forgotten. No, he had taken the hairs from her comb, had planted them in Lawton's room when he had sneaked in at dusk three days before to rip the knaki patch from the ragged work shorts.

One more thing. It would be natural for him to turn on the cabin lights. He did so, and leaving the door open, he ran down the hill yelling hoarsely.

"Help!" he shouted. "Murder!" Even as he ran, he wondered why she had been in bed with that nail file in her hand. Could it be that she was going to . . .? No, that was absurd.

The investigation seemed to be going nicely. Jay Kelso sat at one of the round tables near the soda fountain.

The two police cars were parked out by the gas pumps. The men in charge were up in Cabin 11, investigating.

"Why haven't they picked Lawton up?" Kelso demanded angrily of a man in the doorway.

"If they haven't, they will," the man said grimly.

Finally he heard the crunch of steps on the gravel. The tall man in charge half turned and said loudly, "There's nothing more to see. All you people go on back to your cabins."

"Have you got him yet?" Kelso demanded.

"We know where he is. I just want to check the identification again with you. You say you came back to the cabin after a short walk and you saw the door open."

"That's right," Jay said. "It surprised me, so I stopped. I was in the shadows. The moonlight hit the door. Lawton came out, sort of crouched. I saw his face as plain as day. He was wearing those ragged old work shorts of his.

"He stood for a minute as though he was listening for something. Then he went off into the darkness. It worried me. I knew he'd been acting funny lately. Mumbling to himself. In fact, I mentioned it to Mr. Bright a week or so ago. Lawton was a mental case. There's no getting around that."

The officer yawned cavernously, said, "Well, Mr. Kelso, we can sure wrap this up like a Christmas package if you can stand back of that identification."

Jay pretended annoyance. "I tell you I saw him like I'm seeing you. No possible doubt about it." Secret glee replaced the fear he had felt before.

The officer turned in his chair, looked back at the old man and said, "Jonas, let me have that thing you showed me a little while back."

Without looking at Kelso, Jonas Bright shuffled over and handed the officer a small folded slip of yellow paper.

The officer opened it, read it, his lips moving with each word. Then he slid it across the table to Jay Kelso. "Yes, sir, I guess that positive identification sews this case right up."

Jay felt sudden coldness as he read the telegram.

DON'T BE ANGRY, DAD, THIS WAS MY IDEA AND NOT BEN'S. THE CABINS CAN TAKE CARE OF THEMSELVES FOR A FEW DAYS. I'LL BE MRS. LAWTON WHEN I GET BACK. WE ARRIVED HERE IN DAYTONA AT MIDNIGHT. ALL MY LOVE, SERENA.

Jay tried to speak and his voice was a pitiful squeak. "Dark. Just moonlight. He must have looked like Lawton. You can't think that I—that I—"

The officer opened a big brown hand and put a scrap of khaki on the top of the table.

Jay Kelso almost reached his car before the slug smashed his knee.

State Police Report That . . .

IN THE FIRST gray of dawn he came awake with the alertness of an animal. He was on his stomach in a sandy notch between two rocks and the revolver was a hard lump against his body.

They might have seen him there and they might be watching. His hand closed around the chill metal, and he thumbed back the hammer. Only then did he move, so explosively that nearby birds squawked in alarm and winged off.

He drank from the creek at the foot of the slope and then went back up to the crest. As he neared the crest he dropped to hands and knees, writhed the last few feet on his belly, reaching forward with caution to part the dried grass.

He froze in that position, his pale eyes squinting against sunrise, staring down toward the distant ribbon of highway. His face held all the cunning of a man who skirts the narrow border of death and means to survive it.

It was a narrow face, with a pulled-down petulance about the oddly thickened lips. His body looked flaccid and too thin, but it had a coiled-steel efficiency about it, an animal's economy of movement. A prison number was stenciled across the back of his torn gray cotton shirt. The stubble of beard along the thin line of his jaw was flecked with gray, though he didn't look much over thirty.

At last, when the sun was high enough, it glinted on the white enamel of the trooper cars. The roadblock was established at the place he had expected to find it. With half a break he would have been out of the area before they could have set up the block. The distant cars stopped to be checked, went on again, seeming from that distance to move with incredible slowness.

But the escape siren had gone off too quickly and he had been cut off, had been forced to make his way through the swamp. The black mud had caked to a sick gray on his pants.

He watched the roadblock for a time and his eyes suddenly narrowed as he saw movement halfway between his position and the distant highway. The slant of the sun made vision difficult but he finally saw a thin line of men beating their way toward the hill.

Cursing, he slid slowly back, crawled a dozen feet, ran in a crouch for a time and then began to walk back toward the swamp at a ground-covering pace. Yet there was indecision in his manner. He was a bug in a bottle and they were putting the cork in the bottle.

Then he stopped, thinking that maybe he could ambush the line when they got to the brush, shoot his way through into the clear. But there were flats in the valley and he had seen the long gleam of rifle barrels. The thought of a rifle slug tearing his flesh made him feel ill. It made him forget the hunger that had gnawed at him for twenty-four hours. No choice. The date set for his execution was but a month and three days away. The state wanted that date kept.

Though he knew it was dangerous, some hunch he only half understood turned his steps toward the edge of the swamp where the highway cut close to it.

Soon he heard the roar of cars and, after forty more yards, he could see the flash of sun on chrome as they swept by. With a car he might be able to bluff his way past the roadblock.

But what chance of stopping one of them, when every driver had probably been told an escaped murderer was hiding somewhere along that stretch of road?

He wondered if he could make one of the cars stop. If only they didn't go so fast. A hill might slow them down a bit. He began to move more rapidly, on the alert for any sound of crashing brush that would indicate the nearness of the posse.

A half mile further the road cut away from the swamp, went up a long steep hill. He crouched in the brush and listened until he could hear no drone of cars approaching from any direction. He ran across the road, dived into the brush on the other side, rolled to a stop and held his breath while he listened. There was no shout of discovery, no sound of pursuit.

Twice he heard faraway yells and guessed that it was the men of the posse shouting instructions to each other. Working his way up the hill was slow and laborious. The brush was thin and twice he had to run across open spaces. Once, moments after he found cover, the search plane circled lazily overhead. He cursed it quietly until it was gone—heading back over the swamp.

Fortunately, the steepest part of the hill was a place where the brush grew close to the road. The morning was growing hotter and the sweat made the thin shirt cling to his shoulders and chest. Deerflies began to bother him.

He flattened out on his belly and watched the road. Looking down, the hill did not seem to be as steep. It did not appear to slow down the cars. A red trailer truck ground up the hill and he tensed, then saw the helper sitting beside the driver. Too much risk. Two girls came up the hill in an ancient convertible and it began to labor. But as he shifted the gun to a more comfortable grip, the girl behind the wheel dropped it into second and began to pick up speed.

He wondered how long it would be until the thin line of men came up the hill. Not until afternoon, probably.

The sun was high when he saw the car. He knew the moment it came in sight that it was the car. An ancient touring car. Fifty feet up the hill from where he crouched, a faint unused road cut off at an angle.

The only thing that could ruin his plan would be a car

overtaking this one, or coming from the other direction at the wrong time. He tried to listen through the chugging of the old car, tried to hear other motors. There was nothing but silence.

Partway up the hill the driver shifted. As the tense watcher expected, the car continued, but at a very slow rate.

Lifting himself, he waited on his toes and knuckles like a track star. When the car was opposite him, he bounded forward, ran three steps parallel to it and then jumped onto the running board, leaning in across the woman to hold his revolver on the pasty driver. The driver stared at him.

The convict said, "Do as I say and you won't get hurt—much . . . Turn in right up here."

The driver did as he was told. The car swayed and bounced on the uneven track, the grass scraping the underside.

When they were away from the highway, out of sight of any passing car, the driver looked at him again. "Stop here," he said.

The two towheaded children perched on the luggage in the back seat stared at him with round blue eyes. One was a girl of three or four, and the other was a boy of about nine.

They had their mother's coloring. She sat, slack and bewildered, in the front seat, a baby in her arms. She had a look of acrid poverty about her.

"Sit right there and keep the kids still," he told her, "or you won't see your man again. Come on, you."

He forced the driver ahead of him with the gun, walking him off into the brush. When they were out of sight of the car, he tripped the man so that he fell heavily. The driver was a bigger man than the man with the gun, but he trembled with fear and shock.

"Take off your clothes," he said.

The man's trembling hands fumbled with his shirt buttons. It was a blue work shirt, sodden at the armpits . . . The clothes were in a heap and the man lay quivering on the pine needles. He had a second to cry out, but he didn't.

Once the heavy barrel of the revolver smashed down against the bridge of his nose, there was no sound except the drone of the insects, the distant roar of traffic and the monotonous thud of the heavy gun on helpless flesh, on splintering bone . . . The familiar red mist faded away and he looked down at the dead driver of the car.

The clothes fit reasonably well once he had tightened the belt to the last notch. The worn blackened wallet contained thirty-three dollars and a union card saying that the bearer was Andrew Robelan, a machinist.

He smeared the blood off the gun barrel onto a handful of leaves and went back to the car. The woman was sitting as he had left her.

He got behind the wheel and started the car.

"Where is he? What did you do to him?"

"I tied him up. He'll be okay."

He reached over, took the baby out of her arms, put it between them, its head toward the gearshift. It was asleep.

The motor was noisy. He shouted at the woman, "One wrong move from you or from those kids in the back and I'll—"

He held his clenched fist over the baby's head on the car seat. She nodded, chewing at her underlip.

Backing the car out onto the highway, he put it into low gear and labored up what remained of the hill. The little girl in the back seat began to sob. The woman turned and reached back, patted the child. At his snarled request, she stopped, but she still kept her face turned, her eyes on the two in the back. When he glanced at her, her lips were moving and he wondered if she was praying. Prayer wasn't going to do her much good. Not as far as her husband was concerned.

The roadblock was in the flats a half mile from the foot of the hill. As he took his foot from the gas pedal, shifted it to the brake, he said, "Not a peep out of you, sister. If they ask questions, I do the talking."

41

The car wheezed to a stop and the two troopers, their faces grim, stepped up, one on each side.

He gave the answers in a calm, almost bored voice. "I'm Andrew Robelan. I'm a machinist. We're going to Florida." They wanted to see identification. He showed them the card. But he held it with his left hand. The gun was under the front seat, but in position for a quick hand to grasp it. He kept his right hand on his thigh, inches from the head of the sleeping baby.

The troopers waved them on. He wanted to laugh with crazy glee. The clatter of the old motor was a song of triumph. He felt bigger than life size, enormous with cleverness. Ahead the road was open and free.

She was praying again.

They were on a three-lane highway. Suddenly the world exploded around him, smashing into dark flame and bitter lights. He was dimly conscious of sagging toward the wheel, of her hand reaching out to grasp the wheel. He tried to push himself back up, but the second crushing blow drove him back into utter blackness.

It was dusk when he came to. He was on a cot and his hands were up over his head. When he tried to move them he found that he was handcuffed to a steam pipe that ran down the wall.

The clink of chain on metal brought a big trooper into the room. He clicked on the light and looked down with an expression that indicated both satisfaction and disgust.

"You're going to keep a date, Johnny," the trooper said.

He cursed the trooper, infuriated by the man's grin. But in the middle of the cursing, he stopped and frowned. "What happened?" he asked. "What went wrong?"

"You didn't ask enough questions, Johnny. You took too much for granted. You had a hell of a fine plan and you made us look like suckers, but you weren't as smart as that beat-down Mrs. Robelan."

"I don't get it."

"I'll tell you just to watch your face. Mrs. Robelan gets the reward money, you know. You should have found out more about them, Johnny. If you knew more

42

about them, you'd know how she told the kid to slug you on the head with the wrench that was on the floor in the back.''

"She didn't open her yap!" he said.

"Sure she did, Johnny. Sure she did."

And suddenly Johnny knew. He heard the trooper's words of explanation through the roaring in his ears.

"Yeah, the old lady, the baby and the little girl are okay, but the old man and the boy were deaf-mutes. They both could read lips. She told him to hit you without making a sound."

Johnny turned his face to the wall.

Death for Sale

ON THE WAY to the hotel he sat in the back of the taxi, a broad, sullen-looking man, searching inside of himself for the sense of satisfaction that should be his. There was nothing there but weariness—a dejection compounded of the solid year of search. From the beginning he had known he would win, one day. The perennial cliché of the ever-narrowing world drifted through his mind, and he smiled. No, there is no haven in this world for a man who is hunted.

Once upon a time there had been hiding places. The Foreign Legion, the lonely cattle camps along the Amazon, the fields north of Kimberley. But this is a day of fingerprints, forms, visas, permits, regulations—statistical control of population. "And what is your reason for desiring entrance to this country, monsieur?" "How long do you intend to stay, sahib?" "How do you intend to support yourself, señor?"

Of course, there is always the secret landing by night from a small boat. But then the wheels of bureaucracy grind out the little pink and green forms—work permits, income taxes, census—and it is as though your coming and your forced departure and your name and your secret were written across the sky for all to see.

Even so, it is easier to hide from a government than it is to hide from a man.

Jan Dalquist, riding placidly up Canal Street in the

44

back seat of the taxi, recognized this fact. Particularly if the hunter is provided with adequate funds. The hunter doesn't have to be clever. Jan Dalquist knew his own faults. He wasn't clever. He was dogged, painstaking, stubborn, silent and grim. Not clever. Not clever at all.

But he was an excellent hunter of men.

The huge net of the justice that the democracies dropped over France and Germany after the war was a net of compromise. The diameter of the mesh had to be small enough to entrap the major and intermediate beasts who walked like men. But it could not be so small that it would seine in millions, who, by burdening the mechanism of justice, would make fair trial impossible. As a consequence, thousands of vicious little men had slipped through the meshes and scattered across the world.

Jan Dalquist had been after one of these men for a year.

He was not employed by any government. He was paid by a small group of French industrialists: men who had been beaten to the earth by the German occupation, men who had not known how to compromise, men who thirsted for revenge in the calm, unemotional manner of a banker collecting a debt. They paid for the hunting of other Frenchmen. They were well satisfied with Jan Dalquist. They paid well for the service of a reliable assassin.

Jan Dalquist was after a Jean Charlebois. The facts were very simple. At the time of the Allied invasion, a large band of Maquis were wiped out by German troops. A betrayal was suspected. Only three of the Maquis escaped. Later, after the town was captured, German records indicated that the betrayal had been engineered by one Jean Charlebois, one of the three who had escaped. The son of one of the industrialists who financed Dalquist had been killed in the raid. Thus the assignment to find and kill Charlebois.

The industrialists had little patience with the slow machinery of government. So Jan Dalquist, who had lived in France before the war, and who had gone back during the war as an operative—air-dropped—was contacted and hired as a trustworthy killer.

Had they asked him a bit earlier, or a bit later, he would have refused—for he recognized that he was a man with a profound distaste for taking the tools of justice in his own hands, for acting as judge, jury and executioner. But the offer was made while Dalquist was still in an army hospital where a clever surgeon was attempting to make the ragged flesh and shattered bones of his hands resemble fingers, trying to cover the bone-deep burns on the soles of his feet with skin grafts from the insides of his thighs.

The memory of the basement room in Gestapo headquarters was too vivid. And so Dalquist had said yes. And having once agreed, it was not in him to back out until the job had been completed.

They gave him three names. Dalquist had found the first traitor in Brazil after nine months of search. He still awakened in the middle of the night, seeing again the death of the first. He remembered the man's hand most of all. It had happened in a field outside of Belém. Long after the man had appeared dead, the hand scrabbled at the white dust.

He had found the second one in Montreal after another seven months. The ice was thin on the river. Almost transparent. After he had shoved the body down through the hole he had stamped through the ice, he saw it being borne away by the current, turning lazily so that once the misty face was turned toward him, the eye sockets dark under the film of ice.

And he often dreamed of this, too.

The taxi arrived at the hotel and he registered and followed the boy up to his room. He tipped the boy, locked the door and stood for a long time at the window, his mutilated hands shoved deep in his pockets, staring down fourteen stories at the busy New Orleans streets. A square, quiet man with a grave face which held a look of suffering. He looked across the gilded channel of Canal Street, looked into the narrow streets of the French Quarter. Jean Charlebois might yet be there. If so, it was the end of the third search, the end of the mission. But he wouldn't permit himself to think of what he would do once Charlebois had been found and punished. Such thoughts would dilute resolve.

He unlocked his bag, took out the small black notebook. He sat on the edge of the bed and examined, with little interest, the record of the search for Charlebois. The man had escaped the consequence of his treachery for two and a half years. There was very little writing on the sheet.

> Jean Charlebois left France on foot, crossing into Spain. He remained in Barcelona for three months, perfecting his Spanish and obtaining a passport as a Spanish citizen. He took the name of Ramón Francesco. With a Portuguese visa, he went to Lisbon. He remained there four months, and booked illegal passage on a Portuguese freighter, debarking in Guatemala. He dropped out of sight, reappearing in Mexico City. During the time he was out of sight he assumed the name Pierre Duval. Crossed the Mexican border into Texas illegally in December 1947.
>
> Was unable to locate him until I intercepted a letter he wrote to a Mexican girl in Mexico City. Letter stated that he was working as waiter in a café called the Ancient Door on Burgundy Street in French Quarter of New Orleans. Have arrived in New Orleans twenty-four days after the letter was written. Believe that he is still in the city.

Jan Dalquist slapped the book shut and put it back in the suitcase.

He sat, studying his hands, rubbing the numb tips of his fingers together, looking at the places where there should have been fingernails. There was no sense of accomplishment in him. Only fear. And not of Charlebois. It was an odd fear. It was as though, three years before, in a basement room in Gestapo headquarters, he had ceased to exist. He had become a machine, dedicated to the wishes of a small group of bitter men.

This was the last case. After it was over, he would have to find himself again. There would always be men who would pay him to hunt other men. But that wasn't the answer. He knew that the two and a half years of constant search, of sudden violence, had deadened him, soured him. No, that wasn't the answer. He began to think of himself working with moist earth and growing things, with placid acres on which the sun beat and the rains fell. He could almost smell the rich loam.

After his shower, he strapped on the shoulder holster, checked the clip on the .32 automatic and snapped it into place. It made no visible bulge under the dull gray suit. He sighed heavily, and left the hotel, walking toward Burgundy Street. As he walked, he carried in his mind the accurate picture of Jean Charlebois.

Five foot nine. One hundred and thirty-five pounds. Dark, thinning hair. Sallow complexion. Heavy eyebrows. Gold cap on right eyetooth. Nervous, agile, quick. High voice. Neat and clean. A chaser of women. Likes jewelry. May have small mustache. Weak eyes, but unlikely to wear glasses.

The late sun was gone and the lights were beginning to click on. Jan Dalquist walked through the dusk, feeling at each step the little bite of pain at the soles of his feet—the pain that would be with him until he died. And, in his heart, he carried another type of pain—the pain of an intelligent and civilized man, a man of intuitive delicacy, who has been thrown up against the most brutal and animal aspects of war; who, having discovered that the battle must be fought on the brute level, has made the tools of violence his own, has learned to use them with an incredible efficiency because they are foreign to his essential nature.

He walked and his mind was like a closed fist; the muscles tensed, the kinetic force poised, the entire organism aimed at the careful destruction of Jean Charlebois.

It had to be a delicate destruction. You cannot shoot a man down in the street and walk away. The circumstance must be right. It must be planned like a successful civil murder. Not like military justice.

The trapper baits and sets his trap, and then backs off, removing sign and scent of his passage. He stands for a moment and tries to look at his trap with the eyes

48

*of the animal which he wishes to catch. What are the
possibilities of escape?*

In that way, Jan Dalquist looked at the Ancient Door.
It was in a building set flush with the sidewalk, with
buildings tight against it on either side. Two rooms opened
onto the street. One was a small bar, dim, unclean, with
rough wood walls, old flags and swords on the wall. The
other room was a dining room with a small raised platform at the far end. Between the bar and the dining
room was a big, ornate iron gate with a sign on it which
said "Meals Served in the Court." He noticed, then, an
open door in the back wall of the bar.

He ordered a drink at the bar, picked it up and walked
casually back. There was a small court there, open to
the sky, with an asthmatic fountain bubbling in the center of it. A few tables were covered with soiled, checked
cloths. Another sign said "Dance by Candlelight under
the Stars."

There were only two doors leading from the court, the
door through the bar and one into the kitchen. Except
for one old man who sat at the bar, staring moodily
down into his drink, Dalquist was the only customer.
Through the open grillwork of the iron gate, he saw the
entrance to a stairway that went up to the rooms
overhead. That would bear investigation.

He selected a position at the bar which gave him the
widest view of the dining room and sipped his drink
patiently. Jan Dalquist had a great deal of patience. As
he waited, he went over the several plans which he had
devised to accomplish the destruction of Jean Charlebois,
alias Ramón Francesco, alias Pierre Duval, ex-Maquis,
ex-employee of the Gestapo, ex-Frenchman, ex-human.

Two noisy couples had a drink at the bar, and then
went into the dining room. Jan Dalquist watched carefully without giving the impression of watching. He relaxed internally when their order was taken by a doughy
man who could not conceivably be Charlebois.

A pretty girl, her hair a close-fitting cap of blond
curls, walked into the bar from the street and sat two
stools from Dalquist. She had a wide face, with some-

thing secretive and sensitive about the mouth. He glanced at her hands and liked their square, competent look. It suddenly occurred to him that a couple would be far less likely to arouse Charlebois's suspicions than a single man.

He watched her carefully, saw her look at her own image in the rounded, polished surface of a silver decanter that stood, out of place, on the back bar. He saw the little wrinkle of laughter as she saw her distorted image.

"Not very flattering, is it?" he said quietly.

She turned toward him quickly, startled by the way his words had spoken her thoughts. He saw the flicker of analysis, the debate with self whether to ignore the comment. He knew that his grave, impassive face would weigh in his favor, that she would not rule against him because of his appearance.

She didn't. She smiled and said, "Keep a woman away from anything in which she can see her face."

"Men are just as vain, you know. Before you came in, I was staring at that thing and imagining what it would be like to go through life with the face I saw in there. It made me feel happy about the face I have. That is a pleasure seldom experienced."

She cocked her head to one side and inspected him gravely, a glint of humor in her eyes. "Why seldom? You've got a very good face. Solid and dependable-looking. Nice eyes."

He bowed and said, "Thank you, friend. And what else do you see about me?"

She pursed her lips for a moment and then said, "Let me see. About thirty-six. Scandinavian ancestry. By the way you speak, you've been well educated. Your suit is well cut. There's something sad about your face. As though you've had a great deal of trouble. I'd guess that you're some sort of professional man. Maybe an engineer."

He laughed. "You're observant. However, I'm thirty-two. And I've had an average share of trouble. I have a small job to complete and then I'll be unemployed. How did you learn to use your eyes so well?"

"I'm down here trying to paint. Let me see your hands. I can tell a great deal from hands."

"I'd rather not."

"What do you mean?"

"They're not pleasant. They were injured a few years ago."

He saw the quick compassion. He said, "I'd very much appreciate it if you'd have dinner with me. That is, if you haven't other plans . . ."

Her smile became wooden. "I'm sorry, but I don't think that—"

"I know. You're not accustomed to meeting men in bars and being taken to dinner. But I'm perfectly harmless and I'm lonely. I have no ulterior motives. Please don't disappoint me."

She looked down at her cocktail for a long second and then smiled over at him. "Okay. I'm Jerry Ellis."

"How do you do, Jerry. Jan Dalquist. Now I'll have to give you a second chance to refuse. I told you that my hands aren't pretty. They're insensitive to the extent that I can't wear gloves over them while I eat. For that reason, I haven't had dinner with a woman in a long time." He put his right hand, fingers spread, on the top of the bar. He looked closely at her face, saw her eyes, saw the minute tightening of her lips.

She said, "Sit over here, Jan." He moved over and sat on the intervenig stool. She put her warm fingers on the back of his hand and said, "I'd be delighted to have dinner with you. And you're a very silly man. Very silly."

Something about the way she said it made him want to throw his money on the bar and walk out. No ulterior motives! She was far too trusting to be dragged into what might turn out to be a nasty mess. She seemed to be a nice person.

She said, "Charles, the bartender, is going to be quite astonished. I drop in here several times a week, and at least once each week he has to tell some ardent gentleman that I prefer not to be annoyed. I brush the others off myself. He's going to look at you and wonder why I have dinner with you.''

Jan grinned and said, "Being a bartender, he can see that I'm a harmless type. Besides, I played on your sympathies.'' As he spoke, he saw a man in the white coat of a waiter walk through the dining room. Some small gear clicked in his mind. Jean Charlebois.

The hunter raises one hand and cautiously spreads the brush that impedes his view. The cold blue barrel of the rifle points toward the clearing. The buck stands, nostrils quivering, head turning slowly in all directions. The hunter cradles his cheek against the smooth stock. He takes a deep breath and lets half of it out. His right hand tightens slowly, the trigger pressing against the pad of his right index finger. The sight bead is centered on a spot just behind the flat bone of the right shoulder of the buck. The right hand tightens . . .

"What on earth were you looking at then?" Jerry asked. "You looked quite frightening for a minute. Like a man looking at old ghosts.''

He glanced quickly at her, annoyed that he should have changed expression on seeing Charlebois. It was important to distract her attention.

He said, "That transparent? I was wondering about you. You seem like a person it would be easy to hurt. Obviously then, you have been. You could never grow to be as wise as you are without having been hurt. I was wondering what sort of person would do that to you.''

Emotionally, she withdrew. She was a girl sitting beside him, sipping a cocktail. Physically she was there. But her mind had gone back into the past, and the look of sensitivity about her mouth twisted into something scornful and not fitting to her.

She said, "You sound like you wanted to know. It's all a bit dull. I may tell you sometime, and watch you trying not to yawn. Maybe there's no one on this earth who is the least bit interested except me. And I'm only interested now because the net result of being hurt is that I'm down here alone, trying to do work I'm not suited for, trying to think of what I should do next—trying to make a plan for my life that'll make sense. I don't make sense to myself these days.'' She turned toward him and grinned. "Do all the people you meet start weeping on your shoulder?''

For a moment he dropped the pretense. He said, "Maybe we're both at a crossroads. I'm doing work I'm not suited for, and I don't know why I continue. It'll soon be over and I have no plans.''

They were both silent for a few moments. He said suddenly, "Before this turns into a wake, we better have another drink."

So they talked of New Orleans, of the tourist-consciousness of the French Quarter, of the proper Vermouth for martinis—discovered a mutual liking for frog's legs, hot weather, Mozart and Duke Ellington. They were gay, and surprisingly young, and some of the ghosts left his eyes and the basement room took another backward step into the past.

But while they were talking, Charlebois crossed beyond the grillwork door a dozen times, and the man's habitual way of walking, the angle of his head, the slope of his shoulders, were all indexed, recorded—filed in a compartment of Jan's mind which was as still and cold as a starlit night on the steppes. And he discovered which set of tables were served by Jean Charlebois.

He offered her another drink and she said, "Just one more. That'll finish me. Then you can lead me to a table."

"The blind leading the blind, Jerry."

The Ancient Door had filled up, and it was difficult for Jan Dalquist to estimate the proper interval which would give him assurance of getting one of Charlebois's tables. He managed it. The headwaiter held the door open with a flourish, and Dalquist followed Jerry Ellis into the dining room, unobtrusively guiding her over to a table served by Charlebois.

When Charlebois came with the menus, Dalquist glanced up at him and said casually, in clipped Parisian, "I assume that you speak French?''

"Yes, monsieur," Charlebois said. "Monsieur speaks very well."

Dalquist glanced at Jerry Ellis, ascertaining from her puzzled expression that she didn't speak the language. He said rapidly, "It is very crowded in here, and the young lady has no French. Have you not a quiet place where we might eat alone? With you to serve us?"

"One moment, monsieur." Charlebois hurried off.

Jan turned to Jerry and said, "I'm sorry, but I just happened to think of it when the waiter came to the table. I asked him if there was a place where we could dine alone. I always feel conspicuous when the tables are so close and people can see my hands. I forgot that you might consider such a suggestion a little bold."

"Don't be silly," she said quickly. "I'd love it. I hate being nudged by the elbows of the people at the next table."

Charlebois was back in a few moments. He nodded to Dalquist and said, "One of the private rooms has not been reserved, monsieur. And I can serve you if you wish. Please follow me."

They followed him through the curtains and up the narrow stairway to the second floor. With a flourish, he opened the door to a small room. It overlooked the courtyard. The moon—newly risen—shone through the open french doors and silvered a table for two set just inside the room. An ornate balcony overhung the court. When they were both in the room, Charlebois shut the door, hurried over to the table and lighted the two tall white candles. He held the chair for Jerry.

Jan said, "May I order for you?"

"Please do."

Charlebois departed with the order, and as soon as he had shut the door silently behind him, Jerry began to laugh. She said, "Look at this den of wickedness! I had no idea they had these rooms up here. Moonlight. Candlelight. Huge divan. Draperies. It looks like a set I've seen in about six movies. My husband, if I had a husband, breaks in while we're drinking a toast in champagne to the evening. I scream and you leap off the balcony. Or you shoot him. Or I shoot him. Or you shoot the waiter by mistake and I jump off the balcony. Why is it that there is so much less drama in real life?"

Dalquist was acutely conscious of the weight of the gun in the shoulder holster. He said, "As a matter of fact, I did order champagne. Now, accuse me of having delusions of drama."

"I accuse you of being a man who never did a dramatic thing in his life, Jan. That's why I like you. I'm desperately tired of dramatic people."

Due to Charlebois's downstairs responsibilities, the service was slow, but neither of them minded it. The candles flickered in the warm, fresh breeze. They talked of her painting, and she told him her only talent was good draftsmanship, that she couldn't translate her emotions onto the canvas. At best, she could become only an adequate illustrator.

Jan told her of his life in prewar Paris, of the great automotive plant in which he had been a very junior engineer. How, somehow, the war, the destruction of men and machines through the application of very expert and very deadly mechanical engineering techniques, had soured him on his chosen profession.

When she asked him what he was doing, he said, "I'm an investigator for French capitalists who wish to build up foreign investments. I'm down here bloodhounding a deal for them. When it's over, I'll be through."

"Then what?"

He shrugged. "Probably become a bloodhound for somebody else. I don't know. I daydream a bit now and then. Always seem to picture myself as some sort of farmer. Green stuff growing all around me. Silly idea. Never tried to grow anything in my life."

"I'm a farm gal," she said. "Take me along with you to pick out the land, and I'll give you a short course."

She said it lightly, but their eyes met as she said it and something passed between the two of them—something frightening in its momentary intensity.

At that instant, Charlebois knocked on the door and entered on command.

Dalquist said rapidly, in French, "Bring us some brandy. Good brandy. And I suspect that the lady will leave me for a few moments. When she does, I wish to speak with you privately."

"Oui, monsieur." He brought back a tray with two glasses and a dusty, unopened bottle. He showed Dalquist the label, opened the bottle and poured the two glasses.

Jerry said, "Would you excuse me, please?"

Charlebois held the door for her and then came back into the room. He stood by the table and said, "Monsieur?"

Dalquist noticed the man staring at his hands. He moved them below the table level. "You have been very helpful. What is your name?"

"Pierre Duval, monsieur."

"The young lady and I are very pleased. You impress me as being a man of tact and intelligence." Charlebois made a small, self-effacing gesture. "I am unacquainted with New Orleans, Duval, and I desire to visit many interesting places with the young lady. You are doubtless well acquainted with the French Quarter. The young lady is a new acquaintance. You understand how such things are." Dalquist chuckled in a man-to-man fashion. Charlebois laughed dutifully.

Dalquist continued. "At what time are you off duty here?"

"In two hours, monsieur. Eleven-thirty. Rather late, possibly."

"If I were to come for you at that time, Duval, would you consent to guide us to some interesting places?" As Charlebois hesitated, Dalquist added, "I will pay you well."

"If Monsieur will come to the top of these stairs, to the first room on the left in the outside hallway, anytime after eleven-thirty, I will be ready." At that moment a sudden gust of wind blew out one of the candles. Charlebois hastened around the table to relight it. He stumbled on the rug and had to place his hand against Dalquist's chest to keep from falling upon him. He backed off and apologized profusely. There was something in

his eyes that vaguely alarmed Dalquist. He relighted the
candle as Jerry Ellis came back into the room.

They lingered a half hour over the brandy, and at last
Jan paid the check, leaving a liberal tip for Charlebois.
They walked down the stairs and out onto the street,
with Dalquist fighting against the spell of the night, the
warmth of her laughter, the faint, clean scent of her hair.
And that odd look in Charlebois's eyes troubled him.

They went to three different places, listening to the
music, the poor present-day ghost of the New Orleans
jazz heritage. Dalquist arranged it so that they entered
the third place a little after eleven. He also made certain
that it was only a few hundred feet from the Ancient
Door.

They sat, side by side, on a low bench along one wall
of a large room. With practiced stealth, he unclasped her
purse and dropped his silver lighter into it, forcing it
down into a corner. At twenty-five after eleven he began
to slap at his pockets and look worried.

Jerry said, "What's the matter, Jan?"

"My lighter. Seems to be gone. I bet you I left it at
that last place. If I go back right now, I may stand a
chance of getting it back. You don't mind waiting for
me, do you? It's only two blocks. If it isn't there, I'll try
the first place. Just sit tight and order me a drink."

*The hunter acquires the habit of melting into the terrain,
of blending himself with the brush and the movement of
his passage is as unnoticeable as the stirring of a light
breeze. His every step is sure, his movements deft. He is
gone before you become conscious of his presence.*

So it was with Dalquist. One couple sat in a far corner
of the dining room of the Ancient Door. No waiter was
about. He crossed the floor in his dull gray suit with his
noiseless tread. They didn't look up. He went up the
stairs and knocked at the first door on the left of the
passageway.

"Duval?" he called.

"Come in, monsieur."

Dalquist walked into the room. Charlebois stood on
the far side of the room. It was a small room, ob-

viously used as a dressing room by the help. A row of hooks held wrinkled uniforms. Dalquist's automatic was equipped with what is called a one-shot silencer, a small cartridge of metal containing compressed sponge rubber. It was screwed onto the threaded end of the barrel. Such a device is only effective for the first shot, muting it to about the decibel rating of a loud cough.

With the sixth sense of the hunter, Dalquist, as his hand flashed up toward the shoulder, felt the presence of someone else close behind him. He tried to dodge and turn, but as his fingertips touched the rough grip of the automatic, a stunning blow hit him just under the ear, dropping him heavily to his hands and knees. He shook his head and tried to fight away as he felt a hand slipping under his coat, snatching away the automatic. In a fog of semi-consciousness, he cursed himself for not entering with the weapon in his hand.

He was kicked heavily in the side and he fell over onto the floor, gasping for breath. The room swam around him as he sat up, narrowing his eyes to hasten focus. The door was kicked shut. A stranger, a bandy-legged man with a potbelly, small eyes and cropped black hair, stood grinning down at Dalquist, covering him with his own weapon.

Charlebois stood slightly behind him, also smiling, a slim knife in his right hand. He held it in the traditional knife fighter's manner, the end of the handle against the heel of his hand, his thumb resting lightly on the cutting edge.

Charlebois said, "Crawl slowly over to that chair, monsieur, and sit. Cross your arms tightly and keep them crossed. René, lock the door."

Dalquist did as he was told. He had learned, in the most difficult conceivable manner, that it is best not to speak when at a disadvantage.

After Dalquist was in the chair and René had locked the door, Charlebois said, "René, this is the cow I spoke about. An ex-member of the Gestapo. A man who betrayed hundreds of the brave patriots of France. It is up to us to kill him in the name of France."

René's stupid face twisted with hate. He said thickly, "My brother was one of those betrayed by such a man!"

Dalquist weighed the chances. He said quickly, "René, you are listening to one who is a traitor himself. Look at my hands. Would the Gestapo torture one of their own? Would any group other than the Gestapo do such a thing?"

He extended his hands, ignoring the hoarse exclamation of Charlebois. As René stared at the mutilated fingers, Dalquist said quickly, "And the man behind you is an infamous one named Jean Charlebois, who betrayed the Maquis. I was hired by the patriots of France to track him down."

As René, confused, turned toward Charlebois, the traitor said, "Do not believe this pig, René! He is lying—"

"I want to know why this man you call a member of the Gestapo should come here for you, Duval," René said heavily.

Dalquist felt his heart leap as he read the indecision in René's face. The small eyes looked swiftly toward Dalquist's hands and then into Dalquist's eyes.

There was a sudden loud banging at the door. Charlebois hissed, "Shoot him quickly, fool!"

Wheeling ponderously, René said, "Maybe it is you that I should—"

With a grunting curse, Jean Charlebois took a quick step toward René and drove the ready knife into the man's body. René staggered with the force of the blow and the gun hand sagged. As he tried to lift the gun, Charlebois chopped down with the edge of his hand on René's wrist, snatching up the gun as it fell to the floor.

René did not fall. He hugged his belly and moaned hoarsely. His eyes were shut with the pain in his body. The flat metal handle of the knife glinted, protruding from between his hands. Dalquist sank back into the chair under the threat of the muzzle of his own gun, pointed at him once more.

With another curse, Charlebois snatched the handle of the knife and yanked it out of René's middle. René's life seemed to flow out with the blood that made a widening splotch on his clothes. He dropped to his knees, chin on chest, and then went over onto his face with a damp noise in his throat that sickened Dalquist.

The pounding at the door continued. Charlebois called out, in accented English, "One moment, please." The pounding ceased.

Charlebois said quickly, "Monsieur, you are of a stupidity most amazing. True, you were clever to find me, but before I left Mexico City, I told Pepita that she should unseal each letter from me with great care. I told her that she would find, stuck under the flap, a short single bit of my hair. If it was missing, she should tell me by telegraph immediately. It was missing on the last letter. The letter had been unsealed and read. Thus I knew someone was coming for me.

"I have used great care. You are the first one to have paid any attention to me. I saw your hands, monsieur. I am familiar with the work of the Gestapo. I stumbled against you, monsieur, and felt the bulk of your gun under my palm. You asked me to go out into the night with you, monsieur.

"It is indeed regrettable that you plunged a knife into René. He is indeed dead. I will open the door now, and your gun will be in this pocket. Do not speak."

Charlebois held the knife delicately and rubbed the thin metal handle against the side of his trousers, careful not to spot himself with the blood that colored the blade. He stepped closer to Dalquist and flicked a few drops of blood from the wet blade. They spattered on the dull gray fabric of Dalquist's suit.

He stepped to the door, unlocked it and swung it open. Jerry Ellis walked hesitantly in, her eyes wide, her underlip caught behind her teeth. Charlebois took a quick look into the hall and shut the door again.

He bowed to Jerry and said, "Mademoiselle, this is most regrettable, but this man—who was here with you earlier tonight—appears to be quite mad. That knife on the floor. With it he . . . ." Charlebois waved a nervous hand toward the body of René.

Dalquist knew he could quickly protest his innocence

to Jerry, and Charlebois would not dare use the gun. He needed Dalquist, alive, on whom he could pin the suspicions of the police so as to provide him sufficient time to get back across the border into Mexico before Dalquist could make his credentials known. It was a clever and daring plan. But some perverse instinct in Dalquist made him keep silent. He stared woodenly at Jerry, saw her features pale, saw her take a step backward away from the silent body.

Charlebois said quickly, "Mademoiselle, I have a gun in my pocket and I shall watch this murderer. Will you please go downstairs and phone the police."

She looked at Jan Dalquist, hurt and questioning in her eyes. He stared at her without expression. Charlebois opened the door and Dalquist heard the quick tapping of her feet as she went down the stairs.

Dalquist said, "You won't get away with this, Jean Charlebois." But even as he said it, he knew the scheme would work—that by the time he could divert the attention of the police away from himself, Charlebois would be out of reach. He felt ill as he thought of the additional weary months of search that would be necessary.

He said, "And even if this does work long enough for you to get away, Charlebois, I will soon be after you again." It was not said with defiance. It was said with a tired resignation. It expressed the soul-sickness of him, the cumulative exhaustion of killing and seeing death, the internal, pervading nausea that had been with him for two and a half years.

Charlebois said, "You forget, monsieur. I know you now. I know your face. You will never kill me. Even if you find me, it is you who will die. In this game, once the hunter is known, the advantage is with the hunted. I will seek a place where you cannot approach me without my knowledge. And there I will kill you."

There was a quiet confidence in the ring of his words. To Dalquist, it was like a sentence of death. Somehow, he knew that it would end in precisely that way. For he was too weary with the game to continue much longer.

He would walk blindly into a death that would be but a continuation of his present, purposeless existence.

Charlebois chuckled. He said, "I did not believe that the young lady was in league with you. Had her reactions been different, I would have killed the both of you and escaped immediately. In a way you are lucky. But it will be more pleasant to deal with you at some future time in circumstances that are more to my liking."

"You are an egocentric animal, Jean Charlebois."

"Possibly, monsieur, but of an effectiveness truly surprising."

Dalquist heard the heavy steps on the stairs and tensed himself to spring as Charlebois glanced toward the door. But the slim man looked back too quickly.

They walked in the door, with Jerry Ellis following them, two lean uniformed men. One crossed over and knelt by René's body. He stood up and shrugged.

The other said, "While we wait for Homicide, suppose you give me a quick reading." He stepped over to Charlebois and held out his hand. Charlebois laid the automatic carefully in the outstretched hand.

"Sir, the dead man is my employer and the manager of the Ancient Door, René Despard. That man in the chair came in here earlier in the evening, and we made arrangements for me to be his guide starting at eleven-thirty. He was with that young lady who called you. At eleven-thirty, René and I were in this room. That gentleman came in, quite drunk, and began to call us both foul names. René tried to quiet him. The gentleman pulled out that gun I just gave you and threatened us.

"I circled him and struck him behind the ear. You will find the mark. He fell and dropped the gun. René took out that knife you see on the floor. As I picked up the gun, the gentleman jumped up and rushed at René, striking him violently on the arm. René dropped the knife. The man picked it up and drove it into René Despard.

"The violence of his act seemed to sober him. I threatened him with the gun and he sat in that chair where he now is. You can see the marks of blood on his trousers. The woman came and knocked at the door. I admitted

62

her and told her to call the police. Truly, it seems to me the act of a madman." His voice broke. "René was— was my friend. A harmless man and a good man."

The first policeman said, "Made him drop the knife, picked it up and killed him with it." He glanced at Dalquist.

Dalquist said. "This is a fabric of lies. That man killed René. I saw him."

Charlebois grunted contemptuously. "Kill a man who was my friend and my employer? Any other employee will testify as to our great friendship."

The policeman turned to Dalquist and said, "Mister, you just keep your mouth shut. We're damn tired of people getting crazy drunk in this town."

Dalquist knew that it would be that way. Charlebois was too convincing, too sincere in his expressions of bewilderment and sorrow. He avoided the pitfalls of retelling his story, of showing too much emotion or giving too much detail.

Dalquist was surprised to see, out of the corner of his eye, that Jerry was moving closer to his chair. The room was very silent. One policeman leaned against the door-frame and picked his teeth with a fragment of matchstick. Charlebois stared numbly at the floor. Dalquist pleaded with the Fates for a man of perception among those they were awaiting.

They all started when Jerry said loudly, "You say that the dead man dropped the knife and Mr. Dalquist picked it up off the floor?"

The policeman by the door said, "Stay out of this, lady. We'll ask any questions that need to be asked."

She fumbled with her purse, and her very thin ciga-rette case dropped to the floor. It landed by Dalquist's feet. Instinctively he bent over for it.

As he fumbled at it, he heard Jerry say loudly, "You're fools to listen to that waiter! Look at this man! Do you believe he could pick a knife that thin off the floor when he can't even pick up my cigarette case, which is twice as thick as the knife? Look at his hands!"

It was true. With the numb ends of his manufactured

fingers, with the absence of fingernails, Jan Dalquist could only fumble at the case. He couldn't get a grasp on it. The policeman by the door stepped over. Dalquist straightened up and held out his hands. The policeman's mouth twisted as he looked at them.

There was a flash of movement and the other policeman yelled, "Hey! Stop, you!" Charlebois had melted out of the room. Dalquist heard his feet pounding along the corridor. It was obvious that it had been Charlebois's only possible move. Once Jerry had cast sufficient doubt on Charlebois's story so as to make it essential to hold him, he couldn't risk staying.

Dalquist said, "Stay in this room!" as he ran out into the corridor. He realized that Charlebois hadn't wanted to take the risk of running into the men who would soon be coming up the stairs. He would duck in somewhere.

A gun boomed in the corridor. The policemen disappeared into the small room where they had had dinner. Dalquist followed them. He found them leaning out from the balcony, looking up. One said, "Went up the face of the building on those vines. The leaves are shaking . . . There he is. Wing him, Joe!"

The shot cracked more flatly in the open air. The policeman said, "Got him. Look out!"

They ducked back away from the railing as a screaming figure fell down through the night. It struck the iron balcony railing, and as it clanged like a bell in a minor key, the scream stopped abruptly. There was a noise in the court a second later. A noise that might be made by a soaked rag slammed down onto a basement floor. A woman in the court screamed. A man cursed softly and fluently. The policeman who had fired the shot said, "Al, I feel kinda sick."

She was waiting in the shadow of the building when he walked out of Police Headquarters with orders to return and sign statements at ten the following morning.

He glanced at his watch as he walked up to her. Three-fifteen in the morning.

She said, "Mister, where were we when we were so

rudely interrupted? I know a place where you can buy a short girl a small beer."

She began to walk and he fell in step beside her, grinning. Somehow a weight had been lifted off his heart.

He asked, "Why did you follow me?"

She said, "Lipstick is a fine thing. Just as you left I looked in my purse for mine and found your lighter. At first I thought I had picked it up by accident. Then I realized that you must have put it there for a reason. I hurried after you, not certain of what to do. I saw you turn in here. You weren't in the bar or in the dining room. I tried upstairs and heard some sort of thumping behind that first door. I listened and couldn't hear you. Maybe the brandy got me. After a while I started to kick the door. You know the rest."

"I suppose you've got a million questions to ask me?"

"Have I asked you any?"

"Not a one."

"Jan, two people have to have some sort of a code. Let's make ours a code of no questions. When either of us wants the other to know something, we'll tell it without waiting for questions. Okay?"

She put her hand on his arm, stopped him. She held her hand out. "Shake on it, mister."

He took her hand quickly. Her clasp was firm and warm.

"No questions?" she asked.

"No questions," he said, smiling down at her.

"And no regrets?"

"No regrets, Jerry," he said.

"And now you buy me that beer."

A Corpse in His Dreams

IN HIS DREAM, as in a thousand dreams before, Alicia Crane called to him, her voice thin, sweet, clear.

"Matthew! Matthew, darling. Matthew Otis!"

"But you're dead!" he said in his dream. "Dead, dead, dead, dead."

Odd that she couldn't or wouldn't believe. And what was she doing here in China? There was a battle coming up.

Above the sound of her voice he could hear the sound of battle. The distant slap of rifles, the surly crump of mortar, the guttural whack of a grenade.

"You're dead, Alicia Crane! Dead!"

But he couldn't make her hear. "Matthew! Matthew, darling!"

He awoke, his leg cramped from being braced against the green plush of the seat in front of him. The train, huffing laboriously along the coast toward Cranesbay, rocked and jolted on the uneven railbed. The vivid dream made everything unreal. Yes, Alicia was dead. He had killed her just nine years before. Nine years this month. November 1939.

He turned to peer out into the darkness. The lights of a farmhouse appeared, then fled off into the night.

He picked the magazine up off the littered floor, and turned to the article he had been reading when he fell asleep. "Cheap Death in China," by Matthew Otis. With a wry smile he reread the editor's introduction:

> As this is being printed, Matthew Otis is on his way back to this country after three long years with the Chinese armies. In order to gather the news, Mr. Otis has lived as a Chinese soldier. Only those who have seen the Chinese armies know the incredible hardships that Mr. Otis has endured in order to bring you factual reporting of the Chinese Civil War. Matthew Otis is a tall, powerful man who looks older than his thirty-two years. His face is tanned, and in his gray eyes is a dim reflection of the misery he has witnessed in his . . .

Matthew yawned and put the magazine on the seat beside him. Maybe one day he'd write an article that would tell them the motivation behind his efforts. Maybe one day he'd tell them he had lived in the distant places of the earth because he fled from a girl who would not stay properly dead.

And he would have to tell them that he was returning to Cranesbay for the first time since it had happened, hoping that in some way he would be able to rid himself of the nightmare that had been his ever since the day of her death. The night of her death.

He smiled. That would be a fine article. He would tell how during that first year he had carried her, fresh and vivid, in his mind. The tone of her voice. The warmth of her lips. The proud, high way in which she carried her head.

But in nine years his memories had grown more, rather than less, vivid. He could not escape her. She made all his days of danger tasteless, his vain seeking of delight insipid.

He knew that he was afraid to come back.

And yet if he was ever to be able to live in the present and in the future, it had to be done.

Guilt is a hand across the eyes, a knife at the heart. There can be no peace, no joy, no ecstasy, no pride in accomplishment. With guilt all there can be is a pseudo-life where one goes through the motions expected of an adult, and carries in his mind the horrors imagined by a child.

The aged coach jolted and the gray smoke hung in wet strands across the stale air yellowed by the coach lights. Across the aisle a doughy woman reached for a whining child that fought to get away from her. In the seat ahead two sailors, two tired blue-and-white memories of wartime, slept noisily with their mouths open.

He felt the rising tide of excitement, a chill that ran down his back, a hollow feeling in his stomach. But it was the excitement of a man who, alone in a factory at night, has caught his fingers in slow-moving gears and knows that the gears will inevitably pull in his arm, elbow, shoulder, killing him at last.

The excitement of a man whose car is plunged into a dizzy skid across sheer ice toward the inevitable precipice.

Matthew Otis on vacation!

Matthew Otis returning to appease the ghosts of long ago. A private Munich.

Matthew Otis returning to the overgrown village of Cranesbay, where he had become an adult, fallen in love with Alicia Crane and killed her.

The train's whistle was a lonesome call at a deserted crossing. Out there in the darkness was the ocean. To his left were the high hills, shrouded by night. Ahead would be the crescent of Cranesbay, a city carelessly arranged on the shelf of land between the hills and the sea. The train whistled again and something within him answered the lonely cry.

There was no way to leap out into the night rain, turn back across half the earth. It was done. The symbol of fulfillment was the little orange cardboard ticket wedged into the window lever. In his mind was the memory of her echoing voice in his dream.

It was mingled with the memory of long ago, when her voice had been different. When her eyes had looked on him and found him good. When her hand . . .

Alicia Crane reached her hand across the table and traced the blue vein on the back of his hand.

The dance floor was crowded and the band was giving a not ineffective imitation of Goodman.

"Matt," she said softly, "what are the words you use when two people are like this?"

He smiled at her. "Meant for each other."

"Don't sound so flip, darling," she said.

"I can't help it, Alicia. Nineteen thirty-nine is a wise-crack period. A hundred years ago I'd be swearing eternal devotion and getting my tight pants all dirty by kneeling in front of you, my right hand over my heart."

"Couldn't you do that now, Matt?"

"Sure, but you'd think I was clowning. No, honey. I have to tell you I love you as though it were the punch line in a wisecrack and then you believe me. I love you, honey."

"I want to be kissed," she said firmly.

He began to get up, saying, "We can take a walk out to the car."

"Yes, but later, Matt. When I was a kid I always saved the icing until last. Let's just sit and think of how nice that kiss is going to be. Then it will taste even better."

She smiled and something about the way her gray eyes looked made his heart pause in its beat.

Suddenly the smile faded as she looked toward the door.

"What is it?"

"Roy Bedford, Matt. I was afraid for a minute he was drunk. He hates you, Matt."

"I don't blame him, honey. He had the nicest girl in the world and she belongs to me now. Let him hate me."

"If he comes over, please be nice, Matt."

"If he's nice, I'll be nice."

He glanced across the dance floor. Roy Bedford was with a girl who had her hair frizzed out in a mop. Her mouth was dark with lipstick. Roy led her to a booth and Matt saw him glance over, murmur something to the girl, then cross over toward them.

He had an easy smile on his face. He was tall, with a

sharp, aquiline face, crisp dark hair and eyes set so far apart as to give him an odd opaque look.

He walked up to the booth, smiled down at Alicia and said, "How're the lovebugs getting along, lovely?" There was a slur in his voice.

"Just fine, Roy," Alicia said blandly.

Matt said, "Sit down a minute and have a drink, Roy."

To his surprise Roy sat beside Alicia and said, "Thanks."

They stared across at each other and behind them was the history of a vicious competition that had begun in grade school. Roy Bedford had seemed to depend on winning as much as on breathing. And this time he had lost. Once before he had lost. Back when the high school basketball coach had tried to start a boxing team . . .

(Through puffed eye, through maze of blood and pain, standing on wavering legs, Matt looked down at Roy Bedford, who, with blind fury, was crawling to his feet to be smashed to the floor again. The hoarse sound of Bedford's breathing was loud in the deserted gym.

Matt said, "Had enough?"

Roy rushed him, staggering, blundering. Matt, his arms like lead, beat him once more to the floor. Roy Bedford didn't get up. Instead he rolled onto his stomach and began to sob, loudly, hoarsely. Matt untied the gloves, walked slowly to the showers and washed away the blood and part of the pain. When he looked back Roy was sitting on one of the stools, his face in his hands. Matt knew he would never be forgiven. That ended the boxing team.)

Roy Bedford was defeated again—and by the same person. Alicia is mine, Matt thought. And he knows it.

The drinks came; Roy drank his quickly. Matt looked curiously across the room. The girl Roy had brought still sat there.

Matt said, "Maybe your girl's lonesome, Roy. Maybe you better trot on back."

"Alicia doesn't want me to go," Roy said lightly.

"Don't be so silly, Roy," Alicia said. Her tone was

also light. "We've got nothing to talk about. Ever. You'd make me happy if you'd just go away. Don't think that you make me uncomfortable. You just bore me."

Across the room Rose Carney snapped open her purse, took out her cigarettes and ripped the cellophane from the pack. She had seen Roy sit down with Matt Otis and that Crane girl.

What does he think I am? she thought. How much does he think I'll stand for?

But she knew that there was no limit to what she would stand for from Roy Bedford. Still it would be wise to let him know he had angered her. Be cool with him. Push him away, even when the touch of his hands turned the whole world swimming.

He wouldn't go over there if he didn't still want that Crane girl, Rose thought. It gave her a feeling of great loneliness.

The waiter sauntered over and said, "I see you come in with that fellow, but is he joining that party over there? The boss don't allow no women without an escort."

"If you think he isn't with me, try throwing me out and see what he does. That's Roy Bedford, friend."

The waiter arched his eyebrows. "Is that supposed to mean something?"

"It doesn't right now. But it will."

The waiter walked away. Rose knew how much the name Roy Bedford was going to mean in Cranesbay. She sensed the hard quality of his indomitable ambition, his need to acquire power. In the soft, secret silences of the night when he had talked of himself, he had told her a little.

("Dad was the town drunk, Rosie, and I can see them looking at me and thinking about how I'm going to turn out to be a bum like he was. I'm glad I didn't go to college like the rest of them. Rosie, I was learning how to do things the hard way. College punks, that's what they are. Matt Otis, Evan Cleveland, the Furnivall girls. I'll show every last one of them. Okay, so I got grease under my nails now from working as a mechanic for Jud Proctor. But last week he let me buy into the garage. In a year or two I'm going to edge him out. The garage will give me dough to get into other things, Rosie. Lots of other things.''

"Like marriage, maybe?'' she had asked hopefully.

"No time for that, Rosie,'' he had said, reaching for her.)

Suddenly he slipped into the booth opposite her. She said quickly, "Thanks, Roy. Thanks a lot! All they were going to do was throw me out because they thought I was alone. I should think—''

She stopped because then she had seen the rigid fury in the set of his mouth, the dark shine of his eyes.

He took her wrist. He smiled at her and his nails dug into her skin.

She moaned softly, "Oh, don't, Roy. Don't!''

He let go of her and the blood stood where his nails had been. "We'll go now,'' he said quietly.

Alicia watched Roy's straight back as he walked away from the booth. She turned back to Matt and shuddered.

"He frightens me, Matt,'' she said.

He smiled. "What can he do, honey? Besides, he wasn't ever in love with you. It's just that your name is Crane and your ancestors gave their name to the town where he was born. He's driven by demons, that lad. He's the original teapot tempest. Now, let's settle down while you tell me how nice a guy I am, Alicia.''

The conductor stuck his head into the coach and said, "Cranesbay in five minutes.'' Matthew Otis turned from the window where he had been staring out at the memories of nine years before.

Fear was Alicia's face outside the train window, looking at him. Fear was Alicia's voice, repeated in a thousand dreams. Fear was the small city of Cranesbay, waiting in the darkness ahead.

Gradually the train slowed, the wheels clicking in slower cadence. Lights began to flash by the windows, and at last the train rocked wearily into the dingy station, the soot-smeared platform roofs damp in the feeble glow of the naked bulbs.

A Corpse in His Dreams

He buttoned his topcoat, walked awkwardly up the aisle, his big suitcase thudding against the seats.

The wind that touched his face as he stepped down onto the platform was the cool breath of Cranesbay. Dampness and the sea. Night, rain and the sea. The station was a square ugly room with a white tiled floor, a smell of coffee and rest rooms.

A drunk sat on one of the benches, mumbling eternal truths which no one would remember. Behind the ticket window a sallow man in a green eyeshade was reading a magazine.

It was as though he had never been away.

The Ocean Bay Hotel, six blocks from the ocean, was but two blocks from the station. He walked it, with the moisture, half rain, half mist, beading his face.

The lobby was empty. Behind the desk a man in a gray smock placed the registration card on the counter, read the upside-down handwriting with practiced ease.

"Ah, Mr. Otis!" he said, rubbing chubby hands together. "We wondered if you'd have time to visit Cranesbay."

Matt looked at him in sudden surprise. He had begun to think of himself as having no interest for anyone in Cranesbay.

"Oh!" he said. "There was something in the papers?"

"Two columns, Mr. Otis. A review of your new book and sort of a biography and a little about your work in China." He laughed. "You've become one of Cranesbay's favorite sons, Mr. Otis. I can give you a nice suite on the eighth-floor corner. You can see the ocean from there."

Matt said, "Fine. Thank you."

A lean, yawning bellhop materialized and the desk clerk handed him the key. The bellhop ran the elevator, left it with the door open while he carried the bag down to the suite.

When he was alone, Matt took off his coat and hat, turned out the lights, flung the window up and stood looking toward the sea.

He could hear the distant whisper of the surf against

the rocks. It made the same noise as it had on that night long ago when . . .

He grew conscious of the sound of the sea and thought at first that he was in his bed and he wondered why the sea should sound so loud. A storm? He lay with his eyes closed, listening to its muted thunder, gradually feeling the beginning of the pain.

The pain crept slowly over him, and he wondered almost objectively if the pain would pass some mystic boundary where he could no longer remain motionless, but must thrash about and scream.

His cheek was against wetness. He grew conscious of being fully dressed. He opened his eyes, moved his fingers about. He could see nothing. His hand touched grass, a twig, small stones.

The pain came back and part of it was above his ear. He touched it, felt the huge lump, the opened gash across it. The rest of the pain was in his hips, his loins. He touched his hip with his fingers, felt the unfamiliar shape. Distortion.

I am hurt, he thought with sudden surprise. I am on the ground and I am hurt. My body is the wrong shape.

When the pain came back the third time, it dragged him down into darkness.

When he awakened, the pain was not so bad. The cold numbed him. He reached out and his hand brushed against something that was soft and like ice. He tried to identify it, but his hand was too numbed. With infinite effort he rolled onto his hand, warming it with his body.

At last, the warmed hand outstretched, he traced with gentle fingers the outline of brow, the gentle arch of nose, the softness of lips. When he touched the eye, the lid was up, and his finger rested for a moment on the naked eyeball, feeling the moistness, feeling no quiver.

It was then that he screamed for the first time . . .

Feeling enormously weary, Matthew Otis turned away from the window and switched on the light. All of the strain that had gradually increased since the day he had walked up the gangplank at Hong Kong seemed to break within him, leaving him impossibly weary.

He pulled off his clothes, flung them carelessly aside and dropped onto the soft bed, the light still shining. Down into sleep, down into vast sleep . . .

He had told General Soong that the position was bad. The Honorable 21st Division had dug in on the forward slope of the hill. During the long, hot, dusty morning the artillery attached to the 8th Route Army had marched up the slope, pounding across the shallow holes, the places scooped in the earth, while from beyond the crest their own artillery answered. To his right a fragment caught a Chinese soldier in the throat. With a strange bubbling scream the man plunged up out of the hole, ran in a staggering, blundering stride down the slope to fall at last, rolling to a stop.

During a lull in the shelling, two men crept out and stripped the corpse. At noon the body had begun to bloat.

Far down on the plain they began to advance. The small slow figures of the soldiers of the 8th Route Army. Seeking shelter behind the rocks that littered the slope. Coming constantly closer.

Near dusk they were within rifle shot. At a signal they burst from cover, running up the slope, their faces showing the strain of fear and effort.

Then he saw her. She was running through the dusk. She was naked. Her long hair fell, golden and shining, down her back. She smiled as she ran toward him, and her voice, echoing, was saying, "Matthew, darling! Matthew Otis!"

He jumped up and screamed at them to stop shooting at her. But his voice was gone and the scream came as a soft whisper. He wanted to run to her, to drag her out of danger. But he could not move.

Even as she leaped over the naked body of the bloated soldier he saw the slugs write a wavering message across her white body. She came toward him in a stumbling run, falling as the dusk turned to night.

75

He reached out a hand in the darkness, traced the line of brow, the arch of nose, his fingertip resting for a moment on the unquivering eyeball.

"You're dead, Alicia," he said softly.

"That's right, Matt. Dead, dead, dead, dead, dead . . ."

He woke with a start, his body wet with perspiration. He felt weak and nervous. He padded into the bathroom, and stood under the shower, trying to wash away the memory of the dream.

In 1872 James Furnivall, blacksmith, walked into the village of Cranesbay. Three days later he had set up his shop. He was twenty years old.

Sixteen years later his only son, Roger Furnivall, was born. In 1908 James, then fifty-six, and his son, then twenty, enlarged the shop to take care of repairs for those new gadgets called automobiles.

When Roger was thirty, he married a Boston girl named Patricia Bowen and incorporated the company as the Furnivall Pneumatic Tool Company. It covered an entire city block, having acquired nearly two million in war contracts.

In 1927 Roger's father died one week before Patricia died in childbirth, leaving Roger with two daughters. One four, named Patience, and one infant, named Susan.

In 1948, at nine o'clock in the morning after Matthew Otis' return, Patience Furnivall stood in her bedroom and looked toward the sea. To her left she could see the Furnivall Pneumatic Tool Company. Beyond it was the shining steel threads of railroad sidings. Beyond the sidings was the ocean. On the horizon a coastwise vessel made a gray pattern of smoke.

The plant buildings were old, badly in need of repairs. The recent war years had not been profitable. She and Evan Cleveland, plant manager, had made a bad guess on equipment purchases.

She sighed and turned away from the window. The maid knocked quietly at her door and said, "Mr. Bedford is in the sun room, Miss Furnivall."

A Corpse in His Dreams

She took a quick glance in the mirror, neither approving nor disapproving what she saw. She saw a tall woman of twenty-five. Tall and pale with black hair drawn back so tightly that it gave her high-cheekboned face almost an Oriental look. Her lips were full and warm, the only spot of color in her face.

Here it is, she thought. Just walk downstairs and sell out something that started when my grandfather walked into this town with a pack on his back and a sledge in his hand. I can remember him. Tall and strong and straight until the day he died. If only Dad had lived as long as he did. The war killed Dad. Sixteen hours a day in the plant killed him. Square your shoulders, Patience. Go smiling down the stairs and sell your birthright to Roy Bedford.

As she walked toward the sun room and caught sight of Roy Bedford, she felt the quick rise of hate. He was so sure of himself. So positive. So determined.

He jumped up and took her hand. "Hello, Patience. Nice to see you alone like this."

She smiled, sat on the couch, and he sat across from her. She knew she was supposed to bring up the question first. That would give him some sort of an edge.

"What's your proposition, Roy?" she asked bluntly.

Studying the glowing end of his cigarette, he said, "You've passed every dividend since the war. The forty thousand shares of stock outstanding have an over-the-counter value of twenty dollars a share. That's thirty dollars under par. You and your sister own twenty-two thousand shares—eleven apiece. I own or control seventeen thousand three hundred and forty-one shares. It's only a question of time until I get hold of the remaining six hundred and fifty-nine outstanding. You and your sister vote against me, giving me no hand in management.

"I have two propositions. If you and your sister will sell me fifteen hundred shares apiece, I will give you seventy-five thousand dollars each, or a bonus of forty-five thousand dollars each over market value, permitting each of you to retain ninety-five hundred shares each. The other alternative is to buy you out completely, and frankly I'd rather do that. It will take me six months to get the actual money, but I will pay you half a million apiece for all your stock. That's two hundred thousand dollars over the present market value of the stock. That could be invested so as to give both you and Susan a life income of twenty thousand apiece."

Patience smiled. "You make it sound so generous, Roy. You offer us a million for what we could have got three million for four years ago."

"That was four years ago, Pat. I'm offering you a million for what you can get half a million for a year from now."

"Evan doesn't think so."

"Evan is a dreamer, Pat. He'll be out five minutes after I get the controlling interest."

"Aren't you a little hard, Roy?"

He smiled broadly. "Pat, I didn't parlay a one-third interest in a little repair garage into big money in nine years by being soft. I'll put my own men in. If this new line of hammers and special tools that Evan has developed is any good, we'll take over. If not, we'll toss it out."

"It's a good line, Roy. If we could only—"

"—get the steel. I know. You buy the gray-market steel and the increased cost bumps your production cost so high you can't make money."

"And you can?" she asked, smiling crookedly.

He lifted his chin. "Of course I can!"

She said slowly, "I'd like to sell out, Roy—"

"It's a deal?" he asked eagerly.

She shook her head. "But I don't want to do it this way. I don't want to be licked. I don't think Dad and Gramps care if I decide not to run the company, but I don't think they would like to see me quit while I'm behind."

Bedford smiled confidently. "Pat, that's why you can't ever make any money. You're too sentimental."

"Come back in six months, Roy. We'll talk about it again."

His face turned pale with anger. He jumped up and said, "These things don't work that way, Miss Furnivall.

I'm warning you. This offer is going to be good for exactly one week. Unless I get a decision at the end of that time, you may get a lot of surprises.''

She looked at him calmly. ''You wouldn't be threatening me, Roy?''

''I'll make it my business to run that shabby little outfit of yours right into the ground and you right along with it!''

''Please get out of this house,'' she said.

His mouth twisted in a humorless grin. ''Polite even when you're sore, hey? Sure, I'll get out. But you better come around on your knees before the week is up.''

She stood up slowly and said distinctly, ''Mr. Bedford, I don't have to wait a week. I'll tell you now. The Furnivall Pneumatic Tool Company will go into receivership rather than make any such deal with you. Good-by.''

''I suppose you think you're talking for Susan, too?''

He didn't wait for her to answer. The door slammed behind him and Patience stood leaning against the hallway door, weak and trembling.

He had defeated her. Through Susan.

Susan will see through him, she thought. She must!

That was the weak link. Susan. Gay, reckless Susan, who did not share her feeling of family pride in the name of Furnivall.

She called the plant, got hold of Evan Cleveland. She told him that she'd be down in a half hour to discuss something of importance . . .

Evan Cleveland had been in the same high school graduating class as Roy Bedford and Matt Otis. At the time of Alicia Crane's death, Evan was just finishing his third year of engineering. He started out at Furnivall running a bank of automatic screw machines, eventually functioning as troubleshooter, assistant foreman, foreman, second assistant to the plant superintendent and finally, after the death of Roger Furnivall, factory manager.

He was short, broad, quick and naturally cheerful. He had red hair touched with gray, freckles across his pug nose and calm blue eyes with a glint of humor in their depths.

After Patience had finished telling him about the conversation with Bedford, he leaned back in his chair and glared at the papers on his desk.

"I did do right, didn't I?" Patience asked.

"That's just it, Pat. I don't know. Yesterday I would have said yes. Today I don't know."

"What's the trouble?" she asked, alarmed.

"Yesterday we were pretty sure of getting a hundred and fifty tons of steel at a price that wasn't too bad. It would arrive by next Wednesday. But another bidder sneaked in and grabbed it. A week from today we're going to either shut down or buy steel at prices that will make your eyes stand out on stalks."

"There's more than that," she said, suddenly calm.

He stood up, walked over to the window and looked down at the plant yard, his blunt hands knotted behind him.

"You're right, as usual, Pat." He sighed. "Got a phone call this morning. A man named Feeney in Rochester, New York, is bringing suit against us for patent violation. The whole line of stuff we're working on. Claims he had it first."

"But I thought your patents were unchallenged!" she said.

"The courts will have to decide that. They may slap an injunction on us to keep us from turning out any of the new line." He turned around suddenly and she saw that he looked old. "Pat," he said, "I've an idea that if Roy Bedford didn't have his eye on this place, we would have got our steel. Also, Roy owns a piece of Delansey Tool in Rochester. This guy Feeney worked for Delansey. You figure it out."

She frowned. "Can he do that to us?"

Evan Cleveland gave her a tired grin. "Honey, he's doing it. And you know as well as I do that if it doesn't work this way, he'll get us through Susan, marrying her if he has to, to get control of her stock. That boy is dynamite."

"I'd better talk to Susan," she said.

"Or take Bedford's offer."

She smiled with an effort. "Evan, if I took his offer now, I'd never again be able to think of my ancestors without blushing."

She smiled at him and left his office.

Evan Cleveland sat down, rolling a yellow pencil between his blunt fingers.

Maybe it would be a good thing if she fights him, he thought. Maybe it would be a good thing if she loses every dime in the world. Maybe then I'd have the courage to tell her that I've loved her ever since the day she fell out of the pear tree and broke her wrist and didn't cry.

The pencil cracked suddenly, with a loud snap. In a quiet tone he called Roy Bedford every name he could think of.

The phone rang and he picked it up. A voice said, "Evan?"

"Speaking. Who is it?"

"Your favorite correspondent in the Chinese armies, chum."

"Matt!" he yelled. "Where are you? Are you in town? When can you come over?"

"Slow down, boy. It's ten minutes to noon. We'll have lunch together in the grill of the Ocean Bay—unless you've got other plans. You can find me at the bar."

"A deal," he said, hearing Matt's laugh, then the click of the line.

Standing at the bar of the Ocean Bay, Matthew Otis watched the man mix a martini. Evan Cleveland should be along in a few minutes. He hoped that no one would recognize him before Evan arrived. He wanted to think. The ghosts were thick in the bar. Over there, at the corner table, he and Alicia had sat one night. She had broken a date with Roy Bedford to be with him.

A heavy man with white hair and a yellowed face walked in, stood at the end of the bar and glanced incuriously at Matthew before ordering a drink.

It was a face out of the past. The man with the white hair was John Bernard, coroner.

The coroner's jury had returned a verdict of accidental death. Bernard had wanted more than that . . .

"Dr. Green, please describe the injuries suffered by the deceased."

"The car, driven by Otis here, was a convertible. Both occupants were thrown clear when the car overturned the first time. The deceased was thrown clear in such a way that the handle which fastens the top tore her throat open. She bled to death in seconds, as the carotid artery was completely severed."

"You have treated Mr. Otis?"

"Yes, I have."

"Describe his injuries, please."

"Thigh broken near the hip joint. Pelvis crushed. Bad concussion. He was thrown clear but the car evidently rolled over him on its way down the slope."

"He sustained no permanent injury?"

"We can't tell as yet. That cast you see on him can be taken off in another month. He'll be confined to that chair for some time, however. The concussion has destroyed all memory of the accident."

"Could alcohol have the same effect?"

"Yes. It would be possible. When the percentage of alcohol in the blood reaches a certain tolerance, memory is often impaired."

"Thank you, Dr. Green. Call the next witness, please. . ."

"Your name and occupation?"

"Anthony Dorio. I'm a waiter at the Ocean Club."

"You served the deceased and Mr. Otis on the night of the accident?"

"Yes, sir."

"How many drinks did Mr. Otis have?"

"I think it was five."

"Do you know?"

"Not for sure. It was at least five."

"Was he drunk when he left there?"

"I wouldn't say he was drunk. He was happy."

"Happy? What degree of intoxication does that indicate?"

"Just happy, sir. Laughing, kidding with the girl and tipping me a whole buck when he left . . ."

"Your name and occupation, sir?"

"Stanley Hoornbeck, highway engineer."

"You have looked over the site of the fatal accident?"

"I have."

"Would you please describe it."

"Halfway between the Ocean Club and Cranesbay, the road goes up over the hills, because there the hills reach to the waterline. The road climbs around two sharp curves, then straightens out. There is a long straight stretch with a ten percent grde, a three-lane road with a sharp drop of about seventy feet off the right side. Since the road is straight at that point, there is no guardrail on the right. The skid marks were still on the road, hadn't been washed off by the rain. Otis apparently drove toward the edge, then jammed on the brakes too late and went on over . . ."

"Matthew Otis, sir. Unemployed. I'd just got out of college when—"

"We don't need explanations. Tell us what you remember of that night."

"I remember sitting in the booth and talking to—to Alicia. After that, nothing."

"You were drunk, then?"

"No, sir. I was not drunk. I was hit on the head and—"

"Do you have any idea why you drove off the road?"

"No, sir. I can't understand it. Dr. Green says it may come back someday and I've been trying—"

"Limit yourself to answering the questions, Otis. What was your relationship to the deceased?"

"We were going to be married."

"Had you quarreled that night?"

"No, sir . . ."

At last he sat in the wheelchair and looked into the yellowed face as the coroner said:

"Matthew Otis, you have heard the verdict of accidental death. My hands are tied. But my opinion, sir, is that you are a murderer. Your intent makes no difference.

This girl died through an act of yours. You have caused her parents, her friends and, I hope, yourself immeasurable sorrow. According to Dr. Green, you will walk again. It would not be too heavy a cross for you to bear, in my estimation, if you never walked again.

"Possibly, you would have lonely hours in which to sit and think of Alicia Crane, great-granddaughter of the founder of this city. You could think long of this girl, brutally killed in the flush of youth. When you killed her, Matthew Otis, you killed her potential children and children's children.

"It is obvious that if you were not drinking, she would be alive today and you would not be facing me. I do not envy you, Matthew Otis . . ."

Matthew Otis turned suddenly at the rough grasp on his arm and stared down into the smiling face of Evan Cleveland. They shook hands warmly and exchanged the customary banalities.

It was only after Evan had ordered his drink and they had carried them over to a table that Matt noticed the lines of strain in Evan's usually cheerful face. Evan said, "I ought to be thrilled sitting right here with a national figger."

"Lay off!"

"No, in an unpleasant sort of way, I mean it. How long are you staying?"

"Maybe two days. Maybe two weeks."

"You ever have any trouble from getting smashed up the way you did before you left, Matt?" Direct mention of the accident reminded them both of the death of Alicia, and put constraint on the easy conversation.

"I got around on crutches for over a year. Nowadays I can tell when it's going to rain, and that's about all. Stop quizzing me and give me the pitch on the locals. How's the Furnivall girls?"

"Lush and wealthy, as usual. Pat worked like a fool at the plant after her father died. Things haven't been going too well there. Susan came home from Wellesley last year. She doesn't take any interest in the place so long as she can keep her purse full of cash."

"You married, Evan?"

"No. You?"

"No. How's Roy Bedford?"

"Obnoxious. In forty he eased into that garage deal as sole owner. By the end of forty he'd put in machine tools and had a contract from the British Purchasing Commission. He plowed the money back in and went way into hock to build a big plant south of town. Aircraft parts. With the dough from that, he has a finger in every pie all up and down the coast and some interest in distant pies. Knitting in the sunny South. A foundry in Buffalo. A tool works in Rochester. I guess he's still coining dough. He bought the old Crane house on Perkins Street. Alicia's folks went out to California the year after she died."

"Did he marry that girl he was running around with when I left?"

"Rose Carney? No. He's fixed her up with a nice little beach house about three miles out of town. He entertains out there. She makes a good hostess. She's thinned down and she acts like a lady. She's kept up with our boy Roy all right."

"How about Maura Gissing?"

"Her? Oh, sure. You went around with her before you got engaged to Alicia. She's still in town. A widow. She married a boy named Barton who got killed overseas during the war. She works in the phone company and is active in civic affairs. No kids."

"I might look her up."

"Oh, so you came back to pick a wife?"

"Relax, boy. I've got no time for wives."

"Got yourself all lined up with some Chinese talent, hey?"

During lunch Evan told him about the current problems of the Furnivall Company, told how anxious Roy Bedford was to get his hands on it.

His face a mask of despair, Evan said, "What I can't

understand is why he should want the outfit. He's got enough irons in the fire.''

Matt sipped his coffee, then said, ''The pattern is pretty clear, Evan. Roy was the kid that everybody expected would end up like his old man. Look at him now. At thirty-two he's one of the biggest guys in town. Who were the two top families when he was a kid? The Cranes and the Furnivalls. Now he lives in the Crane house. He won't completely justify himself until he controls the Furnivall Company.''

Evan smiled tiredly and said, ''It's pretty tough to combat a psychosis—with dough behind it. I wish I knew what to do.''

''Can you fight?''

''Pat wants to fight. She's got an ancestor complex about the plant. And she hates Bedford and everything he stands for. But our working capital is scraping bottom. If we have to close down, it will just about force us under.''

''What will happen to you, Evan?''

''Oh, I'll start punching somebody else's time clock.''

''I wish I could help you,'' Matt said.

Evan frowned, stirred the dregs of his coffee. Matt, looking toward the door, saw Roy Bedford come in, following a young girl. She was quite tall and looked oddly like Patience Furnivall. But there was more life and exuberance to her. Her eyes were brighter, her mouth larger. She walked with an air of vitality and health, smiling back over her shoulder at Roy Bedford.

''Here's your problem,'' Matt said softly.

Evan looked back and then stared at Matt, consternation plain on his face.

''That's nice!'' he said. ''That's Susan Furnivall.''

Roy Bedford had changed little in nine years. His crisp dark hair had receded a bit, but the sharp, vital features were the same; the eyes, set far apart, had that same opaque, bland look. He was well dressed and had an air of confidence.

Matt saw him glance toward the table, say something to Susan, and they came over. Evan stood up as Matt did. Roy Bedford said, "Well, hello there, Matt! Heard you were in town."

"You must have your spies out," Matt said.

"I keep track of things. This is Susan Furnivall, Matt. Hello, Evan."

Susan sighed. "You were one of my heroes, Mr. Otis. When I was in the fifth grade you were on the football team in high school. I cut your picture out of the paper and slept with it under my pillow for months. Hello, Evan."

"I can't live up to that buildup, Susan. How's Patience?"

"The female industrialist? Grim. Why don't you drop out and see her? The way I lost that picture, she took it away from me and it ended up under her pillow."

"You had quite an effect on the whole family," Roy said. "Well, see you around. Drop up to the house for a drink if you have time."

They walked off and took a table in the corner.

"She owns eleven thousand shares of Furnivall stock," Evan said. "She's young and pretty. It's time Roy got married. That would be the easy way for him to beat Pat."

"You're dreaming up trouble for yourself," Matt said.

"Am I? Take a look over there when you get a chance."

As they left, Matt looked back. Susan was leaning toward Roy, her face animated and eager, her eyes soft. Her fingers rested lightly on Roy's wrist . . .

Susan took her hand away as the waiter approached. She ordered and, as Roy studied the menu, she thought of Matthew Otis. There was such a tremendous gap between the dreams of childhood and the actualities of an adult.

Matthew Otis had always been young, laughing, surrounded with sort of a shining halo of success. There were two males named Matthew Otis. One was forever back on the green field, leaping high in the air to catch the long pass, running with the ball while the cheering section screamed. The new Matthew Otis was a heavy man with a brown face and an impassive look.

She looked at Roy. Roy was different. She had gradually begun to think of him in one of those odd curved helmets that the Spaniards had worn when they sought gold in the New World. He had a look of lean cruelty that awakened something deep inside her. Something exciting.

"That's a very unflattering expression, Susan," he said. "You look as though you expected me to reach over and hit you."

"You're a conquistador," she said.

All expression left his face. He said softly, "That's not bad, Sue. Not bad at all. They came here in the sixteenth century and took over. And that's what I'm doing."

"You frighten me sometimes. You know, I didn't expect you to know what a conquistador was."

He was suddenly angry. "You college snobs! You got it in nice airy classrooms. I got it at night. And I got a lot more than you did."

She laughed. "A sore point?"

His anger faded. "Sure, kitten. Why do I frighten you?"

She took time to pick the right words. "When I was a little girl I used to go in the plant with Dad. There was a room with a concrete floor and in the room there was a huge machine that nearly touched the ceiling. It had a big hammer thing in it that used to come down with a thud that you could feel against your feet. I used to think that nothing in the world could stop that machine. It was ruthless and relentless. It used to scare me and I used to hold Dad's hand so tightly that he'd laugh at me. But every minute, I wanted to run to where it came down and be smashed to nothing."

He smiled crookedly. "Not too flattering, kitten."

"You don't care about me as a person, Roy," she said softly.

"Don't be silly!"

"Oh, I know. I'm young and healthy and clean and I dress well. But this is just a big deal for you."

"Big deal?"

88

"Sure. I know how you operate. You want me because along with a nice clean young girl to wife, you'll get control of the company. The daily double." There was scorn in her voice.

He looked at her steadily. "That's exactly the way it is. And there isn't a thing you can do about it. Your dad isn't around to hold your hand so you won't jump into the drop forge. It's just a question of how long before you jump." He reached out and his fingers were tight and hard on her wrist. She looked into his eyes and all the rest of the room faded into mist, with just those eyes the only thing visible to her.

She felt her breath come fast. Then he leaned back in his chair and smiled at her. The room swam back into focus.

"I think I hate you," she said softly.

"That's a strong enough emotion, kitten. That will do."

The food came, but she had lost her appetite. She wanted to disturb his calm confidence. She said, "Rose Carney will hardly be pleased, Roy."

He took a sip of water. He said, "Rose Carney does, thinks and believes what I tell her to do, think and believe. I will tell her to be glad about this."

"And you will tell her to pack her undies and take a train ride to California, Roy. Without a forwarding address."

His face was blank. Then he smiled brilliantly. "You know, kitten, you have possibilities! Okay. Rosie gets a one-way ticket. The dough I get for the beach house will give her a going-away present."

"And you will be nice to Pat."

The smile went away. "Don't push your luck, Susan. Your stately sister isn't like us."

Susan said with anger, "You shouldn't say that!" But she knew that, deep down, she resented Patience and had never admitted it to her conscious mind.

Matthew Otis walked through the growing chill of dusk up the hill that led to the Furnivall home. He tried to analyze his interest in Bedford's attempt to take over the Furnivall Company, because the real reason he had returned to Cranesbay was to rid himself of the ghost of Alicia Crane. Her dream image had grown stronger over the years, making the daylight hours into unreality, making night the only reality—night when he could hear the silver tones of her voice.

He had intended to rent a car. He hadn't driven an automobile since that night. He had intended to drive to the Ocean Club each night until there was a rainy, misty night like the night when she had died.

He would then drive over that same road, possibly park and climb down over the rocks to where his smashed body had lain. A lonely vigil and then, in the gray of dawn, a visit to her grave. Her ghost would be appeased. Or he would find out why she returned in his dreams.

He had imagined that by reliving that night, memory might return. The doctors had said that in most concussion cases, the direct memory of the events immediately preceding the accident is wiped out, to return gradually over months, or even years. In his case, there had been no return of memory. Maybe if he could remember . . .

He was afraid to relive that night. He had seized on Evan's difficulties as an excuse to keep from reliving that night. Even this visit to Patience Furnivall was an attempt to delay the moment when he would drive up that lonely mountain road toward the scene of death.

The Furnivall house was Victorian, its unlovely lines concealed by elms. Patience opened the door when he rang the bell. "Matt!" she said, warmth and greeting in her voice. "Evan told me you were in town. It's so nice to see you again. Come in."

She clicked on the lights in the small study. The room was warm and pleasant, and peopled with shadows of long ago when Matthew Otis and his younger brother had been brought to the big house by his parents. He had been twelve, full of scorn for six-year-old Patience, barely aware of the existence of Susan. The study held the same smell of furniture polish and leather bindings. The small pane in the breakfront was still cracked from the time that Pat had thrown the book at him.

A Corpse in His Dreams

They sat and looked at each other. There was no tension in their silence. Pat had turned into an interesting-looking woman. Rather severe, with her dark hair pulled back so tightly. She had dignity.

As she grew older she would retain her looks, her quiet eyes, her air of warmth.

"It's good to see you, Pat," he said quietly.

"You've changed a great deal, Matt. You've entirely lost that long-legged colty look you had. That Airedale puppy look."

"You aren't exactly in rompers, Pat. Let me see. When I left, you were sixteen. You wore dirty white shoes and ankle socks and your legs were too thin."

She excused herself. He sat in the small comfortable room feeling at peace with the world. She came back with martinis and said, "One of the advantages of being famous, Matt. I read in a biographical sketch in a magazine that you like martinis."

He lifted his drink, said, "To the Furnivall Company, Pat."

She drank with him, said wryly, "That's about all we can do to help it, Matt. Drink to it. Evan said he gave you the complete picture."

He stared down into his drink. "The old order changeth, Pat. If your grandpop were alive, he'd know how to handle it. We're too soft. Psychopaths like Roy Bedford are inheriting the earth. The age of industrial piracy has begun. It got its start in the black market, gained strength through war surplus and is fattening on shortages."

"I want to fight him," she said.

He was surprised at the deadly earnestness of her tone.

She smiled. "I guess I sounded pretty grim then. But it's the way I feel. I could cheerfully shoot him. Oh, it isn't that he's an upstart. I'm not being a snob, Matt. It's just that he's a home-grown fascist. If he gained his ends through work, that would be fine. But he's ruthless and clever and crooked."

"I'd like to help, if you can think of a way," he said.

She sighed. "There isn't enough time. With time we

might prove that he has interfered with our steel deliveries, that he is financing a nuisance suit against us. It might give us the basis for a damage suit."

She tilted her head as the front door slammed. Then Susan walked in, her face flushed from the chill, her eyes bright.

She saw Matt and said, "Well! You do get around, Mr. Otis! What's the subject of conversation? How to save the mighty Furnivall interests?"

"If you thought more of the mighty Furnivall interests, Susan, you might be able to help us," Patience said quietly.

"Oh, wake up!" Susan said with annoyance. "You've got an industrialist complex. Why don't you let Roy take over? Maybe he'd make some money for us. All you and Evan do is put us further and further in hock."

"Susan!" Patience snapped.

"Well, it's true. And brace yourself, sister mine. I've got another little shock for you. I'm going upstairs and pack. In half an hour Roy is picking me up. We're going to fly down to Maryland and be married. He told me to tell you that the plant will get the steel and that some man has dropped some sort of a suit against the company."

Matt was looking at Patience. She had been sitting very straight, her cheeks flushed with anger. The flush faded and her shoulders slumped. She buried her face in her hands and whispered, "Oh, Susan! How could you?"

Susan had the grace to blush. She said, "You'll get over it."

She left the room. Matt heard her running steps on the stairs, the slam of an upstairs door. There was no sound in the study except Patience crying.

He went over to her and put his hand on her shoulder. She lifted a tear-streaked face and said, "But the man is—ruthless! She'll—never be happy. Never!"

Matthew realized that it was an indication of Pat's character that she was weeping, not over a battle lost, but over the emotional mistake Susan was making.

He frowned. "Mind if I go up and talk to her, Pat?"

"It won't do any good. You don't know how stubborn she is. Her room is the second one on the left from the head of the stairs."

Matt knocked on Susan's door. "Who is it?" she called.

"Matt Otis, Sue."

"Go away. I'm in a terrible rush."

"I want to talk to you. It's important."

After a long silence she said, "Okay." She opened the door. The pleasant bedroom was brightly lighted. Two open suitcases were on the bed, half packed.

He offered her a cigarette, lighted it for her. "Make it fast," she said. "If Pat thinks you can talk me out of this, you've both got holes in the head."

He smiled. "I wouldn't think of talking you out of it, Sue. This is a great opportunity for you. Everything you want. Money, position. Everything."

"Are you being sarcastic?" she asked, frowning.

"Not at all. You're a beautiful girl. I don't blame Roy for falling in love with you. He always did like nice things."

He saw the shadow cross her face. She murmured, "Love is a dandy word."

"Isn't that what it is?"

She sat on the edge of the bed. "I wish I knew. I don't think there's room in his head for love. He's an element. Like wind or fire or storm."

"It's that stock that bothers you, isn't it?"

She looked up quickly. "That's right. I keep wondering if that's the only reason he's going through with this. He says that he wants me, and the stock isn't important."

"Half a million dollars plus control of a good company is a nice dowry, Sue. Do you want to try something?"

"What kind of a something?"

"Suppose you sell your shares to your sister for the consideration of one dollar down and the balance within a year. Sell them at the market price. I'll make out a bill of sale and witness it and we'll get another witness. Don't say a word of it to Roy until you get down to Maryland. Then tell him you no longer have the stock and see what happens.''

"Why not tell him right away?"

"It won't be a good laboratory test."

She stared up at him, stubbed out the cigarette on an ashtray on the bedside table. Her eyes narrowed. "You think he won't go through with it."

"What do you think?" he asked gently.

"Why did you tell me this, Matthew Otis? Now I've got to do it. I must know."

"Sure you have to know, Sue."

He went downstairs and told Patience. She brought him the writing materials and he made out a bill of sale, listing the stock certificates. Susan came downstairs and signed it, gravely accepted the dollar from Patience.

When the doorbell rang, Susan hurried to the hallway. They heard the low, familiar tones of Roy Bedford's voice. A few minutes later a car motor started in front. Matt and Patience stood at the window and watched the car drive away.

"She won't tell him until just before the ceremony," Matt said.

"He'll never go through with it."

"Susan believes he will."

"You know, Matt," she said, "I can—somehow feel the effect he has on her. He's completely unprincipled. He has the fascination that high places or snakes or great speed in a car has."

Her voice sounded so weary that he was filled with sudden sympathy. He put his arm around her, and kissed her gently on the lips. It was meant to be a kiss which would express his sympathy. But it turned into something else entirely.

When at last they parted, her eyes were wide and shining and his breathing was shallow.

"Where—did that come from?" she asked.

"A special import from China. Always take advantage of a troubled woman."

"Fool!" she said softly. "Let's go tell Evan what's happened."

Evan stood on the sidewalk, and watched Pat's car drive away, Pat at the wheel and Matthew Otis beside her. Even after the twin red taillights went around the corner and the sound of the motor faded he stood there, his fists so tight his knuckles hurt.

At last he shook himself like a shaggy animal aroused from sleep and trudged up the stairs to his room. He clicked on the lights and sat down on the edge of the studio couch that served him as a bed.

He looked around the room as though seeing it for the first time. A drafting table, a couple of framed diplomas, a row of texts and reference books. The wallpaper had a design of faded roses.

He ran his fingers along the stubble on his jaw. His mouth ached from smiling.

Oh, it was a gay and happy smile. All evening. See, folks? I'm your friend. I'm Evan Cleveland, the patient beast. I didn't want to come back here to Cranesbay. I came here because she is here. I went to work in the plant because I would see her more often. I watched her with quiet adoration. As time goes by, as she is twenty-two, twenty-three, twenty-four, twenty-five—I am glad. She will be mine. I wait in fatuous complacency for her one day to recognize my great love.

Evan Cleveland, the great lover.

She is cool and calm and slim and lovely—and I thought that I was the only one who could see the fire burning brightly under that placid surface. Susan burns brightly on the surface.

And then tonight the two of them come to me and she has at last awakened. I can barely hear what they are telling me! Something about Susan and a sale of Susan's stock. She is vivid and lovely. And then I see the way she looks at Matthew Otis. It is hard to realize that I hate Matthew Otis. But he has stolen her from me. He doesn't know it and neither does she.

He stood up, walked to the closet and took the bottle from the top shelf. As he walked woodenly back to the couch he tore the paper wrapping from the metal top. He sat down, tilted the bottle and swallowed. The liquor burned his stomach. He tilted the bottle again. When he set it clumsily on the floor it was half full.

He put his elbows on his knees, his square hands hanging limply from his wrists. After a bit he began to rock from side to side, making a low, moaning sound.

He fell heavily to the floor. He tried to get up, then cradled his head in his arms and wept. After a long time he fell asleep . . .

The cockpit of the little plane was finished in blue leather. Susan sat beside Roy Bedford, the palms of her hands cold and sweaty. Roy took the small mike from the clip and talked to the tower as he circled the small field.

The lights along the runway clicked on. The little plane settled down at last, the tires making one furtive squeal as they touched the concrete.

"Four hours," Roy said. "Not bad."

He taxied over to the hangars. She stood off to one side, her suitcase by her feet, as he talked with a man who had appeared out of the darkness. Within minutes a car appeared. Roy climbed in beside her, groped for her hand and held it tightly as the car hurried off into the night . . .

The beach house had been built so that at high tide the waves crashed against the rocks ten feet below the sill of the twelve-foot pane of flawless glass that faced the sea.

During early evening the waves had grown bigger. At midnight, the big swells punched the rocks with solid force, sending spray up to run down the huge window. With an impulse that she but vaguely understood, Rose Carney had put on a white strapless evening gown. Her bare white shoulders were perfect.

The Capehart thundered the bass in the Debussy *La*

Mer. She had it turned too high. Tall candles shone with motionless flames. The wine was the deep color of blood.

A song of the sea. A minor chant to sadness and to the sea.

She thought of Rosie Carney of nine years back. Rosie Carney in love with Roy Bedford. Rosie Carney who had seen the strength of his incredible will, who had sensed his enormous drive. Rosie Carney who had loved him.

But this was Rose Carney. A slim woman who drank wine by candlelight while the sea touched the rocks below her window.

He had taken everything she had from the beginning. Her individuality.

My soul, she thought, if there is such a thing. He has made me over in the image of what he has wanted. A modern-day courtesan. A woman to say the right things, do the right things, cater to the right tastes.

Somewhere along the line she had lost the essence of Rose Carney. She had become a creation of Roy Bedford. Music and words by Roy Bedford. Gowns by Bedford. Sets by Bedford. Produced by Roy Bedford, from a script by Roy Bedford, from a play by Roy Bedford, from a cheap novel by a garage mechanic named Bedford.

Aloud she said, "What will become of me?"

She knew that he had enjoyed coming to her, telling her that it was all over. She had met him at the door, had lifted her lips to be kissed.

"Not this time, Rose," he had said, grinning at her.

She had frowned. "What do you mean, Roy?"

"Baby, you're talking to a man about to be married. About time, don't you think?"

For one incredible moment of joy she had thought he meant her, then had seen the look in his eyes.

"A nice young article, Rosie. Cheeks like apples and smells like a load of hay. Miss Susan Furnivall will be married tonight to Mr. Roy Bedford, and you are not cordially invited to attend the ceremony."

"But us, Roy!"

"No problem, Rosie. You must have a nice little nest

egg saved. You're good-looking and you've learned a lot. Tomorrow when I get back, I'll put this place up for sale. By then you can be at the hotel. As soon as I get a buyer, I'll give you cash in the amount of the sale. Then you can go anywhere you please, just so long as it isn't Cranesbay.''

It was as though she were dreaming the words. It didn't seem possible he could be saying them. She had always thought that one day he would marry her.

"You can't do this to me!" she had screamed. "I won't go!"

Still smiling, he had slapped her across the mouth. She had staggered back against the wall.

"Pretty please, Rosie? Pretty please?"

When he had stepped toward her again, she had cowered back and said, "I'll go away, Roy."

Her answer had been the door slamming behind him, the high whine of the motor and skid of gravel as he turned out of the drive.

She lifted the glass to her puffed lips and drank deeply of the tart red wine. Holding her arms out, she turned slowly in ritual dance to the tempo of the music and the sound of the sea.

She laughed. She laughed until there was salt on her lips mingling with the taste of the wine.

Long after Matthew had left Patience Furnivall, he walked down past the hotel to the docks. Clouds hurried across the slim face of the new moon. The wind was rising and he could taste the sea on his lips. He stood with his hands shoved deep in his topcoat pockets, his head tilted, listening—to voices of long ago.

With sudden resolution, he turned away from the sea and walked back through the silent heart of the city, back toward the distant hill. It was an hour before he arrived at the cemetery. The iron gate was chained. He stepped over the low stone wall. The moon was just bright enough so that he could make out the shadowy names on the headstones.

A Corpse in His Dreams

The family of Crane had the place of honor, directly opposite the gates. The third match he lit showed him the headstone. "Alicia Belle Crane 1919–1939." The earth was damp. He walked over to the family stone, sat on the edge of it and lit a cigarette.

Below the surface was the body of the girl who had haunted his dreams for nine years. Through all his dreams she had called to him, and it was as though she were trying to tell him something.

"What have you been trying to tell me, darling?" he asked softly.

There was no answer but the sigh of wind in the pines, the far-off whisper of the surf.

He had been afraid to come to that spot and yet, sitting there, he felt a sense of peace.

He flipped the cigarette away and stood up, enormously tired. He stepped over the wall, and walked down the hill toward the city.

Back in the hotel he took a shower and climbed into bed. He lay in the darkness, listening to the sea, thinking of Alicia . . .

He was back on the stone and in the silent air was the echo of his voice. He stared at the ground where she was buried.

Suddenly there was a call, a distant call—her clear, thin voice in a vast place of echoes. He jumped up, and turned. She was walking through the silent stones, with a radiance about her. She wore the white dress that she had worn at high school graduation. Her face was younger than he had remembered it.

"Matthew, darling! Matthew Otis!"

"Alicia!" he called, but as in other dreams, his voice was frozen in his throat. He turned and began to run toward her.

"What have you been trying to tell me?"

His voice was loud and clear. They were no longer in the cemetery. They were in a huge room like a railroad station. The floor felt odd and he looked down and saw that he was running on the moving belt of a treadmill. She was also on a treadmill, running in the opposite direction. They moved ever steadily apart.

"Matthew!" she called. "Matthew, darling!" Her voice was lost in a thousand echoes against the great dark ceiling.

Suddenly she stopped running, stood still and was carried off into the darkness, her figure diminishing until at last it was a tiny white glowing spot against the black horizon before it was gone altogether.

He stood in the blackness and the loneliness.

He awakened standing near the windows, cold and trembling. Exhausted, he found his way back to the bed.

Susan lay rigid in the darkness, her mind filled with loathing. Beside her, Roy Bedford stirred in his sleep and his hand touched her shoulder. With infinite care she moved further away so that he no longer touched her.

It had gone wrong. Incredibly wrong. They had stood in the small cheap parlor of the marriage mill and she had said, her voice trembling, her tone light, "By the way, Roy. I sold all my stock to Patience just before you picked me up at the house."

His lips had drawn back from his teeth in a parody of a smile. "You what!"

"Oh, it was legal enough. Bill of sale and everything. It was Matt Otis' idea. I suppose you don't want to marry me now."

He had looked at her with those unreadable eyes for long seconds. Then, while the man waiting to marry them had coughed and fussed with the book, Roy had laughed. Humorless laughter. A senseless bray that twisted his body.

When he could get his breath he said, "Matt Otis' idea? Oh, that's great! Yes, Susan, I want to marry you. Very much."

The tears stood in her eyes as he fitted the ring on her finger. But his wedding kiss wasn't tender. He had put a hard hand at the back of her neck and brought his lips down on hers with ferocity. His teeth had bruised her lips and she had gasped with the pain. When she had pushed him away, tasting the warm blood from her lip, he had laughed again. The man who still held the book was embarrassed and a bit angry. Roy had laughed at him, too, and had flung a ten-dollar bill at him. His hard fingers had bruised Susan's arm as he led her out to the car.

He was asleep now. She felt soiled from the touch of him. She wanted to go and scrub her body, but she was afraid she would awaken him. She felt lost and young and hopeless.

It was at that moment that she began to wonder if she had the courage to kill him one day.

The bedside phone rang insistently. Matthew Otis reached up out of his sleep, lifted it from the cradle and held it to his ear. The luminous dial of his wristwatch said that it was a quarter to four.

"You're Matt Otis?" a woman's voice said.

"That's right," he mumbled. "Who is it?"

"Rosie Carney. I saw you a long time ago." Her voice was slurred. He could imagine the loose drunken lips, the wet eyes.

"I remember you," he said.

"I'm glad you remember me, Matt Otis. I saw you that night your girl died. She was Roy's girl, you know."

"Look, it's four in the morning. What is this? A little talk about old times? Save it until tomorrow, will you?"

"Save it?" She laughed. "Sure, old Rose Carney'll save it. For a long time. Wanted to tell you' bout that night. Wanted to tell you Roy took me home and left me. And came back later."

She hung up. "Hello! Hello!" he shouted.

He put the phone back on the cradle. Drunken woman. Probably went off the deep end when she heard about Susan. Talking nonsense. He went back to sleep . . .

Rose Carney stood in her stocking feet on the sand and looked up at the beach house. She held the bottle of wine by the neck. She could hear distant fragments of music. The night was cold, but she didn't feel cold.

It was like waiting for something exciting to happen. She lifted the bottle and drank deeply. She threw it from her, heard it shatter on the rocks.

At last the little glow touched the windows. Breathless, she watched as it grew brighter.

All my nice clothes, she thought. All the records. They'll melt and burn. All the wine bottles will break. Present for Roy. Li'l present for my boy Roy.

At last she could hear the crackle of the flames above the noise of the sea. The flames flickered up from the flat roof into the night air. The huge front window went and she felt the heat against her face.

"Too hot out here," she mumbled.

She put her fingers in the neckline of the white dress, ripped it down, stepped out of it. She tore off the bra and pants and threw them aside, standing naked on the sand.

She heard the distant wail of sirens and it was like a signal she had been waiting for. She turned and walked down the slope of beach into the water. Oddly, it felt warm. As a wave smashed against her thighs she stumbled and almost fell. When it reached her waist, she began to swim straight out with a smooth crawl.

She was all-powerful. She could swim forever. She felt the lift and drop of the waves. Her body was warm, clean and strong.

After many strokes she paused and looked back at the beach house. It was a pillar of flame. Dark figures passed between her and the flame.

She floated for a long time. Then, rolling over onto her stomach, she resumed her long, strong stroke, swimming straight out into the night.

Patience met Matt at the door. She was looking lovely in a dark green dress.

"Just a minute while I get my coat," she said.

She came back and he asked, "Do you know who's going to be there?"

"Just you and I and Evan and the bride and groom, as far as I know," she said. She handed him the keys. "Will you drive?"

Drive to Roy's party at the Ocean Club. Drive on the mountain road. Oh, fine. Better let Patience drive. Better tell her that she might end up staring up at the dark sky.

He found himself reaching for the keys. He said, "I'm a little rusty."

He got behind the wheel, took a moment to find the starter. It was a dark green coupe, fairly new.

"I never thought he'd marry her," Patience said softly.

"Maybe it was my fault, Pat."

"Nonsense! If he was going to marry her anyway, it's a blessing that he doesn't get his filthy paws on the company at the same time."

He backed out of the garage, turned down the drive.

"Did Sue ask you or did he?" Matt asked.

"He did. I thought that a little strange. He said it was just a small intimate dinner for friends of the bride and groom. He said that Susan has particularly asked that you and I come. And Evan, of course."

"Evan is in love with you, Pat."

She looked at him quickly. "Don't be absurd!"

"I think he always has been. What a tangle of emotions this little dinner party will be! And I suppose the guest of honor will be Rose Carney, who burned the house down and skipped out."

"She got a raw deal, Matt."

"Who doesn't get a raw deal from the great Bedford?" As they drove through town and turned left on the road to the Ocean Club, a fine rain started. Patience turned on the windshield wipers.

The wheel felt strange under his hands. Time had been turned back. He was going to the Ocean Club on a night like that night nine years before—

Patience reached over to the dashboard and turned on the car radio.

". . . the body was identified as being a Miss Rose Carney. There is no evidence of foul play. The nude body was washed ashore early this evening near Toll Point six miles south of town. Police state that Miss Carney's garments were found near the scene of the fire that destroyed her home last night. It is believed that Miss Carney set fire to her home and committed suicide by swimming directly out from shore."

Patience clicked off the dial and shuddered. Her voice trembled as she said, "Another mark on Roy Bedford's sterling record."

Matt stared ahead and frowned. "I must have been the last living soul she talked to. If I'd known—"

"What!"

"She called me up at four this morning. I couldn't make out what she was driving at. She was drunk."

"Poor Rose."

"Poor Susan," he said.

The road climbed higher and higher. Twice he had to shift into second to ease the laboring motor. At the very top was a wide parking place, a favorite spot for sightseers and the high school group. Far ahead, down on the flats, he could see the lights of the Ocean Club. The road dipped down. It turned into the long straight stretch where, nine years before, a blond girl had lain, her sightless face turned up toward the misted sky.

His jaw ached with tension. The dark night sped by. Ahead were the sharp turns.

"It happened right along here, didn't it?" Patience said softly.

"That's right," he said, amazed at the calmness of his own voice. "On a night just like this one—nine years ago."

He pressed down on the brakes, slowed for the sharp curves and, minutes later, turned into the parking lot of the Ocean Club.

As it was an off night, there were few cars in the lot. Also, the Ocean Club trade usually arrived later than eight-thirty.

The man at the door said, "Mr. Otis? Follow me, sir."

He led them to a stairway at the far end of the dance

floor, and said, with a smile, "The room at the head of the stairs, sir."

Matt followed Patience up the stairs. Roy, affable and urbane, met them at the door, took Patience's coat, told Matt where to put his, then led them over to the table where Evan stood talking to Susan.

Patience kissed Susan and said, "How are you, dear?"

"Very well, thank you," Susan said.

Matt was shocked at the change in the girl. She seemed to have lost that quality of exuberance. Her eyes were large and there were dark shadows under them. Her lips curved in a careful smile and she stood very straight.

As Evan shook hands with Matt, Roy put his arm around Susan and pulled her against him as he said, "Now isn't she a beautiful bride?"

Matt noticed the sudden twist of Susan's lips, the haunted eyes.

"She certainly is, Roy," he said, with forced joviality.

"That's right," Evan said, matching Matt's tone.

There was a tall shaker of martinis. Roy poured two for Patience and Matt. Evan was obviously drinking too much. Roy did not appear to be drinking. Susan sipped her drink with downcast eyes.

"A toast to the bride," Evan said, lifting his glass.

"To the bride," they echoed. Susan smiled her careful smile and her eyes were dead.

Roy laughed loudly. "Say, you folks thought you were pulling a fast one on me, didn't you? Getting Susan to sell that stock of hers! What kind of a guy do you think I am? I'm going to take over that company anyway, you know. I married Sue for her sweet self."

"You make it sound so easy, Roy," Patience murmured. "I mean, the way you're going to take over the company."

His eyes showed no expression, but his smile revealed his white, even teeth. "It is easy, Pat. When you know how. How about dinner, folks? The house recommends steak or lobster."

The round table was set for five. A fire was lit in the fireplace.

Roy sat with Susan on his right and Patience on his left. Evan sat between Patience and Matt. Susan was on Matt's left.

The food was excellent, and Roy skillfully kept the table talk away from any personal topic. Matt was almost enjoying himself. Susan said little. Patience kept glancing across at Susan, her eyes puzzled. Evan talked loudly and expansively and, between topics, glared at Roy Bedford.

After a time Roy switched the conversation to China and Matt found himself talking about some of his experiences. Patience seemed to be the only one who gave her undivided attention.

At last there was a pause in the conversation. Patience said firmly, "It was too bad about Rose Carney, Roy."

He frowned. "Too bad? The house was insured. She'll get the insurance money when she shows up."

Matt tried to warn Patience with his eyes, but she kept on. "Oh, I thought you'd heard." Matt saw Susan's hand tighten on her coffee spoon. "They found her body early this evening. She drowned herself."

Susan slumped against Matt. Roy merely said, "Now that was a stupid thing to do, wasn't it?"

Matt carried Susan over to the leather couch by the fireplace. She was unconscious. Evan rubbed her wrists while Patience swabbed her forehead with a wet napkin.

Roy said in a low tone to Matt, "She seems a bit upset. I think I'll run her home. I was going to get her back early anyway. Excitement, you know."

He bent over Susan as her eyes opened. She looked up at him without recognition, and then her eyes narrowed.

"Get away from me!" she said in a low tone. Low and deadly.

It made no dent on Roy Bedford. He said, "You're a little upset, darling. Come on. I'll take you home." The calm assumption of authority overcame Susan's momentary revolt.

Roy got her coat and helped her into it. "There's no

reason to break up this little party," he said. "All Susan needs is rest. I've ordered some decent brandy for after dinner. You folks stay around and we'll be with you in spirit."

He and Susan went down the stairs together. Evan sat down heavily, suddenly quite drunk, and said, "Come on, folks. Cheer up! This is a party. Remember? A big celebration."

"That's right, Evan," Patience said.

They finished the coffee and the waiter came in with the brandy.

Patience pounded lightly on the table with her fist and said, "What has he done to her? What on earth has he done to her?"

"Acts dead," Evan said.

"Exactly," Matt added. "Just as though he had cut the heart right out of her. Did you see how meekly she went along?"

"She's frightened of him," Pat said, as though discovering a great truth.

After that they sat and talked of Roy Bedford, of Susan's future, until the fire burned low and Evan put his head down on the table and began to snore softly.

Matt moved over beside Patience, put gentle fingers under her chin, tilted her face up and kissed her. It worked the same magic as before.

"You look different," he said softly.

"I've felt different. All day. I've felt as though all the problems I've had have belonged to someone else."

"In my own way," Matt said, "I'm being as unfair to you as Roy is to Susan."

"How do you mean that?"

"I came back here to get rid of a ghost with golden hair. Alicia. She's been in my dreams for nine years. She won't stay dead. She tries to tell me something. At last she drove me back here. I've got to be honest with you, Patience. You're something very rare and very sweet. Maybe I'm in love with you. I don't know. But Alicia has been very close to me for nine years. The only time she is really away from me is when I kiss you.''

She looked at Matt for long moments, her eyes brimming. "That's good enough for me, Matt,'' she whispered.

"Has it happened to you this quickly, too?" he asked.

"Stupid! It happened to me back in those days when I wore the filthy white shoes and the ankle socks and my legs were too thin. It happened when I took your picture away from Susan a million years ago. I knew you'd come back. I knew it!''

Suddenly they both looked at Evan and began to smile. He looked so peaceful, the lines of strain ironed out.

Matt said, "I hate to wake him up.''

"Why do it, then? They don't close until four. It's just a little after midnight now. We can get him over to the couch and he can get some rest. He's got his car and after some sleep he'll be in shape to drive. We can tell the manager.''

Evan, half awake, blundered across the room and fell on the leather couch with a sigh of relief. Matt clicked the lights out and, holding Pat's hand tightly, walked down the stairs with her.

The manager nodded with quick understanding and said, "Certainly, sir. We'll wake him up when we're ready to close. He'll be all right then, I'm sure.''

They walked out into the parking lot and he saw the mist form in shining droplets on her dark hair. The sound of the sea was a whisper in their ears. He reached for her as they stood by the small green car. She came into his arms with a small purring sound.

After a moment she said, "Don't we know enough to get in out of the rain?''

"You drive,'' he said.

She looked up into his face, her head tilted on one side. "Scared?''

"Maybe.''

"Then you drive.''

"But, Pat, it was a night just like this. The same

place, the same road. Now that I've found you, I can't take a chance on it happening again. Ever."

"You drive," she said.

"But I can't remember what happened that night. I can't remember what I did! For all I know, I've got some compulsion neurosis that made me drive it right off the road."

"You drive," she said.

At last he got in under the wheel. On the way down the hill it had been bad enough. This was immeasurably worse. This was nightmare. Already he had gone beyond the bounds of memory. On that night nine years before he must have walked out of the Ocean Club and driven out of the parking lot onto the wet highway that reached, dark and shining, toward the hills.

Patience sat with her hands folded in her lap. He glanced at her quickly and saw that her face was calm. Her calmness lent him strength.

A dream, he thought. I am living a dream. I sit here, tense in the midst of nightmare. Nothing will happen. I will drive up the hill and down into the city and it will all be over.

Somewhere in the back of his mind a thin silver voice was calling him: "Matthew Otis! Matthew, darling!" The thin voice echoed as in a vast, empty room where she stood frightened in darkness.

The road began to lift toward the sharp turns. His hands were tight on the wheel and his mouth was a thin, hard line. His shoulders ached from the tightness of his grasp.

"Matthew, darling," the voice called. Thin and far away. A voice that reached over nine years.

He hit the first turn a shade too fast, braking as the car rocked. Patience said nothing. The night was dark. The mist was thick in the blue-white headlight beams. The muted lights of the dashboard were an orange glow.

On the second turn he had to shift into second. The gears made a ragged noise as, rounding the curve, he dropped back into high.

Far up the straight stretch a car was coming toward

them, its twin lights shining. Some fragment of memory stirred in the back of his mind.

Another night when the rain was thick in the headlight beams. Another car coming down the straight stretch.

Suddenly it was Alicia beside him. Not Patience. The lights coming toward them were bright. The lights and the rain blinded him.

He blinked his own lights rapidly. The lights bore down on them. It was then that he remembered.

The girl beside him—and it was Alicia—screamed as the wheels on the right dropped off the road onto the wet shoulder.

Off to the right was death. It was a death he had lived through once, but he could not live through it again. On that night nine years ago the onrushing lights had forced him over the edge. Cursing, he spun the wheel violently left. A crash was preferable to death down among the wet rocks.

Alicia-Patience screamed again as the lights leaped at them.

There was a ridiculously light impact and the other car was gone. His car swerved madly. He fought the wheel. His left headlight was gone. The car headed back toward the edge and he yanked it back onto the road. At last it nudged into the mud on the far side of the road and the motor stalled.

In the sudden silence Patience exhaled slowly.

His voice strangely high, he said, "That's how it happened before! I remember now! Bright lights coming down on us. I got over as far as I could. The car rolled and I knew I was being thrown through the darkness, right through the canvas top. Then blackness."

He put his arms around her and held her close. She was shivering.

She said, "If I'd let you talk me into driving, we'd be over the edge."

He frowned, "I don't get it. We should have hit him with a smash. I thought we were dead ducks. Got a flashlight?"

She clicked open the glove compartment and handed

him a flashlight. He climbed out into the rain. The car was at right angles to the road, with the rear wheels barely on the pavement. The bumper was nosed into the muddy hillside.

He inspected the damage. An odd iron bar was wedged into the grill. There were fragments of glass on one end of it. The other end showed the bright face of fractured metal. He grabbed it and pulled it free. The left headlight had been smashed by it. The bar had punctured the radiator.

He climbed back in and put the bar on the floor. "We'll ruin the engine if we try to make the rest of the hill. All the water has run out of the radiator."

"Can we coast back to the Ocean Club? Do you think the other car went over the edge?"

"I didn't hear anything. And I saw taillights going down the road in a pretty orderly fashion."

"He could have stopped."

Matt didn't answer.

"What was that thing you put on the floor?" Patience asked.

"Something I want Evan to look at . . ."

Once more the three of them were in the private room in the Ocean Club. Evan began to respond to hot coffee. He sat nodding, as Matt told the story of the near-accident, made him repeat it.

Only then did he examine the odd bar which Matt had wrenched out of the grill of Pat's car. He lost his sleepy look, became the competent engineer.

He said, "See here? This outside shell is hollow. This solid bar with the gear teeth on the bottom moves back and forth through it. This was a lamp socket. A headlight was fastened to the solid bar. See the slot in the shell so it could move freely?"

Patience frowned. "What does it mean? What is it?"

Evan said, "This thing goes on the front of a car. Suppose a guy is coming down that road and there's a car coming up he wants to wreck. He can't take a chance on moving over toward it. He might get clipped and go over himself. So he rigs up the gimmick. Maybe

111

he's got a little handle on the dash. As he turns the handle, the solid bar, carrying the lights with it, moves out to his left, activated by a little gear that fits against these slots.''

Pat's eyes widened. ''And the people in the other car would see the lights and they wouldn't know that the lights were moving out toward them but the car itself was staying over on its own side. They'd get out of the way.''

Matt said slowly, ''And our pal Roy was a part owner of a garage when Alicia and I went off that road. I remember being forced off.''

''This isn't a new gimmick,'' Evan said. ''See the rust spots. This thing was out in the rain a long time ago. Nine years ago, maybe.''

Patience sat down suddenly. ''He couldn't!''

''Who did, then?'' Matt asked. His voice was hoarse with hate and anger. Was this what Alicia had been trying to tell him for so many years?

''But why would he do it tonight?'' Patience asked.

They looked at each other, bewildered. Then Evan began to smile. It wasn't a pretty smile. He said softly, ''Who inherits when you die, Patience?''

She put the back of her hand to her mouth. Her eyes were wide.

''Exactly,'' Matt said. ''And that's why he went through with the wedding. He knew that if he couldn't get the stock through her, he could work it another way. That's why he had the party out here. Why, after Sue fainted, he said that he had been planning on taking her home early anyway.''

Evan was frowning.

''How would he know which car you'd be in?''

''There's a parking spot at the top of the hill. You can see the Ocean Club from there. With a decent pair of binoculars, you could see who was getting into their cars. The lot here always is floodlighted.''

''Then he watched for you and Alicia nine years ago?'' Patience asked in a tight voice.

Matt smacked his palm with a clenched fist. ''Rose

Carney suspected what had happened. She tried to tell me when she called me up, but I was too stupid to listen. She said he took her home from the Ocean Club nine years ago and left her. And that he came back later. That was when he drove us over the edge. He hated me for taking Alicia away from him. He must have made the gimmick in the garage after hours. Why, on that evening he even came over for a few final words with the condemned!"

Patience shuddered.

"The guy is crazy," Evan said.

"Crazy, and efficient," Matt said.

"What will we do?" Patience asked in a small voice.

"Get to a phone," Evan said. "His car will still have some stuff on it to show where this little toy was attached. This rain won't wash away the marks you made on the shoulder. We ring the cops in on this quick and have him picked up for attempted murder before he can dispose of the evidence."

"I've got to get to Susan," Patience said . . .

The man at the high desk picked up the phone and said in a tired voice, "Sergeant Rolph speaking."

"This is Evan Cleveland, Sergeant."

"What can I do for you, Mr. Cleveland?"

"I want Roy Bedford picked up immediately on a charge of attempted murder."

The sergeant's hand tightened on the phone. "You got enough for us to go on?"

"Plenty. And I don't know anything about the statute of limitations, but I think I can prove he killed the Crane girl nine years ago."

"An accident case, wasn't it?"

"Look, Sergeant. I know how it is when anybody asks you to pick up a man like Bedford. He has influence and—"

"And Rose Carney's sister is the wife of the deputy chief, Mr. Cleveland. We aren't too fond of Bedford. Any idea where he is?"

"We're at the Ocean Club. Twenty minutes ago he

was in his car on the hill between here and town. I don't know where he went from there."

"We'll see what we can do. Suppose you come in here. Ask for Lieutenant Canady. I'll give him the pitch."

The sergeant hung up, clapped a fist into a meaty palm and headed for the radio room . . .

Patience and Matthew stood on the wide porch of the Crane house. Matt rang the bell for the third time. The house was dark.

"You don't suppose he came back here?" Patience asked softly.

"I wouldn't think so."

After a few moments a dim light shone in the hall. Matt, looking through the glass, saw a husky man in a bathrobe walking toward the door.

He opened it and said, "Yes?" The quiet, dignified voice of a trained domestic.

"We wish to see Mrs. Bedford, please," Matt said.

"Sorry, sir. Mr. and Mrs. Bedford have retired for the night."

"This is urgent."

Smoothly the man said, "It certainly can wait until morning, sir."

"It will not wait until morning," Matt said.

The man's eyes flickered dangerously. He said, "Very sorry, sir," and began to close the door.

Matt drove against the doorframe with his shoulder. The man staggered back, his face ugly, his hand dipping into the pocket of the bathrobe. Matt rushed him. The hand flashed up and, as it started to come down, his wrist smacked into Matt's palm. Matt tightened his fingers on the wrist and twisted. The man was powerful. He put a beefy arm around Matt's neck and the dark hall filled with the hoarse sound of their breathing.

Matt realized he would never be able to twist the thick wrist hard enough. He released the wrist suddenly, brought his fist down in a diagonal blow against the man's jaw, jumped back as the heavy sap in the man's hand grazed his shoulder. The force of the blow swung

114

the man off balance. Matt brought his left fist up and the jolt of the blow sent needles of fire up his arm to his shoulder. The sap dropped from nerveless fingers. But the man didn't fall until Matt snatched the sap from the floor and laid it above the man's ear. He caught him as he fell and eased him down onto his face.

"Chinese Army technique?" Patience said, her voice shrill with hysteria. Matt grabbed her wrist and pulled her toward the stairs.

The first upstairs room was empty. A still form lay in a huge bed in the second room. Patience found the light switch. Susan lay on her back, breathing through open lips. There was a bubble of saliva at the corner of her mouth and her eyes seemed sunken.

Patience said, "Sue! Wake up!"

Susan's head wobbled on the pillow, but there was no break in the rhythm of the deep breathing.

"Doped," Matt said. "That way she could give Roy an alibi. We've got to walk her."

Patience found a robe in the closet and Matt sat Susan on the edge of the bed while Patience got the robe on her. Matt threw the inside bolt on the door and, with one on each side, they tried to walk her. Her head hung limply and she moaned. At first her feet dragged and she was an inert, awkward lump. In a few moments she began to walk in a stumbling fashion, tripping frequently on her own feet. Her walk grew better articulated and her head lifted, the eyes still closed.

At last she opened puffy eyes and said, "What—wha' you doing?"

"We can get her out of here now," Matt said. "You get her dressed. I'll wait in the hall."

Matthew stood in the hall and heard, through the closed door, the murmur of their voices. He looked down into the lower hall. The husky man was on his hands and knees, shaking his head from side to side.

A thick skull on that one, Matt thought.

He hurried down the stairs, making plenty of noise. He got in the lower hall just as the man scrambled drunkenly to his feet. Matt drove him over against the wall and put a forearm across his throat, the sap poised.

"Try anything," Matt said, "and you get it across the bridge of the nose this time. Shut up and listen." The man stopped his feeble struggling.

"Your boss is wanted for murder," Matt said, watching the man's eyes widen. "Too much trouble out of you and we can think up some rap to pin on you in connection with the murder."

"Cop?" the man said hoarsely.

"No. But I'm on the same side. Will you be good?" The man nodded. Matt stepped back. "Where's Mr. Bedford?"

The man looked genuinely surprised. "Isn't he up there?"

"No. Did you think he was?"

"Yes, I did. I don't want any part of any trouble, mister. I thought he was up there and my job is to keep people from busting in. A lot of people get sore at him."

"A mastery of understatement."

There was a sound of sirens in the distance, whining through the night, descending at last to a low growl and then silence, followed by the stamp of heavy feet on the porch. Matt flung the door open. A spidery little man with a sharp red nose stood with a uniformed patrolman hulking large behind him.

"Who're you?" the little man demanded.

"Matthew Otis. Bedford tried to kill me and Miss Furnivall."

"I'm Canady. You should have come in when you dropped Cleveland at headquarters. You got a warrant to swear out. We're going on the basis you've signed it. You won't back out?"

"Don't be absurd!"

"Where's Miss Furnivall? Who's this man?"

"Miss Furnivall is getting her sister ready to leave this place. This man works for Bedford. Bedford isn't here."

"I figured he wouldn't be. We've put the plates of his Chrysler on the tape in case he left town. The troopers'll get him if he tries the coast road."

"I don't think he'll run," Matt said. "He's got a genius complex. He doesn't think anything can touch him."

"He'll run, Otis. Suppose you get the women over to the Furnivall place. Then get yourself back to the hotel. We'll get hold of you if we need anything. Leave the keys to Cleveland's car at the hotel desk."

The two women came down the stairs. Susan still had a drugged look, a faraway look. Patience held her arm and walked carefully with her.

"Mrs. Bedford!" Canady snapped.

Susan turned her head slowly and looked at him blankly.

"What happened when you got home?"

"I got it out of her," Patience said. "Don't snap at her. When she was ready for bed Roy Bedford gave her a capsule. He told her it would quiet her nerves. That's all she remembers."

"Otis will take you home, Miss Furnivall. You and your sister. Stay there until you hear from me . . ."

After Matthew had helped Patience get Susan out of the car and up to bed, he held Patience tightly for a moment, kissed her and left.

He drove through the wet, deserted streets wondering where Roy Bedford could be. Roy must know that the unexpected maneuver on the part of the car he was trying to force off the road had carried away a piece of the mechanism he had designed so long ago. He would know that there had been no chance to identify him as the driver of the murder car.

The evidence would be circumstantial. Damage to the Chrysler. Roy had three choices. The first was to run— and that didn't seem practical. It didn't match Bedford's character. The second was to provide himself with an alibi and to pretend that his car had been stolen. That seemed a feeble defense.

The third bet would be to remove from the Chrysler all evidence that it had been used on the hill.

The last idea made the most sense. Roy could either attempt to repair the car or dispose of it. Burning would

117

be too risky. Evidence might remain. The ocean was handy. There was deep water at the end of the docks. Or he might even drive the car into a tree, planning that the impact would remove evidence of the previous lighter one.

The idea of the plunge off the dock didn't seem too practical. There was too much chance of the car being recovered. A crash that would obliterate all evidence. Better than burning. Better than driving it into the sea.

Pleased with the logical procession of his thoughts, Matthew stopped, lit a cigarette and tried to carry his reasoning further. Before Roy could risk a collision, he would have to remove from the car the rest of the mechanism which made the lights movable. He would have to dispose of that. To remove it meant tools, working space, lights. A garage, preferably.

He began to wonder if Roy had ever disposed of the garage which had given him his start. It would be typical of him to retain ownership of the garage so that he could point it out to people he wished to impress. He could almost hear Roy say, "Ten years ago I was a grease monkey in that shack."

With sudden resolve, Matt started the car, made a U-turn at the next intersection and turned back toward the garage where Roy had been working nine years before.

It was in a neighborhood of narrow flats, grocery stores, liquor stores, gas stations. It was in back of an ancient rooming house, the unlighted sign hanging out at the curb.

MORGAN STREET GARAGE—REPAIRS ON ALL MAKES—DRIVE IN

He drove beyond the entrance and walked back. The garage was dark. The structure of reasoning collapsed.

He glanced down. A tire had made a deep hollow in the dirt. The tread marks were crisp. Water from a nearby puddle flowed with a slow current into the deep track. He felt a sudden excitement. A car had gone in there not over a half hour before. It was a little more than an hour since the accident. To be safe, Roy would have taken the long way around to get back to the city.

With training born of night fighting, Matt drifted over into the thick shadow of the rooming house, headed back toward the garage. His steps made no sound on the moist earth. He moved close to the door, put his ear against it.

With startling clarity, he heard the clang of a tool dropped onto a concrete floor. The padlock was gone from the hasp on the wide sliding doors. He got his fingers in the crack between the doors and heaved suddenly. The door slid back with a deafening shriek.

The black Chrysler, moist with rain, stood in the middle of the small garage. A mechanic's light, with birdcage bulb, lay on the floor near the front wheels. Roy Bedford, the light shining up onto his face, outlining the high cheekbones, squatted motionless, looking toward him. "Hello, Matt," Roy said softly. "Want something?"

Matt could not see Roy's hands. Doubtless he held some sort of tool.

"I was looking for you, Roy. I thought you might be here."

"Couldn't sleep," Roy said easily. "Nothing relaxes me as much as doing a little work on the wagon. You know how it is."

"Sure, Roy. I know how it is."

Every muscle tense, he walked closer. For a moment he had the idea that Roy was going to let him circle behind him. The urge to maim, to kill, was acid in his throat, was cold sweat and tensed muscles.

But Roy stood up without haste and moved back into the shadows away from the car. Matt could not examine the car without permitting Roy to get behind him.

It was a play where the lead actors circled each other on the dim stage, touched by the clever lighting, speaking in soft tones, the desire to kill carefully masked.

Matt kicked a piece of metal. It rang across the concrete. He stooped quickly and picked it up. Roy seemed to have moved a great deal closer to him during the moment his eye was off him. The metal had a famil-

119

iar feel in his hand. It was wet, and there were serrations on the edge of it. It was too short to be a weapon, unless hurled with great force at too short a distance to be avoided.

He lifted it high so that he could look at it without taking his eye from Roy. It matched the piece that had been wedged into his grille.

"Funny-shaped piece of metal," he said softly.

"All sorts of queer scrap in an old shop like this, Matt," Roy said.

"This piece is damp."

"The car is wet. Probably dripped on it."

He still could not see Roy's hands. The caged light was a blinding thing, making the shadows velvet black, making sparkling highlights on the metal skin of the car. The rubber cord on the light stretched back across the concrete near his feet.

"Why did you kill Alicia?" Matt asked, his voice almost tender.

Roy was silent, his face impassive. "You talk like that, Matt, and they'll come and throw a net over you."

"Over me? You're the mad one, Roy. You couldn't have Alicia. So you tried to kill both of us. As it worked out, I lived and she died. You liked it that way. You hoped I'd be crippled for life. You've squashed everybody in your path. You married Susan knowing that you would kill Patience. The method had worked once, so why not twice? Everyone knows how you did it, Roy. A pity you're not more insane. If you were, you might end up in a nice institution. This way, they'll shave the leg on the great Bedford and strap him down in a nice armchair and put a hood, a black hood over—"

"Shut up!" Roy screamed.

Matthew stood on the rubber cord with one foot and kicked it with the other. The sudden blackness was as violent as a shot. Noiselessly Matt moved toward the car. He stood, strained with the effort of listening, his fingers clenched around the piece of metal, his hand poised to throw.

120

Suddenly the car creaked, as though bearing someone's weight.

There was a chance that he might be silhouetted against the lesser darkness of the open door. He moved away from the car, stepping cautiously. As he moved, his foot touched some tool on the floor. It shifted with an almost imperceptible grating sound.

He staggered and fell as Bedford leaped onto his back. He fell forward trying vainly to turn, his arms pinned, trying to avoid hitting his head on the concrete floor.

The dark garage exploded into pinwheeling lights, into nothingness . . .

He was being jiggled and it made his head hurt and something was digging into his cheek. He bit down on the moan, stifling it, as the vivd memory of the moment of falling flashed back into his mind. Slowly he realized that he was in a moving car. The thing against his cheek was the door handle. The inside of the car lightened briefly as they passed under a streetlight.

He knew that if he lifted his head and Bedford was driving, he would probably be pounded into immediate insensibility. It was hard to think clearly.

He felt as though one whole side of his head had been shattered.

When the car went around a corner he permitted himself to lurch, turning his head slightly. Through slitted eyes he saw Bedford, oddly relaxed behind the wheel, a small smile on his lips.

A confident smile, Matt thought. What has he got to smile about? What can he be planning to do? Matthew had no way of knowing where they were. Roy was driving slowly, so as not to attract attention.

Suddenly, out the window beyond Bedford's head, he saw the high outline of a building, barely made out the white letters VALL. The Furnivall Company! The road passed the plant, then turned down across the sidings, down a gentle slope toward the main railroad tracks.

As they went slowly around the corner, Matt heard

121

the distant huff of the train, the lonely call of the whistle. Why should Roy be smiling?

He shut his eyes as Roy turned and looked over at him, counting slowly in his mind to ten, then risking opening them again.

Roy took the car out of gear. They were on the slope headed down toward the main track. Roy opened the door on his side, stood up with his head and shoulders out in the night, one hand on top of the wheel, steering.

The roar of the train was closer. Much closer. The way Roy was standing he couldn't see Matt. His mouth dry with sudden desperate fear, Matthew raised his head, saw the Cyclops eye of the pounding locomotive. The crossing signals flashed red.

Matthew, a hoarse cry in his throat, opened the door on his side. He grabbed Roy Bedford's wrist, pulled with all his strength, pulled until Bedford was forced back in through the door, falling awkwardly across the wheel. Matt released his hold, rolled backward out of the door he had opened, thudded with sickening force against the steel upright of the crossing signal, hearing above the deafening roar of the locomotive one thin, high scream, cut off by a crash which sounded almost faint against the pound of the big steel wheels.

As the twin brakes screamed and slithered, steel on steel, Matt put his cheek against the wet gravel and began to cry like a heartbroken child.

Patience trudged over to the flat rock and sat down with a sigh. Her cheeks were flushed from the walk along the beach. At Matt's urging, she had unpinned her severe hairdo. The wind whipped at her dark hair.

He gave her a cigarette, lit it, then sprawled on the sand at her feet, looking out across the gray sea.

"You were wrong, you know," she said.

"About what?" he asked. "I'm wrong once a day like clockwork."

"About Evan being in love with me. He went out to the rest home again this morning to see Sue. He'll bring her back to life. He said she smiled at him the last time

122

he went out. When he talks about her his eyes shine and he gets hoarse and funny.''

"Don't laugh at men in love. I know they're funny. You can reach out and kick one from where you're sitting.''

She didn't answer and he looked up at her. Her eyes were grave and steady.

"Matt, tension can do odd things. We were living in a nightmare. I don't hold you responsible for anything you might have said.''

"Tonight I'm arranging soft lights and music and I'm going to say it again.''

"Isn't it—too soon? After Roy's death, and all that went with it?''

He laughed. "Roy was just pitiful, honey. As soon as he matched muscles with that locomotive, he became as extinct as the dodo. I can hardly remember what he looked like, even though I did just get the bandages off my skull yesterday. You're trying to ask me if Alicia is out of my system. Right?''

He looked up at her. She looked away and said in a small voice, "I guess so.''

"In the fourteen days since Roy died, I've dreamed about her once. Want to hear about it?''

"If you want to tell me,'' she said, her lips compressed.

"In my dream I was walking at dusk in a big city. The streets were empty of cars and people. I was going to meet Alicia. But I couldn't remember the address. I was worried because I'd forgotten the address. All the streets looked alike. There were no signs, no numbers on the houses, no one to ask.

"Suddenly I heard someone calling me. It didn't have that hollow, echoing sound that Alicia's voice has always had in my dreams. It sounded as though it was right in my ear. I turned around and you ran into my arms. You, not Alicia.

"You were laughing and crying at the same time. Excited. I held you close and after a bit I asked you where Alicia was. You told me that she had gone away and that she had sent you to keep her date. I asked you what Alicia had been trying to tell me. You said that it wasn't important any longer. I looked around then and all the sidewalks were filled with people and the streets were filled with cars and all the people were bustling by, paying no attention to us.''

He stopped talking, picked up a handful of sand and let it trickle through his fingers.

On the horizon a coastwise vessel left a smudge of smoke against the horizon. He looked up at Patience. Her lips were parted and she looked out at the ship.

"They say the best honeymoons are available on tramp ships in the South American trade," he said, smiling up at her.

She moistened her lips and said, "Give me time to pack.''

I Accuse Myself

IT WAS A siren buried under the flesh. Not the up-and-down rollercoaster kind of siren, but the constant wail—the steady shattering scream.

In one part of his mind he heard the ward noises, heard the clink of a spoon in a glass and the snap as sheets were drawn drum tight. But they wouldn't become familiar noises. Always he turned mentally away just as he was about to listen carefully and remember where he was. There was also the prick of a needle, but it was dull beside the grind of the siren. He would fade away and the siren would become a screaming woman, or a hot white light—bringing him back to the restless muttering.

On some days he could see the pain. That was when the siren was not so loud. The pain looked like the edge of a razor held close to the eye. It stretched off for miles toward a Dali horizon, each bitter blur on its edge grating like teeth on crushed glass.

Then there was a heavy bearded face close to his own. He saw it vaguely and then it was gone. He was handled, moved. He felt a sense of movement and it looked as though a long wall was slowly passing his bed. Then sharp lights and suffocation . . .

On one hot summer between grade school and high school he had gone with Tom and Rod out to Corey's Creek, to the black pool. They had often dived from a high limb down into the center of the blackness. But they had never touched bottom. On this day Rod had started to ride him about his diving. And finally he had gone out onto the limb, exhaled most of the air in his lungs and dropped straight and clean into the black depths. He had gone down until his ears had throbbed, but his outstretched hands touched nothing. Then, in the deep blackness, sudden fear had sent him struggling up toward the surface. The little air in his lungs contributed no buoyancy. He had fought his way upward, seeing above him the dim light of the sunny afternoon. He had seemed to rise so slowly, fighting the involuntary sucking of his lungs by keeping his throat tightly shut. And when he thought he could fight no more, he had burst through into the bright light, his chest aching, his throat making a rasping sound as he sucked in the sweet air. The sun had felt warm on his face . . .

But this time when he broke through it was all different. Rod and Tom swirled back into the far past, remote and sweet. And he was on crisp sheets in a hard bed in a large white room. It seemed suddenly silent—and he realized that the siren was gone. The sharp pain had left him and it was as though the turning world had stopped on its axis. With a long spent sigh he shut his eyes and drifted off into a velvet sleep.

It was daylight again. Somehow he knew it was a new day. He turned his head weakly, feeling the pull of adhesive on the skin of his forehead. There were two other beds in the room, but they were empty. The window showed him a square of gray sky and the green tops of trees. There was no clue. He wondered, but was content to rest.

It must have been a half hour later when a nurse brought the woman in. The woman was tall, with pale hair and colorless eyes. Her face was wide and white. She chewed at her underlip as she tiptoed across the room and sank gently into a chair by the bed. He stared at her, knowing that he had looked at her ten thousand times. Her face was familiar and unfamiliar. It frightened him to look at her and feel the pull of long association combined with strangeness. He looked into her pale eyes, wondering who she was, and saw the quick tears brim up. She crouched with her forehead on the edge of his bed and he felt her soundless sobbing shake him in dull rhythm. Her hair was parted and with the clarity of weakness he could see tiny flecks of scurf along the gleaming whiteness of her skull. He remained motionless, dreading the moment when she would lift her head and he would have to find out who she was, what their relationship had been. He felt too exhausted to puzzle over it. He wanted to hold back his questions until he had rested again. Until he was so strong that the answers he might get would not bring back the siren shriek.

The man in white walked in, the nurse following respectfully a few steps behind. He ignored the woman, stopping a few feet behind her and looking down at the face on the pillow. There was an intent expression on his long heavy face, a look of curiosity in his eyes.

"How do you feel now?" he asked. It wasn't a question of compassion. His high sharp voice was medical curiosity—like a question written in a case history.

His lips felt dry and his voice sounded rusty in his own ears as he answered, "Better." He had tried to speak loudly, but the tone sounded as though he were speaking through a mass of cotton. He wanted to tell them all to go away—tell them to leave until he could find the strength to wonder, to question. But he couldn't find the words.

"You will feel strange for a time. Maybe a year. Maybe two. The technical name for what was done to you is a frontal lobotomy. Used on manic-depressives in extreme cases. First time it was ever done on a sane man to relieve the internal presure of a complex skull fracture. It will play tricks with your memory and might even effect minor changes in your personality. But don't be frightened. It was a long chance, and we saved you. You will recover rapidly, Mr. Warlow." The tall man leaned forward and touched the still-crouching woman on the shoulder. She looked up at him through a shine of tears. He made a small motion toward the door and she stood up obediently. They both smiled at him before they walked quietly out. His was a smile of professional pride. Hers was a smile of bravery and uncertainty. In a few moments he felt sleep drifting across him. All of the other words had faded, except his name. Warlow. He would cling to that. Yes, he would remember that. It was a stone on which to anchor the odd, shifting memories. He slept.

On the third day the little man came. He sighed wearily as he sat on the bedside chair, and brushed with a fat white hand at the gray ash on his dark blue lapels. His nose was long and fat, with the tip covered with little wandering red veins like a miniature road map. He squinted little blue eyes and looked down his nose at Warlow, like a man aiming some strange weapon. He sighed again.

"Now, Pete," he rumbled, "it's time we got some of the answers. Jackson says your memory is going to be mixed up, so I got to help you. My name's Kroschik. I'm a cop. Do you remember anything about what happened in the office?"

"Office?" Peter Warlow felt the strangeness of it. Of course, there must have been an office. He must have worked in an office. And then he saw it. Saw the rows of desks, heard the clatter of the typewriters and the ringing of many phones. His desk was on the end, near the windows. He could even see the small black sign with his name—Peter J. Warlow—printed in discreet gold.

"Yeah. Benson and Coward, where you worked."

"I remember, but I don't know what happened. Was I hurt?"

"All we know is that four of you were working late on a Friday night about a month ago. Three guys and a girl. She was a little blondie named Clarissa Paine, but everybody called her Sandy. I'd say she was a cute little piece. The other two guys were J. Howard Jones, a fat guy who is your boss, and Trent Welch, a red-headed college kid who does part-time stuff for Jones.

"Jones says he heard a big argument going on out in

128

the big room. He stepped out of his office and you and this Sandy were yelling at each other. He heard her screaming something about telling everybody. Then he says you pulled a gun out of your desk drawer and shot her in the head. He grabbed one of those heavy gadgets that hold Scotch tape and flung it at you. It caught you smack in the forehead and he called up and reported both of you as dead. But you've been lucky. They fixed your bashed-in head and stirred up the front half of your brain with some kind of a stick or knife or something. This Welch came back from the men's room just as Jones was calling us. Now, do you remember shooting the little lady?''

Peter could hear his heart thudding. The horrible words seemed to belong to some other situations, to other people. It didn't fit his slowly returning concept of himself. It was like a puzzle that he had read in a magazine, or the first half of a TV play. He couldn't feel that he had done such a thing. He could remember the faces of the others, but they seemed far away and unreal. He couldn't remember working late. He couldn't even remember the sound of Sandy's voice. He rolled his head from side to side on the pillow and stared at the veins on Kroschik's nose.

"Can't remember a thing, hey?''

"But, if . . . if I . . . why do you ask . . .?''

"You mean if we got you hooked why do I ask you questions? The reason is that we like to know reasons and background. We can't figure why you should knock her off. Your books are all in shape. You got money in the bank. But you could have been in love with her and she wouldn't play. You're our killer, but we need some more blanks filled in. Like where you got the toy gun. We can't trace the twenty-two target job you used, and the surface of it is too corrugated to leave any prints. I don't like to bother a guy who is just getting well, but this thing has been dragging on for a month now, and I want to get it off the books. You understand?''

The mists in his mind wouldn't clear. He tried to force his mind back to the office, tried to imagine the sound of a shot in the office. But no stimulus of the imagination would give him any clue to what had happened. At last Kroschik left, with the promise to return on the next day. Peter lay motionless in the bed, forming countless pictures in his mind—trying to fit the shifting impressions into a coherent self-history. But all he could get was a series of quick snatches of past events. In no one of the scenes was there a shot fired. He couldn't imagine himself shooting anyone. And yet, what if in his previous mental life he had been the type of person who could take a life? What if he had deliberately . . . ?

He awakened with a jump. It was a different awakening than he had experienced before—the slow drifting up out of black curtains of sleep. He tried to move and then remembered, slowly at first, and then with a rush that brought back everything—the white-faced blond woman—it was Jane, his wife. The late work on Friday. The mass of correspondence that had to be gone through, with countless dictations into the office tape equipment. Then he saw it. He shut his eyes and he could see the brown weight turning over slowly in the air as it hurtled toward his eyes. He could even see the glint of light on the shining roll of tape. Yes, it had spun slowly toward him and then a great blackness—a sense of spinning away into a black depth. But what had happened before that? His own hand around a slim, long-barreled gun—he could see his own index finger clenched around the trigger. Could even see the deep semi-circular scar across the back of his finger as it tightened on the trigger. There was the crack of a shot and Sandy sliding down behind the desk, her eyes narrowed, quick blood matting her hair. Yes, he had done it. It was too clear—too vivid. It could have been no one else.

He felt helpless as he lay on the bed in the dark room. He couldn't move. He heard the hum of traffic in a far street, and the click of heels in the corridor outside his room. Above all, he heard his own breath, shallow and quick. He smelled his own acid perspiration brought on by fear. He had nearly died. The great pain had been defeated and now he must get well only to give his life to the state. But why should they kill a man who had changed—a man who flinched at the thought of firing a shot at a human being? The small night light threw motionless shadows against the wall. One of them was the shadow of a chair. A freak effect of the lighting made it look as though there were straps on the arms of the chair. He knew that if he were standing he would feel faint. Nausea made the room spin slowly around him. Yes, his finger had pulled the trigger. The lead had smashed into the brain of the girl Sandy. He began to call, a feeble monotonous sound, more like a groan than a signal. It was many long minutes before he heard steps coming toward his room. A vague form walked in.

"Get the police! Get Kroschik! Tell him I can remember." The figure left and he tasted blood, realized he had sunk his teeth into his underlip. It was an endless period of waiting. The temptation to tell Kroschik that he had seen Jones shoot the girl was impelling. Then there would be a chance. But if he won, then Jones would pay. And he knew that he had killed the girl. Maybe it would be better to say that he could never remember. But he had already sent for Kroschik to tell what had happened. He felt trapped by his own haste and weakness. He tried to move, to get out of the bed, but found that he couldn't even lift his arms. The struggle made him sweat more profusely.

The lights clicked on with a blinding flash that sent sharp pains deep into his eyes. He squinted and saw Kroschik standing by the bed, a cigar stub in the corner of his wide flat mouth, his shirt open at the neck.

"Okay, Pete. Give it to me."

Peter Warlow started slowly, his speech hesitant and fumbling. "I remember that somehow . . . when the thing hit me, I could see it coming through the air. Before that—before I was hit, there was a vision of Sandy sliding down out of sight behind the desk. But . . . the worst . . . I could see my own hand . . . a long gun, sort of thin, with my finger on the trigger. I could see the scar on the back of my finger, a scar like a new moon . . . I saw it squeeze the trigger. I must have done it. I don't see how I could have, but I must have. And I'll have to take whatever I've got coming to me."

There was silence in the room. Peter couldn't meet Kroschik's gaze. Then the little man said, "So you saw your hand on the gun, with the scar on your finger? Saw that finger pull a trigger?"

"Yes. I remember it."

Again the silence. He looked up and saw the small blue eyes narrowed. Saw the expression of satisfaction. "Okay, Pete. That cooks it. You'll testify formally, won't you?"

"Anything you want. All I want to do now is sleep and see if I can forget. I want to forget the look on her face . . ."

After Kroschik had left, Peter Warlow lived in a strange world of tangled dreams. A world where a girl named Sandy had two slim guns fastened to her wrists instead of hands; where he stood behind a chair with straps on the arms and tried to duck as dozens of brown tape holders came turning slowly through the air; where a spreading red stain matted blond hair and a trickle ran down a white part like muddy water down a clean gutter.

The pale morning sun was slanting into his room when he awakened. He felt the bed shake and saw the same blond head in the same position on the edge of his bed. Once again he felt the tremor of the quiet sobs and realized that it was Jane, his wife, and he knew that she was mourning the wreckage of her life and the ruin of her husband. He tried to think of something that he could say which would convince her of his love and his own sorrow.

But the only words that would come were a halting "I'm sorry, darling."

She lifted her head and in her eyes there was a strange light of joy and triumph. It startled him. She should be mourning him! Wasn't he as good as dead?

Then with the words dancing over each other she said, "Oh, Peter. Mr. Kroschik told me. Now the case is over."

"It's over, certainly. I've confessed."

"But, darling, your confession proved it wasn't you. The scar on your finger." He tried to lift his right hand and couldn't. She sensed what he was trying to do and lifted it for him. The fingers were like a fragile bundle of gray twigs. There was no scar. His world reeled around him.

"You see, Peter," she continued, "you are still mixed up. Your memory will play tricks for a long time. But you're still the same sweet guy. You saw Jones's finger on the trigger and some part of your poor mind made it seem to you that you had seen your own hand. Then he tried to kill you and blame the girl's death on you. But when you spoke of the scar, Kroschik remembered seeing it on Jones's finger. He understood. With that clue, he broke Jones down after he left you last night. Now they won't want you—but I do. I want you to be well again."

After his wife left, Peter lay for a long time in delicious relaxation. All the pieces were beginning to drop into place. He felt bemused at the memory of the alarm he had felt during the night.

Memory was still fragmented. It was like riding a bus through the night, looking out rainy windows at fleeting glimpses of unknown towns. Bits of memory had no relation to time. He could not tell if a vivid scene had happened ten years ago or ten months.

Suddenly he was in a motel room, propped up in bed, lights from the parking area shining in, lighting the room. Sandy stood naked at the window, looking out, hair tousled. There was an old black-and-white movie on television, the sound off. Cowboys rode down a long slope, firing silent guns at invisible foes.

Sandy said, her voice listless, "Fat Jones told me if I don't go back to him, he'll fire you."

The scene faded away, dwindling to a bright white dot.

So that's the kind of man I am, he thought. Or was. And Sandy hadn't gone back to him. Did Jane know about him and Sandy? Was that the reason for some of the triumph in her eyes, knowing the girl was dead?

When he was on the edge of sleep, another scene

flashed bright in the back of his mind. He was in a pine woods on a cool day, walking silently, carefully on the soft carpet of brown needles. Ahead, through the trees, appearing and reappearing, he saw a woman in a red-and-black-plaid wool jacket, strolling slowly. He leaned his left shoulder against a pine trunk and raised the rifle and looked through the scope at Jane, his wife. She would reappear in a few seconds on the other side of a deadfall. He aimed the cross hairs at that height where her pale head would reappear.

He was wide awake. The scene faded. The sense of delicious relaxation was totally gone.

What had happened? Had it been some sort of game?

The neurological surgeons had scrambled his brains. Was this the sort of man he had been? Was this the sort of man he was now?

Or was it a glimpse forward into time, of the sort of man he would become?

A Place to Live

THE RED NEON flickered, making bloody glints on the wet sidewalk. Sometimes the rain-filled wind paused for a moment, and he heard the hoarse chuffing of the switch engines in the freight yard. He walked endlessly, his raincoat belted tightly around him, his brown felt hat pulled low over his eyes, leaning into the gusts of wind. He shielded his cigarette from the swollen drops that would have hissed it out.

He was tired, exhausted—weary to the bone with the events of the past two weeks. Just a little while longer. Not even an hour now. And it could be turned over to someone else. The whole dirty burden could be flung to someone used to that sort of thing. And then he would have to look for a new place to live. The city of Amberton would be far too unfriendly. There would be people left around the town who would like to see him on his back in an alley with his eyes wide open. But until the train arrived . . .

He looked nervously behind him. The street was deserted. A taxi roared by, the springs and shocks smacking hard against the holes in the road. Holes in all the roads. Amberton was a stupid city. A fat, complacent, poorly run little city, full of bland, greedy politicians. The tax rate had climbed above fifty-five dollars a thousand, and factories stood idle along the river. New industry wouldn't come in.

135

And still the politicians smiled, the citizens paid their taxes, the slum sections widened. The death of America, he thought. Right here in Amberton. And in the heart of every other fat little city where nobody cares—but the politicians. Well, he was doing what he could. And then it would be time to get out.

Time to get back to the station. He turned and began to walk more rapidly. He walked through the echoing station, across the dirty white marble, past the scarred wooden benches. He bought another pack of cigarettes at the newsstand and waited.

In ten minutes the train came in, and a few passengers walked listlessly out the gate toward the taxi line. Anxious to get to a bed. They looked crusted with sleep. All except one. A slim man who carried a briefcase.

Bill Davo walked over to him and said, "Berman?"

"Right. You're Davo, hey? Where's the sack?"

"Hotel Amberton. Half a block. One thing, though. They may grab me in the lobby. That's okay with me— it just means I won't be able to give you the dope until you can get to me tomorrow. Don't try to make a fuss."

Berman was slim, dark, alert. When he spoke he didn't change expression. "That way, hey? Let's go."

They walked side by side diagonally across the street and up the block to the side entrance to the Amberton. Bill Davo felt so tense that he couldn't manage to swing his arms naturally. In spite of his casual words to Berman, fear tensed the muscles of his stomach.

He stood near Berman while he registered, not daring to look around the lobby. They rode up together in the elevator. It was only when Berman tipped the hop and the door clicked shut as the boy left that Davo let his breath escape in a long sigh.

It was a bitter, antiseptic little room. Davo looked around and said, "Notice the smell of this shack? Dry rot and dust. Just like the rest of this town. Just like the rest of this stinking town." He heard his own voice climb up and up.

Berman put a hand on his arm. "Take it easy, Davo.

136

Relax. Hold it a minute, and I'll get my pint out of the case. Yeah, there's two glasses in the john.''

Bill Davo sat on the edge of the bed, the glass cupped in his hand, the bite of the liquor sharp in his throat. Berman sat at the small desk, a pad open, a pencil in his hand. He grinned at Davo. "Let's have it, friend."

"Okay. I'll make it short and you can ask questions later. Two years ago I got out of the service and went to work as a junior engineer in the city engineer's office here in Amberton. I used to live in Santon, a few miles up the river. I know a few people around here and this seemed like a good place to go to work.

"The work went okay until a month or so ago. I felt like an outsider, but I did what I was told. Then I made a survey and found out that a retaining wall that holds up a mile and a half of Western Boulevard ought to be condemned. I made a report in writing, had the girl in the office type it and sent it through my boss, Stanley Hoe, to Commissioner of Public Works Wescott. One other guy in the office, a fellow named Jim Danerra, son of the city treasurer, knew about it.

"Nothing happened. Then, three and a half weeks ago, I found out that a contract had been let to tear up and repave two miles of Western Boulevard. The low bid was put in by Benet Brothers Construction Company. Five hundred and ninety thousand. I went around and got hold of the specifications and couldn't find out anything about the wall being fixed. Finally I went to Arthur Wescott and asked him what the hell. He told me to mind my own business, only he used bigger words than that.

"I don't know whether you know anything about road construction, but it's plain damn foolishness to put in a new road over that faulty wall. I couldn't figure it out. It didn't make sense. Then, two weeks ago, I went down on my own to see how Benet Brothers were making out. I figured maybe I could show them the wall. I found out that instead of doing the job they bid on, they're just spreading a thin coat over the old road. It's a four-lane job. Then I got the angle.

137

"Somebody from my office will approve it and they'll finish the job at a cost of maybe a hundred and fifty thousand. It'll be opened to traffic, and then the wall will be officially condemned and torn up again. This time, the second time, they'll fix the wall. With the big profit on the first deal, Benet will be able to bid low on the second job, and thus cover their own tracks. They ought to make a clear profit of about three hundred and fifty thousand—at a minimum. I got mad. I went—"

Berman broke in. "Hold it a minute. Let me get this straight, Davo. What they're doing is botching a job because they know it won't have to stand wear. When they get it down, it'll be torn up again within a few months?"

Davo grinned wryly. "Right," he said. "Somebody got the idea when they read my recommendation to condemn the wall. I went back and saw Arthur Wescott and threw the whole thing in his face. He called me a damned visionary, an impractical dreamer. I made a few threats about spilling it all to the public and about not being a party to that kind of thing.

"When I went back to my desk, I was just in time to have Stanley Hoe find a bottle of liquor that had been planted in the drawer. There's an old ordinance about liquor on city premises. I was out of a job and out of the building in twenty minutes. But not before I grabbed this. My copy of the original memo on the retaining wall, dated and with Jane Fay's initials. She's the girl in the office."

Berman looked at it and frowned. "This won't be much help with just your bare word, Davo."

"What if she is willing to swear as to the date and the contents?"

"That makes it good. Does this Wescott know about the girl?"

"I hope not. But he knows I have this. I mailed it to myself, care of General Delivery. That same night some of the boys came around and beat me up, but good. They went through my room looking for it. Spoiled a lot of my private papers. I spent six days in bed. My ribs are still taped.''

Berman whistled. "They love you in Amberton, don't they?"

Bill managed a twisted grin. "Looks that way. Anyhow, as soon as I got out of bed I paid a visit to the newspaper. Talked to the managing editor, a quiet little man named Johnson Vincens. He took me into his office, listened to the story, wept on my shoulder and told me that it would mean his job to mention it. The city political boss, an ex-brewer named Stobe Farner, owns fifty-one percent of the paper.

"Vincens told me that if I want to snitch, to get hold of you people at the state capital. And he told me not to let the machine know that he'd told me, or he'd be fresh out of business. That's when I phoned and talked finally to you and we made the arrangements.''

Berman said, "Let me check now. Stanley Hoe and James Danerra in the city engineer's office know of this deal. Also Wescott, Jane Fay and this editor fellow—Vincens. There are others, but you don't know who.'' He paused a minute, thinking. "How come this girl is willing to testify to back you up? A little gone on each other?"

Davo grinned. "I am. And I'd like to think she is . . . Hey, I forgot the most important thing, almost.''

Berman started as Davo pulled a small wad of fifty-dollar bills out of his side pocket. "This is a thousand dollars. I just happened to check my bank statement and found it had been deposited. The bank says somebody came in and deposited it in cash. These boys play safe. They figured I wouldn't notice it maybe, or if I did I might keep quiet, thinking the bank had made some mistake. Then they could discredit me by making me explain where it came from. And here's a photostat of the deposit slip. Typed. Maybe you can find out what machine it was typed on.''

Berman took the money, counted it and stuck it in his pocket. He made out a receipt in pencil and gave it to Davo. He lit a cigarette and stared at Bill Davo oddly.

At last he said, "Have you got any angle you've left out? What I mean to say is—what is your motive in all this? Why are you trying to buck these people?"

Davo studied the floor. He said, "It sounds silly, but I just guess they made me mad. First of all, they didn't let me in on a thing for a long time. Then they insult my intelligence by letting that road contract without a word to me. Maybe I'm no more honest than the next guy. I think sometimes that if they'd buttered me up before they let the contract, I might be right in there with them, skimming off a little cream. But they didn't. And when I yawped, they had me fired and then had me beat up.

"I'm just mad, that's all. Besides, I hate to see a town taking the tossing that Amberton has been taking. This guy Stobe Farner has figured out a hundred variations of taking graft. I bet you this city could be run for half of what it's costing. And if you could halve that tax rate, this town would start to come to life again instead of slowly drifting off the deep end."

"Well, you've done your job, Davo. You better leave all this in my hands. Get out of town. It won't be healthy for you here. I'll get some men in and we'll go to work quietly. If we make a fuss, Benet Brothers will get the tip and handle the present road job the way the contract reads instead of putting that thin coating on top. Then we won't have anything to go on. Better let them think that they've scared you out of town. I imagine that Arthur K. Wescott is pretty astute."

Bill Davo looked up from the floor and studied Berman for a moment. "Maybe you're right. Of course, they won't suspect you unless we're seen together. You've never been in this town before, and you don't know a soul in it."

"Not a soul."

"That's odd." Davo looked at Berman intently. As Berman looked up, Bill Davo put his shoulder behind a short right that smacked neatly against Berman's jaw. The dark man bounded backward off the chair. His shoulders hit the floor and he moaned as he tried to lift his head.

Davo picked him up off the floor by the lapels and threw him on the bed. He held the man down and pulled a flat .38 out of a shoulder holster. Then he moved over and sat where Berman had been sitting. Davo was breathing hard. In a few seconds Berman sat up, his eyes narrowed. He felt his jaw with gentle fingertips.

Davo said, "If you're really Berman, I'm going to be doghoused. But you're a stranger to this town, and you came out with Wescott's middle initial. You didn't hear it from me. Empty your pockets and throw the stuff on the floor between us."

Berman said, "Look here, Davo. This has gone far enough. You can't—"

"Empty your pockets!"

Berman eyed the steady muzzle of the automatic. As he did so, Davo noticed that he tensed slightly. With quick comprehension, Davo worked the slide, jacking a shell into the chamber. Berman began throwing papers on the floor.

When the man's pockets were empty, Bill Davo said, "Now stretch out on that bed. On your face. And don't move."

After a full minute, Davo said, "Okay, Vittano. Sit up. What did you do with Berman?"

Vittano grinned. "Go find out if you know so much. Berman decided to take a longer train ride than he thought. He talked a lot. Hell, I told him I was you."

"What do you mean?"

"We have a little friend in the capital who gave us the tip. I went a hundred miles up the line on the train with Berman. Told him the thing had blown up and I was leaving town. Told him there was nothing to go on." Vittano laughed, seeming to regain most of his poise. "He got off at Frereton, fifty miles up, and caught the limited back, sore as hell."

Davo got up and paced the floor, careful to keep the gun ready even though Vittano showed little inclination to try anything. Checkmated. He cursed himself for not having the sense to exchange descriptions with Berman over the phone.

"Stobe Farner's going to get a bang out of this," Vittano said. "What're you going to do now, chump? You better take my advice and leave town. You gave me all your ammunition on a silver platter. For example, that Fay woman."

"Shut up!"

"And Stobe'll be happy to know about Vincens. There isn't much room around this town for guys like that."

Davo whirled, raising the gun. Vittano shrugged his shoulders and said, "Go ahead, sucker. Slug me. What'll it get you? You can't keep me from reporting to the boys."

"I can slow you down a little. Take off your necktie and roll over on your face."

In three minutes Vittano was securely bound—his wrists were knotted behind him, his ankles tied with a strip of sheeting, a face towel crammed into his mouth and secured by another towel tied around his head. Davo picked him up easily, dropped him on the closet floor and shut the door. He slipped into his raincoat and shut the door to the room quietly behind him. Not much time. A few hours. No more.

It was raining again and the bars had closed. The neon had clicked off and the streets were dark, wet, soiled. The gun in the side pocket of his raincoat thumped against his thigh. He crossed the street and paused. The station was a few steps away. He had a thousand dollars in cash. Time to take any train. Anyplace. Time to get away. A new job somewhere else. Forget the whole dirty deal. A new start.

He waited and the rain whipped against his cheek. For a moment he wanted to laugh. Melodrama. Bill Davo stowing a gunman in a hotel closet. Bill Davo walking the night streets with a gun in his pocket. Somewhere Stobe Farner would be dreaming of large profits, sleek cars, imported liquor. And Jane Fay would be . . .

That thought stopped him. He suddenly knew that he couldn't go—couldn't leave Jane to the political wolves of Amberton. He walked to the station and startled a dozing cabdriver as he climbed in and slammed the door. He gave Jane's address and settled back into the corner, his jaw set. The tires made a swishing sound on the wet pavement.

Davo climbed out of the cab and said, "Wait here." His heels were loud on the wooden porch. He leaned on the bell and waited. Rang it again. At last lights clicked on in the hall and he saw her come down the stairs, a robe held around her, trying to see who was standing outside the door. Her blond hair was tousled and her makeup was off—but she looked good to him. Very good.

The porch lights snapped on and he saw the worried recognition. She unlocked the door and opened it. "Bill! What in the world?"

"I've got to talk to you. I've messed everything up."

"Come on in." She grinned crookedly. "At least they haven't put you in bed again."

They sat side by side on the couch in the darkened living room.

"This is worse than a beating," Davo told her. "I reported the whole deal, including your willingness to testify, to a man from the Attorney General's office. He turned out to be a plant. The real guy never showed up. I was a fool."

She was silent for a long minute, not looking at him. She said softly, "I don't care much for myself. I can always get work in some other city. But my mother owns this house. They won't stop at driving me away. Her assessment will go up a few thousand. There'll be building inspectors here, forcing her to make unnecessary repairs. They'll find a dozen ordinances to make her life miserable.

"And they may do more than drive me away. There was a girl in the assessor's office once. She tried to make a stink. They found two hundred dollars' worth of office supplies in the back of her car. She went to the county jail for six months."

He said hoarsely, "Okay, then! Tell me I'm a fool! Tell me I've ruined things for you! Tell me to get out of here!"

She reached over and her hand was warm against his. "It's a little late for that, Bill. Maybe we can still fight."

"How? Johnson Vincens is going to get it too. He's right in the soup with us. Our only chance was surprise and I muffed it. Oh, I've done a great job. A wonderful job."

She snatched her hand away. "Stop feeling sorry for yourself! Does Farner know yet?"

"No. I made like a tough guy and put the plant in a closet down at the Amberton. I don't think he'll get out until morning. I thought it would give us more time. More time to run."

"I have a hunch that neither of us is the running type, Davo boy."

"Any ideas?"

Jane said slowly, "There's three of us in the soup. Right? Well, three heads are going to be better than two. You phone Johnson Vincens while I get dressed. Tell him we're coming over. And phone a taxi."

"Got one outside. All this doesn't make much sense to me—"

"Can you think of anything better?"

"Go get dressed and stop needling me. Maybe the three of us can still make some kind of stink."

She ran up the stairs. He went into the hall, looked up and dialed Vincens' number. The phone rang six times before it clicked and he heard Vincens' sleepy "Yeah?"

"Mr. Vincens, this is Bill Davo. I'm coming over to talk to you."

"Look, Davo. I need my sleep. It can wait until morning."

"Maybe it can, but you can't."

A few seconds' silence. Then: "What does that mean?"

"You may be out of a job in the morning."

At last the weary voice said, "Come on over."

Davo hung up.

When the cab pulled up in front of Vincens' house, the downstairs lights were on. Vincens met them at the door, looking very small and very helpless in a gray robe that matched his gray hair.

144

"Come back to the kitchen. I've got some coffee on. You're Miss Fay, aren't you?"

They followed Vincens back through the house and sat around the kitchen table while Bill Davo told once more the story of the deception.

When he was through, Vincens said, "That was a broken promise, Davo. I don't know why I trusted you. Should have kept my mouth shut . . . Well, it's done now. I can see why you thought it wouldn't go any further."

They sat and looked at Vincens. His shoulders slumped and he stared down at the porcelain top of the table, his mouth slack. He murmured, "A long time ago I figured that I'd be a crusader. I'd use the power of the press to clean up the rotten spots in this fair land. Hah! Ended up as a hack dancing on the end of a string. Three kids. One in the first year of college. Come home, laddie. Daddy's unemployed."

Suddenly he balled his small fist and banged it on the table so hard that the cups danced. He looked up with a mad light in his eyes. "You know, damn it, I'm almost not sorry! I've been on the dirty end of the stick for so long that I began to think I belonged there. Then, after eight long years I make one little gesture of revolt and that's the one that creams me. Hell, I'll become one of those guys that clean out sewers with a long pole. It'll be cleaner work . . . Run along home, kids. Let an old man lick his wounds."

They didn't move. Davo bit at dry lips.

Jane said softly, "How about really doing it, Mr. Vincens? How about going out in a blaze of glory? How about hitting this town tomorrow morning with a front page that'll tear the heart out of the organization?"

For a moment, the fervor of her words got him, and he straightened up, a new light in his eyes. He slumped again and shrugged. "Grandstand stuff. What good will it do? Maybe if I get down on my knees in the morning and lick Stobe Farner's shoes he'll let me stay on. I'm too beat to do anything else."

Jane leaned forward and put a hand on his arm. "Stobe

doesn't know about it yet. Bill locked up his man down in the Amberton. We still have time. Maybe the people of this town will come to life and lick Farner if they know the facts.''

"Look, lady. The morning edition is locked up, ready to roll. Stobe has got spies all over the place. And besides, the public wouldn't give one single damn. Not in this town. The ones that vote throw it just the way Farner wants it thrown.''

Bill said, "But if you get tossed out in a blaze of glory trying to upset Mr. Big, won't that give you a better rep to land a good job on a real paper? At least you would be taking a shot at killing the dragon.''

Vincens scuffed at the gray stubble on his chin with the edge of his thumb. "That's not a bad thought, Davo. Hmmmmm. Not bad at all. But it's going to be rough. Very rough.'' He glanced up at the kitchen clock. "Nelly! Not much time.''

They heard him at the phone. "Sam, is she rolling? Not yet? Good! Unlock the first page. No, leave it as is. We'll give 'em a bargain. Two first pages. Who cares? Wait till I get there.''

Vincens dressed in a matter of minutes. Davo had the cabdriver gun it on the way to the newspaper building. Vincens ran up the stairs ahead of them, filled with sudden and surprising energy. His gray cheeks were flushed and his voice had a new edge in it. He shucked off his coat and shoved Davo and Jane into a small office adjoining the newsroom.

"Miss Fay, you type out Bill's statement and your own in detail. Put everything in you can. Names, places, times, people. Everything. I've got to yank some people out of bed and get them down here. Tonight we're putting out a paper!''

Jane sat at the typewriter. Davo paced back and forth in front of her. He started: "Up until thirteen days ago I was employed in the city engineer's office. The following story explains why I was fired, beaten up, threatened. It is a story of graft on a large scale. It is a story of little men who are planning to milk the public of hundreds of thousands of dollars . . .''

The typewriter rattled, and the words spread across the paper. Facts. Figures. Names. An indictment of all that was vicious in Amberton. And all that was sly and diseased in the hearts of Farner, Wescott, Danerra, Hoe . . .

The rain had stopped. The gray dawn touched the mists rising from the river. The specialists, giving Johnson Vincens odd, sidelong glances, had slipped into their coats and left. The trucks were lined up at the side entrance for the morning edition. The drivers were across in the bean wagon, drinking coffee. The building was shuddering with the thump and roar of the big presses. As the copies piled up, men slid them away from the press, tied them and slid them down the chute to the waiting trucks. The first truck was filled and roared away.

In the office of the managing editor, Davo and Jane Fay stood behind Vincens reading the new page one, the ink still damp.

FARNER AND WESCOTT ACCUSED OF FRAUD . . . DANERRA IMPLICATED . . . FORTUNE IN HIGHWAY SWINDLE

Fat, wet headlines. Pictures of Farner and Wescott. Facts. Figures. A cut of Western Boulevard.

Vincens smacked his palm against the wet sheet and said, ''I like it!'' At that moment the presses stopped. They looked at each other. Vincens' face suddenly acquired new lines. He led them in the crazy run down the stairs, down to the room where the presses stood silent. The pressmen stood in a small group. Two stocky men, their faces shadowed, stood by the presses, hands shoved deep in their pockets.

''What goes on here?'' Vincens demanded.

''Stobe Farner's orders,'' one of them said flatly. ''No paper published today.''

Davo stood motionless as Vincens took a slow step

toward the two men. And another. "There will be a paper today."

"Not this one," the nearest said, and spat on the top one of the pile by the press.

Vincens took another slow step toward them. His face was a gray mask, his eyes wild. His fists were clenched tight.

"Don't get excited, mister. Back up. Back up, I said!"

Vincens took another step. He was five feet from the nearest one of the two. The man's hand came out of his pocket, gray morning light glinting on the blued steel of the gun he held.

"Back up!" the man shouted.

Vincens reached for the gun, moved in close. The sound of the shot smashed hard against the concrete walls, the silent presses.

Vincens backed up then. He took two slow backward steps, holding both palms tightly against his stomach. He didn't fall. He let himself down slowly and carefully, bracing with his elbows and knees. He went over onto his side and died with his eyes open, with his face suddenly washed into the cool and placid look, that familiar look—of the battlefield . . . or the morgue.

The man who fired the shot looked stupidly at the gun in his hand.

The other said, "You poor damn fool!"

The man with the gun wheeled and crashed two shots into the intricate gears of the press, walked with quick steps to the door. They left without a backward look.

Jane Fay sobbed then. She sobbed, turned and half ran from the room. Davo felt ill. One of the pressmen walked, as if in his sleep, toward the phone on the bench along the wall.

There hadn't been time for Stobe Farner to have gotten a copy of the paper. Davo realized that somehow Vittano had gotten loose, had gone to Farner with his information. Farner had probably phoned Vincens' home, found he was out and guessed at what had happened. Then he had moved fast, sending two men with instructions to find out what was being printed and stop the presses if they thought it necessary. It wasn't the sort of job Farner would tackle himself. Not with the tough intelligence on his payroll.

The drivers had heard. They came in, gawped at Vincens' body. Davo went to one of them. "Did a load of papers go out?"

"Huh? Yeah. One truck. Sammy Bart."

"Do you know his schedule?"

"Sure. Residential stuff."

"I want you to drive me after him in your truck."

"Mister, I'm on company time. I don't take any runs like that. I've got the sheets to deliver and—"

"Hold your hat, mister."

The tires screamed as the man yanked the panel delivery around the first corner. The dawn streets were empty. A similar truck headed toward them, going back to the plant.

The driver said, "What the hell! That was Sammy! He hasn't had time to drop his sheets."

"Follow him."

He spun the truck around in a roaring U-turn and caught Sammy's truck just as it stopped near the delivery chute. Sammy Bart climbed out, another man beside him.

Davo hurried over and said, "What goes on?"

The stranger with Bart said, "Orders from Farner. These newspapers go back in."

"That's what the man says," Bart sang out cheerfully.

Davo looked for a long moment at the narrow, silent face of the man with Bart, then turned and walked back into the plant.

The police were there. Somebody had thrown a worn blanket over Vincens' body. Bart struggled past Davo with some bundles of papers. A stranger was standing near the press, giving orders. "Bring them all back in and round up two other drivers. These all get carted into the furnace room."

Davo saw what was happening. All copies of the papers were being gathered in to be burned. Chief of Police Lanker was one of Farner's men. The police were studiously taking no interest in the newspapers still standing on the shallow platform as they had fallen from the press. Of course they wouldn't look at the newspapers. They had their instructions. They were concerned about the murder of Vincens. Motive unknown. Murderer unknown. Unexplained tragedy.

All the copies of the paper were taken away while he watched. Davo felt a deep amazement at the speed and efficiency with which the group had moved. They knew it was hot. And they sewed everything up. No opening.

He suddenly thought of Jane, and turned toward the stairs. Two of the policemen were walking toward him, angling in from two directions. When he turned away, they came toward him quickly.

"William Davo?"

"That's right."

"Come on along. There's a warrant out for you. Assault. Sworn out by a fellow named Vittano."

One of them slapped the side pocket of his trench coat and said, "My! My! You got a permit for this thing?"

"No."

"Sort of unlucky this morning, aren't you, Davo? Did you see Vincens shot? One of those guys over there pointed you out to me and said you saw it, that you and a girl came in here with Vincens just before he got it."

"I saw him shot, by Farner's man."

"Farner's man! Are you taking the stuff in the leg or sniffing it?"

"Don't argue with him, Al," the other one said.

"Okay, Junior. The county can for you. Material witness for now, and they'll talk to you about the other stuff later."

Davo sat in the back of the sedan beside the fatter of the two cops, who whistled tunelessly between his teeth all the way down to the county prison. Davo knew Marion Kelz, the sheriff.

"Got me out of bed for a welcoming committee, Bill," Marion said.

He was a lean, pulpy man who looked as if he had been roughly constructed of rotting leather. Davo knew that Kelz cleared about thirty thousand a year on his percentage of upkeep of the prisoners. Of that thirty he turned back about ten to Farner, who kept some and split up the balance. The county allowed seventy cents a day per prisoner for food, and Kelz fed them on less than thirty cents.

"So I'm a guest," Davo said bitterly.

"Don't fuss about it, Bill. We'll take this dough you got here and keep books on it. The boys'll be glad to buy your food down the block."

"At double cost to me."

"They got to make a living, Bill. Take him down to number eight, Jud."

Number eight was a two-man cell, about eight by eight, lighted by one small, high window. The dampness was peeling the cheap white paint off the wall. There were sheets on the bunks, black from the previous occupants. The flat felt mattress stank.

Davo sat on the edge of the bunk and lit a cigarette. He was directly across the corridor from the women's tank. There were eight or nine of them in there, ranging from about thirteen to fifty. They were dirty, noisy and, somehow, strangely alike. White brittle faces, ragged dyed hair. He noticed that they had access to lipstick, caked thick and red on their mouths.

They called across to him, thinking it a great joke.

Hr grinned wearily at them and said nothing.

"Toss over some butts, mister," one of them yelled.

He took three cigarettes from his pack and threw the rest of the package across, through the bars of their large cell. One of the young ones grabbed it, and as she stooped she got a knee in her face that smashed her nose. She screamed and dropped back out of his sight. One of the older women shoved the pack down the front of her dress.

Davo sat on the edge of his bunk and thought how hopeless his position was. He had tried, but they had been too quick, too efficient, too merciless. He knew that he could look ahead to possibly two years in prison. They'd never call him as a witness in the death of

Vincens. They'd let him rot on the basis of minor charges, and not take a chance on his bringing Farner's name into the Vincens case.

He doubted that the editor's murder would ever come to trial. It would be an unexplained death; and without a newspaper to whip up public interest, the citizens of Amberton would accept the mystery with the same dull, unthinking lethargy that they accepted everything else.

The proof was gone. He had no chance. All the papers destroyed. Vincens dead. Jane running. Running fast and far, he hoped.

He wondered that he felt so little anger, so little fear. His mind and his body felt numb, dead, unresisting. What was there to do? Sit and take it. The chance to fight was gone. He should have run while he had the chance.

Sure, there were people who would feel sorry for him, who would know that he had been framed—but they wouldn't dare buck the system. It wasn't healthy. It was better to smile when you met Stobe on the street and say, "Good morning, Mr. Farner," accept his grunt graciously. Never mention that Davo guy. Never ask what happened to him. Davo might get a small paragraph on page eight of the paper, and he might get nothing.

He stood up and stretched, his fingertips touching the damp ceiling. Just relax and take it easy. Let the time go by—wait for the day when you can walk out of the cell and go away. Far away. Hell, they aren't going to kill you, Davo. They're just going to keep you a little while. Teach you a lesson. Teach you not to try to be a reformer. Teach you that when you see fraud, try to cut yourself a slice instead of ripping the lid off it.

Suddenly he heard steps in the corridor, heard a familiar voice. Marion Kelz came into sight. He held Jane Fay by the upper arm. There was a bruise across the left side of her face. Her expression was stiff, tight; her lips thin and straight. Her eyes were enormous and Davo felt the fear in her.

Kelz said, "Here's your playmate, Bill."

Davo jumped up off the bunk, held to the bars on the door, looked into Jane's eyes. "She hasn't done anything, Kelz. Nothing! What's she here for?"

"Material witness in the death of Vincens, Bill."

The one known as Jud came along with the keys and unlocked the door of the women's tank. Davo said, "You can't put her in there!"

Jud swung the door open. Kelz shoved Jane inside and the door clamped shut, the lock clicked. Kelz grinned at Davo and said, "She's nice and close to you, Bill. You ought to like that."

They went back up the hall. Jane stood looking across at Bill, her lips parted. Then, as she felt the women gather around her, she turned quickly, her back against the bars.

The big woman who had grabbed the cigarettes said, "You got ten bucks, angel?"

"What for?" Jane asked.

"Sort of an entrance fee, angel."

"I haven't got it."

"Now that's too bad, angel, because that means you got to work out the ten bucks. This place is filthy. You'll clean it twice a day and get a dime a day until you're paid up. Get to work, angel."

The woman reached out, grabbed Jane's wrist and yanked her back into the cell.

Kelz had left a few small bills in Davo's pocket. Davo called across, "Hey, you with my cigarettes. I'll pay her shot."

He wadded up a five and five ones and threw them across. They disappeared into the same place the cigarettes had.

The big one said, "Now I'd call this a real sweet situation. We got a case of love here. Now you look close, mister, because we got a treat for you." She turned her head. "Bring her up here."

Somebody shoved Jane up close to the bars.

"What's your name, angel?"

"Jane."

"There's a lot of wear and tear on clothes in this tank,

angel, and they get sort of dirty. Seeing as how you're fresh meat, you got to turn your clothes over to the ones who have been here longer. You'll get clothes in exchange.

"Now, I wouldn't fit into anything except maybe your stockings, so I'll take those and you can have mine. Let me see now, you're about the same size as Mabel. Get over next to her, Mabel. Let me see. Yeah. They'll fit. Peel down, sister."

Jane didn't move.

The big one took a step closer to her and lowered her voice. "I'm the boss here, angel, and I told you to peel. Do it nice or we'll give you a treatment that'll make you wish you had that pretty face back in one piece."

Jane gave Davo one despairing look, and slipped out of her suit coat, fumbling with the snaps on her blouse. She took the blouse off as Davo turned away, stood looking at the wall under the window.

The big one called over, "What's the matter, mister? Don't you want a good look?"

Davo neither answered nor turned. His ears burned with shame and he knotted his fists. He heard them giggling and making coarse comments about her. He tried not to listen, tried not to think of what they were doing to her.

At last Jane was dressed in the clothes Mabel had taken off—a sleazy crimson dress with a torn sleeve and food spots on the front of it. On her feet were broken, run-over black shoes, white cracks showing the cheap cardboard underneath the shiny surface. Her legs were bare.

The big one said, almost softly, "You did fine, angel. Here's a cigarette. Light it for her, Penny. Now just don't try to buck the system. Keep your mouth shut. You'll sleep on the top deck there in the corner. Don't yell, grab for food or argue with anybody. I got a hunch you'll be here for a long time. The next girl comes in, maybe you'll get some of her stuff. Now climb up into your bunk and stay there until I tell you that you can come down."

Jane walked off without looking over at Davo. When

she was out of sight, he climbed into his own bunk. He found that he was sweating heavily and there was a sour taste in his mouth. His hands trembled as he lit a cigarette. A cockroach scuttled across the floor. The morning traffic began to be heavy in the street outside. The rumble of trucks shook the ancient building. The women were quiet. He could hear the deadly sobbing of the young girl with the smashed nose.

Jud came in to see Davo just before noon. He stood laughing against the bars, grinning cheerfully at his prisoner. "Get you something to eat, Davo?" he asked finally.

"Sure. Not much. And get a lunch for Miss Fay over across the way."

Jud grinned. "She won't get any of it, chump, unless you buy for all of them, and she may not get any even then. Those dames can eat like horses."

"I want to talk with Miss Fay, Jud. Suppose you bring her over into this cell when you come back with the food."

"That's against the rules, Davo. No can do."

"Just a few minutes. Just—say, twenty bucks' worth of time for us to talk."

"With twenty bucks, mister, you can make your own rules. We run this place honest. We got your dough out front, and when I take twenty, I'll make the debit on your sheet. You don't have to worry about me taking more than the twenty."

"Sure. You don't want the place to get a bad name."

He was back in forty minutes with the watery soup and hash for the women's tank, and with two hamburgs and coffee for a dollar for Davo. He said, "Now?"

"Yes, as soon as she eats."

Jane had been listening. "I couldn't eat, Bill."

Davo said, "Now, then. Bring her over."

Jud leered at Davo, shut her in with Davo. The whole front of the little cell wasn't a door. There was a small part of it cement, forming a corner where Davo and the girl could get out of sight. She came quickly and quietly into his arms and her body was trembling. The women across the way made such a howling, jeering racket that he couldn't talk to her. He stepped to the doorway, looked across at the big woman and said loudly, "How about a break?"

The woman shut them up and Davo went back to Jane. The dress they had given her smelled soiled. The bruise on her face was purple.

"Who hit you, darling?"

"It was my fault. They caught me in a phone booth in an all-night drugstore. I tried to get away."

"I can't tell you that everything is okay. Things couldn't be worse."

She looked up at him quietly. "I know that, Bill. I've always tried to talk a good game. The hard little gal in the politics business. I don't feel hard now. I feel all soft inside."

"Don't let it lick you, Jane."

"It won't lick me." Her arms tightened around him, and she leaned her unbruised cheek against his chest.

He said, "I should have told you before that I love you. This is going to be a long engagement. That is—if you want an engagement." He tried to say it in a joking manner but his voice was too hoarse.

"I want it, Bill," she said.

"You'll get out before I do. You'll probably be here for at least six months."

"When I get out, I'll get you out," she said fiercely.

"Take it easy. We've got to do it this time like the boys tell us to do it. After it's over we'll go away."

"Bill, maybe we'll—" She stopped.

"We'll what?"

"Forget it."

"What were you going to say?"

"I was going to dream out loud." She tried to laugh. "This isn't a good place for dreams, is it, Bill?"

"As good as any," he said bitterly.

Jud looked in. "Okay, kids. Back home for you, girlie."

She was gone and he was alone again. He ate the cold hamburgs, forcing the food down, drank the chilled coffee.

* * *

They came in at five o'clock, Kelz and Jud. They were grim and silent. They took Davo out of his cell. Kelz turned to the big woman. "Where's the girl's clothes, Annie?"

"She give 'em away."

"Get them back on her, quick!"

"Who says?"

"I say it. Unless she's got her own clothes on in three minutes, I'll take you downstairs myself and work you over with a hunk of pipe."

Jane changed in a dark corner of the big cell. One of the girls tripped her as she walked to the door.

They were steered to Kelz's office, a big room with golden oak furniture and brilliant maps on the walls.

A pimply girl sat by the window, chewing gum, her waiting fingers resting on the keys of a stenotype. A dark, sullen man in immaculate tweeds sat behind Kelz's desk. Davo recognized him as John Kroydon, the district attorney. The chief of police, Walter Lanker, was there. He sat with a fat hip on the corner of the desk, his thumbs in his lower vest pockets, a damp cigar butt clenched in his teeth.

A stranger, a meek little man with silvered hair and rimless glasses, stood by the windows, looking at one of the maps on the wall. A muscular young man in a sloppy sports jacket and gabardine slacks leaned against the far wall, a small smile on his lips, his hands shoved deeply in his pockets.

Jud took two of the chairs from the far wall and placed them squarely in front of the oak desk. He motioned Davo and Jane to sit down.

Kroydon turned to the pimply girl. "Get all this, Miss Arkle." He looked at Davo. "You first, Davo. Tell this whole thing from the beginning."

The keys of the stenotype began to click as Davo started to talk, the ribbon unwinding from the machine. In a flat voice, Davo told it from the beginning, told of Western Boulevard, Arthur Wescott, Danerra, Vittano, Benet Brothers Construction, being beaten up, the newspaper, the death of Vincens—every detail of the whole affair. He limited himself to facts.

He finished. Kroydon said, "Thank you. And now you, Miss Fay."

She told it rapidly and well. Davo knew all of it right up to the death of Vincens. Then as she went on, he turned in amazement and looked at her.

Jane said, "I was sick when I went back upstairs. I knew that somehow they had caught on and the paper wouldn't be printed. I knew they would destroy every copy. I wanted to run away. Then I saw the copy Mr. Vincens had brought upstairs. It still had a mark on it where he had touched the wet ink, smearing it.

"I took the paper, folded it and got it into a large envelope I found in Vincens' office. I found stamps, and after I looked in the phone book, I addressed it to the local office of the Collector of Internal Revenue. I marked it special delivery. I sneaked out the side door to the office and mailed it in the corner box. Then I went to an all-night drugstore and called the state capital.

"I got the number of Mr. Berman's home, called him and told him what had happened. I told him he had better get down here fast with help. Then I phoned Mr. Lord at his home. He's in charge of the local office of the Internal Revenue Service. He said he would contact the FBI. The police found me in the phone booth and cut off the call when they yanked me out of the booth. I tried to twist away and fell. They brought me here."

"Why didn't you tell me all this?" Davo demanded.

"I didn't want to get your hopes up. I thought that nothing might come of it. They brought me here and put me in a dirty cell where the women took ten dollars and my clothes and—"

Kelz said angrily, "He don't want to hear about that."

District Attorney Kroydon said, "Shut up, Kelz. We'll make this jail and the conditions here part of the record."

Dave and Jane added statements about the county prison. Just as they had finished, the office door opened so violently that it banged against the wall. Farner strode in, followed by two men. His wide, beefy face was sullen and dangerous.

He snapped at Kroydon, "What the hell goes on here, John?"

"I'm getting statements from these people," Kroydon said quietly.

"Why? You've had your orders."

"Orders? Orders? What do you mean, Mr. Farner? . . . There are two men here in the room you haven't met, Mr. Farner. That man by the window is Mr. Berman of the State Comptroller's office. And the young man over there, Mr. Feldman, is with the FBI.

"For your information, Mr. Farner, I am asking Chief Lanker to pick you up along with Arthur Wescott, Stanley Hoe, the officials of Benet Brothers Construction, Vittano, Danerra and as many of your personal strong-arm men as we can find."

Farner spun on the chief of police. "Are you in this too, Walter? Damn it, man, I can prove you're part of my organization! And you too, John. If you try to crucify me, you'll go right down with me."

Lanker didn't answer. He looked toward the windows.

Kroydon said, "I've told these gentlemen that you would probably try to implicate the two of us, even though, as you know, we have no connection with you, Mr. Farner."

"You lie, John!"

"There is no connection. There are no written records to involve us. Good day, Mr. Farner. Walter, you might pick him up right now. Tell your men out in the prowl car."

Farner, with a speed amazing for his bulk, kicked the door shut and pulled a short, heavy revolver out of the side pocket of his overcoat.

His face was twisted. "Rats leaving a sinking ship! This is warning that the ship isn't sinking. I'll get you two if it's the last thing I do." He turned and spoke to the two dark quiet men with him. "Cover me, you guys. This setup stinks to me. I'm leaving."

One of them said, "Too big, Stobe. This is federal stuff. You're all by yourself."

The other one nodded agreement. They both drifted away from him. Everyone in the room was silent, all eyes watching Farner. The sweat beaded his cheeks under his eyes. He looked at Kroydon's impassive face, at the small smile on the lips of Feldman.

"Don't be a chump," Chief Lanker said gently.

Farner put the gun on the edge of the oak desk. He seemed to deflate, to sink in on himself, to suddenly become very much older.

District Attorney Kroydon smiled at Davo and Jane. "You can rest assured that there will be no charges against you. This was an unfortunate error. You are free to go where you wish. We'll be in touch with you."

Davo stood up and walked with Jane to the door. He pulled it shut behind them, and they walked out past the front desk and across the long corridor, out into the dusk.

"I'm starved," Jane said.

Davo grinned. "The upkeep on you is going to be expensive, lady."

They walked along, side by side, toward the restaurant down the street. His fingers touched the bills that had been given back to him.

He laughed.

She said, "What is it, darling? What could possibly be funny?"

"I was thinking, Jane. We were talking about going away. You know, I have a hunch this might turn into a pretty fair town in which to live."

She took his arm. "Anything you say, but let's talk about it after we eat. I'm starved!"

Neighborly Interest

SHE CAME TO the back door of the cheap new frame house, and Stan Ryan didn't ask her in. He went out, pulling the door shut behind him. The back porch was a six-by-six platform, without roof or railing, supported by cinder blocks. New unpainted steps, giving promise of a short life, descended steeply to the muddy, grassless soil of the backyard.

Stan looked at her, saw that she was young and too thin, a vanishing prettiness in her pale face. Her brown hair was coarsened by a cheap permanent, and great blobs of yellow-brown mud were stuck to her shoes. Her hands were reddened, the skin rough, the knuckles swollen.

He gave her a polite and distant smile, and she opened her mouth to speak, but had to wait because of the whining grind of a trailer truck going by on the highway that led to the city eight miles away.

When the truck roar faded, she put on what was obviously a social smile and said, "I'm Mrs. Clarey and I live right down there." She pointed, laughed thinly and added, "I guess I must be your nearest neighbor, Mr.—"

"I guess you are," he said, still wearing the cool smile, ignoring her request for his name.

Obviously that was all she had planned, the conversation up to that point. Her smile began to have a strained quality, a smile painted on a thin face.

161

"George and I, we saw the baby carriage on the front porch and we thought that being neighbors and all . . . your wife . . ." She lost the sentence and flushed.

"She isn't well," Stan said.

"Oh, I'm sorry. Is there anything that I—"

"No, thanks."

She scraped some of the mud off her shoe onto the edge of the top step, then decided that she shouldn't have done it, as she bent over and shoved the clod loose with her thumb. She straightened up, rubbing her thumb on the palm of her other hand, her smile gone.

"I guess I'd better go and come back when Mrs.— when your wife is feeling better."

"You do that."

She went awkwardly down the steps, picking her way across the mud toward the strip of pasture that separated the two houses. The back of her neck under the tighly curled hair looked flushed. She turned and glanced back quickly and went on, moving as though she wanted to run from him.

Stan Ryan waited until she had crossed the rise in the middle of the pasture and disappeared on the far side. He could see the green roof of the Clarey house. He spat out into the mud, turned and slowly moved back into the house.

Sticky dishes were piled high on the kitchen drainboard and a neat row of empty bottles was lined up under the sink.

Stan Ryan was drenched in sweat, as though he had run a long way or lifted a great weight.

Art Marka stood in the dining-room doorway, his hands in his pockets, a stubble of black beard on his face, a cigarette in the corner of his mouth. His pale blue shirt was stained dark in wide patches at the armpits.

"How are your nerves, kid?" Art asked.

"As good as yours."

"You know, kid, we really got an asset in that honest puss of yours. Even freckles you've got. Everybody trusts a man with freckles. She take it okay?"

Stan shrugged. "Guess so. She won't be back. She'll

probably tell her punk husband tonight that we're pretty unfriendly. No more than that. I told her my wife was sick."

Art sighed and stretched. "Kid, I wish you had a wife and I wish she was here and I wish she wasn't sick. This place gets on my nerves. I need a break."

From the dining room, where the shades were drawn, Howie Jadisko said, "Stop dreaming, moon boy. Come on back. I'm about to knock on you."

"Rummy, rummy, rummy," Art muttered. "Go take my hand, kid. I'll stake you. I'm going to take a nap."

Stan went in and sat across from Howie at the cheap new maple table. The top had long dark scorch marks from cigarettes, pale rings from careless glasses.

Howie Jadisko was short and squat, with a face like a gray paving stone, an underlip that hung pendulously away from yellowed teeth. He looked like a moron, but Stan knew that Howie was probably smarter than Art Marka, who had planned the kidnapping.

Stan picked up Art's hand and began to plan mechanically. The word "kidnapping" had an alien and foreign sound to it. An unreal sound. It was a word that brought on night sweats. Even though it had happened over three months before.

Howie knocked with eight, added up Stan's hand, marked the score.

Marka had picked the family right. They had paid the four hundred thousand without a whimper, and the small bills weren't marked. Art had insisted that the kid be kept healthy because then, if things went wrong, there was a better chance of a jury recommendation for mercy.

Howie had been the one who was in the second car when the exchange was to be made. He had the kid on the floor in back in the basket. Art had picked up the bundle and run back to the first car, and as soon as Art had checked the bundle by ripping open a corner, Stan had given the two beeps on the horn that was the signal to Howie to unload the basket.

But when Howie had shown up at the crossroads, the kid was still with him. Still in the basket. The kid had started to bawl, probably for food, and Howie, getting nervous, had pulled the blankets up over its head to stop the yammer. The kid had stopped.

Before Howie had unloaded, he had taken a look and found the kid's face blue because it had smothered.

So at the crossroads, Art had made Stan take it back into the brush and scoop a hole in the leaf mold. The cold sweats came at night when Stan dreamed of how the body had felt in his hands, how still it was, how incredibly heavy.

So, of course, the family had blatted their troubles to the FBI, and it hit the papers the day after the Boy Scouts had found the grave, and now it was Murder One for sure. Stan Ryan thought a lot about death. Often he found himself clamping his solid thigh between strong fingers and feeling the aliveness of himself, picturing the blood rushing through the veins and arteries. It was a hell of a thing that they wanted to take him, Stan Ryan, and make him dead.

There had been no point in getting rough with Howie Jadisko because it was done and nothing could change it. Sometimes in the night Stan woke up and thought he had heard the kid crying the way it had cried in the cellar room where they had kept it for those five days before the payoff, five days while the family got the cash together.

Art had planned the hideout. A month before they had taken the kid, Art had bought the house two hundred miles away, eight miles from a big city. A cheap and lonesome house, a get-rich-quick venture by a small, sloppy building contractor.

Stan had lived in the house for two weeks before the kidnapping, following the routine that Art had set up for him.

After the kid was buried, they had split and gone to the house. The only car they kept was legitimate, a gray '68 Plymouth. Registered. Stan Ryan did the buying. Art and Howie hadn't left the house in three months, hadn't been seen by a soul.

It had died off the newspapers, except for an editorial

now and then. "Why haven't the brutal murderers been apprehended?"

Stan sorted his new hand, sighed and said, "How soon do we leave, Howie?"

"Hell, kid! You know as well as I do. Another month and a half. Then we divide and split up."

"Where are you going, Howie?"

"Kid, if I should tell you and if they should grab you, they got ways to make you tell them. If you don't know, you can't tell them a thing."

Stan knew where he was going. To Mexico and from there to Guatemala. He had heard they couldn't extradite you from there. And it was cheap. If he was careful, his hundred thousand might last the rest of his life. One seventy-five to Art and one twenty-five to Howie.

For a long time Stan had been nervous about them killing him and leaving him in the house. But Art had explained that nobody should try anything funny because it might give the cops a quick lead and it would be easier to follow a trail from a known place, and if anybody got wise, they might well be signing their own death warrant.

Howie glanced at his watch. "Time for your housework, Mother," he said.

Stan walked to the front door, took a cautious look around, then stepped out, grabbed the baby carriage and wheeled it into the front hall. Dust from the traffic had collected on the pale blue blanket. He took it out and shook it.

Testing the front door to make certain it was locked, he went out onto the back porch, across the muddy yard, and untied the end of the clothesline that was fastened to the corner of the garage. It was a lot easier to take in the line, clothes and all, than to take the clothes off each day and then hang them back on the line. He held them high to keep them out of the mud, untied the end fastened to the house and took the whole wad inside, dropped them in a corner of the kitchen. The line held aprons, women's underthings, T-shirts, shorts, a couple of sheets. All the things necessary to show that the house was occupied by a man and wife.

The following day he would hang the washing back out, push the carriage out onto the porch, bringing it in at regular intervals, putting it back out. There was a celluloid rattle with a red plastic handle that had to be placed on the front porch steps or on the dirt below the front porch railing.

Howie came into the kitchen, looked over the larder, said, "Kid, you'll have to go to town tomorrow. We're getting low."

Stan felt a deep tremor in his gut. He dreaded the strain of shopping, the strain of keeping from looking behind him as he walked from the car to the store, the strain of keeping the car at a speed of not over thirty-five as Howie had instructed him.

In the evening they had a regular routine. The front-room shades were not drawn, and Stan had to spend a certain amount of time seated in the window, reading. Art and Howie never showed themselves by an unshaded window. All lights had to be out by ten.

Howie moved ponderously around the kitchen, his hands deft and quick. Stan watched him for a moment, and said, "Ham and eggs again?"

Howie straightened up. "Maybe you'd like this job, Ma?"

"No. Go ahead. I'm not bitching."

When the meal was on the dining-room table, Stan went up and awakened Art. Asleep, Art's face had settled into flaccid lines, the skin under the stubble of beard looked like a rancid crust on a bowl of grease. When Stan touched him, Art jumped violently, his eyes staring and startled. Then he relaxed, swung his legs over the side of the bed, his face in his hands.

"Shouldn't sleep during the day. My mouth tastes like the bottom of a dishpan."

He followed Stan down the stairs. They ate silently and quickly. The coffee was hot, strong and black. Howie hissed out his cigarette in the dregs of his coffee.

"That's a dirty habit!" Art snapped.

Howie laughed flatly, without humor. "Sensitive, Arthur? Go to hell!"

"I'm going nuts in this place," Art said petulantly.

Neither of the other two answered him. Stan carried the dishes out to wash them and Art got the cards, brushed the crumbs away and started to shuffle them.

When the dishes were done, Stan watched them for a time, yawning. He went and sat in the lighted front room, turned the light out at nine and went up to bed. He lay in the darkness, thinking of the thin woman who had called. Not bad eyes. Maybe with a little meat on her bones . . .

Well, there'd be women in Guatemala. Women who would look more than once at a young guy with a hundred thousand U.S. dollars. The memory of the weight of the dead kid in his hands was trying to push its way up out of his subconscious, but he fought it back. Hell, they didn't have a line on the three of them yet. No, it had been played smart. Careful.

Sleep was black soft water that lapped at him, finally washed over him, carrying him down into a frightening place, a sweaty sickening place . . .

Suddenly he was wide awake, a cry stifled on his lips. Sweat was cold on his face and he sobbed softly. In the darkness he glanced at the luminous dial on his wristwatch. Only nine-thirty. He had only been asleep twenty minutes. He pounded the pillow into a new shape, tried to relax.

From a distance he heard the drone of voices. Art Marka and Howie Jadisko. He frowned. Usually they were quiet over the rummy game. He wondered what they were talking about. There was no chance of getting down the stairs, because already the new staircase creaked badly.

He was sleeping in his underwear. Silently he rolled out of bed, padded down the hall and into the end bedroom, the one where Howie slept. The dining room was under that bedroom.

He knelt in the dark on the bare floor, stretched out on his belly, and put his ear to the varnished hardwood.

When he stopped breathing, he could just make out the words. Howie's voice: ". . . but he's the cover, Art. You can't do it until we're ready to haul."

"I know that. The way I figure it, we stuff him in the furnace and they don't find the punk until next winter. When he starts to stink, it goes up the chimney. We get all set before we do it. We split his end even."

Stan got slowly to his feet, went silently down the hall and got into his bed. He lay with his eyes wide open, looking up into the darkness. He did not feel the least bit afraid. Instead he felt a cold wrath. He was the cover. He was the fall guy. Kill him when his usefulness was over.

Oh, fine! Then he felt a deep, excited thrill that ran up his back. They had given him his freedom. The take was in the brown suitcase in the back of Art's closet. Kill the two of them, take it all and leave. Four hundred thousand sounded a lot better than one hundred. Maybe with four hundred he could stop remembering the dead kid and the picture in the paper where the father was holding up the kid's mother, where she looked as though she'd slip right down onto the floor if he let go.

Killing them was easy to say, not so easy to do.

He turned on the light. Quarter to ten. He pulled his clothes on, went noisily down the stairs.

"Hi, guys!" he said airily.

"Thought you folded, kid," Howie said.

"Couldn't sleep. Thought I'd get myself a drink." He went on into the kitchen, rinsed out one of the coffee cups, sloshed it half full of rye. The liquor was warm and he almost gagged when he finished the big jolt. But it began to radiate warmth through him, and that was good.

He heard the slap of cards on the maple table, heard Howie say, "Knock with four, sucker. Catch you big?"

"Lemme see. Twenty-eight, thirty-three, thirty-six. Satisfied?"

"That takes care of the first two games, and damn near a schneider on the third."

Stan forced himself to be calm. The odds were that

the kitchen circuit and the dining room were on the same fuse. There was a pinup lamp over the breakfast booth, with a fake parchment shade. He strolled over, out of sight of the card players, pulled the plug out of the wall. With a kitchen knife he quickly unscrewed one of the little brass screws that held the wire tight, wrapped the loose wire around the other post. Then he plugged it back in. There was a crackle, a spit of blue sparks, and both the kitchen and the dining room went dark.

"What the hell?" Art said in a hushed tone, and Stan smiled in the darkness as he heard the fear.

"Nothing. I turned on this lamp out here and I guess it's shorted. Must have blown the fuse. I'll take a look. Maybe one of you guys ought to come along. I'm no electrician."

Howie was the one who joined him. Howie clicked the cellar light on. Stan felt afraid. He hadn't thought of the cellar light. He had wanted it to be in darkness.

Together they went over to the fuse box, and Howie opened the black metal door. He peered in at the fuses. "Here it is. This one," Howie said. "You got a penny, kid?"

"Don't think so."

"Wait. I got one." Howie twirled the fuse out, pulled the switch on the side of the box, and the cellar lights went out. Stan heard the clink of the penny, the grating of the fuse being turned back into the socket.

The cellar lights went on. Howie, his hand on the switch, yelled, "Okay up there?"

"Okay," came Art's answering yell.

At that moment Stan struck with the kitchen knife. Right under the left shoulder blade. The metal grated on bone and slipped away. Howie grunted in pain and whirled with uncanny speed, his eyes narrowed, his mouth twisted with pain. He reached toward his hip pocket.

Stan grunted with the force of the blow as he blindly stabbed down at Howie's face. Howie stood perfectly still for a moment, one eye suddenly wide. In the place of the other eye was the dark protruding handle of the paring knife.

169

As he fell heavily on his side, rolled over onto his back, Stan looked down at him and giggled. Then he made a soft retching sound, turned away, weak with the sudden sickness, his hand against the rough, whitewashed wall. He pulled the switch down.

"Now they're out again!" Art called. "What are you guys doing down there?"

"Just a minute," Stan yelled hoarsely. He tugged at Howie, rolled him over onto his face. The knife handle gritted against the cement floor. Stan got the flat automatic out of Howie's hip pocket. He worked the slide, heard the clink of a round hitting the floor. He thumbed the safety off and went up the stairs.

As he stepped into the kitchen, he called back, "I'll see if Art's got one, Howie."

He knocked against the doorframe, blundered into the dining room. "Say, Art, we need a penny to fix the fuse. You got one?"

"I hope you guys know what the hell you're doing down there. The lights going off like that gives me the creeps. Did I hear Howie laughing?"

"Yeah. He was laughing. Now you can laugh, Art."

"What are y—" That was all.

It was as though the slugs drove the breath out of Arthur Marka's chest. The darkness stank of smokeless powder. Stan stood and listened. A heavy truck went by, and then two cars.

Slowly he exhaled. He lit a match, shook it out. Three in the chest and the last one in the face. Art was slumped in the chair, his chin on his chest, both arms hanging straight down.

In the darkness, Stan pushed him off the chair. He hit with a sodden, dead sound. Stan found his heels, dragged him to the cellar stairs, got behind him and pushed. Art Marka's body rolled noisily down the steep flight, thudded against the cement at the bottom.

He turned out the cellar light, went up to his room, saving the money until last. He packed his few clothes, walked through the darkened house to the back door.

170

Very simple. Two suitcases on the kitchen floor. One full of money. All for Stanley Ryan.

The car was gassed up. Lock the door and leave. The clothes and the carriage were in and the front door was locked.

Three feet from his head the bell shrilled. He started violently, stood shaking in the darkness. He cursed. Crouching, he ran to the front of the house, looked cautiously out the front-room window.

A white trooper car was parked in front, the motor running.

Caught like a rat in a trap.

He slipped out of his coat, threw it aside, transferring the gun to the right-hand pocket of his trousers. With trembling fingers, he unbuttoned his shirt down the front.

He turned on the hall light, opened the front door, yawning, and said, "What do you want?"

Two tall troopers stood there, and behind them, her eyes wide, stood the thin woman who had paid a call in the middle of the afternoon.

The trooper nearest the door looked disgusted. "Mister, we got funny stories and we have to look into them."

"He's the one! He's the one!" the woman said shrilly.

"Yeah, lady. We know. Mister, I understand your wife is sick. Is that right?"

Rising hope gave Ryan the courage to smile. "Not very sick. Just a little under the weather. You know how it is. She only had the kid about four, five months ago. If I'm not too curious, what is all this? What did this woman say to you? She called this afternoon and I thought she acted a little off her rocker."

"I might as well tell you, mister," the trooper said. Ryan moved out onto the porch.

Suddenly the woman darted into the house. Ryan made a grab for her and missed.

One of the troopers grabbed Ryan and the other one went after the woman. The trooper who had taken Stan Ryan's arm said, "Joe'll grab her. She's just a harmless nut, I guess."

Stan, listening, heard the woman go up the stairs, the

171

trooper pounding behind her. He knew that there wasn't much time. The woman would be looking for a woman and a baby.

The money was in the kitchen. There was a small chance. He turned half away from the trooper, let his hand drop down until his fingertips touched the cool butt of the gun.

From somewhere upstairs the woman yelled loudly. Stan yanked the gun out, shot twice at the middle of the trooper.

He ignored the clothes, grabbed the brown suitcase. Someone shouted hoarsely. A more authoritative gun roared.

The engine caught the first time, and he was glad that he had backed it into the garage.

It jumped down the drive and a figure ran out from the side of the house, an orange-red jet of flame spurting toward the car. The car swerved, thumping on the rim, wedging against the side of the house.

He ran fifty feet before the slug smashed his shoulder. The impact drove him over onto his face and he rolled, sobbing, yelling with pain and fear and the knowledge that he would die.

Two days later, after Stanley Ryan had dictated his confession to the police stenographer who sat by his hospital bed, he said to the lieutenant, "I've been thinking. Why did that Clarey woman bring the troopers around?"

The lieutenant, a weary-looking man in his fifties, inspected the end of his dead cigar and said, "Why, son, she thought you'd gone out of your head and killed your wife and kid."

Stan puzzled over that. "Why should she think anything like that?"

"She has two little kids of her own, son. She found the weak spot in your window dressing."

"Weak spot?"

"Sure, Ryan. Weak as hell. You see, you had those things on the line every day, and every day she'd take a look, because she missed the one thing that should have been out there. She missed the one thing real bad. And finally she had to come over to talk to you. If you'd given her a chance, she was going to ask about it. There was one very necessary thing that wasn't out there every day blowing in the breeze. And young Mrs. Clarey knew there wasn't any diaper service that far out of town.''

The Night Is Over

THERE WAS SOMETHING infinitely irritating about the puffed, water-wrinkled hands of the man behind the bar. He was wringing out a rag with soft ineffectuality, humming a nasal tune that had been beaten to death by the jukeboxes.

Walker Post stifled the impulse to snarl at him. It was pointless. You can't climb a man because you don't like his hands, or you don't like the tune he hums. He hadn't been in that particular bar before. A quiet neighborhood spot, drowsing in the heat of an early July afternoon. One other customer, an old man with a ragged yellow beard, sat at a table and sweated in the sun that came in the wide window. Walker Post realized that he was holding himself tense and rigid on the barstool. His shoulder muscles hurt. He made himself slump and forced his eyes away from the bartender's hands. He swallowed the last inch of rye and water and slid the glass down toward the bartender. He looked across at his own face in the blue-tinted mirror behind the bar. It's so hard to look at your own face and know what you look like, he thought. What do I see? Dusty hair and pale gray eyes and lips that are thin. Thick shoulders and a sullen look around the mouth and chin. New lines from the corners of my nose to my mouth. The hair has gone back a bit further. A wrinkled and soiled collar. What am I and where am I going and why don't I give a damn?

The Night Is Over

There had been people who had given a damn. Four years ago when he had been twenty-seven, when he had married Ruth, she had given a damn. His mother had always cared. Faulkner, the drafting-room chief, had cared, once upon a time.

He realized that going back to work for Faulkner had been a mistake. They had all been so kind and had tried to be so understanding. He shuddered, remembering the soft touches of their hands on his shoulders. It had been so unreal to stand and see the January snow piled so deeply across the trim new graves of Ruth and his mother. He had brushed the snow away so he could read the dates on the stones. Nineteen forty-six. The paper had used the term "common disaster." Sure. It was a disaster and they seemed to be common enough. He could crawl up seven beaches with his eyes clouded with cold sweat and his fingers slipping on the gun and the grit of fine sand in his teeth, while Ruth skids the car through the side of a bridge.

It had been a reflex going to work for Faulkner again in January. He had been used to it. He had thought it would give him something familiar to hold on to. It hadn't worked. Where is the point in drawing fine clear lines on white paper while the spring sun melts the snow on the soft earth near the stones? He had known he was being careless—his work had been sloppy.

He remembered the afternoon several weeks before when Faulkner had taken him into the empty office of the boss and given him a cigarette. Faulkner had perched his lean frame on the edge of the table and said, "I've been trying to go along with you, Walker. I can only imagine what you've been through. But, man, you're not helping yourself. You're being a fool. I can't cover you much longer. What are you going to do about it?"

There had been a long silence in the small office. Walker Post had sucked on the cigarette while the room had seemed to darken around him. Then he had dropped the butt onto the rug and ground at it with his heel.

He had spun on Faulkner and cut into his objections with a string of the foulest words he could think of. He had gone on and on in a low tone, watching the expressions of shock and anger color Faulkner's long face. At last he was through and Faulkner had slid off the table and walked out the door.

Post had gathered his few personal possessions together and left the same hour. He hadn't been back. Once he had met Faulkner on the street. He had turned his face away. They hadn't spoken. It was like that.

He had put the furniture in storage and moved his clothes into a furnished room on Plant Street. He hadn't tried to find work. There was still more than two thousand dollars of insurance money left in the bank. He knew he wasn't drinking himself to death. Just enough liquor each day to cloud the pictures in his mind. Just enough to dull the constant irritation with everything around him. He slept in the cheap, sour room between the gray sheets. He ate heavy fried foods. He walked the streets slowly and wondered what there was to care about. In some distant corner of his mind he was uncertain and frightened. Some mornings he would remember and realize that it would have to end sometime. There would be no more money. But that was a long way off.

He spoke to no one. He didn't read. He didn't go to movies. He sat and drank and ate and slept and walked, fighting down the mad thing in his heart that wanted to flash out at the people around him. He wanted to strike and crush and batter the faces of those around him.

The bartender placed the fresh drink in front of him. "Sure is hot, hey?"

Walker Post looked up into the man's mild eyes. He looked for several long seconds, expressionless and motionless. Then he said shortly, "Yeah."

The man shrugged and walked back down the bar. Post sat and tapped with his blunt finger at a spot of water on the dark bar. He sipped the drink. The traffic noises seemed to be softened by the heat. A woman walked past the open door pushing a baby carriage. One of the wheels squeaked piercingly. Post wondered what it would have been like if Ruth had left a child for him to care for. Would it have been different? Maybe. Maybe it would have been no different if Ruth were still alive. Maybe the sullen core of him had been slowly growing through the years. Maybe nothing that had happened had really changed him. Maybe it was all inside himself. He scratched at the stubble of beard on his chin with his thumbnail. He dug the last cigarette out of a pack, crumpled the pack and tossed it onto the bar. It slid across and fell behind the bar. The bartender walked heavily over and grunted as he picked it up. He stared at Post and half opened his mouth to speak. Post stared steadily at him. The man closed his mouth again and licked his underlip. He walked back to his spot at the end of the bar.

Some more customers came in. Post glanced in the mirror as they walked behind him. He noticed idly that there were three of them. They were noisy.

They climbed onto the stools. "And a fine afternoon it is, Mr. Donovan. Hessy here is buying us some beer. Right out of his own pay, too. Three superior beers."

The bartender grinned and drew three. He swiped the foam off and set them down. Post noticed that the three were young. Their hands were greasy. They wore T-shirts and soiled work pants. He figured them for mechanics or truck drivers. One had a silly bubbling giggle. Post shifted restlessly on his stool.

The bartender started to walk away and one of them said, "Hey, Donovan! Get back here. We need a cultured citizen like you to settle something."

Donovan beamed. "And sure, what do you want to know?"

"This is important. We got two bits on it. What the hell is a cygnet?"

"It's a ring. A signet ring."

"Nuts, Donovan. You tell him, Hessy."

"This kind of cygnet is spelled with a c-y, Donovan. I say it's a female swan and Fenelle here says it's a baby swan. You ever heard of it?"

"Never did. Sorry, boys."

The one they called Hessy looked down the bar at Post. "Hey, you. You know what a cygnet is?"

Post felt the quick rush of irritation. What right had they to drag him into their silly argument? He turned slowly around on the stool so that he faced them. His arm hit his glass and knocked it over. The chill drink ran across his wrist. He realized that they had caused him to spill his drink, and that made the room darken before his eyes.

"Get somebody else to settle your damn argument. Don't bother me."

The one they called Hessy slid off the stool and strutted over. He was a slim kid with cropped hair. He had a smear of grease across his cheek. His nose was slightly twisted. He stuck his thumbs under his belt as he walked. The muscles on his brown arms looked tightly woven and efficient.

He stopped with his chest a few inches away from Post's shoulder. Post had turned back to the bar and stood his glass up again. Donovan hurried toward them, an anxious look on his face.

Hessy stood quietly for a moment, his eyes small and his mouth compressed. "Turn around, honey, and look at me," he said gently.

Post turned around slowly.

"When I ask a guy a civil question, I kinda like to have a civil answer. Understand?" Post stared at him, expressionless. He wondered if he could take the kid. The kid looked rough and willing.

Donovan coughed. "Hey, now. None a that, boys. Skip it. You go sit down, Hessy. None a that around here." His words were bold but his voice was apologetic.

"Shut up, Donovan. This punk needs a course in manners. Who the hell is he?"

"I don't know, Hessy. Please leave him alone, hey?"

The talk sounded blurred in Post's ears. His back felt tight and strained. "Get away from me. Don't talk to me."

"Come on, honey. Take it sitting or standing. Any way you like it."

"Please, boys, let's drop it, huh?"

Post spun quickly and threw his left hand like a club

178

at the boy's head. He missed as Hessy drew his head back a few inches. The force of the lurching blow dragged him off the stool and he tramped on the edge of the brass spittoon. It tilted up, throwing stale water into his shoe. He couldn't see clearly. He heard someone say, "Nice and easy now, Hessy. Nice and easy. Make it last."

The boy took his thumbs out of his belt and moved easily around Post. He carried himself well. Post swung again, and as he realized he had missed, a fist splatted lightly against his mouth. He tasted warm flat blood. He felt blundering and clumsy. He realized the boy was good. Probably had been in the ring. He felt suddenly afraid. He wanted to drop his arms and let the boy hit him. Anything to get it over.

The boy skipped around him and he circled slowly. The fist hit him again on the mouth. He hadn't seen it coming. It hurt. Then the boy started clowning, leaping high in the air and landing in grotesque positions. He chanted at Post, "How do you like it, honey? How do you like it, honey?" Again the hard fist smashed into his mouth. Each blow was a bit harder than the one before.

Suddenly the dancing, posturing figure in front of him became the personification of all the blind and bitter luck that had hung on his heels. Post forgot where he was. He forgot what it was about. He couldn't see and he couldn't hear. There was a dancing face in front of him that he had to beat down to the floor. He felt the fury roll into his arms. He felt his nails biting into his palms.

He rushed the white face, swinging blindly and grunting as he swung. He was moving forward and the face receded. Then the room seemed darker and he felt stabbing blows on his eyes and mouth. For the first time he felt the jar of his fist striking bone. He dug his chin into his chest and hammered with his two arms, short chopping blows as his mouth grew dry and his breath was an acid gasp in his throat. He couldn't feel the blows on his own face anymore, and suddenly the white face wasn't in front of him. His fist smashed into wood. He stepped

back and looked down. The white face was there, sus-
pended a few feet off the dim floor. He swung his right
leg and felt his shoe smack something. The face was
white and red and it was lower. He swung his leg again
and somebody spun him around. He clubbed his fist at
another face and it went back into the mist. He could
see the white rectangle of the doorway. Something hit
him on the side of the head and he tried to run toward
the door. It was like running through deep water.

Then somebody had hold of his arm, pulling him out
through the doorway, where the bright sun smacked
down against his face and blinded him. He was pulled
toward a car, and he fell into the seat, still unable to see
clearly. He felt the car move and heard the roar of the
motor. He was tossed over against the driver as they
turned around a corner. He pulled himself back. Then
another corner. He lurched against the door. It was an
open car. The wind blew through his hair.

The world began to clear. He heard his own sobs as
his breath kept catching in his throat. He had a deep
sharp pain in his side, the same pain he used to get as a
kid when he ran too far. He looked around, realizing
that they had turned into Carmody Road, heading out of
town by way of French Hill.

He looked at the driver. He was a swarthy man, a
small man, with dark hot eyes and a wide firm mouth.
He was dressed quietly and well. He had a faint smile on
his lips—a smile of amusement and condescension. It
annoyed Post. He decided not to speak until the driver
did. He pulled out a handkerchief and dabbed at his lips.
He felt dried blood on his chin.

The man didn't speak. He drove fast and skillfully.
The car was a new maroon convertible—a Ford. They
drove beyond the expensive new developments, out to
where the farms begin. The road climbed and there were
fewer farms. At last the man pulled off onto the wide
shoulder near a small patch of woods. He switched off
the motor and opened the glove compartment. He handed
Walker Post a wad of Kleenex.

"Better go and mop off that face. You'll feel better.

There's a stream right down there beyond those rocks. I'll wait."

Post took the tissues and climbed out. He felt stiff, sore and shaken. His legs quivered as he climbed down over the rocks. The stream widened to a dark pool under a thick willow. Water bugs skated across it. A dragonfly hung in the air over a weed.

He knelt down and dipped the tissue in the cold water. He mopped his face and it felt good. The damp tissues were stained pink with the blood from his lips and the cut beside his eye. He took his time. He bathed his knuckles. The air in the moist hollow smelled dank and sweet.

He brushed his hair down with his fingers and walked back up to the car. The man was smoking a cigarette. He silently handed Post one when he climbed back into the car. The dash lighter clicked out and Post lit it. It didn't taste good. His heart still thumped from the exertion of the fight.

"I might as well let you know who I am. Dr. Benjamin Drake. I've no right to the title Dr., but I like to use it." His voice was soft and seemed to be filled with gentle self-scorn.

"I'm Walker Post. I suppose I owe you some thanks."

"You're a mean citizen in a scrap, Post."

"I wanted to kill him. I never did anything like that before. If I hadn't been stopped, I would have, I guess. How much did you see?"

"Walked in just as you backed him against the wall. He lost the grin when you hit him the first time. You were lucky. He could have taken you."

"What's your object? What do you get out of this?"

"Probably nothing. You don't look either friendly or grateful."

"I don't give a damn whether you came along or not. I wouldn't have given a damn if I had killed him."

"You don't have to tell me that. I can read it on your face. Something has given you a kicking around. Right?"

"What if it has? I don't want sympathy and I won't answer questions."

"Maybe I could help you."

"Nuts."

"You can't make me mad, Post. Here, let me show you what I do." He pulled a wallet out of his inside jacket pocket and leafed through it. He found a clipping and handed it to Post.

He read: "MERIDIN LAKE SOLD. The Republic Lumber Company announced today that they sold eight square miles of land, including Meridin Lake and the deserted lumber camp, to Mr. Benjamin Drake of Chicago. Mr. Drake stated that he will open up a combination summer camp and health resort restricted to a few patients at a time. The camp will open on July 1. Tax stamps on the recorded copy of the deed indicate that the sale price was in the neighborhood of $110,000."

Post handed it back to him. He was puzzled. "What's that got to do with me? I'm no patient. I don't need a cure."

"You don't know what you need. I'm what you might call an amateur psychiatrist. I don't want you as a patient. I want you to work for me. You don't look as though you have a job. You look like you need some outdoors in your system. You look like you could use the very small pay I'll give you."

"I don't need a thing from you or anybody else. I got plenty of bucks in the bank. I'm getting along. Just drive me back or let me out here." He snapped the cigarette butt off into the highway.

"I did you a favor; now you do me one. Just take that chip off your shoulder for five minutes and don't interrupt me. Okay? You owe me that much."

Post shrugged. "Go ahead, Doc." He knew he couldn't be talked into anything.

Drake slumped down behind the wheel and stared down at the horn button, a frown of concentration on his face. Finally he looked up at Post and smiled.

"I was trying to find the best kind of approach to your type of closed mind. Let me put it this way. Life has slapped you down. I don't know how and I don't care. You're down. You have no interest in anything. Sometimes you wish for death but not strongly enough to kill yourself. Back in your mind is the furtive little idea that someday you'll be okay again. You don't really know. You wonder about it and then force your mind away from it. What are you doing? Nothing. So long as you have that idea in your mind that someday everything will come back—energy, enthusiasm, ambition—you owe it to yourself to put yourself in circumstances that will do the most for you. Right now you revel in drab surroundings. You won't admit it, but you do. You're punishing yourself for something. Get away from it. Come on up to Meridin Lake and get brown and healthy. Healthy on the outside. The work isn't hard. I need another man. You can have your drinks there. I won't pay much. Fifteen a week and your keep. Get away from this town for a while. It won't cost anything. Nobody'll expect you to be friendly. Just do it on a hunch of mine. Now don't answer quickly. Wait a few minutes."

Post sat and looked at his skinned knuckles.

He made himself yawn. He said, "I don't give a damn whether I go up there or stay in town. I don't care one way or the other. You're nosy and you got a lot of cracked ideas. I don't even know what you're talking about. Make it easy for me and I'll go on up. What's the difference what I do?"

Drake grinned at him. "I'll get through that shell yet. Meet me right here at eight tomorrow morning. You can catch a bus out from town. I think the one you want leaves at seven-thirty. Buy some work clothes. That's all you'll need. Try to be on time."

He turned on the motor and yanked the little car around in a screaming U-turn. He didn't speak on the way back to town. He dropped Post off at the corner of Plant Street. Post walked down the street, conscious of the stiffness in his legs, wondering whether he would bother to buy the clothes and show up at the appointed place. He doubted it. He wanted to rest for a while, and then get something to eat. It wouldn't be convenient to buy the clothes. It was going to be too much trouble. There was something about the man, Drake, that he didn't like. Something superior and cold.

He stood in a chill morning rain under a maple across the road from where Drake had parked. The water dripped through the leaves. He was still stiff and sore from the fight. He wondered for a moment whether or not Drake would come. He felt annoyance as he realized that he wanted Drake to come. He stood quietly and forced himself into a state of mind where he didn't care whether the man came or not. Then he relaxed. A few cars whoomed by him, their tires making a tearing sound on the wet concrete. He was lighting a cigarette when the familiar maroon coupe bounced over onto the shoulder. He picked up his bag and strolled through the rain. He tossed it over the back of the seat.

"Good morning, Post."

"Dandy."

"I have things on my mind today. I won't talk to you on the way up. It's five after eight. We'll get to the lake at about two. Just relax."

"You're hurting my feelings." Drake didn't answer. They drove up through the hills that grew almost to mountains. Post watched the road ahead until it made him sleepy. He wedged his head in the corner and went to sleep.

He woke up with a bad taste in his mouth and saw that Drake was getting gas. He glanced at his watch. It was eleven. He stretched his legs and in a few minutes they rolled back out onto the highway. Drake drove at a good rate. His nervous brown hands were firm on the wheel. He cursed softly when cars ahead were stubborn about moving over. Post went to sleep again.

Finally he woke up. Drake was saying, sharply, "Post! Snap out of it!"

"What is it?"

"Nearly there. It's one o'clock."

"Better time than you thought."

"I never make careless estimates, Post. Get used to

184

that. We have four miles to walk through the woods before we're there."

Drake glanced at the rear vision mirror. He slowed down to twenty. An old car rattled by. Drake watched the woods on the right side of the road. He slowed down to ten and then to five. The car ahead disappeared around a curve. He glanced in the rear vision mirror again.

"Now," he muttered, and swung the wheel hard right. The little car lurched across a shallow ditch and scraped under low branches. The back wheels were spinning on the wet earth. He twisted it around another turn and the state road was out of sight. He slowed down. Directly ahead, across the faint trail, was a massive log, nearly a yard in diameter and about eight feet long. The lower third of it was embedded in the trail.

"Get out and move the log, Post."

"Are you nuts? That thing weighs more than a ton!"

"That thing, as you call it, weighs precisely forty-five pounds. Hop along."

Post got out of the car. The rain had stopped. The huge log looked immovable. He wondered if it was a gag. He grabbed the end of it and it lifted out of the soil. He carried the end around. It was a log. Drake drove past and he replaced the log the way it had been.

He climbed back in the car and Drake started down the narrow track.

"What is that thing? What kind of a tree is it?"

"Just what it looks like. I had it sawed into short sections and the center hollowed out. Then I had the boys fit the sections back together with glue and wooden pins. It's strong enough to stand on. The marks are concealed. A stranger would have to kick it or try to lift it to find out what it is. It discourages visitors."

"What are you running down here, Doc? A counterfeiting plant? What goes on?"

"Relax, Post. You'll find out all the answers in time. I run a health farm and I like to keep it private."

After a quarter mile of winding trail through dense brush, they came to a small clearing circled by tall spruce. Drake ran his car under the close branches. They climbed out. Post hauled his suitcase out. As they walked across the clearing, Post saw the rear bumpers of several other cars hidden deep under the trees. He wanted to ask Drake about it. Then he shrugged and followed along in silence.

For a long time the trail wound upward and the vegetation grew denser. Slim branches whipped back, lashing Walker Post across the face. He lowered his head and plodded along, considering only each step at a time. He began to imagine that if he had to stop, he would fail. He wondered where his ability to hike thirty miles in a day had gone.

Suddenly he stumbled against Drake's back. The man had stopped. He stood calm and cool and pointed ahead down the trail. They stood at the crest of a hill.

"Meridin Lake," he said with obvious pride.

It lay below them, a thousand yards away. It was small, possibly a mile long and a half mile wide. A large patch of the sky had cleared and the still water threw a deeper blue back toward the sky. It ran east and west. They stood above the west end. Wooded hills rose steeply from the lake on every side except the west. Ahead Post could see the outlines of weathered gray buildings against the evergreens. It was very quiet, strangely quiet. Post felt a momentary uneasiness.

"Like it?"

"It's okay."

"There's one thing you should know about it. This is wild country. The only decent way to and from the lake is the way we've come. The thickets and brambles and hills are so bad on all the other sides that even hunters never come near us. Remember that."

"So I'll remember it."

Drake started down the trail. The rest of it was easier for Post. It was downhill. He was so tired that his heels thudded against the hard earth with blows that jarred him. He wasn't so tired, however, that he didn't look around at the two buildings as they came out into the clearing.

186

The Night Is Over

They were two long, low buildings of wood weathered gray by the sun and rain and snow. They were of simple construction with gradual slopes on the peaked roofs and overhanging eaves. The square windows were netted. They appeared to Post to be each about forty feet long and fifteen to eighteen wide. They were set parallel, about twenty feet apart. Looking down the alley between them, he could see the blue glint of the lake about fifty feet beyond their farthest edge.

Drake shouted when they emerged into the clearing. There was an open door at the end of the building on the left. A tall man in faded blue denim with flame-red hair hurried out. A stockier dark man followed slowly after him.

They met in the middle of the clearing. Post dropped his bag with a hidden sigh of relief.

"Boys, this is Walker Post. Post, that tall one is Rob Strane, the man who has been with me the longest."

Strane grabbed Post's hand in his big red fist and said, "Hi ya, Post." He was tall and rangy and looked as tough and hard as a pump handle. Post noticed that his eyes were a strange shade of faun, almost a yellow. He acted nervous and anxious to be liked.

"And this is Sam Frick."

The stocky one nodded, and then looked idly off into the woods. He looked impassive and casual. His face was masked and the expression in his eyes hidden by the massive ridge of bone across his brows. Post noticed that the man's lips were tightly compressed, as though by an inner tension that he couldn't permit himself to show.

Frick spat on the ground and said, "Thought you were coming back with Jorder, boss. Told us you'd bring Jorder. Who's this Walker Post?"

"Take it easy, Frick," Drake snapped. "I do as I please." He stopped and smiled. "Jorder is unfortunately detained. He won't be able to come out. Post will be okay when he gets in shape. You might say he's halfway between a patient and an employee. Be easy on him."

187

Frick said, "Oh," and looked at Post with silent amusement.

"How are the patients, boys?"

"All quiet," Strane said eagerly. "Benderson and his daughter are taking a walk around the lakeshore. He seems okay. Mr. Burke and the girl are in their cabin."

"Good. I better go visiting. Take Post in and give him a bunk and answer his questions, if any. He doesn't talk much." Drake headed off toward the lake.

Frick nudged the bag with his foot and gestured with his thumb toward the door they'd come out of. "Lug it in there."

Post picked up the bag and walked into the long building. It was lined with double bunks on both sides. He stopped and stared.

"Used to be the bunkhouse when it was a lumber camp. The other building was the kitchen and mess hall. We still use the kitchen, but use the mess hall for storage of supplies. Grab any bunk except these two lowers on this end. That one by the window there ought to be as cool as any."

Post tossed his bag into the bunk and sat down on it. He sat on the bare slats. The bunk above him was high enough so that he could sit upright.

He waited until his breath was coming more slowly. Frick and Strane stood by the door and stared at him with frank interest.

Post felt that they expected him to ask questions. He decided that it would be easier to satisfy them, even though he couldn't generate much specific interest.

"What kind of work am I going to have to do around here? The boss didn't tell me that. He just said it wouldn't be hard."

"It was hard when we were fixing up those two cabins. Damn hard," Strane answered. "Easy now, though. Nothing to it. Issue them the food out of stores. Bury garbage in the woods. Cut wood for the fall. Just hang around. We have to go out and get stuff once in a while, but the boss probably won't want you to do that. Just hang around and kind of watch. We take turns on our

188

own cooking. With you around, it'll come up every three days."

"Are there only two of these cabins?"

"Yeah, two sets of guests at a time are plenty, hey, Frick?"

"Shut up, Rob. What else you want to know, Post?"

"Where do I get some bedclothes—mattress and blankets?"

"Go right in next door and pick out what you want. Grab some bug repellent, they get rough when it gets dark. Take it easy for the rest of the day and get used to the place. Really, there are three cabins. They were built when the camp was. They're along the south shore there, about a hundred yards from here. The boss lives in one. We had to fix them up."

They followed him out, and then headed toward the lake. He poked around in the litter on the floor of the supply building and found what he needed. He carried the supplies back in and made up his bunk. As soon as it was ready, he felt drowsy. He hadn't had as much exercise in months. He lay on the bunk and drifted off to sleep. His last conscious thought was that the pine woods smelled crisp and clean.

Post gradually came awake and heard voices.

He recognized Rob Strane's voice. "You sure that guy won't wake up, boss?"

"He's too tired and it won't make any difference if he does. Relax. He's all set. Now, here's the deal. Things are going to get a little tight for a while, so don't be too liberal with the food. I got to go back out in the morning. Don't ask me why. I'll be gone maybe two days. You know your orders."

Then Sam Frick said, "You want we should keep Post away from the patients?"

There was silence for a few seconds. Then Drake said slowly, "I can't see as that's going to make any difference. Just let him wander around. He's a funny guy. He isn't going to give much of a damn about anything. He'll turn out to be a good man. You'll see."

Post couldn't catch the rest. They lowered their voices. After a time they left and he could hear a bird calling a hot-weather note in the trees outside. He drifted off again.

When he awoke the second time he felt more rested. The sun was out and he could tell from the slant of the rays outside the window that it was getting late. He stood up slowly and stretched. He could smell food cooking. Suddenly he realized that he was ravenously hungry—hungrier than he had been in many weeks.

He walked out the door and saw the setting sun resting on the top of the hill they had walked down. He remembered that they had told him where the kitchen was. He walked toward it. Smoke wisped out of a crazy-angled stovepipe that stuck through the roof. He found a door in the end of the building nearest the lake.

Strane looked up from the wood stove. "Sleeping Beauty awakes. Hungry?"

Post yawned again. "Yeah."

"Sit down there at the table. I'll eat with you in a minute."

"Where's Frick?"

"He'll be in after a while. We'll eat first."

Post sat down by one of the enameled plates. In a few minutes Strane carried the frying pan over to the table and dished out some of the potatoes and meat. It smelled good to Post. He ate rapidly and then leaned back and lit a cigarette. Strane was still eating. He chewed with his mouth open and the cords in his neck worked. He bent low over the plate and shoveled the food in with jerky scooping motions.

He got up and shoved his chair back. "Tomorrow you can cook, Post. That'll be all you have to do. Ever done any?"

"Camp stuff. That's all."

Strane left and in a few minutes Sam Frick came in. He grabbed the frying pan and heaped what was left on his own plate. He sat down and started to eat without a word. Post stared out the open door and saw that the lake blue had darkened to gray as the sun had gone

190

further below the hills. He finished his cigarette and snapped it out the door. Frick's head was bent low over his plate.

Suddenly Post tied two things together in his head. The two of them didn't eat together. Strane had said they had to "hang around and kind of watch." He realized that the two men might be guarding the exit from the lake. He wondered if he ought to risk having some fun with Frick. He felt full and strangely contented.

"I suppose you guys take turns eating first?" he asked casually.

Frick stopped chewing and looked up. His small eyes were shadowed. "What gives you the idea we take turns, chum?"

"You can't eat together. Who'd watch the patients?"

Frick waited a few seconds and then said softly, "I don't know what you're driving at, Post. Maybe you better let the whole thing drop."

Post hid a grin and stood up. He stretched and walked to the door. The lake was quiet. He walked down to the shore and sat on a flat rock. The waves lapped against the rock. Blackflies gathered around his head and he lit another cigarette to keep them off. The sky grew darker. He heard frogs grumbling in a distant marsh. He noticed that there were no boats.

He stared up the lakeshore and saw a light flicker in the thick brush. He guessed that it was a light in one of the cabins. He couldn't see the other cabins. It had grown too dark. He could see a strange patch of sun at the peak of a mountain in the east, but in the deep valley of the lake it smelled of night.

He sat and wondered what sort of an arrangement he had dropped into. It seemed strange, somehow, but he couldn't work up any great interest. He felt the familiar dull lethargy creeping over him. He shivered in the sudden chill that swept in from the lake. He walked to the bunkhouse and climbed into his bunk.

Just before he fell asleep, Sam Frick came in and climbed into his bunk. He lit a kerosene lamp and found his place in a ragged magazine. He didn't speak. Post watched the sullen face for a time, watched the man's lips moving as he read. Post fell asleep, after deciding that maybe it would be a good thing to leave. He decided he would leave without finding out what it was all about. He drove the growing curiosity down into himself and commanded it to be still.

He climbed out of bed when the air was still chill. Strane was asleep, a nasal snore rattling in his throat. Frick's bed was empty. He wandered across to the kitchen and looked around. He decided to wait until either Frick or Strane could show him where to find the supplies. He wondered how they kept the food cool. He walked down to the lake and skipped flat stones out over the still water. His aches and stiffness were gone.

After a time Strane came out and showed him where the food supplies were kept. They used a crude windlass to lower supplies which had to be kept cool down into a narrow hole that appeared to be at least twenty feet deep. The butter was hard and the eggs were fresh.

He cooked the breakfast and they ate it separately, without comment. After he had cleaned up, Strane came in and made up two baskets of food supplies to take to the two cabins. Post walked over to the bunkhouse and picked up his suitcase. He walked out of the building and toward the entrance to the trail. He decided to walk slowly and enjoy the morning.

He hadn't gone more than twenty feet up the trail when Sam Frick suddenly stepped in front of him.

"What's the matter, Post? Don't like cooking?"

"Cooking's okay. I just don't like the setup. I'm leaving."

Frick didn't move out of the narrow path. He put his big hands on his hips and turned to a bush and said in a mincing way, "Mr. Post doesn't like it here. He's leaving." Then he turned back to Post. "Get on back there, sucker. You love it here. Besides, you told the boss you'd work. If you want to quit, you got to talk to him."

"They keep telling me it's a free country. How about getting out of the way?"

The Night Is Over

In answer, Frick put his big hand against Post's chest and shoved. Frick was on higher ground. Post tumbled backward onto his side and rolled into a bush. His suitcase snapped open and the clothes slid out onto the dirt.

Post got to his feet. Frick still stood above him, a half smile on his face. He said, almost kindly, "Get on back, Post. You're not in shape for this sort of thing. Don't make me hang one on you and drag you down. Let's keep it pleasant, hey?"

Post stood and looked at the broad chest, the thick wrists. He thought of how quickly the man had moved when he had pushed against his chest. The smile faded from the heavy face and Post knew that the man would move again in a few seconds. He knelt in the trail and gathered his clothes back into the suitcase. He turned and walked back down the trail. He walked into the bunkhouse and slid his bag under his bunk. He sat on the edge of the bunk and lit a cigarette. His hand trembled. He felt angry and vaguely frightened. He tried to retreat back into the calm of indifference, but he couldn't do it. He knew that they weren't going to let him leave.

He wondered what kind of a chance he would stand with either Frick or Strane. He peeled off his shirt and tried to look at himself in the battered steel mirror hanging on one of the bunk posts. He could see flashes of white flesh, of a roll of fat around his waist. His arms looked soft and formless.

Within a half hour he was standing out beyond the kitchen stripped to the waist. He could feel where the axe handle was going to raise blisters. Sweat was soaking him around the waist of his trousers. He set another chunk on the block and split it cleanly through the middle with the double-bitted axe. It was as easy as a problem in addition. He could sense trouble ahead, and for some reason he wanted to be ready for it. The better shape he could get into, the better chance he would have. He stopped and wondered why he wanted a better chance. He stared out across the small lake. Maybe he just didn't want to be pushed around. He set another

193

chunk on the block and imagined that it was Sam Frick's hard head. He sunk the blade so deeply into the block that he had to smack the handle up with the heel of his hand to loosen it.

After he had split a sizable pile, he sat on the block to rest for a few minutes. The sun felt warm on his shoulders. He heard footsteps behind him and glanced around. A soft fat man, with crisp curling black hair and white jowls that sagged below his chin, stood with his plump hands on his hips and stared down at Post. He wore a tan sports shirt and flowered shorts. His hairless legs were scarred with a hundred insect bites.

"So there's another one of you guys, hah? What's he running, an army?"

"Are you Mr. Burke or Mr. Benderson?"

"Burke, and I always thought I was a smart operator until I walked into this with my stupid eyes wide open. Where's your boss? I want to talk to him now."

"Not around."

The man turned and looked toward the cabins. A tall tanned blonde in a yellow playsuit stepped carefully across the uneven ground. She looked blankly at Burke and Post. Her face was puffy. Her eyes were wide, brown and dull.

"Millie, this new guy says the boss is away. When'll he be back, fella?"

"Don't know."

Millie pouted. Post saw that the roots of her bright hair were streaked with black. "Gee, Burky, I got to get outa here. All the time you keep telling me to wait. I got other things to do. Maybe they'll let me go now."

"You shut your face and get back to that cabin. You're not getting out until I do."

They walked back toward the cabins. Burke tried to grab her wrist but she twisted away from him. Burke raised his fat clenched fist and then let it drop wearily at his side. He stopped just before he was out of sight, bent over and vigorously scratched both legs.

He didn't meet the others until late afternoon. When his hands were too blistered to continue chopping wood,

194

he found Strane on the trail. The lanky man was leaning against a tree peeling the bark from a slim stick.

"You guys got any objection to me walking around the lake before we eat?"

"Why should we care? Go ahead. Only don't make us wait supper."

He circled the lake, walking along the north side first. The brush was so thick that at times he had to splash through the shallow water. Once he stumbled and soaked himself to the hips. But he made better time than he expected. As he came back along the south shore, he found the walking easier. There were long stretches of flat gray rock slanting down toward the water. The slant wasn't so steep that he couldn't walk across it.

Finally he saw the gray buildings of the camp ahead of him. He looked up into the brush and saw a small gray cabin. It was surrounded with half-grown spruce. Beyond it he could see a part of the roof of a second cabin.

As he stood and stared, he caught a flash of movement down on the rocks. He turned. A slim girl was stretched out on her back in the sun. She was wearing a scanty white bathing suit laced with red. She had a book, sunglasses and a bottle of white lotion. The sun had turned her the soft brown of coffee with cream.

She raised her head. He was standing ten feet from her.

"Hello, there," she said. He recognized the flat clear accent of Beacon Hill. He walked over to her, and because it seemed awkward to stand above her, he sat down and wrapped his arms around his knees.

She stared at him with calm appraisal. Her face was a shade too narrow with the brown skin tight over the high delicate cheekbones. Her eyes were gray and her eyebrows thick and black. She made him think of the women in the fashion magazines that Ruth used to buy. He sensed breeding, money and chill selfish charm.

"I'm Nan Benderson. I imagine you're one of the men who work here."

"That's right. Walker Post."

She rested her dark head back on the rocks and shut

her eyes against the sun's glare. "Tell Mr. Drake that Dad would like to see him. Dad is much better. He hasn't had so much rest and quiet in years. I haven't told him how bored I'm getting."

"I'll tell him."

Suddenly she braced herself on one elbow and looked at him. "Mr. Post, are you certain Mr. Burke is entirely safe? Mr. Drake told us about his delusions of persecution, but he comes to our cabin and says strange things in such a wild manner."

Post wondered what he should say. Burke didn't act like a man with delusions. He acted like a man who was trapped and knew it. He shrugged. "Far as I know, he's harmless."

She continued to stare at him. "You're an odd one!"

He started. Then he shrugged and looked away. He couldn't permit himself the luxury of being curious. He looked back at her. She still stared and suddenly she looked away.

"That was rude, wasn't it? I'm sorry. But your face looks . . . so dead. As though you . . . I can't explain it. You look hurt and glum, like a whipped child, only there's something more. I don't know why I'm talking like this. I guess it's just being alone so much up here and having time to think. Don't pay any attention to me."

He got to his feet and looked down at her. He looked into her eyes for a few seconds. "It's okay, Miss Benderson. Don't think about it." He walked along the shore. He began to wonder what he could find to cook for supper. There wasn't much food left on the platform lowered deep into the ground.

After supper he thought he would try to exercise, to harden himself more. It suddenly seemed pointless. He watched Sam Frick stand on the shore, stoop and lift an immense boulder. He held it high in the air and then shoved it from him. It landed in the shallow water, throwing a sheet of water high in the air to sparkle in the last rays of the sun. Post stood silently for a few minutes.

Then he got the axe and cut a short thick club. It fit his hand nicely. He wondered idly why they let him use an axe. An axe can be used as a weapon. He hid the club carefully. He guessed that Frick and Strane were probably armed. It seemed logical to him that they would be.

Drake didn't return the next day—or the next. They were reduced to tinned foods. Post spent the long quiet days sitting in his bunk. He circled the lake once each day. The first day, he saw the girl out on the rocks again. She didn't lift her head. He stepped by quietly.

Burke came down to complain about the food. He didn't bring Millie with him. Frick and Strane ignored him. He stomped back toward his cabin, anger showing even in the lines of his back as he walked away.

Post felt a definite tension in the air. He couldn't reason it out and he shrugged it off. He ate and slept and watched the lake. He knew that nothing was mending inside of him. And it didn't matter.

Drake returned on the third day at eight in the morning. He had a small man with him. Post watched them walk across the clearing. The stranger staggered and swayed. His eyes were almost shut and his face was slack. Drake walked behind him, shoving him in the back with his left hand. In his right hand he carried a light rifle. Drake's dark face was twisted. He pushed the man through the open door of the bunkhouse. The man tripped and sprawled face down on the floor. He was breathing heavily. He didn't try to get up.

"Frick. Toss him on one of the bunks. You don't have to watch him. There's enough stuff in him to keep him out for hours. He won't remember how he got here."

Frick gathered the man up and held him in his arms like a sleeping child. Post noticed that the stranger's clothes were ragged, his face unshaven. Frick stepped over to one of the bunks and tossed the man onto a top bunk. His head and heels thumped against the wooden slats.

Drake sat on a bunk and wiped his head. "What a job,

getting that joe through the woods. I bet he fell a hundred times." He handed the rifle to Frick, who balanced it in a corner. "How are things?"

Frick didn't answer. He sat down on a bunk across from Drake and jerked his thumb at Post, his eyebrows raised.

"Go ahead. Mr. Walker Post isn't in the way."

"If you say so. Burke has been yapping about the food and about getting out of here. His dish wants me to ask you if she can go even if Burke can't. She's talking about appointments she's got."

"She stays. Pay no attention to Burke. We'll let him steam for a while longer."

"Right. Benderson and the daughter are still in the clouds. She's bored. He's getting healthy. No attempt to get out. He wants to talk to you. She's worried about Burke. Wonders if he's dangerous."

"I'll talk to them. Anything else?"

"Yeah. Strong and silent here tried to leave with his stuff a few days back. I stopped him on the trail and I had to push him around. He hasn't said much since. I told him he had to see you."

Drake looked at Post. His dark eyes were full of amusement. "Restless, hey? I wouldn't have expected that of you, Post. I thought you didn't care where you were. Why try to leave? The work too hard?"

"I suppose you want the truth."

"Why not?"

"These two big clowns of yours got on my nerves. They both handed me smart talk about this place. I don't know what you're doing here, but I can see it isn't kosher. Just tell me what it's all about. I don't care what you're doing. I just don't like not having a question answered when I feel like asking it."

Drake turned to Frick. "Take the panel job and go after the food. I'll have Rob help you pack it in after you get back. Same place." Frick strolled out.

The unconscious man in the top bunk moaned softly. Drake picked at his teeth with a fingernail. He studied Post. Post looked back at him without expression.

The Night Is Over

"You remember, I told you that I'm an amateur psychiatrist? Well, this place is an experiment in applied psychiatry. Science at work. You can't have outside factors intruding in a controlled experiment. So I've made it tough to get in or out.

"I'll give you a case history. We'll take Burke. I needed a lusty playful guy with a rich wife who has a narrow moral outlook. After a little research I located Burke in a city about two hundred miles from here.

"He fit my requirements. He was supporting this character he calls Millie. He's been married for eighteen years to a fantastically ominous woman. She's a modern-day dragon. I saw her. The kind of a woman who can word-whip you till your ears bleed. Burke's never worked. He has a drawing account. She keeps a pretty close watch on him, but he's been clever enough to keep this Millie on the side.

"I met Burke at a bar. I told him about this place I had bought and promised him that he could come up here and nobody would know where he was and nobody could find him. I got him a doctor's prescription to take a rest. He asked me if Millie could come along. He trusted me. I told him that she could. I brought them in here.

"In my safety-deposit box I've got a series of negatives of Burke and his Millie. I haven't made him any offer. He doesn't know what I want, but he's pretty damn sure I want money. I do. I want lots of it. Now comes the psychology. I just keep him here and let him stew, imagining what will happen when his wife tosses him out without a dime. That frightens him. At the proper moment I'll make a contract with him that will give me a neat little income each month for as long as he lives."

The little man licked his firm lips and grinned at Post. "That's one case history. We've just started here. There'll be lots of them. I got the idea that you isolate people and they lose courage. They can't go out on the street and see thousands of other people around them. They sit and look at the lake and think. Things bother them. I like to think that I'm a doctor of mental ills. I don't cure them—I rub a little salt in them and let the bucks drop into my hand. The trouble with most operators who start this kind of a racket—they're out of touch with their customers. I just bring the customers right here to me and let them sweat it out. Then they don't get out of hand."

"How about the Bendersons?"

"A good question. I got him up here on the spur of the moment just because he has more bucks than anybody I ever met before. His pappy founded shipbuilding outfits and clock companies. He's lousy with it. I've done research on him, and the guy has never stepped out of line far enough so I can put the pressure on him. It's taken me a couple of weeks to get an idea. I've got one now." He gestured toward the sleeping man in the bunk.

"Why tell me all this?"

"Because you're staying here and you're going to be right in it with the rest of us. I needed another guy and the one I was looking for is a guest of the government for an indefinite period. I was mad. I stopped the car and went into that little bar for a drink. There you were. Pennies from heaven. All wrapped up in a fight. I figured that I might be able to use you, and I turned out to be right."

"I still don't get it. How the hell can you use me? I'm not interested in your racket. I'm not interested in any racket. I just want to be left alone. That's all. First chance I get, I'll leave. It won't be worth my time to go to the cops. I'll just leave."

"I don't believe it, Post. I think you'll be glad to stay. I got something I want to show you." He slipped the familiar wallet out of his jacket pocket and found a clipping in it. He handed the clipping to Post.

He read: "HESSLER KILLER IDENTIFIED. Police today stated that they have identified Walker Post, age 31, as the man who brutally kicked Victor Hessler to death in Donovan's Bar on West Street four days ago. Post is still at large. After Hessler died a few hours after the fight, police checked all places in the city where transients stay. Mrs. Mary Cortez of 88 Plant Street stated that a man named Walker Post had checked out of her rooming house a few hours after the fight. She stated that Post left no forwarding address and that he seemed nervous and upset. She stated that his face and lips were cut and bruised. A picture of Post was obtained from his previous employers, a prominent architectural firm, and the picture was positively identified by Mr. Donovan and the two companions of Hessler as the man who had kicked Hessler to death. Police expect an early arrest. Post is described as being of medium height, brown hair, gray eyes, wide shoulders. He is sullen and dangerous. He is a veteran of the war in the Pacific.''

Post sat and read it again. It gave him a strange feeling, as though he were reading about someone else. So he had killed the one they called Hessy. He remembered the boy's brown arms, the way he had hooked his thumbs in his belt. He felt sudden regret and contempt for himself. He glanced up. Drake was wearing his superior smile. Post wanted to smash him in the face. Instead he handed the clipping back, holding his hand as steady as he could.

Drake took it and tucked it away. "So you won't leave?"

"I don't know. I may still leave."

The smile didn't fade. "Here's some more amateur psychiatry, Post. You are now running up against a primary instinct for self-preservation. I admire you. You can make yourself look calm. You know you've got to be cold. But it's only on the outside. On the inside you're afraid. No man is so depressed that he won't fight against an outside force that wants to kill him or imprison him. A man on his way to a high building from which he wishes to leap will skip out of the path of a truck. Your face is a lie."

Post shrugged. "Those are pretty words, Drake. Maybe you're trying to talk yourself into the idea that you got me hooked here because I killed a man. I can't tell you right now whether you have or not. I may leave. I may not.''

"You leave and they'll pick you up.''

"So I get picked up.'' Even as he said it, he felt a quiver of alarm. He knew he didn't want to go back out to where they could find him. He wanted to stay hidden in the woods. Suddenly the quiet lake seemed like exactly the proper spot to be. The proper spot in which to stay. He kept all expression off his face. He had killed and he had run away. If they caught him, he would grow old in prison. The free existence which had become so unbearable during the past months became suddenly desirable. He stared steadily at Drake and shrugged again.

"You're pretending, Post. No man willingly goes to the cops on a thing like this. I'm going to prove you're pretending. If you're so anxious to go, I'm going to do you a big favor.''

He got up and walked to the doorway. He called Strane. The tall man shambled in. "Rob, we've got an experiment here. Post killed a man back in town and the cops want him. He says he doesn't care. I'm going to let him go. Don't stop him. Pack up your stuff, Post, and shove off.''

Drake came and stood in front of him. Strane was in the doorway. "So the great man of indifference starts to care. Suppose I force you to leave?''

"Then they pick me up and I tell them what I know about this place.''

"And what do you know? Burke won't talk. Benderson's got nothing to talk about. You saw the other clipping. This is a health resort. I think you better write me a check. Strane, go through his stuff.''

Post tried to grab the suitcase but Strane brushed him aside. He sat while Strane pawed through his clothes. He found the checkbook inside one of the flap pockets. He handed it to Drake. Drake riffled through the stubs.

He handed it to Post. "About two thousand ought to be fine. Make it two thousand even. Don't make it out to me. Make it to cash. I think I can get it cashed without identifying myself with a guy the police want.''

Post held the checkbook and his hands felt numb. He wondered how Drake had known about the checkbook. Strane and Drake stood over him. Drake handed him a pen. He didn't try to write a check.

"I promise you, Post, that if you don't write it, you'll be out of here and in the hands of the police in two hours. Consider it a fee for being at my rest camp. You'll still get your keep. I'm not a bad guy. I won't even stop your wages."

Somehow the money didn't seem important. He knew that it was his last crutch, his last chance to spend idle empty days in small rooms stinking of stale beer. If Drake hadn't demanded it, it would have gone slowly and the day would have come when there would have been no money to buy liquor or food or a roof. He wrote out the check and tore it out. Balance: twenty-one dollars and fourteen cents. He wrote that down at the top of the next stub.

He stood up. He wanted to walk down by the lake. He wanted to sit and think it all out. It had happened so quickly. He walked toward the door. Drake leaned against the doorjamb. He said softly, "I like to have a man know who's running the show. I want people to jump when I talk. Suppose you call me Mr. Drake for a while."

Post stopped. The smaller man's head was near his right shoulder. Without looking he slapped his left hand around, palm open. Drake clattered onto the board floor. Post walked heavily toward the lake, his hand stinging.

He heard Drake call, "Strane! Get him. Bring him in here."

He turned as he heard heavy feet pounding across the clearing toward him. He didn't turn quickly enough to meet the rush. Strane's shoulder caught him in the chest and slammed him onto the ground. He jumped up and Strane grabbed his wrist. There was a sharp pain in his arm as he was spun around. Then his hand was held up against the small of his back and he was marched back to the bunkhouse.

Drake stood in the door. His dark eyes were narrowed.

There was a dull red discoloration across his swarthy right cheek. His nostrils were dilated.

His voice was hoarse as he said, "How about the suckers, Strane? They likely to come around this way?"

"Not this time of day, boss."

"Then give this chump a going-over. Make it last."

Post braced himself. The fight in the bar had given him a certain amount of confidence. He wanted to hit something with his fists. He wanted to wipe out the fear that was in his heart.

Strane came in slowly, his face solemn, his big hands swinging low at his sides. When he was close he stuck his left arm out. Post knocked it aside. Drake slid in and sat on the edge of a bunk. He kept licking his lips. He leaned forward and his eyes were bright.

Post tried a quick chop at Strane's jaw. He never knew if the punch landed or not. He went spinning back into blackness with fire against the side of his face.

He came to on his back on the floor. His shirt was soaked with water. His hair was wet. His face felt swollen. He heard Drake say, with annoyance, "He's coming out of it. Now get him up on his feet and make it last a while." Strane mumbled something.

"That'll do, Strane. Put him in his bunk." He was dimly conscious of being carried. He lay in the bunk after they had gone and became conscious of the stinging pain in his face. After a time he climbed out of the bunk. He held on to the side post for a time. When he had the strength, he walked over to the steel mirror. A stranger's face stared back at him. His lips were puffed. One eye was already dark. The entire left side of his face was so swollen that the lines of the cheekbone and jaw were gone.

He poured water into the chipped basin and washed his face. It didn't feel any better. He sat for a long time on the bunk. He looked down at the floor. A small green caterpillar humped its way across the stained boards with anxious urgency. He heard the far-off murmur of voices. A breeze rushed through the pines.

He had no clear idea of his own thoughts and feelings. He was confused. He wanted to retreat into the lethargy to which he had become accustomed. It escaped him. He felt no anger. He felt no humiliation. In his mind was a feeling of disgust. And there was something else growing inside him. It was something new for him. He hadn't felt it for a year. It was a growing sense of excitement and anticipation. But as yet it wasn't strong enough to guide him. It flickered in the back of his mind like a candle behind blinds.

After a half hour Drake came in. He stood for a moment, looking at Post. Post didn't look up.

"Are you okay now?"

"Fine."

"That was necessary. I can't take chances on discipline. I'm carefully guarded. Frick and Strane are careful of me. Each month I have to mail a letter to the West Coast. If I should die suddenly, and not mail the usual letter, Frick and Strane would be hunted by the police with the same energy that they're hunting for you. A friend holds the information, which he'll turn over to the police the first month he doesn't hear from me."

"Sure. You're a brilliant man. You're a genius. But you enjoyed watching Strane slug me, didn't you? You got a real bang out of it." He stared up at the slim man and his face felt hot.

Surprisingly, Drake looked uncertain. He turned slowly and walked out. Nan Benderson met him at the door. She was wearing slacks and a halter. She looked calm and poised.

"I wanted to ask you something, Mr. Drake. I couldn't ask you while you were talking to Dad. Have you got a moment?"

He took her arm and led her away from the door. She glanced back over her shoulder. Post thought he saw her eyes widen as she saw his battered face. He couldn't be certain.

In the afternoon he sat on the lakeshore in the sun. Later he walked around the lake. As he came down the south shore he felt a sense of anticipation. He thought that he might see her on the rocks. He slowed his pace as he saw that she wasn't there. He was well beyond the Benderson cabin when he heard a scuffling on the rocks behind him. Miss Benderson and Drake were there. He turned and stopped.

They walked up to him, and Miss Benderson put out her hand to him. He took it awkwardly. "Nice to see you again, Mr. Post," she said. "Stop up at the cabin and visit with us sometime, won't you?"

He felt something pressing into the palm of his hand. He started to stammer and Drake interrupted smoothly. "I'm afraid that Post won't have any time for social gatherings, Miss Benderson. Besides, I don't believe your father should have visitors."

She released his hand and he closed it around the small object in his palm. The girl and Drake stared at each other, and Post felt the cool animosity in their eyes. She nodded and said, "Well, I must get back up to the cabin and start dinner." She walked quickly back across the sloping rocks. Post shoved the thing she had given him deeper into his pocket and followed Drake back to the compound.

When they were near the bunkhouse, Drake turned to him. "Tomorrow you take a one-third guard trick. Four on and four off. Fix the hours with Rob and Sam. Just keep your eye on the trail and keep our four guests from trying to use it. Be polite, particularly with the Bendersons. Use any excuse you can think of. But don't let them get past you. Understand?"

"Yes, Mr. Drake," he answered, his voice flat. Drake left him and he walked into the kitchen. It was empty. He fished the item out of his pocket. It was a small wad of paper. He unfolded it partway, not so far that he could see the writing. He held it in his hand. He realized he didn't want any complications. He didn't want to owe anyone anything, or have anything owed to him. With cool precision he tore it into scraps and dropped it into the wood stove. He looked at his watch. He'd have a chance for a nap before supper.

*　　*　　*

The Night Is Over

He realized that it was his last undisturbed night, and yet he slept poorly. When the gray dawn outlined the window near his head and the birds began to clamor, he finally drifted into a restless sleep. Once the low moans of the unconscious stranger awakened him and he listened. All he could hear were the snores of Frick. He went back to sleep.

When he awoke the second time, the sun seemed high. He dressed slowly and walked across to the kitchen. Breakfast was over. There was a cold fried egg in the greasy pan. He opened a tin of orange juice and drank it. He heard voices outside the kitchen window and he walked over.

Drake was giving Strane orders. "I've talked to Burke. I scared him. He and that woman won't move out of the cabin all morning. That'll give me the time I need. You go up to Benderson's cabin and send the old man down here to me. You stay there and make sure the girl doesn't come down here. He may call out to her and she may hear him. Keep her there. But if you lay a hand on her, except to keep her from getting out the door, I'll make you wish you never met me. Understand?"

"Sure boss. Sure."

Drake looked up and saw Post's face in the kitchen window. "There you are. Come out here and watch. I want to educate you a little more. This lesson is called how to make a half million dollars. Let's go look at my new guest while Strane sends Benderson down here. Frick'll be back in a couple of minutes."

Post followed him over into the bunkhouse. He helped Drake lift the small man down from the high bunk. The man was blue around the eyes and his clothing stank. Drake put him on the floor and slapped him on both cheeks. The man didn't open his eyes.

"Good. He'll last until I'm ready for him."

Post noticed that Drake was excited. His dark eyes were wide and he walked around nervously. He was dressed in a yellow-orange sports shirt and trim gray gabardine trousers. The orange shirt made his skin look more sallow than it had before.

Post wondered who the small man could be. He asked.

"This, Post, is that unique man, the man who has nobody and nothing. He has no home, no relatives, no friends and no money. He's the essence of anonymity."

Drake hurried out of the bunkhouse. Mr. Benderson was coming down the alleyway between the two buildings. He walked carefully. It was the first time Post had seen him. He was a tall, frail old man with a gray hairless skull. He wore rimless glasses over his faded blue eyes. The gray folds of his cheeks sagged over the bone structure. Even though he was slightly stooped, he had an air of pride and authority.

He glanced up as they stepped out to meet him. "Ah, Mr. Drake! Your man said you'd like to talk to me." When he smiled his eyes were young.

"Yes, Mr. Benderson. This is Mr. Post, another of my men. Mr. Post is going to sit in on this little conference—that is, if you don't mind."

"How do you do, Mr. Post. Why should I mind? I'm feeling excellent, sir. Excellent. This air, this quiet, it's worked wonders for me. And for Nan too."

"Post, you better sit over there out of the way. Lean against the bunkhouse. Mr. Benderson and I will have our little . . . discussion out in this cleared space. Are you certain you're not too tired to stand, Mr. Benderson?"

The old man tapped himself on the chest. "Sound as a nut. Now, what is all this about?"

They stood in the middle of the alleyway, the early sun slanting across them, throwing their shadows in long strips toward the woods. Drake stepped closer to the old man and looked up into his face.

"You know, Benderson, in addition to running this place, I'm a philosopher. Did you know that?" There was something secret and dangerous in Drake's tone.

The older man looked puzzled and stepped back. Drake's face was so close to his own that Post could see that it made him uncomfortable.

"Yes, I'm a philosopher. This is a country where we value human dignity, Benderson. We bow deeply to the rights of the individual . . . I don't think the individual has any rights."

"But what has that got to do with . . ."

"Don't be hasty, Benderson. Let me finish. You're treated with what amounts to reverence because you stink with money. Money that was handed to you. I don't think I'll give you any reverent attention, Mr. Benderson."

The gray cheeks flushed and Benderson coughed. "Look, Drake, I didn't come down here to listen to any silly theories. I didn't come to be insulted. Now get to the point. I believe that I may leave here today. Yes, I'm certain of it."

Drake stepped forward again, slightly crouched, his head tilted sharply upward. "You're quite right, Benderson," he said, his voice soft and strangely warm. "Neither of us is interested in theory. We're men who like to see theory in practice."

His thin hand flashed up and the smack of hard palm on flesh resounded in the narrow space between the buildings. Benderson staggered back, bewildered, and stared in silent appeal at Post. Post could see that he felt he was dealing with a man who had gone suddenly mad. The red mark on Benderson's cheek reminded Post of the mark he had made on Drake.

He glanced over and saw Frick leaning against the end of the building, watching Drake. Frick's face seemed masked as usual. His heavy arms were folded.

"Now, Benderson, we start the practice. Now tell me. What did that do to you? How did it affect your immortal dignity? Tell me."

"You're mad," Benderson gasped.

"Not mad. Just curious. Let's try it again." Benderson tried to duck but he was old and stiff. The force of the blow staggered him and he held his hand against his cheek. He looked as though he wanted to run. Drake darted around him and blocked one exit. Frick stood at the other exit. Benderson turned and faced Drake.

"You still seem to retain your dignity, Benderson. How about this?" Drake stabbed the old man in the

diaphragm with a rigid forefinger. He gasped and doubled up, holding his stomach. Drake slapped him across
the eyes. The glasses splintered and fell into the grass. A
bit of glass cut the gray cheek and a trickle of blood
started slowly down, following the line of a deep fold in
the flesh. Before the old man was breathing properly
again, Drake slapped him hard on the cheek for the third
time. It knocked him down. He scrambled to his feet
and looked again at Post and Frick. He seemed to Post
to look like an old gray horse being worried by a yapping terrier.

Drake stepped toward him again and the old man put
his hands up to ward off the blow. Then, he seemed to
remember, to reach deep into his past and call up the
forgotten motions of youth. He clenched his fists and
held them rigidly in front of him. It was pathetic and as
brave as banners in the wind.

Drake stepped to the side and hooked a short left into
the old man's stomach. As he slowly fell, Drake slapped
him twice. The man lay on his back, gasping. He rolled
over onto his stomach and pushed against the ground.
He stood up and staggered against the building for support.
Then he rushed at Drake, stumbling, his thin arms flaying
the air. Drake stepped aside and he rushed into the side
of the building. Drake laughed at him.

"The dignity is leaving, Benderson? Where could it be
going? Where is that charming calm?"

He walked up to the old man and grasped the loose
clothes under the old man's chin with his left hand. With
his right hand he slapped, firmly, in monotonous tempo,
forehand and backhand across the sagging cheeks and
mouth. Blood came on the lips and was sprayed across
the lower half of his face with each slap.

"Any dignity left, Benderson? Any guts left?" He
stepped toward the old man again. Benderson covered
his face with his hands.

His voice was more of a bleat than a moan. "Don't hit
me. Don't hit me again." Drake dragged him to his feet
and turned him around so that Drake's back was toward
the building. He shut his fist and released Benderson.

The old man swayed but stood erect. Drake swung with all the power in his wiry back and shoulders. The small hard fist cracked against the lean jaw and Benderson fell with his gray bloody face against the green grass.

"Too hard, boss," Frick said quietly.

Drake grinned and made a dusting motion with his hands. "Nonsense, Sam. He's a tough old citizen, and he's got to be sore as hell when he comes to." He stopped smiling and stared at Post. "You look a little green. What's wrong? This one isn't dead. Don't tell me a little rough stuff gets you down. Maybe I figured you wrong." He stood and thought for a minute.

Then he turned to Frick. "Samuel, you better take Sister Ann away for the next act. There's such a thing as knowing too much. Bring him back in an hour. Take him up the trail a ways."

Frick stirred and pushed himself away from the building. He waited until Post got up and walked ahead of him. Then he followed along.

They walked across the clearing and entered the mouth of the trail. Post slowed and stopped.

"Move along. Get up the hill a little further."

"Relax, Sam. This is good enough. Why climb that damn hill?"

Frick shrugged. "Okay. It's hot. How'd you like the way the boss worked on the old gent?"

"Very pretty, if you like that sort of thing."

"The boss and I can do it okay. Strane can't. Anytime he hits anybody, it's got to be for keeps."

Post stood and tried not to look as ill as he felt. He couldn't get his mind away from what Drake had said about human dignity. He suddenly realized what it was that had made him feel so peculiarly about Drake. The man barely concealed an enormous contempt for everyone around him. The small flame of excitement that had been burning secretly inside of him flared up a little higher. He'd like to show Drake how much dignity there is in being on the wrong end of eager fists. The color of the growing flame turned to red, the color of anger. He wanted to go back and have a few short words with Drake.

He moved over toward the familiar aspen. Frick blocked his way and looked at him peculiarly. "Move over, Sam. I want some more shade." He stood under the aspen and yawned. He yawned again. Finally he stretched, moving his right hand around until his fingers grasped the familiar handle of the club he had made.

With one convulsive movement he tore it loose from the tree and crashed it across Frick's head. Frick stood, his eyes half shut, swaying. Post raised the club and slammed him across the temple. The square man spun half around and dropped face down in the dirt. Post grabbed his arm and turned him over. He slapped at his clothes. No bulge of any gun. On a hunch, he slapped the stocky legs. He felt something against the solid calf of the left leg. He pulled the trouser leg up. There was a thin heavy knife in a stained cloth scabbard strapped to Frick's leg. He ripped it out and threw it off into the brush. He picked up the club and walked quietly back to where he could see across the clearing. He angled off to the side and ran quickly around to the other side of the bunkhouse.

He knew that Benderson must be in the grass almost opposite where he was standing. The club was awkward. He laid it down. He grasped the low edge of the roof and slowly pulled himself up. His arms cracked with the strain. With infinite care, he got his body up over the edge. Then he wriggled slowly up to the peak, up to where he could look down into the open alleyway on the other side.

When he was near the peak he stopped and rested, waiting until his breathing was more regular. He knew that he had made a foolish move, that he had cut himself off from the safety of the lake. It was too late to turn back. He realized vaguely that he was enjoying himself. He tried not to think of the fight in the bar.

At last he could breathe quietly and his arms had stopped quivering. He raised himself slowly until he could look down into the open space. He saw Benderson first. The man was still on his side, but one hand was moving feebly, combing at the thick grass. Then he looked toward the lake. Ten feet from Benderson's form, Drake lay stretched out on the grass on his face, his arms spread wide. Post couldn't make any sense out of the scene. Drake didn't look like a man who was resting. He knew that Benderson couldn't have come out of it and flattened Drake. And yet it looked as if Drake was injured.

Then, with infinite caution, Benderson began to crawl toward the silent form of Drake. After each few feet he would stop and peer behind himself. He found something in the grass. He picked it up and looked at it. It was a short heavy club. He waved it in the air as though testing it. He carried it in his right hand and continued to creep. At last he was poised over Drake. He sank back onto his buttocks and grasped the club in both hands. Then he raised it high in the air and brought it down on the back of Drake's head.

Post felt his mouth go dry as the club was lifted. Then, as the blow fell, he relaxed. He knew what had happened in the heart of the old man. There had been the idea of quick and brutal murder. But as his arms swung the club, some gentleness about him that he had almost forgotten softened the blow. It wasn't a blow that would kill.

He left the club by Drake's form and crawled over to the far wall. He grabbed it and pulled himself to his feet. He was shaking visibly. He panted and stared at the form on the grass with dull eyes.

Drake came walking around the end of the kitchen. Post almost gasped aloud. Drake was wearing different clothes. He was smiling. Benderson fell back against the wall and slid to the ground. He sobbed aloud. Drake leaned over and carefully hit him again. The old man's lean form lay stretched out in the angle made by the wall and the ground. Drake turned him so that his face was against the building.

He stepped quickly over and picked up the club that Benderson had dropped. He stood over the form that

Post had thought was Drake. He lifted the club and swung it down with the force with which a man would swing a mallet at a country fair. He grunted as he swung. When the noise of the blow hit Post's ears, he pressed his face against the shingles and his stomach lurched. He felt dizzy. He knew that the man dressed in Drake's clothes was the little man who had slept in drugged stupor in the top bunk. He knew that Drake had picked him for size as well as unimportance.

Drake whistled a gentle tune as he walked back toward the kitchen. He was back in the yard in a few moments. He fiddled with a small movie camera. He stepped over and took a close-up of the smashed back of the stranger's head.

Then he walked over and looked down at Benderson. He spoke just loud enough so that Post could hear him. "Beautiful! A half million bucks' worth of home movies. Just wait till I run it off for you and your haughty daughter, grandpop. Drake, you're a right smart boy."

There was a crashing noise in the brush across the clearing. Both Drake and Post looked over. Frick was coming across in a blundering run. He looked white.

"Where's Post?" Drake snapped.

"I don't know. I just come to. He slugged me somehow. I didn't even see him do it. I got two knots on my head."

"How long ago?"

"I don't know. I don't know how long I've been out. It was maybe five minutes or so after we got up there. Maybe ten."

"You're a fool, Frick. Where'd you hide the rifle I brought in?"

"Under the mattress on my bunk."

"That wasn't very bright, either. Go on up and get Strane. I'll get the old guy into the shade and get the rifle. I can't figure that Post guy out. He should be scared as hell about making me mad."

Frick hurried off toward the cabins. Drake took the old man by the heels and dragged him around the corner

214

into the shade. Then he darted into the bunkhouse. Post crawled along the roof peak until he was at the end above the door. Quickly he reversed his position so that his legs hung over the edge. He sat on the peak. It was a twelve-foot drop to the ground. He heard Drake's footsteps hurrying across the board floor toward the door. He dropped, spinning as he dropped so that he'd land facing the door.

He had the punch wound up before his feet touched. Drake's face was in front of him, at the right distance. He swung a short heavy right and felt the meaty flattening of the proud slim nose under his fist. He dashed through the door. Drake lay on his back, scrabbling with his fingers on the floor.

Post scooped up the rifle and the camera and ran out. He turned to the right as soon as he was outside the door, and pounded off into the thick brush. After he estimated that he had gone a hundred yards he turned to the right again. He tried to gauge the slant of the sun through the leaves to keep his direction right.

The rifle was awkward to carry. The ground slanted steeply upward and he climbed for a time and then struggled along parallel with the slope. He kept looking to the right, trying to catch the glimmer of the lake below him.

At last he found the spot he was looking for. Gray rocks climbed up out of the slanted forest floor. He circled the rocks and climbed up behind them. Then he walked to the edge. He was above the tops of the trees which grew on the slope below the rocks. He could see the entire lake, the two long buildings on his right and the three cabins almost directly across from him.

He sat down on the mossy top of the rocks and put the rifle and the camera beside him. His shirt stuck to him and he pulled it away from his damp skin. He took deep breaths until his wind was back. He watched across the lake.

Frick came running from the bunkhouse down to the lakeshore. He dipped what looked to be a tin pail into the lake water and hurried back. Post grinned as he thought of Drake nursing his crushed nose. He regretted that he hadn't had time to stay and enjoy it. He hummed softly to himself.

He saw the slim figure of Nan hurry from the Bendersons' cabin and head toward the long buildings. There was something frantic in the way she was running. He stopped humming and watched her. Strane ran from the bunkhouse and met her when she was in front of the last cabin. Post could see that he was shouting at her.

She tried to squeeze past him. He grabbed her wrist and looked around for a long second, staring at the long buildings. He ignored the blows she was flinging at his head. He turned back to her and grabbed her around the waist. He clamped a big hand across her mouth and carried her, kicking and struggling, into a nearby clump of brush. Post jumped up and then realized that there was nothing he could do.

She broke out of the bushes, Strane behind her. She poised for a second on the rocks as the tall man reached for her again. Then she went out in a long, shallow dive. Strane hesitated. He waited long enough to give her ten yards' start and then he went in after her.

At first it looked to Post as though he couldn't possibly catch her. She surged through the water with a smooth-flowing stroke, her dark hair plastered against her head. Strane slapped the water with his arms and kept his head high. He looked clumsy. But as he watched, he saw the distance begin to narrow between them. It narrowed slowly, but he could see that he would catch her before she reached the middle of the lake.

He wondered if he could put a shot between them. He aimed and sighted. It was too long a shot. He estimated it at six hundred yards. He was afraid he would hit the girl.

Then Strane seemed to tire. He wasn't closing the gap. He stayed the same distance behind the girl. Post realized that he probably wasn't tiring. He was probably content to stay up with her, a dozen feet behind her, and catch her on the far shore. She looked around and saw him and increased her speed. He stayed at the same distance. They drew nearer. They were both going much more slowly. She began to roll in the water with each stroke.

Post suddenly realized that when they drew close enough to the shore beneath him, the trees would block his view. He saw Frick come out and peer across the water, then go back into the bunkhouse.

He aimed the rifle again. He realized that it might take two shots to discourage Strane, so he decided to fire before they were too close to the trees. He checked the clip and then worked the bolt. They were about two hundred yards away. He aimed carefully at the strip of clear water between them. He steadied his arm and slowly squeezed the trigger.

The gun cracked and jerked against his shoulder. He looked for the splash of the bullet. There wasn't any. The smack of a bullet hitting a hard substance echoed back to him. Strane's head sank slowly out of sight. For a second he saw the glow of the red hair just below the surface and then that too was gone.

He laid the gun down and plunged recklessly down the hill, slowing himself by grabbing the trees. He burst through the bushes at the edge of the water just as she touched bottom and stood up.

She took a few steps and fell and struggled to her feet. He waded out to meet her. Her face was twisted and she was making a high continual sound that was neither laughing nor crying. He slapped her and she stopped suddenly. Her slacks and halter clung to her.

At last he led her around the edge of the outcropping of rock and she stretched, exhausted and panting, on the thick moss. He saw her glance at the rifle. The ejected case lay gleaming on the moss near her hand.

He sat and watched the long buildings. No one came out. His mind kept circling back to the way the red hair had looked as Strane had sunk slowly under the surface. He realized what he had forgotten—that guns fire high when aimed downward. He cursed his stupidity and forgetfulness.

At last she was relaxed. She said in a weary tight voice, "I'm glad you killed him. I'm glad."

"Shut up. I didn't try to kill him."

"We have to get my father. Now. What's happened to him? Why are you over here?"

"Your father's in no danger. They'll take good care of him now. You and I are the ones in a spot. We're not going back over there." He told her what had happened to her father. He told her about Drake. He made it considerably less brutal than it had been, but it was still bad enough. She shivered and rolled over so that her head was buried in her arms. Then he told her that he had come under false promises by Drake and that he had quarreled with Drake.

When at last he was through, she sat up and brushed her drying hair back with her fingers. She looked solemn and capable.

"What do we do now, Walker?" she asked. He felt pleased that she had remembered his name, his first name. Then he remembered the way Ruth had said it and the black lethargy crept into him. Suddenly he realized that he didn't know what to do—where to go. The world was again a pointless place and he wondered why he had gotten so interested that he had bothered to slug Frick when they stood on the trail. For a time she had been a friend. He looked down at her. She wore the face of a stranger.

"You're odd," she said gently. "Don't be angry. For a while you looked . . . alive. Now you're the way you were when I met you. Why?"

He didn't answer her. He looked off across the lake. There was no point in trying to come alive again. How can a man live in a prison? He waited for long minutes and then he began to think of a plan.

At last he said, "Here's what we do, Miss Benderson. Somehow we get through the brush back to the road. We can get a ride. I'll see that you get dropped off in the nearest town. You can get the police to go back with you and get these men and your father. Without the film that's in this camera, they have nothing to threaten him with. I'll go on. I've done you a favor. As soon as you can manage it, put two thousand dollars in an envelope and mail it to John Robinson, General Delivery, Albuquerque, New Mexico. Remember that. I'll be there to pick it up. Don't tell anyone about it."

Just at that moment he saw Frick and Drake walk down to the edge of the lake. Frick was pointing in their direction. Drake was holding something white to his face. Post leveled the gun and fired, aiming short. He saw the splash of the shot and saw the two men run back toward the bunkhouse. He fired another shot in the air and stood up. She seemed eager to start. He knew that she must be worrying about her father. He felt anxious to get out, to drop her in a village and be on his way. He longed to return to his unthinking quiet, though he knew that he would carry with him a small spot of horror—carry it until he was caught. He didn't doubt that he would be caught—eventually.

The sun was directly overhead when, after a half hour of sweating effort, they gained the top of the first hill. The brush was too deep for them to see ahead. He worried about the direction, knowing that with the sun in the center of the sky, they stood their best chance of wandering away from the line they should follow. He hoped to parallel the regular trail.

When they reached the valley beyond the first hill, they were both scratched and shaken. She twisted an ankle stepping over a rotting log, but she refused his help. She limped along, her lips white and compressed. In a matter of minutes the ankle had swollen so that it puffed against the strap of the sandals she had worn in her swim across the lake.

After the first hour, he judged that they were halfway to the road. He knew they couldn't be more. He made her rest, even though she was anxious to continue.

"Take it easy, Nan. That ankle must be killing you."

"It isn't so bad. It keeps my mind off of other things that hurt. It's a clear sharp pain that I can understand."

"How so?"

219

"I don't want to think about Dad. And I don't want to think about you."

He knew that she wanted him to ask why. He sat in silence. Deerflies found them and buzzed around their heads. He cut her a leafy branch to swish them away. When her breathing was normal, he ripped a long strip from the bottom of his shirt and bound her ankle tightly. She gasped once, but that was all.

They started again. There was only the sound of insects in the darkness under the trees.

After the second hour he called another halt. He felt that they should have reached the road. She was too exhausted to talk. He tried to look confident. After ten minutes he helped her to her feet and then plunged off into the brush. She had trouble keeping up. He made her take hold of the back of his belt. Her weight was a drag on him and he went more slowly.

Finally he stumbled and fell forward. He didn't want her to know how tired he was. He climbed to his feet and saw, ahead of him, the warm gray-blue of asphalt shining between the leaves. They stood at the edge of the road and, on impulse, shook hands solemnly.

After two sleek cars had roared by them, she stared ruefully at her thumb and said, "Wrong technique, Walker. Modern advertising says that you have to awaken the curiosity of the potential consumer. See that hunk of cardboard over there in the ditch? Get it, please."

He brought it back to her. She picked an open place where she could be easily seen from any passing car. Then she spread herself out on her back on the ground, limp and helpless.

"Now, chum, you kneel here beside me and hold on to that cardboard. When you hear a car coming, you fan me as hard as you can. Pretend you don't see the car until the last minute. Then jump up and wave your arms. When he stops, carry me to the car and tell the nice man that your wife has a touch of sun."

He heard the far-off noise of a car and started fanning. She lay with her eyes shut, enjoying it. He fanned until he was certain the car was very near. Then he jumped up and turned, waving his arms.

Tires squealed on the pavement and an old black sedan lurched to a stop practically beside him. A man with a round red anxious face stuck his gray hair out of the window and said, "Trouble, son?"

"I think my wife's got a touch of sun. How about a lift to the nearest town?"

"Sure. Need help getting her in?"

"I can manage." He hurried over and scooped her up. He turned with her to find the rear door already open. He placed her gently on the rear seat. Then he ran back and got the rifle and the camera. He put them on the floor and then wedged himself in on the edge of the seat. As the man started, he picked up her hand and began to stroke it. He saw the man's anxious eyes framed in the rear vision mirror as the old car rattled briskly along.

They turned onto a straight stretch and the man turned his head around and shouted out of the corner of his mouth. "Let 'er sit up now, son. That's a right cute trick you two got there."

"What do you mean, mister? My wife's sick." Nan opened one alarmed eye.

"Don't think so, son. Her color's too good for a sun case. Doesn't breathe right. And wives usually like wearing some kind of wedding ring. Also I just come down the road here about twenty minutes back. Didn't see nobody. You don't get a touch of sun hikin' around in the woods."

Post was about to object again when Nan sat up with a sigh. "Okay, so you're a bright-eyes. We just got tired of cars going right by us. Are you mad?"

"No hard feelings, lady. I get a kick out of it. Any special place you want to go?"

"Just the next town. My wife wants to stop off . . . I mean, Miss Benderson wants to stop off there. If you're going further, I'd like to go along with you."

"Sure, glad to do it. Where'd you come from? Been off in the woods there?"

"We've been down at Mr. Drake's camp on Meridin Lake. He's the man who bought the lake," Nan answered.

"That so? Didn't know anybody was down there. Hmmm."

They joggled along in silence for a while. Nan sat on the edge of the seat. Then the man hitched up to where he could look back at Nan in the rear vision mirror. "Seem kind of upset there, Miss Benderson. Got something on your mind?"

"I'm just anxious to get to the next town. How far is it?"

"Maybe another twenty minutes. Maybe a little less."

"Please hurry, won't you?"

"Doin' the best I can right now."

The narrow road wound through banks of thick green. Post sat back and realized that he had a feeling of regret at leaving the girl so soon. There's nothing I can do about it, though, he thought. No point in fretting. Just get along to a new state and a new city. Find a room and sit through the empty days until they find me. Then the state can support me.

After another few minutes, the man turned around again. He had to talk loud to be heard over the motor roar. "Thought you ought to know I've decided not to take you two into the village. Figure we ought to stop at a trooper station just this side of the village and get a couple of things straightened out. Thought you ought to know."

Post reached down and picked the rifle off the floor. He held it in his lap and Nan looked at him with wide eyes. He stared at the back of the driver's red neck.

"I figure you're going to tell me you're holdin' a gun on me, son. I can't say as I like that. Gives a man kind of a cold feeling up his back. But I'm going to drive you right into the station and you can explain a couple of things to the trooper on duty."

"What sort of things?"

"Well, for instance, how come you're carrying a rifle around in the woods this time of year? Nothing open that's worth shooting. Who's been beating you up? What kind of talk is this about Meridin Lake being sold? That ain't changed hands in forty years.''

''How could you know that?''

''I'm the county clerk, boy. I record all the deeds for land around here. I can remember the deeds for longer than you'd think. No sale on Meridin Lake land for a long, long time. Something funny here and I don't want to drive you on out and then have to tell the law I thought you acted funny but I didn't do anything about it. No sir.''

Post lifted the gun and reached the muzzle over until the barrel rested lightly against the back of the man's neck. He shivered and sank a little lower in the seat, but he didn't slow the car.

''Look,'' Post said. ''I can give you one through the head and grab that wheel. What makes you think I won't?''

''I'm a little scared you might, son. But after fifty years or so you get so you size up people. You look kind of mean-tempered, son, but you don't look like no killer to me.''

''Then slow down and stop. You get out and I'll drive on from here.''

''Not in my car, son. And you try to climb over here in the front seat with me and I run it off into a ditch and nobody goes nowhere.''

Post didn't know what to do. He knew he couldn't pull the trigger. Nan was looking at him with an expression that was half pity and half satisfaction. The woods began to clear and ahead he saw the small white sign which read ''State Police.'' The man didn't slow down. He turned into the front yard in a wide curve which ignored the driveway and tore the sod in the yard. As he slid to a stop, he leaned on the horn button and the old car yapped like a tortured thing.

For a second the yard was silent, the small white bungalow dreaming in the sun. Then the screen door slapped open and a burly man in gray ran out and down the steps. He started to demand explanations of the driver, and then he noticed the rifle in Post's hands, noticed the battered face and the wide-eyed girl. He fumbled at the flap over his revolver and said, "Drop that gun, you!"

"Now you just take it easy, Bobby. This here fellow's a friend of mine. He and his girl've just got a little explainin' to do to the law. No call for you to get so official. You might get him excited and he might shoot somebody."

Post climbed out of the car and handed the rifle to the trooper. Nan stepped out with great hauteur, which disappeared at her first limp. Post looked back and saw the camera on the floor of the car. He knew that somebody would get official and have the film developed. His own testimony might be discredited because of the killing he was wanted for. He reached in and pulled the camera out. Before the trooper could snatch it, he slammed it hard against the fender of the car. The bent metal sprung open and he tore the roll of film out.

"What did you do? What was that?" the trooper demanded.

"Half a million bucks' worth of film. Why? Let's get this over with."

They walked into a narrow hall. On one side was a standard living room, with overstuffed furniture. On the other side was a small bare room in one end of which was a desk with a high railing in front of it. The trooper waved them into the bare room, shut the door and hurried around to sit behind the desk. He opened a notebook, licked a pencil stub and looked up expectantly.

First the driver, who turned out to be a Mr. Benz, told about the rifle and the story about Meridin Lake.

Nan interrupted him. "Please, we're wasting time. My father's back at the lake and he's been beaten up and he's being held by blackmailers. He's Thomas Finley Benderson, owner of Benderson Shipbuilding. Unless you do something quickly, you'll spend the rest of your life explaining why you didn't. This man rescued me and brought me out. That's why he has the rifle. Now get on the ball and quick."

The trooper spent three stupefied seconds staring into

the cold gray eyes, and then he grabbed the phone. It took him five minutes to get his call through to a trooper station in a town forty miles away.

They listened to his conversation. "Carl? This is Bobby. Is Gloria in shape? . . . Good. Hop over to Meridin Lake." He held his hand over the mouthpiece and said, "How many of them are there?"

"Two of the gang and my father and another two people they're holding."

He talked into the phone again. "You and the new guy ought to be enough. Blackmailers or something holding three people there. Round 'em up. Leave the new guy and you fly back out with a man named Benderson, an old boy. Fly him down to Main Lake and shove him in the hospital if he needs it. If the radio's working again, you might keep in contact with station eleven and let them send me the dope on the tape. Got Benderson's daughter here and she's anxious."

He hung up and leaned back in his chair, smiling in appreciation of his own efficiency. "Gloria's a float plane we use up here for search jobs. Carl'll be in there in a half hour or so. Quicker than we could make it. Now you two just go on in the other room and sit tight until I get a report."

Mr. Benz smiled at them as he left. At the door he turned around and said, "You're too anxious to use that gun, Bobby. Get you into trouble sometime." The trooper growled at him.

Nan and Post sat across from each other in the quiet sitting room and listened to the loud tick of the clock on the mantel. He looked at the open window and wondered how far he could get before being picked up. It was tempting. Her obvious honesty had relaxed the vigilance of the trooper.

She glanced up and saw him staring at the window. She caught her underlip between her teeth and shook her head. "No, Walker. I'll get you off before he finds out. Wait."

At last the trooper stuck his head in the door and waved a paper. "Got it."

Nan jumped up and met him at the door. Post walked over to where he could see her face as she read. She turned white and swayed. They each took her arm and led her over to the couch. Post snatched the paper out of her hand and read it.

"Everything as reported. Leaving Carmody guarding two prisoners. Benderson okay. No hospitalization needed. Taking him back to eleven. He wants to see daughter. Will go back in and leave two more men to take prisoners through woods. Wheeler."

He looked down at her and she was smiling up at him. Then she turned her head and looked at the trooper. "Mr. Post has been very nice to me and he's in a hurry. Couldn't you people take a statement or something from him and let him go? He didn't have anything to do with all this."

The trooper rubbed his chin. "Why, I guess so, if Mr. Post lives close enough so that he can get back here if we need him. Sure, miss. I'll do it."

She smiled up at Post again and there was pity and farewell in her eyes. He stood looking down at her and suddenly it was as though a curtain had rolled back in his mind. Suddenly he had pride that was stronger than his fear. He knew that he couldn't start running. It was too late to run, even though she had given him his chance.

"I don't think that's so good, Trooper. You see, you didn't take my name. It's probably in your wanted files. I'm Walker Post. They want me for killing a man in a fight in a bar about a week ago. I killed a man named Victor Hessler. Also, there were three of the gang up there. I shot one through the head as he was swimming across the lake. Maybe you better keep me around."

The trooper opened his mouth and left it open. He shut it slowly and said, "Well, I'll be damned. Wait till I see Benz."

Ten minutes later Post sat on the edge of a bed in a small bedroom in the back of the bungalow. The windows were barred. The door was locked. It looked solid. The trooper had told him that it was temporary until he could be transferred to one of the customary places. He slipped out of his clothes and stretched out on the bed. He felt peaceful and relaxed.

He awakened several times during the late afternoon and early evening, but no one came in to tell him what was happening. He heard many people moving around and heard voices he couldn't identify.

A strange trooper brought in a plate of food and a pitcher of water at seven o'clock. He didn't volunteer any information and Post didn't ask for any. There was nothing else he had to know. He didn't let himself wonder how long his sentence would be. He ate and then stretched out on the bed.

He awoke with a start and saw that it was morning. The door was open a crack and somebody was pounding on it.

He recognized Nan's voice saying, "Hey! Are you decent?"

"Just a minute," he answered, and pulled on his shirt and trousers. He walked to the door and pulled it open. She stood there smiling at him. He stepped back and she walked in and sat on the bed. He stood beside the window.

"You fixed yourself up nicely, didn't you, Walker?"

He shrugged. "Didn't seem to be much point in doing anything else. Call it corny. Just say I was paying a debt."

"To whom?"

"Maybe to myself. Maybe to you."

"Why to me?"

"If I hadn't gotten in this jam, maybe I would have asked you to let me come and see you in a year. I need another year to burn this black cloud off my mind. Maybe because I can't do it now, I've got the courage to tell you. I would want to get a job on a construction gang or in the woods. Work each day until I dropped. In a year I'd be okay. I know that now. I found out too late."

She fished in her bag and found a clipping. She handed it to him.

He read: "POST AND LIMPING DISH WIN OUT. Valiant Walker Post and his skinny gal friend, heiress to the Benderson hundreds, battled their way through seventeen thousand bushes yesterday, only to collapse on the highway. Happy couple refuse to explain why her ankle was bandaged with his shirt."

He looked at her in amazement. "What's this? How come?"

"You're a little thick, friend. I printed it myself. Printed it with the stuff they found in the back of Drake's car. Drake isn't his name. He's a confidence man who was expanding. He didn't buy that lake either. Both the clippings he showed you were fakes. Had his own newsprint, ink and hand printing set. Nobody ever heard of a Victor Hessler. He just wanted to get his hooks into you so he could use you. He confessed to the whole works. The three of them killed a 'patient' out West somewhere, and moved here. He found the lake and took over. Bold guy, I'd say."

"How did he know so much about me?"

"He said he got some information from your landlady. She apparently was annoyed at you. Didn't you wonder how he knew you had a checkbook? Didn't you wonder why, if the police had a picture of you it wasn't printed in the paper, instead of your description? You need somebody to take care of you, Walker. You shouldn't be around loose. You might hurt yourself."

"How about Strane? I didn't exactly mean to kill him, but I did."

"The police don't say that they'd exactly hang you. I heard one of them say something about an award of merit or a pension. You probably saved a western state a few execution expenses. They say you'll be out this afternoon sometime. Oh, and by the way, we're not to mention the Burke man. He and his lady were smuggled out to go separate ways. I saw her. She was wearing a handsome purple eye and an injured expression."

She stopped and he looked at her. She had been gay and bright and glad to tell him that he would be free. She looked at him steadily and her smile faded.

228

She looked away and said, "And you'll come back in a year?"

He waited for long seconds. He wanted to be certain. At last he said quietly, "I'll be back."

She stood up and walked quietly out of the room that was no longer a cell. She left the door ajar.

Secret Stain

THE GIRL WAS young with a dancer's body and a dress that clung expensively and just right. She was the hostess and knew everyone around her. He stood over near the draperies drawn across the windows against the dusk, watching her drink heavily, hearing the dissonant tautness of her voice—and he thought how incredible it was that she had given up all the things she could have become in order to marry Gus Lench, in order to have this Westchester home. And in this long room softly lighted, here in the mechanical babble of the cocktail party, she had become the assistant executioner.

He saw that murder did not become her. He saw that her mouth was too wide and too thicky-shiny. The many drinks did nothing to glaze the faintly feral alertness of her eyes.

Of course, the others did not know, and thus they did not feel the strain of it.

Most of the guests had come up from the city. Lawrence Hask stood near the draperies and took his eyes from Gail Lench for a moment to look around the room. Often he thought that these cocktail party guests had no reality, that they were rented for such affairs, wound up by a key inserted in the small of their backs. Men with gestures, and pouched eyes and deft conversation. Women who posed, holding one stance, moving slowly to another, with sleepy words of idle warmth.

At the far end of the room a sallow man played muted and professional show tunes at a baby grand. A girl, her face putty overlaid with glaze, stood raptly behind him and foolishly massaged the nape of his lean neck as he played. He seemed not to know she was there.

He replaced his empty glass on a tray, took a fresh drink. It seemed so obvious, the tension in the air, that he wondered that Carter didn't feel it. Halfway down the room August Lench sat on a couch with a puffy little blonde. She giggled too much. August Lench, at sixty, carried two hundred pounds on his five-foot-four frame. His naked skull was marked with discolored spots. He appeared to be the incarnation of evil, and this in itself was his greatest business advantage, people saying, "Of course, no man who looks like that could be as wicked as he looks."

And, of course, Lawrence Hask knew that Lench was exactly what he seemed to be.

Carter, carefully marked for death, stood in the group near Gail. She favored him with her most animated moments, with the huskiest of her strained laughter. Lawrence saw Lench glance over from time to time, his eyes flickering across Carter's broad back, and Lawrence wondered that Carter, through the well-tailored suit, could not feel the icy cold of those casual glances from Lench's colorless little eyes.

The room was smoke, and rustle-hum of conversation. The room held the pale flower-stink of gin. The room was suggestion and countersuggestion. And, of course, the room was death.

Lawrence Hask stood, tall and lean and detached, a half smile on his lips, a casual, cocktail party smile, and he caught the gesture when Gail self-consciously touched her hand to her dark hair.

She took three steps out into the room and said, "Everybody! Your attention! With this party the House of Lench inaugurates the all-weather pool. As it's a surprise and we knew you wouldn't come prepared, we've laid in a stock of swim togs for guys and gals. Come along, now. The pool is in the new pavilion. Steam-

231

heated, my dears. With bar. Men's dressing room on the left, women on the right."

Lawrence quickly drained his drink. This would very probably be it. He glanced over and saw Carter's bodyguard, Lochard, pull himself together with an effort. The tall redhead clung to his arm. Lawrence knew that she would not be in on it, that, under pressure, she would merely say that she had been told to be nice to Lochard as he was a friend of Mr. Carter.

The pool was large, oval, the water in it placid and green. The pavilion had glass walls, steamed with the thick heat. The chill glasses on the tiny bar were beaded with moisture.

Hask knew that it was in a style that Lench would well afford, and only Carter could more easily afford. With Carter out of the way, it would be that much easier for Lench to afford it, because then Lench would not only receive his own cut, he would get Carter's also. And that made a proper motive for murder. Lawrence guessed that Gail's few improbable ad-lib courtesies to Carter would figure very small in Lench's mind, if at all. Lench had arranged Carter's murder with care, and, in the mind of Lench, it would have the same importance as the purchase of a new gross of stitching machines to be planted in Brooklyn lofts to enlarge the daily issue of treasury pool tickets, thus enlarging Lench's personal cut.

As Lawrence Hask followed the other men into the dressing rooms, as he selected a garish pair of trunks, he wondered what Gus Lench would say if he knew that Lawrence Hask not only knew about the pending murder but planned to prevent it.

In a way, Lench's weakest point was his inability to think of any motive beyond profit. Given another few days, Lawrence could have ferreted out, from Gail, the precise method. But there hadn't been time.

If Lench had thought of there being any motive except profit, he might have been a bit more wary on the day that the three route men had brought Hask, bleeding, to Lench's office.

The biggest one had said, "Gus, we found this cutey peddling on our route."

Lench had frowned. "You look like somebody I knew once, friend. Who are you?"

"Larry Hask. West Coast. A big fix on a number broke my little combine out there, so I came here where it's soft."

"Soft, he thinks it is!" Lench had said in slow wonder.

"Soft is right," Lawrence had said. "You've got no penetration in your area. Stinking little candy stores and horse rooms and newsboys. Hell, you've got half a hundred big plants in your area. One out of every three foremen and sweepers and setup men ought to be peddling for you."

Lench had picked up Hask's crude pool tickets and had looked them over. "Amateur work," he had said. "Hand-stitched, mimeographed. How could you unload these?"

Lench had flinched when Larry reached for his inside pocket, but one of the route men had said, "He's clean, Gus." Larry had thrown a pack of stubs onto the desk.

"You sold all these?" Lench had said.

"Yes, and right in the middle of your area, friend."

Lench had put his fat white fingertips together. After a long pause he had said, "I can use you."

"So can a lot of other people. But I come high. Three hundred a week and expenses."

"You think a lot of yourself, eh?"

"So much that I don't like your pet poodles laying their fat little hands on me. That's the offer. Take it or I go in business for myself. And I import some talent for protection."

Lench had hedged for two days, and Lawrence knew that he was checking higher up. Approval had come through and Lawrence Hask went on the combine payroll at the figure he requested, under the very sedate title of promotion manager. And it had taken a full year. One full year of gently prodding Gus Lench, of telling him how smart he really was, of how unappreciated he was by the higher-ups.

Carter was the top and Lench was one of the three main underlings. Carter, at Lench's party, looked as out of place as a banker at a crap game. Tall, heavy, he had a massive dignity.

Lench had asked plaintively, "Why are you all the time pushing me? Why should you want a bigger cut for me, Larry?"

"Bigger for you, bigger for me," Larry said.

And so the germ, once planted, had grown.

Two nights before, he had arranged the meeting with Gail. She had left Lench snoring at the city apartment, had stood on a corner with the spring wind whipping her long coat, standing where the streetlight touched her face.

When he had parked on a quiet block in the Seventies, Gail had come into his arms, half moaning, half sobbing, "Why so long, Larry? Oh, why do you make us wait so long?"

"Gus is no dummy."

With her face at his throat, she ground her forehead hard against the line of his jaw. "Oh, how I hate him, Larry!"

He had the bottle in the glove compartment. She tilted it often. Each time, as before, he only pretended to drink, letting a slur creep into his speech.

She giggled emptily then and said, "Gus is going to be really big. Really the tops. It's all set for the cocktail party, Larry. Mr. High-n-mighty Carter is going out."

And then, with a sort of primitive caution, she refused to say any more, and he didn't dare pump her.

He dropped her near the apartment. After she had gone, quickly, swayingly, around the corner, he had mopped the caked lipstick from his mouth, had rolled down the window and spat out onto the dark asphalt.

During the next two days Lench had acted much as usual, moaning because there were three five-hundred-dollar hits to be balanced against a twelve-thousand take on the first day, and gloating because, on the second day, there were no hits at all. The route men left their take at the drop-off points as usual, picking up the tickets for the following week.

Only once did Lench give Larry a slight clue that Gail had been talking the truth. He said, "How would you like a nice fat district of your own, kid? A new district with a lot of promise."

"Carter gives out the districts in this combine."

Lench had pawed at his loose chin. He had grinned. "Maybe he'll let me do that. You could make a G and a half a week instead of the peanuts you're getting."

"When you can give it to me, Gus, I'll take it."

"Having a cocktail party tonight, kid. Out at the Westchester house. You know where it is. Come around about five, hey?"

"Thanks." That solved a problem. It saved having to angle for the invitation.

Lawrence dressed quickly, came out in the trunks onto the apron of the pool before Carter left the dressing room. The water was almost unpleasantly tepid. He came up from the long dive, shook the water out of his eyes, thrust strongly out for the far edge of the pool.

Gail sat on the edge in a brief white two-piece suit. Her feet were in the water. In spite of the heat her smooth shoulders were pimpled with an odd chill and she hugged herself.

He looked up at her from the water and said, "All set?"

"For what, Larry? For what?" she asked in a flat empty tone.

He pushed off and floated on his back, looking up at the night sky through the overhead glass. When he rolled on his side he saw Lench walk out of the dressing room. Lench looked as though he were made of white wax, as though he were a clumsy Buddha that had begun to melt and then had cooled again in the moment of melting.

Lochard did not swim. He stood, sweating in the steamy heat. The redhead had changed to a golden suit. She clung to his arm and giggled up into his perspiring face.

Lawrence saw the color of the man's face and knew that the heat had gotten to the drinks and that he would soon be ill. Carter walked out with dignity and made a fairly respectable dive into the pool. The pool began to fill up, the green water dancing, smooth limbs flashing, soft music coming from the loudspeaker over the bar. No, it would not be long now. But how were they going to do it? It had to be almost foolproof. If murder were suspected, retaliation in the line of work of Lench and Carter was likely to be rather severe.

Lawrence kept his eyes moving. He saw Lench pad wetly toward the light switches. He looked quickly for Carter. Carter was coming down the far side of the pool. Lawrence launched himself toward Carter just as the lights went out.

The air was filled with shrill screams and giggles and hoarse laughter. Closer at hand Lawrence heard a gasp of surprise, then a grunt of alarm and the beginning of a yell for help, smothered by the water before it could attract attention.

He hadn't counted on the lights being out. In sudden fear he made a surface dive, reaching out under the water. He could find nothing. He went up, gulped air, went down again. His fingers lightly brushed smooth flesh, but his wind was almost gone. The third time he went down, his hand tangled in long hair.

He pulled as hard as he could, struggled to the surface. When he broke into the dark air, a hand splatted against his face and teeth sunk into his arm. He smashed his fist out into the darkness, missed completely. And then she was gone; he had sensed that it was a woman.

He then did what he should have done before. He made the side of the pool, hauled himself out and ran for the light switches.

There was a chorus of disappointment as the lights went on, as people moved hastily away from each other.

He said loudly, "I thought I heard Carter call for help."

"Where is he?" Lochard bellowed. "Where's the boss?"

Lawrence did not miss Lench's look of venomous fury. Water stung the tooth marks in his arm.

He walked to the side of the pool, poised, dived deep, keeping his eyes open. Near the tile bottom of the pool Carter floated, his gray hair drifting silkily in the water, his face composed, his eyes half open.

Larry grabbed the drowned man's wrist, got his feet against the bottom, pushed up with all his strength. When he emerged with Carter there were people to help. They got Carter onto the concrete apron of the pool, on his stomach. Larry went into the rhythmic cadence of lifesaving technique.

Lochard stood by, dancing with anxiety. All the others were clustered about. Larry dipped and pressed hard; when he sat back on his heels giving Carter's lax lungs a chance to fill, he saw Gail on one knee beside him, her face a white mask, her hands clenched. Her eyes were venomous.

The group stood, sober now, numbed by the disaster, waiting and hoping. When Carter coughed and then sighed, something like a faint cheer went up.

Water gouted from Carter's lungs and finally, white and shaking, he was well enough to sit up.

Lench said, "What happened? I thought you could swim good. What happened?"

Carter looked steadily at him. "I must have gotten a bit tired." He looked around. "Who got me out?"

Lawrence Hask was pointed out to him. Carter looked soberly at Hask. "You work for Lench?"

"One of my best," Lench said eagerly.

"Help me up," Carter said to Lochard. Carter staggered for a moment, then walked toward the dressing room, leaning heavily on Lochard. He beckoned to Larry. Larry shrugged and followed him.

Once inside the dressing room Carter pulled away from Lochard. He braced himself, doubled his fist and hit Lochard in the mouth with all his strength. Lochard stumbled back against the wall, slipped, caught his balance and stood up. He wiped the blood on his handkerchief.

"Dress," he said to Larry. "You're leaving with us."

"I work for Lench."

"You used to work for Lench. He is out of business. He'll find out tomorrow."

Larry shrugged. "Okay, so I come with you."

Minutes later the three of them went out to the pool. Lench, sitting on the edge beside Gail, struggled up, smiled wanly and said, "We're having steak pretty soon, boss."

Carter said evenly, "I'm sure you can eat my share. Thank you for an instructive party. Thank you very much."

"Accidents will happen," Lench said.

"Yes, they sometimes will," Carter said in a dry voice. "Good night."

But Lench, his wet white body dripping water onto the heavy rug, caught them at the front door.

He said thickly, "Take your choice, Carter."

"Is there a choice?"

"It can work both ways, you know, Carter."

"You wouldn't be warning me, Gus, would you?" Carter asked, almost gently.

"People get too big for their pants, Carter," Lench said. "They lose touch. They don't know how many people they have left in the organization."

Carter leaned against the wall. "Since you force my hand, Mr. Lench, I'll put it this way. You, my greedy friend, may live another twelve hours, or even as much as thirty-six hours if you stay and fight it out. If you run like a rabbit, it may take my people a year to find you. If you want another year—run."

Something inside Lench seemed to collapse. He looked vaguely around the hall, as though weighing his possessions. He said in a smaller voice, "It isn't smart, Carter. These wars. They hurt business. Compromise—"

"No war, Lench." Carter stared meaningfully at Lench's sagging abdomen. "Just a little more worm food."

He opened the door. Before Lawrence left he had a fraction of a second in which to wink at Lench. He saw the little gesture light a fire of hope in Lench. Then Lawrence followed Carter out to the black sedan beside which the driver stood patiently waiting.

Lochard sat in front with the driver. Carter rode in silence for a few moments. Then he said, "That girl he married. Dancer, wasn't she?"

"Swimmer first. But the work was too hard. She picked Lench."

"She amused me at first, but she has no conversation. A bit humiliating to be drowned by a woman."

Lawrence saw then how they had worked it. He said, "How did you know?"

"Perfume. She put her arms around my neck from behind and dragged me down. She drenches herself in perfume, or hadn't you noticed? Has it in her hair."

"I've noticed," Lawrence said.

Carter maintained himself in two adjoining suites in a midtown apartment hotel. He ordered hot rum for himself, scotch and water for Lawrence Hask.

He set the rum on his desk blotter, screened the wall safe with his big body as he opened it. He took out bills, a sheaf of them, turned and counted them out on the corner of the desk.

"For you, Hask. Five thousand. Part of that is for using your head. The rest is for giving me all you know about Lench's routine, his habits and his people. This may become very messy. It will hurt business. It will attract unfavorable attention to our business affairs.

"Our tame politicians and the police on our payroll will have to show signs of activity. Route men will be picked up and fined. Newspapers will sprout scare headlines. Police will smash the stitching machines. Then a master headline will say 'Numbers Ring Smashed.' After that we can go back to work. I know. I've seen it before."

Lawrence picked up the money, folded it once and put it in his bill clip.

He said, "Lench is all set to go on his own. He's been relocating the printers and stitchers and he's been making new friends. He wangled gun permits for most of his route men and he has a big trouble fund to pay them heavy to stay with him. He has sleeping quarters at his office, and he won't stick his head out into fresh air until you're cooked. I'll write you out every pertinent address."

"Wait until I order dinner sent up. Tomorrow I'll change the master ticket design. I'm always prepared to do that. I'll send boys around to tell all the customers that the combine isn't honoring any old tickets sold starting tomorrow. That'll cut into his sales badly."

"But how will you get Lench himself?"

Carter shrugged. "The same way as always. Buy somebody close to him and guarantee their way out of the country. A nice chance for someone to retire."

"Not this time," Hask said slowly.

"What do you mean by that?"

"He has his defenses laid out so that nobody will get close enough. He knows your methods. He has one of those jailhouse items where it will ring a bell if you try to go into his office with a gun. He'll only have one man in his office at a time. He controls the door lock from his desk. And he keeps a gun in his hand until this trouble is over. He told me his plans once."

"What would you suggest, young man?"

"I winked at him as we left. He thinks I have something under my hat. Money will bring him out. So I case your layout, get your safe combination. If I do it right, I can go back to him in secret, explain that I'm living here now, clear him and some of his harder boys through downstairs. You'll have to be out. He'll open the safe himself."

"So what?"

"Set gun. Your safe sits fairly low. Rig a double-barrel in there and it ought to catch him at throat level. So a man gets killed robbing your apartment. You're having dinner at a club when it happens."

Carter said, "Hask, you have a quite extraordinary talent for this business."

"Thank you, sir."

* * *

Lawrence Hask sat slouched in the chair across the desk from Lench. His throat was tight and his lips were dry, but he tried to look amused. Lench sat behind the desk, the heavy revolver aimed directly at Larry's face, Lench's finger on the trigger. "Why should I believe anything you say? You crossed me!"

"You just think I crossed you, Gus. I'm working for myself, and my best bet is through you. I thought you were smarter than Carter, but that thing you tried to pull at your pool is tops for stupidity in my book."

"Swimming accident? The cops would swallow it."

"They might. But Carter kicking off at your place would be just a little too rich for the blood of some of his people. They knew he could swim. Besides, that dopey little wife you bought last year marked his throat with her fingernails. And he recognized her perfume. Sure, she can swim. But she had a little panic all her own. Carter dies in your pool and his people clean his safe. My way is better."

Lench said uncertainly, "Your way?"

"I'm living there now, at Carter's invitation. He sent me down here to cross you up. I'm supposed to pretend to play along with you and suck you into a trap. He has at least three hundred thousand in that wall safe of his. I got a peek at it. Nice dirty old hundreds and five hundreds. Nothing too big so it has to be discounted. I am supposed to tell you that next Friday night Carter will be going out for a big evening. I'll say I'm going out, but I won't go. I'll stay in the hotel and sap the two he leaves there at all times. I can do that easily enough.

"Then I am supposed to tell you that eleven o'clock is a good time. Bring a few boys and call up from the desk and I'll clear you with the desk. I give you a fake safe combination. When you arrive there's a reception party and you all get gunned for trying to rob the apartment."

Lench swallowed hard. He said, "Thanks, Larry. Thanks for telling me. But have you got a plan?"

"Carter is going out, but he's coming back at ten-thirty with a few extra boys. So you come at ten. You can be waiting. And instead of giving you the fake combination, I'll give you the McCoy. For twenty-five percent."

"Ten," Lench said.

"Isn't this a good time not to argue, Gus?"

"Okay. Ten o'clock on Friday night. A quarter cut for you. And I leave fast and leave a hoppie to blast Carter."

"Or do it yourself to make sure it's done."

Carter, standing near the bedroom windows, said, "I've moved the money to a box and the set gun is rigged, all but the trigger string. Did he believe you?"

"Of course. I told him you were fixing the frame for midnight, so he's coming at eleven. That'll give you plenty of time to clear out."

"If the set gun kills Lench, Hask, what will his men do to you?"

"I'll tell Lench that I'd better watch the hall. When I hear the set gun go off, I'll run for it. I'll have a good chance."

"I often wonder about you, Hask. You have a—an educated way of speaking."

"Is that important?"

"No. No, I guess it isn't. Who do you think Lench will bring with him?"

"Hoagie Chance, Shenk, Ullister and probably Murphy. They all have legal permits and they're the least likely to cross him."

"And Lench will open the safe himself?"

"You should have seen his eyes when I mentioned the money. Like a kid with his nose flat against the toyland window."

"Day after tomorrow is Friday. I'll clear out by ten-thirty, leaving you here, with Lochard and Mains on the floor, apparently sapped, as window dressing."

"That ought to do it," Hask said, keeping his voice calm.

Lawrence Hask sat slouched in the armchair, a drink in his hand. He tried to keep from looking at the clock. It was five to ten. Carter was dressing. Lochard and

Mains were playing an aimless gin game at the big table. Heckle and Donovan, the two men Carter was taking with him, were in the next room watching the video.

Every time Larry took a deep breath, his throat seemed to knot and it was hard to exhale. Small tremors ran up and down his spine. A year and a month.

The phone was at his elbow. Carter came out of his bedroom just as the phone rang. Larry took it.

He listened, said, "Just a moment, please." He made his eyes wide, cupped his hand over the mouthpiece, said, "Lench and four men. He's trying to cross me by coming early."

Carter frowned. He jerked a thumb at Lochard, who went in and got the other two men away from the video program.

Carter said heavily, "Okay, we'll play it his way. On your face over there, Lochard. Remember, you're out. Mains, you drop in that doorway there. Make it good. Clear them to come up, Hask. Heckle and Donovan, you come into the bedroom with me."

Hask spoke briefly into the phone and hung up. He went to the bedroom door and said, "He's no dummy. Better shut the door completely."

Lochard lay still. Larry went over to him, slipping the sap from his hip pocket. He said, "Turn your head just a little this way, Lochard."

The lead ball, leather-wrapped, made very little sound as it thudded behind Lochard's ear. He made a small sighing sound. Hask crossed the room quickly and struck Mains. Mains began to struggle weakly. He hit him again, with careful precision.

Moments later there was a knock at the door. Hask opened it. Hoagie Chance came in fast, ramming a revolver muzzle with such force against Hask's middle that it knocked the wind out of him.

"Against the wall, friend," Hoagie said. He moved to one side of the door. Murph came next, took his station on the other side of the door. Then Lench came in, his face pallid with strain, a cigar in one hand, flat automatic in the other. The automatic had a long, tubular silencer screwed to the barrel.

Lench bent and held the glowing end of his cigar near the back of Lochard's hand. Lochard didn't stir.

"Good boy," Lench said to Hask. "Our friend is out?"

This was when it had to be. Hask jerked his thumb several times toward the bedroom door and said, "Left some time ago, Gus."

Gus said loudly, "We'll see about that safe." He motioned to Murph and Chance. They moved, up on their toes, toward the bedroom door.

Chance put out a gloved hand, closed it gently over the bedroom doorknob, then gave a sudden twist, opening the door, slamming it back with his foot as he went in.

The double slam of the shot sounded as Chance went in. He didn't falter in his rush, merely leaned further and further off balance, landing on his face, skidding on the bedroom throw rug. Shenk and Ullister had come in from the hall, closing the door behind them. Shenk carried a .45 Colt, army model. When Heckle appeared inside the room, standing near the body of Chance, Shenk fired once. The heavy slug doubled Heckle, dropped him back across Chance's body.

Carter moved quickly into the doorway, aiming carefully at Lawrence Hask, his face calm, his hand steady and deliberate. Ullister, Shenk and Murph fired almost as one man. The slug from Carter's gun entered the wall an inch from Hask's left ear. The powdered plaster stung his cheek and neck. As Carter fell to his knees, driven back by the impact, he fired wildly. Murph had been standing sideways. The slug tore through him. He moved two weak steps to one side, lowered himself delicately to the rug and was still.

Donovan appeared beyond Carter's body, his hands held high, saying hoarsely, "Okay, okay. Enough."

Lench's automatic made a small sound, no louder than a book dropped flat against a rug. Donovan's hands sagged. The dark hole had appeared just beside the left nostril. He stood for a moment and fell heavily, full length, his head slamming the hardwood floor.

Lench, his fat lip lifted away from his teeth, stepped to Lochard, aimed and fired. Lochard's head moved slightly with the impact. He walked lightly over to Mains, fired again.

"Don't move!" Lench said to Hask.

He went to the safe, spun the dial, his thick, gloved hands trembling. He missed, tried again. Hask heard the tumblers click. He closed his eyes. The blast seemed almost to lift the ceiling of the room. Lench's pudgy doll-body lay on its back in front of the safe.

Ullister stepped around the body, glanced into the safe. "Time to move," he said to Shenk.

Shenk yanked the door open and they raced into the hall. Other doors had opened and people peered out fearfully.

Lawrence Hask counted slowly to five, ran into the hall and yelled, "Stop those men!"

The fire door was slowly closing behind the two. He heard their feet on the stairs. He raced to the fire door, hauled it open, pulled it shut, went quickly up two flights. The little wedge of wood still held the tenth-floor fire door open.

He pocketed the wedge, walked down to the bend in the corridor. The service elevator operator looked at him with frightened eyes. "Mister, I heard shots coming up the shaft. I don't like this."

Hask tried a calm smile. "Do I look like a killer?"

"Mister, you run around with those smart money boys on eight. I'm stopping with you at the main lobby."

Hask held the bill where the man could see the denomination. "Suit yourself, friend," Larry said casually.

"Mister, you go right to the basement." The man grinned nervously.

Lawrence Hask walked four blocks, took a subway downtown, phoned her from a drugstore, met her twenty minutes later in a cheap restaurant.

In the harsh light she looked older.

Her voice masked by the noise in the restaurant, she

said, "Why did you save him? Why did you? It was a deal. Gus was going to give me my freedom if it went through."

"You have your freedom, baby. Gus is dead."

He watched the slow waves of shock, and then the deadly satisfaction.

"And thanks for helping me make sure that he got it," he said.

"Larry," she said. "You and I, we . . ."

He stood up slowly, put coffee money on the table. He said, with an enormous weariness in his voice, "My name isn't Larry and there never was any 'you and I . . .'"

Ray Logan lay in the hot bright sun of the beach at Acapulco. Sally was beside him.

"Darn it, Ray!" she said. "What made you think I'd wait for a year?"

"You waited, didn't you?" he asked teasingly.

"But not patiently. And I was so afraid, darling, that you were going to New York to do something foolish about that kid brother of yours."

He shut his eyes against the sun and it shone red through his eyelids. He said sleepily, "Roger inherited all the craziness in the family. He wanted big thrills and so he started that stupid little numbers racket in New York. The trouble was, the opposition didn't know he was doing it as a sort of game and that he was going to fold it up after six months and write a book about it.

"Yes, Sally, I did go to New York and I found out which organization had removed Roger. It's a big organization. I haunted the police and the District Attorney's office and finally they admitted that they not only didn't have enough evidence to go on, but they had no chance of getting the evidence.

"The big guns of the group were a man named Lench and a man named Carter. I fooled around for a long time, wondering what to do, and then suddenly I didn't have to do anything at all."

"Why, darling?"

"Oh, Mr. Lench got annoyed at Mr. Carter, or the reverse, and they settled their argument by shooting each other and various other people who worked with them."

Later they swam together in the warm and restless sea, and he wondered if the hot sun would bake away the memories, or if the blue sea would wash them away— and yet he knew that fragments of that year would be always with him, and that no man can take his own vengeance without staining some secret place in his heart.

Even Up the Odds

OLD ANGELO MANINI has fired me maybe twenty times and each time all it amounts to is I get a night off from working behind the bar at the Spot Tavern on River Street, which is the joint Angelo has owned for years.

Always it is the same old reason he fires me and the same old reason he hires me back. You see, he gets to reading these magazines on how to run a bar and the first thing I know he is around measuring what is left in bottles and glaring at me and then I am fired and he goes behind the bar. Sure, he can make the drinks, but the Spot Tavern is always loaded with characters spoiling with an urge for fisticuffs and desirous of not paying for drinks.

Angelo is a little old guy with a gray mustache and a nose that twitches and a way of talking very large. Anyway, always he fires me and the neighborhood hears that he is behind the bar and all the characters come around and talk rough to him and he gives away two free drinks for every one paid for, as he is usually nervous of anybody who acts like they want to hit him. Then he begins to think how he would rather be in the back room drinking that red wine and playing some screwy card game with some old guys who come in just to play that game with him. The next day he comes to see me and at twelve noon sharp I am wrapping on the apron and once again Johnny Pepper, which is me, is at the old stand,

248

with that junior baseball bat handy to reach, prepared to handle the business.

It is a Tuesday, about two o'clock in the afternoon, and there is one customer only, and he is asleep with his head on a table, basking in the sunshine which comes in the front window, not so strong maybe, because, as Angelo frequently tells me, the window could be cleaner. But, then, I always say that I am a bartender. I don't do windows.

Angelo comes in from the back, where he lives in a small room with a cot, a gallon of red and a deck of cards, and says to me, "Today, Johnny, you will please to carry down all the crates of liquor from upstairs and put them in the cellar."

"I am weary, Angelo," I say, "but for the consideration of ten dollars, I will do as you ask."

He jumps up and down while I put my elbow on the bar, my chin on my fist, and stare at him. He yells, "You are to call me Mr. Manini and I order you to do it!"

After he has said that about eight times, I start to take off the apron. He remembers that if I quit he will have to miss out on his game and where can he get another bartender as large and as ugly as Johnny Pepper to scare the customers?

He counts out the ten dollars and I say, "Thank you, Angelo, but why does this have to be done?"

In a tired but proud way he says, "Because the upstairs is rented. This morning only, I rented it to a lady and her husband. They will live up there."

"Live up there!" I exclaim. "With only a sink, and with holes in the walls and rats like jackrabbits?"

"This afternoon more plumbing goes in and my cousin comes to put boards over the holes and the lady says she will buy rat traps."

I shrug and he goes back into his back room. I ponder on the housing situation in our town and wonder when Manini will rent his own room and sleep on top of the bar.

They move in the next day, and as it is four o'clock,

with business beginning to thicken, I only have time to give one or two looks at the couple. She is a slim type with good clothes, and she stands out in the wind giving orders to the bums who carry up her furniture. The wind plasters her skirt against her and I see that when the customers are drinking, she better stay upstairs with the door locked, as she is built like what my customers dream about on winter nights.

A guy I figure is the husband, a frail type, leans against the side of the truck and smokes cigarettes and does a medium amount of sneering at the bustle which goes on. He looks like the guys in the movies I see, those guys that take the part of the no-good fellow with bad habits, and I wonder if this new guy is running true to form.

I had a quick chance to forget the two of them along about nine o'clock when Buster Pasternak comes in. Always I hate to see that guy come in. He is even mean when he is sober, which is seldom. He doesn't work at anything, except fighting once in a while when he needs a few bucks. He is maybe thirty-five, blond, half bald, with a beefy face, mean little eyes and a build like Gargantua. But he isn't slow. He moves like a hungry cat.

Often I have wished to work him over with the ball bat, but seeing as how his brother Dave is deputy chief of police, and his brother Harry is alderman, and his brother Francis is behind all the rackets in town, one swing with the bat and Angelo Manini has to fold his tent and sneak. Buster meets nobody but yes men and strangers. He loves to turn the strangers into yes men.

You come down three steps to get into the Spot Tavern, and when I see Buster Pasternak come through the door, I give the crowd a quick look to see if I got any strangers. I get an empty feeling in the middle when I see a big guy at the end of my bar, nursing a beer. He is unfamiliar and about seven feet tall, with shoulders like beer kegs.

Of course, Buster sees the stranger, waves at his friends and stands up to the bar right next to the big guy.

Buster always wears a smile and maybe some people say it makes friends for you, but Buster's smile, along with his little pale blue eyes, always makes me think of a guy I once saw trying to beat a horse to death.

The room gets very quiet and some of the quieter characters slip out the door and go home, the characters who don't like the sight of blood.

Buster edges up to the stranger and jiggles the guy's arm, spilling a little of the beer. The big man glares, but says nothing. Buster says to me, "Johnny, my friend here is buying me a rye and water." Still, the big guy says nothing.

I wish I was a million miles away. I pour the drink and set it in front of Buster. I hesitate a little and Buster says softly, "You heard me, Johnny. This guy is buying."

I reach for the change in front of the stranger, but he knocks my hand aside and asks, "What the hell are you doing?"

"You're buying me a drink," Buster said with a smile.

Then the big guy made the mistake of shoving Buster away. It was a shove that would have sent me back six feet and would have sent Angelo into the bar across the street. It moved Buster back a half step. Buster swung a hook into the big man's middle. It doubled him over. Buster hooked a right up into his mouth. It sounded like somebody whaling a concrete post with a bag of wet sand. The guy flipped over onto his back. But he was game. He rolled over onto his knees and turned around, so he could come up at Buster. He waited too long. Buster kicked him flush in the mouth. It wasn't pretty. Somebody near the door gagged. The big guy fumbled his way over to the wall, and Buster stood waiting for him. The big guy got smart. He felt his way along the wall and then broke for the door in a stumbling run. Buster laughed and a few dutiful souls joined in. I poured out what was left of the big boy's drink, and Buster scooped up his change and shoved it in his pocket. I didn't ask who was going to pay for the rye and water.

In ten minutes the big boy was back with Ray Haggerty, the cop on the beat. They came through the door with the big boy holding on to Ray's arm. He pointed a shaking finger at Pasternak and said through bleeding lips and broken teeth, "That's the guy! That's the one beat me up!"

When Ray saw who he was pointing at, he spun the big boy around and shoved him toward the door, saying, "Get along with you, you stew bum. If Mr. Pasternak beat you up, he had a good reason."

The big guy looked stupidly around the room, and then the door slammed behind him. Ray said, "Hey, Buster, take it easy on those guys. I kind of thought it was you."

Buster laughed again and bought Ray a drink out of the change he had picked off the bar.

On Thursday, the next day, at about three, the slim guy from upstairs comes in. I give him a big smile and say, "I guess you're the fellow who moved in upstairs. I'm Johnny Pepper."

"Yeah," the guy says without a smile. "Straight rye. Water chaser."

I set it down in front of him. His hand was shaking a little when he grabbed it, and he put his mouth down close to it so he wouldn't spill it. He knocked it off with one gulp and I give him another. The second one went the same way as the first. He let the third one sit for a while. He relaxed and his hand stopped shaking. He got a little color in his pale face and said, "The pause that refreshes. I'm Bob Simmonds."

I had him cased. There's only one kind of drinker that drinks like that. I began right then to feel sorry for the wife.

At three-thirty, Simmonds is reciting poetry to me. He talks like a very educated guy and he tells me he is writing a book of poetry. He also tells me that his wife is secretary for a guy who runs a big laundry and that she is working until he can get his book finished, at which time they will be rich.

At four o'clock, he is talking more than ever, telling me all about life and art and culture, only it is getting hard to understand him and he has gone right through a whole bottle. He is beginning to get noisy and having himself a time clinging to the bar when in comes Buster.

I have hopes that Buster will leave the kid alone, and maybe he would have, because you got to say for Buster, he only picks on the littler guys when he's pretty well loaded. But the kid tears it. There is half a dozen guys in the bar, and when the kid sees Buster, he yells, "And here comes an example of the Neanderthal man. The primitive type."

Buster swaggers over, smiling, and says, "You talking to me, kid?"

"Take it easy, please," I say.

"Shut up, you," Buster tells me. "I think junior here needs a little workout."

The kid doubles up a thin fist and slams Buster in the jaw. To Buster it is like a kiss from a mosquito. The kid's eyes bug a little and he tries again. Same answer. Buster doesn't lose his smile. Buster grabs the kid's clothes in the front in his left hand so he can hold the kid up and maybe have the fun of hitting him more than once.

Just then, the door busts open and in comes Mrs. Simmonds. She shoves in between the two of them, her big eyes flashing. I can see little red glints in her hair. She says, very low and deadly, "Keep your paws off him, ape man."

There is a clatter behind her as junior passes out. She turns to me and gives me one of those smiles you wish for and said, "Could you please get him upstairs for me?"

She turns and walks out, her hips moving nicely under her skirt. Buster looks a bit dazed. He whistles softly and says, "That's for me. Boy! That's for me."

"That's her husband on the floor," I mention. But he doesn't seem to hear me. Which is bad. Buster Pasternak has some very violent and elemental ideas about womenfolk. The worst rap his brothers had to fix for him was the time he put the college girl in the hospital for three weeks. They even kept it out of the papers.

Somehow, I didn't want to see him on the trail of Mrs. Simmonds.

Anyway, I got Angelo out from in back and he took care of the bar while I carried the kid upstairs.

She let me in and I dumped him on the sofa. She looked tense and worried. "I'm sorry about this," she said. "You see, Bob doesn't seem to—"

I held up my hand. "Don't say another word. I saw a movie about a guy like him. Only, that guy you stopped would have killed him."

"It would have been better than watching him drink himself to death," she snapped.

"You don't want to think like that, lady. Maybe he'll snap out of it."

"In three years he's had a thousand chances to snap out of it. He's getting worse instead of better. Don't serve him anymore."

"That doesn't make sense. If he hasn't any dough, I won't trust him. If he has the dough, I'll sell him drinks. If I don't, there's nine gin mills in the block that will."

She sagged into a chair. "I suppose you're right. I wish I had the money to take him away where he couldn't buy a drink."

"Look," I say to her, "there's something else. I want you should buy a chain for your door and let me put it on. You know, those kind that let you open it a little to see who wants in."

She stared at me. "Why, for goodness' sake?"

I had to tell her all about Buster. I really laid it on. When she asked me where the law was, I told her that in this town the Pasternaks are the law. I finally got it through her head that she was in actual, physical danger. She was crying when I left, not from fear, but just from having too many problems all at once.

Angelo glared at me for taking so long, and hurried back to his game in the back room.

The next evening I put the chain on the door for her. Simmonds was sitting on the couch. He glanced up at me, but he didn't speak.

I didn't see any of them for nearly a week, except

254

once in a while a glimpse of her on her way home from work.

On a rainy Wednesday, shortly after one o'clock, Simmonds comes in, shaking the rain off his collar. I wait until I see him take a ten out of his pocket before I pour the rye. The performance is the same as before, with him relaxing a little as soon as he downs two shots.

"What'd you hock to get the dough, golden boy?" I ask him.

He leers at me. "From in back of the sugar bowl in the cupboard, if it's any of your business, Johnny." It wasn't any of my business, but I was having the jitters worrying about whether or not Buster would show. I knew that this time she wouldn't arrive like the horses do in the Westerns. He was just medium noisy when a little kid clomped down the steps and peered through the window.

I said to Simmonds, "Bud, you better finish your drink and blow. And put that chain on the door. That kid is off to tip Buster, and this time your wife won't be around to save you. You remember Buster?"

"What I don't remember, Alice told me. And I'm staying. That monkey won't touch me."

"No," I said, "he won't touch you. He'll just put you in the hospital for two weeks while he makes a play for your wife. Buster'll be real gentle, he will."

Simmonds grins at me and shows me the butt of a small automatic. He drops it back in his pocket and says, "I loaded little sweetie pie last night. She's only a twenty-two, but I can put all seven shots into your eye from across the room. I'm ignoring the monkey, but he lays a hand on me and he gets it."

"Look, Simmonds," I say, "you're not the type."

"Maybe I'm just starting to be the type."

I guess it was my fault. As predicted, Buster shows up in five more minutes, blowing hard from hurrying. Two old guys are sitting at a table near the window. The five of us is all there is.

Buster isn't smiling. He stops about six feet from

255

Simmonds and says, "Turn around and look at me, punk. I'm going to rough you up a little."

That was my cue. I should have said, "He's got a gun, Buster." That's what I should have said. But I was too busy remembering the look in Mrs. Simmonds' eyes and too busy remembering the jobs that Buster had done on numerous clients and customers. I had my mouth open, but nothing came out.

I saw the kid's hand dart down into his coat pocket, and he whirled, yanking the gun out as Buster rushed him. There was a small snapping noise. The kid was yanking at the trigger and nothing more was happening when Buster hit him. I expected Buster to pull the punch, but he was like a wild man.

You ever see anybody killed with one smack? It makes a sight and a sound that's right out of this world. You don't want to see it twice. The kid flew back against the bar and crumpled to the floor. Somehow, I knew he was dead.

Buster gave me a weak ghost of his usual smile, pawed at his throat, mumbled, "What the hell?" and folded slowly down across Simmonds' body. One of the old guys tried to get out by way of the plate-glass window.

I was alone and the room was beginning to smell of death by the time the cops got there. I was the only witness they needed.

Buster got one hell of a big funeral. I didn't go. I stayed right behind my bar and got tight. There was a couple of things I wanted to forget.

One thing was the way Alice Simmonds acted. You see, I went upstairs right after the two of them were pronounced dead. I expected her to be working, but she wasn't. She was home. She opened the door and held her hands up to her mouth, her eyes wide, and said, "Is he—?"

I gave it to her quick and caught her as she fell.

I carried her over to the sofa, and as I laid her down, some little brass things spilled out of the pocket of her skirt. Six of them. Six little .22 shells.

She opened her eyes dreamily and stared up at me and

murmured, "I gave him a sporting chance, which is more than he ever gave me." Then she acted like she wanted to bite off her tongue, and looked sick when I handed her the shells.

Another thing I want to forget is Ray saying, "Damn if I can understand why a guy would expect to knock off Buster Pasternak with one dinky little bullet. That's all he had in the gun, you know. Nicked the heart."

They made a routine check for fingerprints, and when they found hers as well as his, it didn't mean a thing to them.

She's gone now. Moved out.

Sometimes on sunny afternoons when I see a slender woman walking on the other side of the street, I think it's her and I run to the window, but it never is. It just never is.

Maybe one of these days, when Angelo fires me again, I'll see if I can locate her.

Verdict

ONE

CHOWDER GAVE ME the assignment one hot afternoon in Chicago. I like to stay in shape and that morning I had gone three fast sets of tennis with a pro at the club. It was one of those afternoons. Chowder was at the big desk he keeps in the front room of his apartment, and I was in sweat shirt and shorts over on the couch. Chowder was going over the coded reports from the outlying districts. Syndicate business.

Gloria was sitting cross-legged on the floor beside me, hunched over a magazine. I had my right hand on the nape of her neck, running my fingers up through her bronze hair. Gloria is a good kid, but not too bright.

Her drink was on the floor beside me, and her cigarette smoke was curling up through the still air. She has never gotten it through her head that I don't smoke or drink just because I don't like the tastes involved.

I've told her that a gentleman is a guy with none of the minor vices, but she merely gives me a blank look.

Chowder got his name because he started in a political way in some small New England town trying to buy the voters with free chowder and beer at picnics. He has a flat white face, no hair and a little mouth like an upside-down U. He is a very rough man indeed.

"Go down to the bar and buy yourself a drink, Gloria," he said.

She gave him a look of quick annoyance. "I like it here."

I took my hand away from the back of her neck, put my palm flat against her ear and pushed. She sprawled over and jumped up, hopping mad.

Before she could start yapping, I said, "Do like the man says, honey."

She walked to the door with an insolent strut that showed off certain clothing concessions she had made to the Chicago summer weather. The door banged behind her.

"Sit up when I talk to you, Wally," Chowder said.

I swung around to a sitting position, yawned and smiled at him. He rapped a report with the back of his fat white hand.

"Now you go to work," he said.

"Who gets roughed up?" I asked.

He stood up, frowning. "Wally, we got an investment in you. You know that."

I didn't know it. For a little AWOL, hijacking and black-market stuff in West Germany, they had given me ten in Leavenworth. The reviewing authority had set me loose after thirty-seven months. With a dishonorable discharge on the record, people like me had best make some contacts in Leavenworth for work on the outside, or else settle down to a life of manual labor. My army background had given me some skills useful to the organization, and I knew who to go to when I was released.

I'd been here with Chowder's group for a little over a year at five hundred a week, and had drawn only four assignments in that time, each one involving using muscle on people who felt that they deserved a larger slice of the sucker money than the organization was willing to give them. Oh, there had been a lot of small errands for Chowder. Go leave off the Continental and pick up the Mercedes. Stop on the way back for that case of wine.

In the real action, I had given them their money's worth.

"Why are you talking about the investment in me?"

"Because this is a different kind of deal, Wally. This one is what you could call maybe a permanent fix."

"Then you should send somebody too dumb to care what happens later. I have this aversion to electric furniture."

He ignored me. "This one comes from the very top. Up until six months ago the company was grossing fifteen thousand a week out of Bruerton. That's in upstate New York. Our local guy is Sid Marion. You met him at the meeting. The gross is from machines, books and grass."

I waited patiently. "So when the gross sagged off to eight a week, the big man called Sid in and found out that a couple of years ago they put the cops on a merit basis, and six months ago the old Chief of Police died, and a younger man, this James Fosting, was put in. He can't be bought. We can buy the number two in line, but that doesn't do us any good while Fosting is there. The loss comes to a total of three hundred and fifty big ones a year, so the big man asked Sid to go to work on the new chief. Smear him. Buy him. Whatever. What happened was that even more of the action got closed down. There are a hundred and forty thousand people in that town up there. It should turn twenty thousand a week, not six. The front office has confidence in you, Wally. He's yours."

"Isn't it work for a button man? Like you can borrow one from St. Louis or someplace."

"No, because then the locals get very upset, and maybe our number two man won't get in after all. This has to be accidental, Wally. Very smooth and very cool. You are coming along nice. You are very bright. I keep telling them that."

"Thanks. I'm bright enough so I know that five hundred a week doesn't buy that kind of work."

"There's a bonus authorized if you make out okay."

"Like how much?"

"Like twenty."

I thought it over and did some mental arithmetic. "Twenty is fine, plus ten percent of the total gross for the first year after he's gone."

Chowder shook his head sadly. "Wally, you should know I can't go back to the front office with a crazy idea like that."

At the door to the bedroom I turned and said, "While I'm dressing, maybe you should contact somebody and get an okay—or go get somebody else."

"Will you drop down just a little?"

"Let's get their offer first. Okay?"

I showered, shaved, put on a white shirt, the new cord suit, knotting the pale blue tie just the way I like it. I looked over the finished product in the full-length bedroom mirror. When I was eighteen, a lady told me that I reminded her of a big sleepy blond cat. She told me my eyes had a cold look.

I always think of her when I look in the mirror.

When I came back out, Chowder said, "He'll go along at seven and a half percent."

I walked to the door. "Okay. A deal."

"Where are you going?" he asked.

I grinned at him. "First, I'm going downstairs and get my girl out of the bar. Then I'm coming back here and draw five thousand bucks advance. Then she's going to pack my stuff, and I'm leaving for Bruerton. Okay with you?"

Gloria was at a corner table, and a slicker type had moved in on her. Gloria likes games. When she saw me coming, she unwrapped her fingers from the glass, and slapped her palm across the dummy's mouth. He was one startled guy.

He looked up at me and Gloria pouted and said, "Honey, this man has been annoying me."

I just looked at him. He knew his cards had come off the bottom of the deck. For three seconds he thought it over. Then he got up and slid away fast. I realized I was getting weary of Gloria's little tricks.

"Why didn't you hit him?" she demanded.

"Come on," I said. "Time to pack."

The eager light came into her eyes. Gloria likes far places. She likes to be on the move.

But she was disappointed. I checked her packing job on my stuff, folded the crisp bills Chowder gave me out of the safe, went in to where Gloria was packing her own rags and said, "Snap it up, baby."

She smiled up at me. I told Chowder what I planned for Gloria and tipped the doorman off too. She was to wait in front for me while I got the car. I stacked her bags on the sidewalk and carried mine around to the car. I grinned to myself as I waited for a light six blocks away, thinking of the expression on Gloria's face when she finally realized I wasn't picking her up and she couldn't get back into the building. The doorman would have a hard time scaring her off. In a week she'd cool off and be back at her job as dice girl in one of the bars.

It's kid stuff to barrel along in a car like a big shot. I kept the needle right on fifty-five.

The bad thing about driving is that it gives you too much time to think. I had hoped to inch my way up in the organization without ever having the pressure on too hard. This was a horse of a new color. It gave me the trembles. It had been a long time since I had killed a man. The last one was in a Hamburg alley two weeks before I was picked up in the big raid. And that hadn't been a pretty one. We couldn't risk a shot, and I had to whip him to death with the gun barrel. He had been softening up and we were afraid he was going to the MPs, to clear himself by turning us in.

But that had been sort of a spur-of-the-moment deal. I remembered how sick to my stomach I had been after it was over. This was worse. This was more cold-blooded. I had the idea that it had been Chowder who recommended me for the job, hoping that I would foul up. I knew that Chowder was afraid of me.

The difference was in the background, I guess. When Chowder was a kid, he had been brought up in comfortable middle-class surroundings. While his mother was tucking him in bed, I had been sneaking out over the orphanage wall with Mick and Chucky, heading through the dark streets down to the waterfront, rolling the drunks we hauled into the alleys.

When I was fifteen, I drove for two crazy guys who specialized in gas stations. They chiseled me on my cut and I quit them the week before they stepped into a trap. It hadn't been pretty. Their new driver caught one over the ear and sheared off a gas pump and they went up in flame and black smoke.

Rufe Ventano was the guy who smartened me up. During the three years I worked for him, making book, he taught me how to dress and act. He taught me the right line of chatter and the proper fork to use. The week he was dying in bed of pneumonia, I was picked up on a breaking and entering, and the court gave me a choice of state prison or the U.S. Army. I enlisted the day they buried Rufe.

After Basic I had another long training session at Benning for the Airborne. I found out I was not crazy wild about jumping out of airplanes and wangled a transfer to the MPs. I took their training and got sent to Germany. After a month of watching the clumsy crooks making big dough, I moved in. During the seven months I was AWOL, I made two hundred thousand dollars. I had it in hundred-dollar bills. When they closed in, I buried the fat stacks behind a rock in the subcellar we used as a headquarters.

As I drove toward Bruerton, I realized that if I could carry off the job they had given me, I could ask for a month off. The dough I would get, if properly placed, would get me legitimately to Germany. I wanted to dig behind that rock.

With the two hundred thousand, I could buy myself a little talent among the syndicate personnel, enough to move Chowder out of my way and take over his job.

So it all depended on how I worked it out with James Fosting, Chief of Police of Bruerton.

* * *

I left the car in a storage garage and took a cab to the hotel. I signed in as Thomas Quinn, giving a Chicago address.

My room with bath in the Stanley Hotel in Bruerton was that size where you can't open the room door and the bureau drawer at the same time. The bed was narrow and hard. But it was a respectable hotel. That was important.

With the room door locked, I sat on the bed and went over, for the twentieth time, a few of the tentative plans I had made on the road. The day was fairly cool for September, so, after a shower, I changed to a tweed coat and gabardine slacks.

I got some of my shopping done that first day. I bought a used portable typewriter, a ream of paper and a briefcase. Then I had the room clerk get on the ball and get a suitable table for my room.

The other little item was more important. I had to be careful about it. After breakfast the second day, I walked around, heading toward the shabbiest part of the business district, until at last I found a print shop that looked next door to bankruptcy.

A bell jangled when I went in, and an old guy in a green eyeshade came out peering nervously through the gloom.

Even though I explained carefully that it was a joke I was playing on a friend, he didn't want to cooperate until I let him see the corner of the twenty-dollar bill. I waited while he ran off the letterhead I wanted. It looked okay, and I paid him the twenty for five copies on his best-quality bond paper.

The letterhead was that of one of the top-flight publishing houses.

Back in the room, I wrote a rough draft of the letter, and then carefully typed it, I addressed it to my fake name, Mr. Thomas Quinn, at the address I had given on the register card when I checked in.

Dear Tom,
    Bill and I are really enthusiastic about the job you've done this time. There certainly is a need right now for this sort of book.

264

Verdict

We would like to go ahead with it as it stands, but Bill says it could be longer than the present 70,000 words.

We talked it over and have decided that, along with the other men, you should include about twenty thousand words on a man named James Fosting who has been doing an outstanding job of cleaning up Bruerton, New York. He is Chief of Police there.

Make it the same sort of intimate biography technique that you used on the others. Find out how he thinks, what he eats, where he goes for amusement—all that in addition to the main job of finding out the reason for his success.

You can use this letter with him, if it will help. By the way, how would you feel about changing the title to "Men Who Make Our Cities"? Sound okay to you?

A check for your advance will go out sometime next week.

Sincerely,
Al Justin

In composing the letter, I was aided by the three years of education I received while locked up. If I made Fosting suspicious in any way, he would check back with the publishing house. I had to carry off the act, and do it well.

My next job was to go to the public library, read some of the articles in municipal journals and make a list of a few men who were written up with loud praise. I was careful to select them from cities with which I was reasonably familiar.

From a drugstore phone booth, I called the number Chowder had given me for Sid Marion. When he came on the line I said, "Sid, just listen and don't ask questions. I've come here to help out. You know who sent me. You met me at the annual meeting. Don't blink an eye if you see me in funny company. I'll call on you, if and when I need help."

I hung up before he could answer. I had the feeling that the further I stayed from Sid Marion, the better I could operate. If he had been on his toes, he would have thrown some syndicate dough around in the Common Council to spike the police merit system before it ever got underway.

I expected that he would be surrounded with the usual group of amateur and semipro sharpies, ward heelers and buck-hungry hangers-on.

For guaranteeing him freedom from competition and a war chest to tide him over the rough times and legal talent to keep him out of the pokey—the syndicate stepped in to take half his net. A syndicate spy had, of course, been sent in to make certain that Sid wasn't holding out.

The way the force was set up, the Deputy Chief had his office at Police Headquarters, and the Chief had an office over in City Hall, adjoining the office of the Commissioner of Public Safety.

I went in, sat on the bench in the outer office and spent some happy moments admiring the talent he had at the secretarial desk before I got the call to enter the sanctum.

James Fosting turned out to be a tall guy with a long leathery-looking face. About thirty-five, I guessed. He wore the local equivalent of a Brooks Brothers suit, and under the high forehead, the blue eyes had a harsh and knowing gleam.

I gave him my best-variety smile and handed him the letter. I didn't sit down until he asked me to. There are cops who claim that they can tell a wrongo in one third of a second. Those cops have holes in their heads. No hick cop has ever made me on first look. You have to have presence. And a nice, open, honest smile.

I sat and watched him read the letter. His eyes flicked down it, then he started in again from the beginning and read it more slowly.

"Hmmmmm," he said. "Very flattering, Mr. Quinn. I'm honored."

"Can I assume that it's okay with you, Chief?"

"With strings. One—I took over a very bad situation here, Mr. Quinn. Very bad. Straightening it out is still a fourteen-hour-a-day job. I can't slight that job. You'll have to get a lot of your information secondhand. Two—I want to read every word you write, and approve the final draft. One wrong sentence, and my political enemies might use it as an excuse to move me out of here."

I knew he was normal, and I knew he had swallowed the hook. I didn't even have to give the line a yank to set the hook.

Already he was thinking of himself in that book. City Builder. Ha!

He had been crisp and businesslike, but now he had that old pleased gleam in his eye. He pushed a button on his desk.

The lush item came in briskly. "Miss Calder, this is Mr. Quinn." I stood up, and we nodded at each other.

"Mr. Quinn is including a write-up of me in a book that has been accepted by a good publishing house. What shape is your work in?"

"I'm nearly caught up."

"Good. I'm assigning you to Mr. Quinn. Have Miss Willington take over your desk. Explain the ropes to her. You are at liberty to give Mr. Quinn any information he may request. Is that clear?"

"Yes, sir."

I was still standing. Chief Fosting stood up too. He stuck his hand out, and I took it. "When she's given you all she knows, come to me to get the blanks filled in."

I sat patiently on the bench again while Miss Calder finished a few letters and got hold of a chubby item named Willington and gave her the routine. Willington acted nervous, but pleased.

She sat on the other side of the booth.

I think of women in terms of music. I don't know why. Gloria was barrelhouse piano with a driving bass.

There have been women who were bright, raw trumpet, or the gutty blast of a trombone. One or two have been a tom-tom beat.

But this Janet Calder was something else. A string section. Violins. The longhair brand of music. But neither cool nor faint nor dull.

She was nineteen or twenty. Blond. A wide, sensitive mouth, with a flare to her nostrils and wide eyes of a blue-violet shade. Keen eyes. They didn't look as if they'd miss a great deal.

Her young body was almost excessively feminine, but she didn't throw it around. She carried herself in a way that showed she could swim, play tennis, ride. Her hands and arms were tanned. Her eyebrows made her hair look dyed, which it wasn't. They were thick black eyebrows, unplucked. They made me want to lean across the table between us and run the tip of my finger along them. They looked as though they would feel like fur.

Fosting knew what he was doing when he attached me to her for information. I scribbled in my prop notebook while she filled in the background.

It was an unusual background. Law degree. FBI before Vietnam. G-2 during that war. He had come back to his hometown in late '77 just as the merit system went in. And he had become a rookie cop. With his talents, he passed the competitive examinations with a rating and performance record that got him up to sergeant in the middle of 1978, lieutenant by the spring of 1979, captain by Christmas of 1979. Oddly, the other men on the force didn't resent his extremely rapid rise. When the Chief died, his grading was tops, and he moved into the hot spot.

I asked a few questions, scribbled down the answers.

"How come you know him so well, Janet?" I asked.

I saw the faint blush. She spun her Coke glass in a wet pool on the black marble tabletop, making a pattern of interlocking rings. She watched those rings as though they were very important and said, "My dad was a policeman for years. I was in business school when Dad was shot and killed on New Year's Eve in 1977. Chief Fosting, then a rookie, took an interest in me and saw that there was enough money for me to finish the course. Then he helped me get a job."

"Nice guy," I said casually.

"It's stronger than that!" she snapped. "He's—he's a wonderful man. I respect him and admire him more than any man I've ever met. He's fair and honest and . . ."

I grinned at her. "How long have you been in love with him?"

For a minute I was afraid I had gone too far. Her face

got white and her lips were firmly compressed. She had been calling me Tom, as per agreement, but she said, "Mr. Quinn, I hardly think that your job gives you any right to—"

"Hey, wait a minute, Janet!" I said. "I was just kidding. Take it easy. He's a nice-looking guy and I thought you two maybe had some arrangement."

Her anger faded. She looked rueful. "You know, he doesn't even know I'm alive. As a woman, I mean. I'm just an efficient piece of office equipment. Sorry I flared up. I guess—well, I guess I am in love with him."

There was no reason under the sun why her words should irritate me. But they did. It was certainly none of my business who she was in love with.

To cover up, I asked quickly, "Where does he live?"

"In a little room in the Stanley Hotel. It's a horribly bare little room. He doesn't seem to care about his environment. He's so wrapped up in his work."

That gave me a jolt. Fosting right in the same hotel with me. It might be a break.

"Any wine, women and song?" I asked.

She shook her head. "I sometimes wish he'd—well, get out sometimes. He looks so tired. But he says that there's too much for him to do."

"You live with who?" I asked.

She tilted her head to one side. "What has that got to do with your write-up, Tom?"

"I just wondered who you'd have to call to tell them I was taking you to dinner."

"Are you?"

"You heard the Chief's orders, Janet."

Her smile was a little-girl grin. It wrinkled her nose and made me want to kiss her. "Okay," she said. "Chief's orders. If you must know, I live all by myself in an apartment complex for singles on Maple Terrace. And now you can take me back there so I can change."

I compromised by putting her in a cab and promising to call for her in an hour.

TWO

I FOUND MYSELF singing in my shower, and wondered why. I picked the answer up an hour later.

Funny how it happens to you. You think you have the world cased, have yourself all set from here on in. And then somebody throws a blond monkey wrench into the machinery. I decided that I was silly to keep the car out of circulation. So I took it out of the garage and called for Janet.

Janet came down looking like one of the girls they should put on magazine covers and don't because they can't find them often enough.

"Yours?" she asked when I opened the car door for her. When I told her it was, she said, "Writing must be pretty profitable. Maybe I'm in the wrong business."

The steak house she suggested was fair, and, over the coffee, in order to make my story look good, I hauled out the notebook again.

I asked her to describe each of his movements on an average day. The guy was a bear for punishment. To the office by seven-thirty, on foot. Half an hour for lunch. Usually not through until nine. I casually worked in the idea that, since he had clamped down so hard on gambling, he must fear personal reprisals and go around with a bodyguard.

She laughed at that one. "Heavens, no! Jim—I mean Chief Fosting has put the fear of God into all the sneaking little men in this town. He'd consider it beneath his dignity to go around with a guard."

I smiled. "Maybe I hadn't ought to put that in the article. It might encourage somebody to potshot him."

"I think he'd like them to try. He carries his own revolver and he's an expert shot with it."

That was an important fact to file away. Not that I was going to gun him down. I had better plans.

I folded the notebook, slipped it into my side pocket. "Working day over?" she asked.

"No. Not by a long shot. Now you've got to give me some of the local color. I can't write a good chapter on

Verdict

Fosting until I know what the city is like. Where do we
go from here?"

"I'm going to demand overtime!"

"Am I that bad?" I asked her.

"You'll do, Quinn," she said softly.

Some dregs of a long-forgotten conscience stirred me.
Maybe some of it showed on my face.

"What's the matter?" she asked.

I smiled. "Where do we go?"

"There's one place I've always wanted to go," she
said, "and I've never had an excuse before. But this
could come under the heading of local color. I want to
go to the Key Club."

"Sounds interesting," I said. "What is it?"

She had a pixie look in her eyes. "A disco where they
gamble upstairs," she said in a conspiratorial tone.

"Hey, I thought your boss closed those all up!"

"He did. All of the ones inside the city. This one is
over the line."

From the way the place was running, I knew that the
fix was in, but good. Thus the peephole setup to get to
the upstairs games was just so much thrill for the suckers,
plus insurance against somebody knocking the place off
with profit in mind.

It was a penny-ante outfit, with a dapper male cashier
dispensing chips at the one, five, ten and fifty levels.
There weren't many fifties in play. I tried to stake Janet,
but she shook her head, took a twenty out of her purse
and bought twenty one-dollar chips. I did the same.

They were getting a college crowd at the place, plus
the old-lady business, plus the beer-salesmen set. There
was a bar in the corner.

Roulette, birdcage and the crap tables were getting a
decent play. Janet stared around like a school kid in the
principal's office. The sign near the birdcage said that
they would take a maximum fifty-dollar bet with a limit
of six doubles. Thus the most that could be placed on a
number on one turn of the cage was thirty-two hundred.
Not good and not bad. The limit on doubles made the
house percentage high enough to keep it honest.

271

I don't know why I felt so proud to be with Janet Calder. She made all the other women up there look like harpies. She was like a fresh breeze blowing through the stale smoke.

She settled for the crap table. When I saw that the table posted no limit, I knew that the house had it gimmicked. With the education Chowder gave me, it didn't take long to figure it out. They were set up to handle a routine switch of the dice, and they were playing on an oilcloth surface. That spelled trippers. It is the simplest dice fix.

The dice can be square and true and properly weighted, but on the side opposite the one they don't want to come up, they have some sticky stuff, not noticeable to the touch. The dice will always roll, tumble and slide to a stop. They don't slide on that sticky stuff. It will trip the dice over.

We found a place at the table wide enough for the two of us, and the pressure of her shoulder against my arm was very sweet indeed.

A florid yokel across the way was betting heavy, the sweat standing on his upper lip.

I told Janet to follow my lead and I started betting the other way, with the dice. The switch was pulled so smoothly that I didn't see it. Sure enough, the red-faced citizen threw two aces, deuce-ace the second time, then tossed a six followed by a seven, while both Janet and I let our bets ride to a happy little total, which we dragged in.

Janet's face was flushed with excitement. She didn't understand what was going on, but she liked winning. I knew that if I was running the game, I'd feed her dice that build up a few naturals, so when they came to her, I told her to try five dollars. I was beginning to get on to the switch. Seven came out and I told her to let it ride. Seven again, the same way, and there was twenty in front of her. Suckers along the table piled on, hoping she was having a run, and I made a quick estimate, decided the stick man would let her get one more natural. Eleven came out and he paid off nearly all the way around. A lot of them were letting it ride, so I reached out and hauled in all but one chip for her.

"Whyn't ya let the li'l lady play her own game, doc?" the stick man said.

I didn't bother to answer him. He'd already pulled the switch. The dice came to a four, and then a seven. I passed them along. We'd each picked up fifteen bucks on the florid man's bad luck, and thirty-four more on Janet's passes. Total of ninety-eight.

It looked like the sort of bust-out house that would hate to have you walk out with even that much. I didn't want a fuss, so I decided to drop my share and get out. A floor man had his eye on us and I guessed that the stick man had tipped him that I might be a little too wise for their good.

I wanted to drop the few bucks at the same table, but then Janet saw a poker game getting underway over in an alcove.

"There's my game," she said. "Come on!"

I didn't like it. At first I was going to sit it out, but then I began to wonder just how far they'd go.

There were eight of us. The house dealt and took a cut of each pot. I took a long look at the other six players. They really had that game stacked. Two of them were house men, though trying not to look that way. The dealer had a mechanic's grip on the deck.

It was five-card stud. No ante, of course. Five-buck bet, and after that it was pot limit. No limit on raises.

To warm the game up, the cards were dealt honestly the first few hands. The house boys were getting the feel of the six suckers. I folded my hand the first few rounds, and watched Janet handle her cards. She seemed to know what she was doing. When she had a ten of hearts in the hole, a nine of hearts up, she stayed once, and folded when her third card turned out to be the trey of spades.

Then the house began to go to work. A skinny citizen across the way, who kept biting his lip, got an ace up. He peeked at his hole card and bet five. A house man bumped him, and when it came around, Skinny advertised his aces back to back by bumping again.

It cost Skinny a hundred bucks to look at his last card. The house man came through, of course, with three sevens, whereas Skinny didn't improve on his original pair of aces.

The next few hands were dull, and then I felt the kill coming. After the opening bet, Janet and me and the two house men were left. I had eights backed. She was on my left with a queen showing. The house man was on my right with a jack showing. The other house man had a ten showing.

I guessed that everybody had them back to back. Janet, with queens back to back, was looking down everybody's throat. And, with my eights, I had to follow. The man with the jack showing bumped, and Janet bumped back, catching me in the middle.

The next card, the third card, didn't help anybody but me. It gave me three eights. To make it look good, I bet fifty. Everybody stayed. The fourth card didn't help me a bit, but it gave Janet three queens, gave the guy on my right his third jack and the other house man his third ten. At that point the two house men started bumping each other, with both Janet and me caught in the squeeze. Janet took the last of her money out of her purse, and I slipped her two hundred over her protest, telling her that she could pay it back out of the pot—if she won.

There was well over a thousand bucks in the pot by the time the flurry stopped. Janet's hands were shaking. I was cold inside, figuring an angle.

It all depended on the first card dealt. That went to the house man with the three tens. If he collected the fourth, we were licked. He got a four. The next card came to Janet. An ace. No improvement.

My timing had to be just right. I waited until the card was free of the pack, the card that I suspected would give me the fourth eight. As soon as it was free, I slapped my cards over and said, "Folding!"

I kept my eye on that card that was free of the pack. I wanted to laugh at the expression on the face of the dealer. It was a stupid thing for me to do, as I could have called Sid in the morning and gotten my losses back. But I had to show off for Janet.

The dealer couldn't stick the card back in the pack. It was frozen in the air for a moment and he said, "You can't fold while the cards are coming."

Without taking my eye off the card he held, I said, "I can fold anytime, brother."

He had to give it to the other house man. My fourth eight. And the unused card on the top of the deck, I felt certain, was the fourth jack that the house man didn't get.

Janet took another hundred, pushed it out into the pot and whispered to me, "Stupid! You threw in the winning hand!"

The house man didn't call. Janet pulled in the big pot. The dealer gave me a long look.

We walked slowly to the desk and converted the chips into cash. The usual bouncer stepped up to me and said, "Sir, there's a call for you on the phone in the office."

"Wait down in the lounge," I told Janet, and followed the guy.

He opened the door, stepped in right after me and leaned against it. An ex-cabby type sat behind the desk, picking his teeth with a split match.

They gave me the silent treatment. I smiled amiably.

"Wise guys we don't go for around here," he said, favoring me with a black scowl.

I thought there was more to come, so I was off guard. The bouncer's fist, cased in brass, caught me on the mastoid bone, and the edge of the desk hit me across the bridge of the nose as I went down.

Through a swirling mist, I heard the man behind the desk say, "Clean him, Al, and roll him down the back stairs."

Al rolled me over onto my face. He started to fumble at my pockets. His necktie hung free. I got it in my hand and yanked down hard as I brought my knee up. The middle of his face made a sound like a ripe apple being run over.

As he fell across me, I reached through the kneehole of the desk, got one of the ex-cabby's ankles in my hand and dragged him under there with me. He didn't seem eager to join me. But he stopped objecting when I got him by the throat and banged his head against the leg of the desk a few times.

When they began to stir, I was seated at the desk talking to Sid. Al held a large handkerchief to the middle of his face. I smiled at them.

I finished my conversation and hung up. I put my fingertips together, my elbows on the desk. "You two shouldn't have any trouble finding a job," I said. "In some other town. Mr. Marion has just advised me that he's replacing you, as of tomorrow night. You can pick up your pay from him. The new man will clean out these thumb-handed mechanics you've got in here and put in some artists. This place could net twice as much, if you let the public win once in a while."

As I came around the desk, they started to make their apologies. I pushed my way out, glad that the brass hadn't broken the skin, and wondering how soon I'd have to cover my black eyes with dark glasses.

Janet stood up as I appeared in the doorway of the downstairs lounge. In her eyes was mirrored the surprise that I had seen in the eyes of the boys on the upstairs door.

"What on earth did—?"

"Not here, baby," I said. I took her arm, and we went out the side door to the floodlighted parking lot.

She didn't speak until we were a half mile away, and picking up speed. Then she said, "You've got to explain, Tom."

I found a quiet spot near a country crossroad, and pulled over. I cut the lights and motor, and held a match for her cigarette. She moved around in the seat so she could face me. "What happened back there?"

"Why do you ask?"

"A horrible little man came up to me in the lounge and said that you'd fallen and hurt yourself and that in a little while you'd be out in the car. I told him I'd wait right where I was. He shrugged and went away. I was getting scared. I didn't know what to think of that phone call." She paused. "I've been doing a lot of thinking, Tom."

There was enough pale moonlight so I could see the lovely planes of her face, the delicate hollows at her temples.

"I did fall, but I wasn't as badly hurt as they thought, Janet," I said quietly.

"What happened at that dice table?" she asked. "What happened in the card game? Why did they act so funny? It was as though they knew something, and so did you, and they didn't like your knowing it."

I was right about those smart eyes of hers. She saw things, and her mind meshed very nicely. By trying to be Mr. Smooth, I had put myself neatly out on a limb.

There seemed to be a very good answer. I put my hands on her shoulders, pulled her toward me, slipped my arms around her. She ducked her lips away from me. But I caught her and kissed her. She went limp and dead, her lips firmly compressed. It's as good a defense as any. I kissed her unmoving lips until I began to feel silly. Then I felt her stir in my arms, felt her arms creep up and circle my neck. And suddenly she was the most alive creature in the world. It lasted while the car seemed to spin like a crazy top, and then she tore herself away and planted a stinging slap, high on my face.

"Damn you!" she whispered. "Damn you!"

She moved over into the corner of the seat near the door and said in a small voice, "Take me home, please."

No words were spoken on the trip back to her place. I let her out and walked up to the foyer door with her. She had been fumbling in her bag. In the darkness, after she had unlocked the door, she turned and thrust a wad of bills at me. As I bent to pick up the ones that fluttered to the porch, the front door shut firmly.

I shrugged, stuffed the money in my side pocket, parked the car in an all-night lot near the hotel and went up to my room.

While I was in the shower, the phone rang. I went to it, lifted it off the cradle and said cautiously, "Yes?"

Her voice. "Tom?"

"Yes?"

"Good night, darling." She hung up.

Once again I found myself humming in the shower. I went to sleep thinking of her.

She must have changed her mind again. During the three days that followed, she gave me, in cool and precise tones, the answers to my questions. She refused to go out with me. I began to run out of questions. I had become an expert on James Fosting. I knew his shirt size, brand of toothpaste and next dental appointment.

On the fourth day, she broke down.

We were awkward with each other during dinner, with more things being said with our eyes than with our empty words.

Then we got in the car and, as I drove out of town, she leaned her head against the back of the seat. Her blond hair was tossed by the wind. We didn't talk.

I found a secluded spot, and she came into my arms with a little sob that started deep in her throat. When I kissed her, I felt the tears on her cheeks. It wasn't the sort of kiss I was used to. It was sort of a dedication. There's no better word.

In my arms, she looked up at me and said, "Who are you and what do you want?"

I held her tight and smiled down at her. "I'm the guy who is writing a book. Remember me?"

She looked up at me, her eyes grave in the moonlight, and shook her head from side to side. "No, Tom. You're not writing a book. Your publishers have never heard of you. No man named Al Justin has ever worked for them."

I sat very still, and something inside of me turned to ice. I had guessed the reactions of Fosting, but I hadn't taken into account the emotional reflexes of a woman.

Before I could answer, she said, "I don't want anything to hurt him, Tom."

"Who wants to hurt him?" I said.

"I think you do. You were at home in that gambling place, Tom. You were at home with those people. I—I don't know what to think. There's something fine and clean and decent about Jim Fosting. And there's something about you as black as the grave."

It jolted me. I tried to laugh it off. "You make me sound like a fiend!"

"Maybe you are, Tom," she said softly.

"Then why are you here?" I asked her, tightening my arms to show her what I meant.

Her voice was broken. "I don't know, Tom. I don't know. I don't trust you and I don't love you and yet I can't help . . ."

I tilted her chin up and kissed her again. She was eager in my arms, and a dull roaring obscured my hearing. I was conscious only of her, and then, as from a great distance, I could hear her saying, half moan, half sob, "No—no—no—no . . ."

I fought my way back to sanity and opened the car door. I stood out in the night, breathing in the cool air in great gulps. When I turned and smiled at her, her face was pale but composed.

"Thank you," she said in a little-girl voice.

I knew it was time to go back. There was work to do. I left her at her door, kissed her lightly on the lips and walked back out to the waiting car.

Chowder had bribed his way into my room. He was sitting on the bed, waiting for me. One of the punks he collects was standing by the bureau, cleaning his nails with my file.

After I shut the door, Chowder said, "The boss thought you were taking too long, Wally. He wants it for tomorrow."

"Okay, he gets it for tomorrow. Bright and early," I said.

Chowder liked the plan I outlined. The best plans are the simple ones. This was simpler than most. Three blocks from the hotel was a small freight depot. Big

279

trucks. Fosting left the hotel at seven sharp every morning. To get to the City Hall, he walked down a street with a narrow sidewalk, walled with red brick buildings.

At a quarter to seven there was only one man in the freight depot, a driver who came to hook his tractor onto a trailer full of groceries.

The plan was to get into the freight yard, sap the driver, hoist him into the cab and time it to move up over the sidewalk and crush Fosting against the bricks. The man handling it, which would be me, could then pull the unconscious driver over under the wheel, slip out and make like he was a witness.

The driver's lack of memory would be taken to be the result of concussion. Shock amnesia. Routine accident. Too bad.

Chowder questioned me in detail. The punk filed his nails as he listened. I explained how the man with the sap could hide just inside the freight-yard gate and lay it gently over the driver's ear as he came in. He'd never be seen.

All the time I was telling Chowder, I was thinking of Janet. She was a clean kid, a good kid. Fosting, in spite of the age difference, would be right for her.

But there wouldn't be any more Fosting. And if there was the slightest slip, she knew enough to point the finger right at me. And that wasn't good.

Chowder had a bottle and he kept nipping at it. He told me his room was right down the hall.

I couldn't stop thinking of Janet, of the smell of her hair and the taste of her lips.

"What's the matter with you?" Chowder asked. "You nervous?"

I was pacing around. I stopped and grinned at him. "Should I be?"

"I don't know. You look edgy to me, pal. I hope you can handle this picnic okay. The front office wouldn't want any slips."

"But you wouldn't mind, would you?"

"What the hell does that mean?"

"You'd like to see me nailed for it, wouldn't you, Chowder?"

He sulked. "Ah, shove it, Wally."

He sat on the bed and I could see that he was getting an idea. It was slow coming to him, and he had to nibble on it for some time. Then, when he had it set, he looked up at me without expression.

"You're too nervous for the job, Wally," he said.

I got it right away. "That's right. Things weren't going good. You came down here. Poor old Wally had a good plan lined up, but no guts. So you took over. Yep, Wally is all right for dreaming up things, but no follow-through. That means Wally wouldn't ever fit into a responsible position like yours. Very cute. The point is, Chowder, how do you make it stick?"

Like a sucker, I had let the punk ease around behind me. I caught the signal that Chowder gave him, I ducked, and the sap nearly tore my ear off. I spun and he gave it to me, backhand across my mouth. I felt the teeth give as I dropped toward the floor. I never felt myself hit the floor.

When I came out of it, I was on the bed. Chowder was in the chair. His jaw sagged open and he was snoring. My ankles were tied together and my wrists were tied to the two bedposts at the head of the bed. Some kind character had stuffed a pair of my soiled socks in my mouth and tied them in place with a necktie. One end of a sock stuck out just far enough so I could see the pattern when I looked down my nose.

My head hurt just enough so that I knew the punk had sapped me again as I was falling.

Chowder slept like he'd had a lot of practice. I had a lot of time to think. And none of the thoughts were good. I knew that Chowder wouldn't do the job himself. He'd get the punk to do it. Then he'd pay off the punk and say he did it. If it went wrong, the punk would be on a limb and Chowder would be out of town.

The organization would never forgive me after a foul-up like that. I'd never be paid more than muscle rates.

And yet, those reasons didn't seem to be enough for

the way I felt. I felt dirty all the way through—as dirty as that pair of socks that kept me from waking up Chowder.

The feeling of being dirty was all tied up with Janet Calder. It was as though I had been living in a box and she had torn off one wall and let some light in so I could see my own pigpen.

There aren't any other words to explain it.

I stayed right there, thinking thoughts that hurt, until, as the windows started to get gray with dawn and the light from the lamp began to look watery and pale, there was the sound of a key in the lock, and the punk came in. He was a dark kid, with a weak mouth and long sideburns.

He saw that my eyes were open and he said, "Good morning, Glory!"

I got a look at his eyes and saw that he was stoned. Chowder was a damn fool to use a snowbird for that kind of a deal.

He shook Chowder, and the broad white face slowly came back to life, the eyes squinting at the light, the little upside-down U of a mouth working as though there was a bad taste inside.

"Whatsa time?" he demanded.

"Six. I just got back from the freight yard. I can get in okay. Everything set?"

"Sure. Get on your horse. Don't let the driver see you when you sap him. You saw the street. And I showed you the picture of Fosting. Cruise along behind him until the street is empty. Then go in fast, Joey."

Joey left. Chowder squinted at me and heaved himself out of the chair. He tested the neckties he had used to tie my wrists. Fifteen-dollar ties. And he had soaked them in water to get the knots tight enough. He cuffed me alongside the head, making my ear ring.

Then he went into the bathroom and pulled the door shut. I pulled hard, but those were good ties.

They hadn't tied my ankles to the footboard. They had just tied them together.

I swung my legs up over my head until I was standing

on the back of my neck. I got my toes on the headboard and pushed. The headboard was a good foot from the wall. They had moved the bed out, apparently, to fasten the knots and hadn't pushed it back.

I got my numb fingers wrapped around the posts.

As I pushed with my legs, wood splintered and with a sudden, startling crash the whole pillow end of the bed dropped onto the floor.

I rolled up onto my feet, bringing the headboard with me. I held it above my head. I struggled for balance, made one hop toward the bathroom door. It was a good thing the room was small.

The bathroom door swung open and a startled Chowder ran out. I swung down with all my strength and the edge of the headboard hit him right at where his hairline would have been if he'd had hair on top.

He went back into the bathroom faster than he had come out. He slid across the short tiled space and piled up half under the john. I turned sideways to get the headboard into the bathroom and hopped in. When I got close enough to him, I jumped up in the air and came down on his face with my heels. It had to be that way because my ankles were tied together. The bad footing spilled me, and I hurt my back as I fell.

I soon found out that I couldn't roll back up onto my feet in that restricted space. On my fanny, I inched over to the sink, reached up and knocked my razor off the shelf above the sink, using the leg of the headboard. It took me a long time to get my numb fingers to work properly so that I could open the razor. The blade fell out. I managed to pick it up, wedge it on end in a crack between two of the tiles. In the process of slashing the damp necktie, I took a piece out of my wrist.

With one hand free, I cut the other one loose, and freed my ankles.

Chowder had stopped worrying about this world. I weigh two hundred and five. Being too eager to keep him out of action for a little while, I had put him out for a long, long while—forever.

By the time I was ready to leave, it was ten minutes of

seven. Knowing Chowder's habits, I felt around his pulpy middle, and felt the hard butt of the belly gun that he kept wedged under his belt. It had no trigger guard, no sights and a barrel about an inch and a half long. But it threw a .38 slug.

I was telling myself that nobody was going to queer me with the front office by knocking off somebody in the method that I was going to use.

But I wasn't believing the words I was telling myself.

They had made me stand to hear the fat jury foreman yell out the verdict. Even though I knew what it was going to be, it still sounded much worse than any words are supposed to sound.

The lawyer assigned to me had done his best, but there was too little for him to work with. Even if I'd told him the whole story, he wouldn't have had enough to go on. He was willing, but he knew when he was licked.

Something was holding me up, but I didn't know what it was.

The case had been pretty simple. I'd made no attempt to cover my tracks as far as Chowder was concerned. A splinter of his cheekbone had been driven down into the brain. My heel marks were on the flesh of his face, and they had found blood on my heels.

There had even been witnesses to the second murder. Fosting was a half block ahead of me. The big red tractor-trailer had come roaring along, not too fast. Not too fast to keep me from angling over and jumping up on the driver's side.

Ahead was Fosting. He didn't turn until the slugs from the .38, at close range, broke Joey's head like a rotten melon.

Fosting turned as the truck bore down on him. I saw the comprehension, the sudden realization in his face . . .

A man with sweat stains at his armpits came over to me and took my arm and urged me gently toward the door where I was supposed to go out. The judge had finished mumbling over me. The jury faces had a sick, yet satisfied look. "I sure hate to do this but I'm doing my duty." That kind of look.

He was urging me toward the door over at the side. Beyond that door was the long corridor, the stairs, the short sidewalk and the waiting police car. And a few months beyond the police car, hazy, and yet promising to grow much clearer, was the picture of a squat chair, a sullen, brooding chair.

A waiting chair.

At the doorway, I turned and looked back at the courtroom. Every day of the trial she had been there. Alone. White, white face and blue-violet eyes. Wide, wide eyes. Lips I had kissed.

Maybe I looked toward her for three seconds before the guy got my arm again. Beside her was the lean leathery face of James Fosting. He had made it for the last day. The kiss-off. I wondered what he was thinking. He knew that I had wrenched the truck out of the course that would have killed him. Yet he had to cover me, to force me to drop Chowder's belly gun onto the asphalt.

They were sitting very close together. Her lips formed a word. "Thanks."

And suddenly it seemed as if a lot of things were worthwhile.

But you can't go soft. Out in the hallway the guard offered me a cigarette. I said, "Don't smoke, friend. I've got none of the minor vices."

As usual, the tired old gag worked. And I was in a slot to give it a little more impact than it usually had.

He caught on and he repeated the tag line. "None of the minor vices." The other guard was waiting in the hall.

Between the two of them I walked down toward the stairs.

He was giggling so that his fat belly shook. "This guy's got none of the minor vices, Harry," he said, gasping, because, to him, it seemed like a very good joke.

The High Gray
Walls of Hate

THE NIGHT HEAT was a violence that reflected up from the pavements, bounced off the stone walls of the city. Sleep was a thing to be trapped and captured on the fire escape, under the still trees in the park. The tires of the cars made a ripping, sticky sound on the asphalt.

James Forbes walked slowly through the streets of the city. He carried the coat to the suit they had given him over his arm. The cheap white shirt was plastered to his body, outlining the lean strength of his chest and back. His sleeves were rolled up tightly over brown biceps. He wore no hat.

Over his head the neon hummed and flickered. Bar and Grill . . . Eat . . . All Legal Beverages . . . Hostesses . . . Try Your Luck . . . Eat . . . Cocktail Lounge . . . Topless Barmaids . . .

A haze had come in from the river with the night heat, making molten halos around the signs.

There was no trace of expression on his face. They had taught him not to show expression. They had taught him that a trace of expression lands you in solitary, if you're a new one.

The fields had been long and flat and hot, the rows of vegetables stretching into infinity, wavering in the dance of heat waves. The calluses were as hard as leather on his palms.

"Yes, Mr. Commissioner, the prison commissary is

286

almost entirely self-sustaining. Except for the staples like sugar, of course. It does them good to work out in the open air. Yes, you could call it a release."

Across James Forbes's temple was a fine white line. A prison screw, sun-touched, had yanked the hoe away from him and struck him down with it. He remembered and could taste again the blood and earth that caked his lips.

The people of the city sat on the high steps of the houses that stood, shoulder to shoulder, beyond the sidewalk. The doughy women fanned themselves and the men drank the cool beer, wiping their mouths with the backs of laborers' hands. The only notice they took of James Forbes was to wait until he passed before spitting out onto the sidewalk. Just a young guy walking. That's all. Just walking through the night heat. Probably been stood up by his girl. Got a nice suntan—you notice?

But there were a few smart ones who sat and drank the beer on the high steps. They saw the stuff of which the suit was made and knew where it came from. They saw the cut of the cheap white shirt and remembered the stink of the prison laundry. They saw the brown face with no trace of expression. Those smart ones drank deeply of their beer, remembered the gray of concrete and uniform, the blind misery of the sun . . . and they were silent.

"Whadya stop talkin' for, Joe? Whassa matter, honey?"
The measured snarl. "Shaddup, woman!"
"Sure, Joe. Gee, I ain't done nothin'. Whassa matter?"
"Shaddup, I said!"

The contemptuous retreat, climbing up through the floors of ammonia salts and the stink of many people to lie sleepless and sweating on the gray sheets and remember the sound of a thousand feet in prison shoes stamping to a halt before the cell doors. The bitter-bright clang of the closing doors. The snug chunk of the lugs entering the doorframes as the screw on the tier spun the big wheel.

Lie in the heat with the sweat running across your ribs and dig your fingers into your palms and curse them.

Remember the look of the young one that went by. Remember his "just out" look. Remember when they gave you your name back and every cop on every corner was a guy who ached to smash what was left of your teeth down your throat.

James Forbes walked the night streets, his feet scuffing through the candy wrappers, the chewed cigar butts, the cellophane off the cigarettes, the clotted spittle, and somehow he kept his eyes straight ahead and resisted the impulse to look behind him.

A woman with frizzed blond hair and a body that sagged under her bright cheap dress stepped out of a doorway and said, "Wanna party, chum?"

Barely moving his lips, he said one word.

As he walked slowly on, she screamed obscenities after him. Two boys leaning against a darkened storefront laughed at her. She turned on them as Forbes walked on. Behind him, he heard her laugh.

He walked and he heard George's heavy voice. George, round and happy and doing a twenty for second degree. George was back there behind the walls and he'd be right there for ten more years. I'll be forty then, Forbes thought with a sense of shock, and felt as though he should do something for George somehow to make it easier.

Then he could hear George's soft and heavy voice. "You're jus' heah for a little time, boy. Just a little time. But they somehow suck the guts out of you in a little time. Why, when I come in I was goin' a head back as soon as I got out an' I was goin' to separate the head from the neck of my fine fren 'at turned me in. I surely was, boy. Now I'm one scared boy. When I get out, I'm walkin' that chalk line. I surely am. I won't be no trouble to noooobody. No sir! I'm leavin' my guts in heah. So'll you, boy. So'll you."

Forbes remembered that he had said, "Not for me, George. I was framed into this place and I'm going to get even."

George had said, "Maybe you was framed, boy. Maybe in kind of a funny kind a way everybody in heah was framed—whether they did what they say they did or not. But you won't have the guts to get even, boy. I tell you now. You left your guts all over them fields out there in the sun with them screws a-standin' and a-watchin' while you spewed 'em out. You'll see, boy.''

He walked through the night streets and clenched his fists and felt the muscles of his arms and shoulders writhe under the skin. He smiled once, his lips flattening against his teeth. They put him up there behind those walls and he grew the muscles that would smash them. He tightened his fists harder, felt the calluses under his fingertips.

Ahead was the street. The well-remembered street. He crossed diagonally and walked down the far side, walking more slowly, alert for any sign of someone who might be watching . . . and waiting . . . They would know that he was out. They would know.

He stopped on the corner, stood absolutely still and looked back the way he had come. A couple passed, their arms around each other's waists, the girl giggling at something the boy said in a low, hoarse tone. A taxi rocketed by, the springs smacking against the frame as it hit the potholes in the asphalt.

Forbes crossed the street, walked back the way he had come. The house was just the same, a battered brownstone with a massive front door, always unlocked. Mrs. Lesnovack would be asleep in the room just off the entrance hall. The street was empty. He hurried up to the door, pushed it open far enough to slip inside and let it close softly.

The twenty-watt bulb left shadows in the corners of the front hall. He looked up the wide stairway. The house was asleep. He held his breath, heard the sing of blood in his ears, the steady fast thud of his pulse.

Up the stairs. Quietly. Watch the third step—three years ago it creaked. Stay close to the railing. Good. No light on the second floor. Down the corridor smelling of age and dust and the disorderly lives of a thousand transients. The girl who drank the iodine lived in that room. The trumpet player lived in the next one.

It was the room beyond that that mattered.

She lived in that room.

He stood by the door, suddenly afraid that she would be out. His fear was a tangible, chilling thing.

Tap, tap, tap. Softly. Just loud enough to wake her. Not loud enough to wake anyone else. *Tap, tap, tap.* How will she look with sleep misting her eyes, with her golden hair falling to her shoulders? *Tap, tap, tap.* She should have heard that. She should be coming to the door. She wouldn't open it. You don't open doors at night if you are a girl and if you live in a place like Mrs. Lesnovack's.

The creak of the floorboard. Sleepy voice. Plaintive. "Who is it?"

Lips close against the stained wood of the door. "Open up. It's Jim."

Hands that fumble with the chain, the door swung wide. Arms high around his neck, the scent of hair against his cheek as he stumbled into the room, shutting the door behind him.

Her broken voice said, lips touching his face, "Oh, Jim! Jim! I didn't know you'd get here so soon."

She left him abruptly, saying, "I've got to look at you."

"No lights!" he whispered softly. "Someone may be watching your window."

She was a vague whiteness against the black. She walked to the window and raised the dark shade. On a building a half block away a sign blinked on and off, on and off. Stanley Beer. . . Stanley Beer. . . Stanley Beer . . .

With the shade up there was a second's space of light in the room, constantly interrupted. In its light, he saw her moving over to the bed. On and off. On and off. It gave her movement an odd quality, as in a very old motion picture—or a penny arcade.

He sat on the bed and held her hand tightly.

"Was it too awful, my darling?" she whispered.

"It's over now. It would have been—easier if you'd come to see me once in a while."

"I know. I know, darling. I should have. But I couldn't bear the thought of seeing you in that horrible place. I'd remember it all my life. It was better that I didn't come. I wrote you all the time. Don't you think it was better?"

"I guess so," he admitted. "You wrote happy letters."

Hotly she said, "What would you have had me write? Tragic things, stained with my tears?"

"No. No. I only meant that I liked the letters. They helped me wait for now."

"I couldn't believe that such a thing had happened to us, Jim. To us! When I sat in that terrible courtroom, heard that horrible man say, 'Five years,' I thought I'd die right there. I really did. As it was, I didn't stop crying for three days."

"How is Besterson doing?"

"Why—all right, I suppose." Her hand tightened on his. "What are you going to do about it?"

The light, on and off, on and off, flickered across her pale face, upturned. Lips red. Shoulders smooth. Pale lace at her throat. Clean lines of throat, of brow.

He shrugged. "Do? What is there to do? I was his accountant. He was hard up. He robbed himself, phoned the police, told them I had the combination to the safe. They came to my room and woke me up. They found bills with the right serial numbers in the side pocket of my jacket. Open and shut. Cut and dried. What is there to do?"

He felt her hand relax. "I'm glad you're not—going after him," she said softly.

"You wouldn't like that, would you?"

"Of course not, darling. It would just mean more trouble. A lot more trouble." He moved closer to her, her head on his shoulder, the warm smell of her filling his nostrils, the sweet, aching smell of her after so long, after so many years.

She stroked the hand that was around her shoulder. Soft woman-fingers. Gentle. Sweet and gentle.

The light flicked across them, across the taut lines that cut down close to the corners of his mouth. No expression on the brown face. No life in the deep-set eyes.

He said softly, "Three years gives you a long time to think."

"You can forget it now." The soft answer. The warm invitation.

"It's hard to forget. How much do you make, Sally?"

"Hundred and forty a week. It's not hard work. I get along."

He reached his left hand over, touched her gown, said, "The fabric is smooth and soft."

"You've been a long time away from such things." Moments of silence, a small tension coming from somewhere and building. Building. The soft fingers stroking his hand again.

"You always know expensive things, Sally. You sense them. On the tier underneath mine was Hans Reichert, craftsman. Fine paper—engraving. He fingered the strip of paper I tore from one of your letters. Told me it was the best money could buy."

The stroking of her hand faltered for a moment. "It was a gift. Oh, an aunt or somebody, I've forgotten."

"I thought you broke with all of your relatives?"

"Not all of them. An aunt and I still exchange gifts."

"If there's only one, why can't you remember?"

"Why do we have to bicker about such a pointless thing, Jim? You're out now, and you're back with me."

"I'm sorry," he said softly.

More silence and the tension was there between them. It could be felt, tasted.

"You know what they used to do with the papers we got?" he asked. "They used to cut out all the crime news, robberies, murders. Give us the rest. Said it wouldn't hurt us to read the rest. You always wondered what had been in those empty spaces. Over a year ago I saw a racetrack picture. Showed the crowd at the races. Besterson was there—with a girl."

The stroking fingers stopped.

He said, "Her back was to the camera. Couldn't recognize her."

The High Gray Walls of Hate

Her fingers moved again and he felt the deepness of the breath she took.

"A man's habits are funny. You notice that sort of thing in prison. You think about them a lot. Now, some men, when they're ready for bed, they stand in front of the bureau and empty every last thing out of their pockets and hang up their suits all right and proper. Me, I just toss things around. I guess I told you that once. Warned you about what an awful guy I'd be to live with. That was before—before they caught me."

She stopped stroking his hand, put her hand down at her side. When the light flicked on again, he saw that her eyes were wide, that she looked up at the dark ceiling.

He continued. "I always had a good head for liquor. Never believed in mixing my drinks. I guess the only time I ever did was the night out with you, Sally. The night before they came and got me."

"Why are you talking about this, Jim?" she said loudly.

"Shh! You don't want to wake up the people. I'm talking because it's nice to talk to people when you haven't been alone with anybody for a long, long time. That's the worst of those places. The fact that you're never alone."

Her breathing was easier, but he saw in the next flick of the light that her lips were compressed.

"You know, Sally, Besterson is a coward. Never fired people himself. Always had somebody else do it. Scared to death. Afraid of going broke. Afraid of getting sick. Always worrying. I figured he was going broke a week or so before I—went to jail. You know, it was funny. For the month before I went to jail, he spent a lot of time out of the office. An awful lot of time. Let me see, it started about the time you lost your job, didn't it?"

She moved quickly away from him.

He caught her shoulders and pulled her back beside him. "What's the matter, dearest?" he said.

"Get it over with!" she demanded, her voice hoarse.

"Sure, dearest. I'll get it over with. You met Besterson when you used to wait for me outside the office. You

293

always had your eye on the best chance. All that time Besterson was out of the office, he was with you. You got me tight. You knew my habits. You planted those big bills in my pocket, knowing that I didn't keep money or cigarettes or keys in that pocket. You made me a sitting duck, darling. They still wonder where I hid the rest of the money that I didn't take.

"And then Besterson got scared. You were the link. He knows I'm smart. If you moved out of here and moved into the big time, I'd know the answer. So he bought you your pretties and told you to stay here. Expensive writing paper. Fancy nightgowns like the one you're wearing. Sure, the girl in the picture had her back turned to me, but I recognized the back.

"I know. Besterson is hiding and trembling someplace and waiting for the word from you. You're supposed to get in touch with him and tell him whether I've gotten wise to what you two did to me. Only you could have planted that money on me. Only you, darling."

She drew a deep and shuddering breath. The light flicked on and off, on and off. In a husky tone, she said, "You're sick. You're talking crap."

"You're right. It was rotten." His hand slid past her face, and his hard fingers fondled her throat.

"No! No, Jim!" she gasped, as his fingers tightened. Then she could say no more. Her nails tore at his face, at his hand. She strained her body up in a hard arc like some strange bow and dropped back. Again and again. Her wide eyes bulged. There was no sound except the tiny tearing noises of her nails in his flesh.

He put his lips close to her ear. "Tell me where Besterson is."

He released the pressure gently. She sucked the air into her lungs and tried to scream. He tightened down again, careful of his anger, nourishing it, knowing that if he released the anger his fingers would crush her throat and she'd never breathe or speak again. He turned his head away as she dug for his eyes.

"Where's Besterson?" he asked, lips close to her ear. Slowly he released the pressure. Her breath rattled as she coughed, holding her throat. "Mountain Lodge. Near Star Lake," she gasped.

"This is it," he said softly. His fingers closed on her throat again. "Good-by, Sally. Good-by, dearest. Good-by, you female Judas."

She found new strength in her terror. But his fingers were tight. Tighter. Tighter. . .

He stood by the window and the light from the sign flashed across his face. Staccato. Pulse of a mechanical city. Pulse of a heat-sodden city, counterpoint for the littered sidewalks, the stains of sweat under the arms of the doughy women, the foam wiped from lips with the back of a hand.

He seemed to hear the voice of George, close to his ear, "But you won't have the guts to get even, boy. You wait and see."

He turned toward the bed, full of a bleak weariness, as though a spring, wound one notch tighter during each day of imprisonment, had suddenly spun free of the ratchets, lay sodden inside him, without tension.

She sat on the edge of the bed, still coughing, gasping and massaging her throat. When the light hit her face he saw the silver streaks of tears across the soft cheeks, the disordered froth of pale hair. With each inhalation, her breath made a rattling sound in her throat, like a parody of a snore. He picked up his coat, stood by the bed, the coat slung over one shoulder, looking down at her as the near-death noises slowly stopped.

She looked up at him and, in the light, her face was cold—the face on a silver coin, the face on a billboard in winter. "You're going after Besterson," she said. It wasn't a question. It was a statement and said in the way she would have said, "He is dead."

He considered her statement. He thought of his hard fists smashing Besterson's soft face, the blood gouting from the split flesh, the eyes puffing shut, the broken mouth working in a froth of red.

"No," he said softly.

She straightened her shoulders and there was contempt in her face. "You couldn't kill me," she said proudly. "You know why? Because you still love me."

He stared at the pale oval of her face, shocked by what she had said. "Love you?" he exclaimed. "You!"

It came then. It started as a small spot of delirium deep inside him, spiraling up through his chest, exploding into laughter at his lips. Loud, raucous, pealing laughter.

Somehow he found the doorknob, let himself out into the dark hall. The hoarse wonderful sound of his great laughter boomed along the corridor, blasted the silent air of the stairwell. He clutched his middle with one hand and caught at the railings with the other.

Slowly he managed the stairs, whooping and gasping in an odd glee that was almost too much to bear. The door slammed behind him and he was out in the night heat of the city, weak and panting.

James Forbes walked off through the night streets, a pain in his side, his lips still twisting, and in his heart he knew that he was at last free.

He could hate the two of them no longer.

Hate was a prison with walls that touch the gray sky.

He was finally free.

Unmarried Widow

HE WAS SITTING in a place called Stukey's on Primrose Street, and he had been there most of the afternoon, alone at a table for two, a table with wire legs and the black scar tissue of cigarette burns. At the far end of the bar, a little clot of beer drinkers were making a two-dollar investment cover a whole afternoon of TV. Max dimly realized that they were so hard up for conversation they even watched the puppets on the late-afternoon kid shows.

He wasn't drinking hard and heavy. But he was working on it. Somehow it had become important to achieve a state of remoteness. Whenever he felt himself sliding back into the uncomfortable reality of the present, he raised one finger and Stukey came out from behind the bar with another shot.

Three days before, the managing editor had climbed up onto a desk in the newsroom and addressed the whole working staff. His words had been as depressing as if he'd played a fire hose on the crowd. The sense of it was that the bankroll had faded, the promised backers had eeled out and thank you all so much for your loyal service and I hope you all find wonderful jobs within the next eleven minutes.

Max Raffidy sat and drank with a careful effort to maintain a detached state that was neither drunk nor sober. Because when he veered toward soberness he began to think that there were no jobs left in this town, in his town, and he'd have to hit the sticks. And when the shots came along a shade too fast he wanted to go out and punch noses. Being a large citizen with heavy bones and having a background of alley fights in this same city when he was a kid, he knew that if he went out nose hunting, he would land in a cage.

He could have taken his sorrows to one of the bars frequented by his fellow sufferers, but he did not wish to weep on shoulders, nor did he want tears on the lapels of his own tweeds, so he bundled up his misery and disgust and had taken it to Stukey's—not to drown it, but just to make it swim a little.

He sat alone, and with his big blunt fingers, he peeled paper matches down so that they looked like little people. These he gave names to, the names of the people whose job it should have been to keep the *Chronicle* running. He laid them, one at a time, with a certain dedication, in the green glass ashtray with the chip out of the rim, and lit their little green heads with the butt of his cigarette, watching them flare up and writhe in unutterable torment.

He was vaguely considering taking his troubles to another bar when the raggedy screen door flapped and banged and the girl came in. She stood a few feet inside the door. The corners of her mouth were pulled down in such an odd way that Max told himself that here was a person with even more trouble than he had.

She saw him then, and her face lit up like a kid's pumpkin. She ran the three steps to the table for two, collapsed into the chair opposite him. He had his arm outstretched on the table. She grabbed his forearm with both hands, her fingers digging strongly into him. She laid her forehead down against his arm, the breath shuddering out of her.

Two large and solid men in dark suits came in and stood a few feet behind her, looking down at her, looking inquisitively at Max.

"Oh, Jerry! Jerry, darling," the girl said, her voice somehow thick and twisted.

Max had been around a sufficiently long time so that

he was about to say, "Take her along, boys." He recognized one of them as Billy Shaw, a district man.

But there was a sudden hotness on his thick wrist and he knew that a tear had fallen there. Somehow this made it all quite different. Tears were oddly in the mood of this day of unemployment, this sultry spring day.

He left his arm right where it was, with the warm pressure of her against it. He said mildly, "Something we can do for you boys?"

Shaw looked at him and said, "Seems she called you Jerry. Wouldn't you be Max Raffidy that used to drop into precinct, reporting police?"

"It's her special name for me," Max said.

"Don't go wise with us, Raff. What's her name?"

"If you want her name, let's do it right, Shaw. Let's all go right down and book her."

Shaw gave him a look of baffled disgust. "You people know too much. There's no charge, Raffidy. She was reported acting funny on the street. Crying and carrying on."

"She's fine now. All my women cry and carry on when they can't be with me."

Stukey came over drying his hands on his apron. "I'd just as soon not have no trouble here, gentlemen."

"Keep her off the street," Shaw snapped. He nudged his running mate and together they walked heavily out.

"Bring the lady a brandy, Stuke," Max said. Stukey shrugged and went back behind the bar.

Now I have a tramp on my hands, Max thought. Sir Lancelot Raffidy roars in on his white horse. She seemed content to make a permanent pillow of his arm. In fact, the arm threatened to go to sleep. The kitteny whine of the woman pretending to be a puppet had covered up the little conversation with Shaw. It still made a certain amount of privacy possible.

"Hey," Max said softly. He burrowed with his other hand, got a crooked finger under her chin, gently eased her up.

Her hands slid down so that she held his big hand with

both of hers, gave him the warmest smile he had seen in many a moon.

Stukey brought the brandy and plodded away. Max gave the girl the Raffidy evaluation. Silly spring hat, worn a bit awry. Hair worn too long for fashion, long and blond and curled under at the ends. Not harsh parched blond. Soft and natural. Short straight nose, unplucked brows, gray eyes, damp with tears, gray-purple smudges of weariness under the eyes. A young mouth, warm and somehow crumpled. As though from recent hurt. Pale, with a smudge on her cheek and the side of her nose.

The tiny bugles blew inside Max. This was no tramp. This might have a very legitimate news interest. Then he smiled wearily as he realized that even if there was a news interest, there was no place to phone it in.

Obviously the kid—she wasn't over twenty-two—had been having a rough time. The side of her hand was scraped raw and her hair was tangled.

The gray eyes bothered him. She smiled right at him, but when he looked into her eyes there was an emptiness there: as though she were smiling, not at Max, but at somebody sitting right behind Max. A faintly creepy dish, this one.

"Drink your brandy," he said.

"You know I don't drink, Jerry."

Max grunted as though somebody had shoved an elbow into the pit of his stomach. "Baby, look around. They've gone. And you need the brandy."

She let go of his hand, picked up the shot glass. "Right down?"

"Down the hatch."

She knocked it back, thumped the glass down, gasping, coughing, strangling, new tears in her eyes. "Fooo!" she said.

He watched color come back into her cheeks. "Sit right here," he said. Stukey was watching too curiously. He went up to the bar, paid the tab, went back to the table and got her and walked her out into the late-afternoon sun. She clung to his arm. Usually Max did not care for the clingers, but this one made him feel very masterful. She was taller than he had thought, and she wasn't too steady on her feet.

"Where are we going, Jerry?" she asked. Her voice had the small and faintly faraway tinge that her eyes had—as though she talked to someone a few feet behind Max.

He stopped twenty feet from the door of Stukey's and said, "Let's straighten this out, kid. I'm not Jerry."

She moved away from him. Her eyes widened. Her mouth began to work. She began to make a hoarse moaning sound. Max had seen many ladies putting on an act. This was no act.

She looked as though she were about to run from him, screaming. He took three steps toward her, grabbed her shoulders and shook her gently. "Hey," he said. "Sure I'm Jerry. I was kidding, baby."

Right in the street, in the sunlight, she came into his arms, saying hoarsely, "Don't do that to me again, Jerry. Please don't."

Some urchins witnessed the deal, and did considerable hooting and whistling.

Max walked down the street with her and he felt oddly like a man juggling a hand grenade after the pin had been pulled. He had begun to feel a certain responsibility. So, if he had to be Jerry, he had to be Jerry.

"When did you eat last, kid?" he said.

"I . . . I don't know."

Hiram's was two blocks away. Not worth taxi fare. They took a booth in the back and she wanted her steak medium well. She ate without taking her eyes from Max's face and he began to think that this Jerry was one lucky character.

Finally he had a play figured out. He grinned at her, his lips a bit stiff, and said, "Honey, we'll pretend we just met, hey?"

"That would be nice."

"Glad to meet you, miss. My name's Jerry Glockenspiel."

"Silly! Your name's Jerry Norma. I'm Marylen Banner." She gravely shook his hand.

Max frowned. He said absently, "Hi, Marylen." The name Jerry Norma had rung a tiny bell way back in his mind. Jerry Norma had, at one time or another, been news. Not big news. Something about the size of a page three quarter column.

In a low voice that shook with emotion, she said, "Why did you do it, Jerry? Why did you run out on me like that?"

Max sighed inwardly. Boy ditches girl. Girl goes off the beam. Tired old story. Better get along with her, turn her over for observation.

"I shouldn't have done it."

"You were just pretending, weren't you?"

"Sure. Just pretending."

She said softly, her head tilted on one side, "The lights, the way they came on so quickly. And that concrete floor. The black drops. You walked away and the lights came on and then all that noise like thunder. You doubled over and fell so slowly, Jerry. And then—when I ran to you—"

She stopped and put the back of her hand to her forehead, her shadowed eyes closed. With the smudges washed off, she was delicately beautiful.

Max shut his jaw hard. He ground out his cigarette and, keeping his voice level and calm, he said, "You thought I was shot, eh?"

Her eyes snapped open. "Shot? I—I—can't remember."

"I walked away from you and the lights came on."

"I think you left me sitting in the car, Jerry. Yes, in the car."

"Then the car was inside. A garage, wasn't it?"

"Now it's fading away, Jerry. I can't remember. I can't."

Suddenly she looked around, at the tabletop, at the floor under the bench. "My purse! I've lost my purse!"

"You didn't have it when you found me in that bar,

Marylen. Can you remember where you were before that?"

"I don't know, Jerry. I was looking for you for a long time."

He realized that she spoke well, that her clothes were smart, though not extremely expensive or shining new.

"I'll take you home, Marylen. Where do you live?"

"Please stop teasing me, Jerry. Please. I'm too tired to take very much."

Max stared at her. "Look, I just plain forgot where you were staying here."

"Don't you remember, Jerry? You met me at the train. We were going to find a hotel for me and then you said that when we were married I could move into your place. But my purse! All my money was in the purse. Everything."

"Now I remember. You came on the train from Chicago."

"Jerry, are you losing your mind? From New Orleans! When you wrote me I gave up my job and found another girl to take over my share of the apartment on Burgundy Street. And I came to you as fast as I could, darling."

Max ran a finger around the inside edge of his collar. "Sure, kid. Sure."

"What will we do?" she asked. "We checked all my things at the station and my baggage checks were in my purse."

"Maybe we could get in touch with your folks."

"You say such queer things, Jerry Norma. I told you what happened to my folks. It was so long ago that I hardly remember them. I told you about my guardian and how there was just enough money for school, and then nothing."

"What am I going to do with you?" Max asked helplessly.

"You have plenty of money, Jerry, darling. Find me a room and tomorrow we'll shop together for what I need—to be married in."

Suddenly she winced, leaned low over the table and said, "Jerry, I'm sick. I'm so sick . . ."

When he had the cab waiting outside, he went back to the table and got her. She leaned heavily against him, walked with her head down, eyes half closed. People stared at them with wry amusement, thinking that she was drunk.

He said to the driver, "Memorial Hospital, and snap it up."

But three blocks further on, he leaned forward and said, "Changed my mind. Take us to Bleecker Street."

He paid off the cab, walked her up the three steps, held her in his left arm while he got the key in the door. She collapsed completely inside the door, and he picked her up in his arms, carrying her like a child. Gruber, the superintendent-janitor, came out into the hall, stared at him, then grinned.

Max snapped, "Pick up her hat and hand it to me. Then get hold of my friend Doc Morrison across the street."

He stepped with her into the elevator as Gruber went out the front door. He had to put her on the floor while he got his door key and opened his front door. The tiny living room of his apartment was rancid with stale smoke, thick with dust. Through the open bedroom doorway he could see the unmade bed. He turned sideways to get her through the narrow door, her head hanging loosely, her arm swinging.

He grunted as he lowered her onto the bed. Then he went to the window, stood smoking a cigarette, his back to her, until he heard the knock on the door.

Morrison was young, dark, quick. He put his bag on the floor, went over to her, took her pulse. "What's wrong with her?"

"You're the doctor. She's not loaded, if that's what you mean."

"Then get out and shut the door."

Max sat in the armchair. He picked up a newspaper, found that he wasn't getting any sense out of the words. He flipped it aside.

In fifteen minutes Morrison came out, leaving the

bedroom door open. Max looked in, saw the girl was snoring softly.

Morrison looked angrily at Max and said, "Somebody gave that girl a hell of a beating."

"Beating?"

"Come here." Morrison led him into the bedroom, pulled her arm out from under the covers. There were two large purpled bruises between her elbow and shoulder. He said, "She's got a round dozen bruises like that. And look here." He rolled her head to one side, pulled the fine blond hair away from her ear. Behind her ear was a large, angry-looking lump. "That looks like she's been sapped. But I wouldn't know. She's suffering from the beating, from shock, maybe from a minor concussion. I gave her a shot of sedative. She'll sleep hard for twelve hours. There don't seem to be any broken bones. I'd like to get my hands on whoever treated that girl that way."

"That's a pleasure I would enjoy too, Doc," Max said gently.

"Twenty dollars, please. I'll stop in tomorrow and see how she is and see if we should take her down for X rays."

Morrison took the twenty and walked out, still angry, slamming the door behind him. Max walked back in and stood by the bed and looked down at her. In sleep her face was composed, childlike. Her blond hair was softly spread on the pillow.

He turned to the lightweight suit she had been wearing, went carefully through the two pockets. He found a balled-up handkerchief smelling faintly of perfume. Nothing else. Then he went over the labels. The shoes and suit had come from New Orleans, definitely. The other items could have.

He opened the window a bit further, looked down at her again, and said, "Honey, you're gradually becoming a burden."

Closing the door gently, he left the bedroom. He locked the apartment. The streetlights had just come on. The air was growing a bit more chill. At the corner, he swung onto a bus and took it down to within a half block of the *Examiner* office.

Townsend, on the desk, said, "Sorry, Raffidy, but we haven't—"

"This is something else, Bobby. I want to see if you got a clip on a citizen of this fair city named Jerry Norma. Jerome, I'd guess."

Townsend, relieved that Raffidy hadn't come about a nonexistent job, gave him the use of an empty desk and, within a few minutes, a copy boy brought a brown manila envelope from the morgue.

Ten minutes later Raffidy had a fair picture in his mind of a young man named Jerry Norma. In 1966, an alert gas station attendant had smashed the eighteen-year-old Norma with a wrench, while Norma was working on the till. He drew a one-to-three. Fifteen months with good behavior. In 1968, he had been implicated in the case against a car-theft ring. Case dismissed for lack of evidence. In 1971, he was under suspicion of having tried to bribe a member of the State Liquor License Board. No case. No trouble with the cops since that time. In 1975, listed as one of the "partners" in an enterprise called Valley Farms, Incorporated. Max knew the place. Riding horses. Whiskey sours for breakfast and a lot of fat gambling. A semiprivate club with the rumored reputation of being "protected."

In 1977, a paragraph about how Jerome Norma, acting as agent for the Concord Amusement Devices, had issued a statement to the effect that none of the equipment located near the public schools of the city was in any sense gambling equipment, but should be considered merely games of skill.

There was a cut with the paragraph. Max studied the picture. Yes, Norma would be about his size. A bit thinner. Same general coloring.

He knew the type. A rough kid who starts out like a chump then finds that you can work close to the letter of the law without actually stepping over. A rough kid who gets smarter and smarter, learning where the four-thousand-dollar convertibles and the plush apartments come from.

But where would the girl fit? He had heard that Concord Amusement Devices was a segment of a national organization. If Jerry Norma was high up in Concord, he could very well take business trips to New Orleans. Gambling was on the way back there. And, meeting Marylen, it was also probable that Jerry could fall for her. She wasn't what he was used to. She had—might as well admit it—more than a little charm and breeding.

He found a phone book, found a J. B. Norma listed. He signaled for an outside line, dialed the number given. The phone at the other end was picked up in the middle of the second ring. A cautious low voice said, "Yes?"

"Mr. Norma?"

"Isn't in. Who's this?"

"I had an appointment with him for five o'clock. He didn't keep it."

"No. He went out of town for a while."

"When will he be back?"

"I couldn't say. If you'll leave your name—"

"Are you a friend of his?"

"Yeah. He loaned me his apartment here until he gets back."

"This is about some—some equipment to be installed for me."

"Oh!" There was a pause. There was a distant sound of voices. Max listened intently, but with the newsroom noise around him, he couldn't catch what was said. The man came back on and said, "If it is in connection with the Concord Amusement Devices, friend, you get hold of Bill Walch tomorrow morning at the Concord offices. Know where they are?"

"On Madison."

"That's right."

Max hung up slowly. The girl had spoken of Jerry Norma falling over slowly in some place that could have been a garage. And now Jerry Norma was out of town. Way out, maybe. He knew of Bill Walch. Walch was also one of the partners in Valley Farms. A big jovial backslapping man of mysterious and varied interests.

He thanked Townsend, walked slowly out of the building. He grabbed a crosstown bus to Primrose, went on back to Stukey's. The crowd was a lot heavier and the place was thick with smoke. He wedged himself into a foot of space at the bar. A variety show was on video.

Stukey came along the bar, poured the shot and said, barely moving his lips, "You had callers."

"Same ones followed the girl?"

"Other side of the fence, lad. Very harsh types. They wanted the girl. All I knew was she left with a stranger."

"Thanks, Stuke."

"They went the same way you went when you left with her."

Max downed his drink, dropped the money on the bar and was out of the door, moving fast before he had thoroughly swallowed the rye. He kept on moving fast until he rounded the corner where Hiram's, bright with green neon, shone in the middle of the block. Two cabs were parked in the stand at the corner.

He went over to the first one. The driver snapped the door open. Max pushed it shut and said, "People have been bothering you with questions?"

"In a nasty way. Why?"

"They were tracking a couple who came out of Hiram's a little after five. Is that right?"

"Am I talking for free?"

"For whatever it turns out to be worth."

"Okay, so they wanted the couple. Vague on the guy but lots of detail on the woman. They let it be known they could be unhappy about it all. Joey saw 'em come out. The guy first to hail the hack, and then he went back and brought out this dish. Drunk, maybe. Or sick. Joey would have had the fare but his boiler didn't catch the first time and so a floater got the fare. These other nosy guys asked Joey about it until they got tired. Unless they can use cops, they can't trace it."

Max's sigh of relief came right up from his shoes, was expressed through his wallet. He went back to his apartment by bus. He had Gruber dig up a cot and install it in his small living room. In the meantime he went in, clicked on the bedside lamp and looked at the girl. She was breathing heavily and she hadn't changed position.

Max tipped Gruber, turned out the light and lay down on the cot, an ashtray on his stomach. He watched the pattern of the car lights across the ceiling for a time. Then he butted the cigarette, rolled over and was immediately asleep. He dreamed of someone coming up the stairs and it woke him up. He went into the bedroom, dug under the shirts, found the Jap automatic. Back in the living room, he went near the window and, in the glow of the streetlights, he jacked a slug into the chamber, clicked the safety on. With it under his pillow, he slept better.

When the knock sounded on his door, he opened his eyes, squinting against the morning sun. His watch said eight-thirty. He shucked on his robe, transferred the gun to the pocket of his robe and opened the door.

Dr. Morrison said, "How did she sleep?"

"Fine, as far as I know. Come take a look." He led the doctor into her room.

Marylen had changed position and her breathing was much softer. When Morrison lifted her wrist to take her pulse, she opened her eyes. She looked around the room, her puzzlement showing on her face. Bewilderment began to be mixed with fear. Behind Morrison, Max put his finger to his lips and made exaggerated gestures for her to be quiet. She saw him and her eyes widened.

"Don't sit up, please," Morrison said. He opened his bag, took out a little thing like a flashlight. He held her eyelid back, shone the thin beam into her eye. Then he did the same with the other eye. He gently touched her behind the ear.

"Hurt?" he asked.

"Yes, Doctor," she said in a small voice.

Morrison straightened up. "Try to rest, today. You took a bad beating. I'll leave these pills. One every three hours, please."

Max went with him to the door. Morrison said, "She's tougher than she looks. Sturdy girl. Keep her quiet today."

Max paid him and hurried back to the bedroom. Marylen looked up at him.

"You told me to be still. Why? Who are you? Was it a train wreck?"

"Train wreck!"

She sat up, holding the covers up around her throat. "Yes. Last night I went to sleep in the berth. Who are you? Where are we?"

Max sat down heavily on the straight chair and said, "Concussion."

"What?"

"Marylen, you have a concussion. Or had one. I am—or used to be—a reporter. I know how concussions work. They kick your memory back to a time before the accident."

"Where's Jerry?" she said, her voice rising in fear. "Is he hurt?"

Max held up his big hand. "Now shut up a minute. Let me start from the beginning. My name is Max Raffidy. I was sitting in a bar."

Slowly he went through it, with her wide eyes fastened on him. He left out her description of Jerry doubling over and falling to the concrete floor. He left out his own guesses about Jerry. But he did report the phone call to Jerry's apartment.

When he was quite through she said, "And I thought you were Jerry?"

"I was beginning to think that was my name."

She looked at him speculatively. "You are a little like him. But not much. Mr. Raffidy, this must have been very difficult for you. I'm very grateful to you. I'll—"

"What? Call Jerry? He's out of town. You haven't got a dime and you've got only the clothes I found you in. You haven't even got a lipstick and you don't know a soul in town. You came here, met Jerry, and somehow you two got separated and you were beaten up."

"I can't stay here, though!"

Unmarried Widow

"Marylen, I'm no hero. I'm a reporter out of a job. Jobs are tight in this town right now. They won't hire me cold, but if I can walk in with a fat yarn, an exclusive, then I stand a chance."

Her lips were tight and she had a frightened look. "But—you sound as though something awful might have happened to Jerry!"

"I'm no alarmist, Marylen. But it could happen."

"I could go right to his apartment and talk to the man you talked to over the phone."

"I found out last night that some unsavory types are hunting for you, baby."

She sank back against the pillow. She looked blindly at the ceiling and said, "But I don't understand!"

"How did you meet this Jerry?"

"A year ago I went to a party with one of the girls who worked in the same office. I wouldn't have gone, but I was bored. I don't care for her. She's too loud. It was a cocktail party at a hotel. I met Jerry there. He's—very nice. He travels around, selling machinery and seeing that it's installed properly. He acted very—well, worldly, but he was funny and sweet and shy with me."

"He came down to see you?"

"Five times. The last time he proposed. He said he had certain details to clean up, business details. He said that we'd go out to the West Coast and that he'd have a little capital to start a business of his own with. He would come down and get me and we'd be married and go West together. Then he phoned me. He sounded nervous, said things weren't working quite right. He wanted me to come up here. I agreed. He wanted to send me money for the trip, but I said I had enough. He always seems to have plenty of money."

It was beginning to shape up a bit more clearly. Max thought for a while and then said, "Trust me, Marylen. You stay right here. I'll whip up some breakfast for you. Then I'm going to go to the place where Jerry worked. I'll see what I can find out . . ." As she sipped her coffee, he said, "This is a gun, baby. To fire it, you shove this little gimmick down and then pull on the trigger. Every time you pull it will fire, up to eight times."

"But I don't—"

"Somebody beat you up, honey, and they might want to try again. If someone knocks on the door, keep quiet. If they try to force the door, let them know you are in here with a gun. If they keep it up, shoot at the door. Okay?"

"If you say so, Max."

"That's what I want to hear."

She called, just as he reached the door, "Please get me an orangy shade of lipstick and a hairbrush and toothbrush and toothpaste."

The waiting room was paneled in honey-blond wood, with the combination receptionist-switchboard operator behind a square glass window. Latest magazines were on the low tables. Framed pictures on the wall were color photographs of snow scenes.

The girl said, "Mr. Walch will see you now, Mr. Raffidy."

He went to the door. She touched the release and he pushed it open. Walch had the first office on the left.

He met Max at the doorway. He said, "Max, I was damn sorry to hear about the *Chronicle*. Tough break, fella. Maybe I can give you a note to a friend of mine."

"No, Bill. Thanks anyway. This is something else."

Bill slapped him on the shoulder. "Sit down, boy. Sit down." Walch went behind the desk, sat down, nibbled the end of a cigar and spat in the general direction of the wastebasket.

Max said, "This is pretty delicate, Bill. A couple of days ago I landed a job fronting for a group of citizens who want to open up a club well outside the city. I contacted a man named Norma. I was told he could get me the stuff my clients want for their club. I talked with Norma about an order of about a hundred thousand. He wanted a guarantee of good faith. I went back to my people and got fifteen hundred cash. Naturally I couldn't expect a receipt. Norma said we had to have a conference about a percentage cut after he talked to his principals. I was to meet him last night at five. He didn't show. I called his apartment."

Walch broke in. "I wondered who made that call."

"It was your boy Max. Now he's out of town and I'm in a spot. My clients want to hold off from making any definite commitment for a month or two. Lease trouble on the property they want. They want the fifteen hundred back. I promised it today. I look pretty sick, Bill. I've been around enough to know that you people can't use written records. So you have to go along on faith. What do I do next? I'd hate like hell to spread the word that your outfit had rattled me for a lousy fifteen hundred."

Bill Walch inspected the end of his cigar. For a moment his face was absolutely blank. He said softly, "I'd hate to think you'd gotten yourself a job with another paper, Max. I'd hate to think this was something fancy."

"How fancy can I get? That's your chance, the same way I took a chance with your boy named Norma."

Bill suddenly smiled, a warm and hearty smile. "We can straighten this out fast, Max, boy. I'm expecting a call from Jerry any minute. When it comes in, I'll ask him and we'll soon know. Okay?"

With sinking heart and with an attempt to match Bill's smile, Max said heartily, "That'll be fine. Fine!"

Within a few seconds the phone rang. Bill said, "Be good and go back out into the waiting room, will you? This is pretty confidential. Big out-of-town deal."

On wooden legs Max went to the waiting room. He had the feeling that the gun had been left in the wrong hands. It would feel splendid in his pocket.

It was five minutes before Bill Walch appeared. He came into the waiting room with a wide smile and a long white envelope, saying, "It checked out, Max. Here's your deposit. Come back and see us when your people get their lease attended to. Tell them that for strictly hands off by the county cops as well as the state boys, we'll take ten percent of the gross, based on a monthly audit."

Max went through the motions like a large smiling

mechanical toy. He mumbled words of farewell, backed to the door, found the knob, went on down the corridor to the elevators. As he waited for the bronze arrow to swing up to the right floor, he peeked into the envelope. A flat sheaf of bills. All hundreds. Fifteen of them. He slipped the money out of the envelope, folded it once and slid it into his bill clip, behind a few tired fives and ones.

Down to the street he looked both ways, suddenly wary. It had seemed almost too easy. The tough part was to come—telling Marylen that the way Walch handed over the money was conclusive proof that her sweetie was no longer a matter of interest to the census taker.

He had worked on some fine fat stories, and in the process the *Chronicle* had chewed lightly on the frayed edge of the Concord organization, on the underlings, on the not-too-smart. But never had a lead opened so nicely. And there was no paper to back him. No organization. It was too early in the game to ring in the law. Yet he grinned with a certain satisfaction, and the grin, as always, erased the somewhat moody lines of his heavy face, made him look younger and even a shade reckless.

Yet the hair on the back of his neck seemed to prickle. He walked casually east, stopped to look in a window. A man who had no place to go. The third window of the department store was rigged out as a bedroom, with a plastic dolly sitting on the dressing-table bench. The dressing table had a mirror. It was in that mirror that he saw the one who sauntered on the far side of the street, pausing to cup his hands around a cigarette, tossing the match aside.

And behind the man who sauntered, a car slid to the curb. But nobody got out of it.

Max turned away from the window, walked more rapidly to the corner. As he walked, his mind was busy. Obviously Walch had ordered the tail. But why? Where had there been a slip? Or did Walch still want to cover in case it was a frame and Max was working, on the side, for another paper, or even for one of the perennial civic improvement groups? If Walch was worried enough to employ the tail technique, it would have been easier for him to play dumb about the fifteen hundred.

The obvious thing was to get back to the girl. He picked up a cab at the corner, glanced back in time to see the saunterer swing into the waiting car.

"Uptown," he directed.

After five blocks he leaned forward, handed the driver a bill. He said, "I might leave you in a hurry, friend. Pay no attention."

The driver gave a quick and startled look over his shoulder. Then he looked in the rear vision mirror. He said, "Friend, I'll make a little time and then slow down by the Casualty Trust. Hop out there and go right through the building and with luck you can grab a downtown bus in the next block."

"You are an intelligent and perspicacious citizen."

"Thank you too much."

Max went through the bank at a semi-lope, looking ahead with the expression of a man trying to catch up with someone.

There was no bus, but there was a cab. Max grabbed it, looked back. Three blocks away he thought he saw a tiny figure come hurrying out of the door. He wasn't certain.

He took the chance of giving his own address. The elevator was in use, so he ran up the stairs, breathing hard. He had his key out and stopped absolutely still when he saw the door was ajar. He kicked it open, moved to one side and called, "Marylen!"

The rooms were empty and dusty, and the tired sun made too much of a point of the frayed rug. The keys that had slid from Gruber's hand lay in the sunlight. Gruber's hand was in shadow. The keys were on a chain neatly decorated with a white plastic death's-head. Gruber lay on his face with his legs spread, his toes pointed in. Max cursed slowly and monotonously as he knelt by Gruber. He got his thumb on the right part of the stringy wrist, felt the strong pulse thud. He rolled Gruber over. There was a deep red spot on the point of Gruber's chin.

The girl was gone, and her clothes were gone. On the

dresser, there was a note in sprawling backhand finishing school writing which merely said: "Thanks for everything." The note was weighed down with the Jap automatic. The safety was off. He noticed with clinical detachment that it was a silly way to leave a gun.

Gruber responded to the water treatment, dopey at first, and then violently and thoroughly angry, with all the heat and force that a stringy, sandy little man can develop.

Max finally got the sense of it. Mr. Raffidy had locked the girl in. This friend of hers had come and the friend had asked to have Gruber unlock the door. The girl had seemed eager to have the door unlocked. He remembered the friend, a small plump man with red cheeks, saying, "Miss Banner, Jerry is down in the car waiting for you."

After he had unlocked the door and the girl was in the bedroom dressing, Gruber had stepped in for the expected tip. The man had reached for his hip pocket and then his hand had come up too fast from his hip pocket.

No, Gruber was going directly to the cops. No fat little so-and-so was going to put the slug on him right in his own place. Max blocked the doorway while Gruber danced up and down in a rage, getting even madder as he found a tooth splinter in his mouth.

Max got hold of one of the crisp hundreds. He crackled it, said, "This is to lick your wounds with, Gruber. This is oil for troubled waters. You can gripe all you want with the hundred in your pocket. Or you can yell cop and the hundred is in my pocket."

Gruber's dance of anger slowly settled down into a shuffling of feet and then he said, "A deal. But what are you mixed up in, Mr. Raffidy?"

"Never mind me. What did the guy look like?"

He didn't get more than the original description. Gruber hadn't seen the car. The girl seemed happy, but worried. At least, that's the way her voice sounded. Gruber went down to the elevator, grumbling about a respectable apartment house, and how the hell was he to know what kind of friends Raffidy had.

"Permanently."

"Oh, yes. And then we discovered the blunder. Jerry had a girl with him. She battled vigorously but was finally quieted. My assistant phoned me. I suggested that the young lady be taken to a certain apartment we maintain on Primrose Street. He put her on the floor in the back of the car. In heavy traffic she managed to get the door open and lose herself in the crowd. It was my idea to find out how damaging a witness she might be."

"Why are you telling me all this?"

"You are clever, Mr. Raffidy, in a gaudy way. We picked up the young lady. She faked loss of memory. But when confronted with the man she saw eliminate Mr. Norma, she had a fine case of hysterics. You spent considerable time with the young lady. Doubtless she told you her story. My question is—what am I to do with you?"

"You spoiled my chance of going to the police."

"That was elementary."

"What harm can I do you, Ledecker?"

"I don't know. How can you prove to me that you won't make the attempt?"

"I can't."

"Then this is a type of stalemate, wouldn't you say?"

"Stop horsing, Ledecker. Make your proposition."

"Impatience and impertinence, Mr. Raffidy. Here it is. My people have a strange distaste when it comes to the question of dealing with the girl. They will have no such scruples about you. You can go free from here, Mr. Raffidy, as soon as you have accomplished that slightly messy job."

Max sat very still. "There's no need to ask you what happens if I say that this isn't my line of work."

"No need whatsoever. Please don't think that I enjoy this sort of thing. If you help us take care of the girl, then your mouth will be closed. You need to have no fear of the law unless you try to cross me. We run an efficient place here."

Now was the time to mention the report to Lowery.

Max opened his mouth to speak of it, then closed his lips.

"What were you about to say?"

"Nothing. Nothing at all." To mention the report would definitely seal the girl's death warrant. Then he had another thought. "Why not throw this trusted assistant of yours to the wolves. That sounds easy."

Ledecker's smile was without humor. "The assistant is trusted because he had the good fortune to obtain documentary proof of an earlier indiscretion of mine. That was when I was younger, and not as wise. His position is far, far better than yours, Mr. Raffidy."

Max slouched in the chair. "Just how am I supposed to kill the girl?"

Ledecker frowned. "Please, Mr. Raffidy. Discuss it in business terms."

"Well, how?"

"There's a choice of methods. We can have her taken over into the woods and you can shoot her. Or you can strangle her. Or you can hit her with a heavy object."

"Business terms, eh? Why such rough ways?"

"For their effect on you, Mr. Raffidy. I would prefer that it be a rough way, as you express it."

"Where is she?"

"Roughly sixty feet from you."

"When is all this supposed to take place?"

"Right after dusk, I believe. That should be the best time."

"Where does the body go?"

"We will take several pictures of the body and then it will be disposed of. There's no need for you to know where or how."

"And then?"

"And then, with my blessing, you go on about your business."

"Why not just pick the two of us off? Why tie yourself in knots?"

Ledecker sighed. "There is too big a chance, my boy, that you might have tried to protect yourself with some silly report to the police."

"Suppose I did. Then all I have to do is sit tight."

"Hurt him a little, Joseph," Ledecker said in a strained voice.

Max spun out of the chair and got his back near the wall as Joseph came in. With the expressionless boredom of a professional, Joseph ducked into Max's swing, taking the knuckles against his forehead. He moved in close, grunting with the exertion of each blow.

When Joseph backed away, Max dropped to his hands and knees, then fell over on his side. He pulled his knees up toward his chest and rolled his head from side to side, pushing against the pain, trying to think and plan.

Ledecker stood above him, seeming to sway, to shift back and forth through the mists that the pain brought. His voice was very far away. "There'll be no more lip and no nonsense, Raffidy, damn you!"

Joseph, torpidly satisfied with his work, had gone back to the couch. Max was spinning toward the edge of consciousness, but, as the idea formed, he fought his way back. He wheezed, "Where'd you lose your British accent?"

He saw Ledecker's neat black shoe coming at him. He snapped his head back at the last moment and the foot went by, throwing the man off balance. Max grabbed him by the ankle and spilled him. He grabbed one wrist, twisted the arm up into a punishing hammerlock, got his thick right hand on Ledecker's throat. Joseph came charging across the room.

Max yelled, "Hold it!" He had Ledecker in a sitting position. He said quickly, "Come any closer and I shut my hand on this throat. With one squeeze, I can crush the windpipe."

When Ledecker reached up to claw at the hand, Max tightened the hammerlock. Ledecker painfully groaned, "Move back, Joseph."

Joseph, no longer expressionless, moved slowly back on the balls of his feet.

"I want Joseph to give me the gun he took off me," Max said softly.

"Don't be absurd," Ledecker said. His voice had more confidence.

Max gave a quick hard pressure with his fingers, released it. Ledecker's body shook with the convulsive coughing.

Max said, "Did you feel that, friend? Just a little more than that. Here, I'll try to give you a little more without killing you."

"Wait," Ledecker gasped. "Joseph, give him the gun."

"Boss, I'm not going to get—"

"Do as you're told!"

Max said, "Hold it by the barrel and slide it along the floor. Slide it right over here."

Joseph hesitated for long seconds. The automatic slid along the rug. He released Ledecker's throat, snatched up the gun, scrambled to his feet. It took an effort to straighten his bruised body.

Ledecker stood up slowly. His face was calm. "What now, Raffidy?"

"You and Joseph line up against that wall, face to the wall, feet about a yard from the baseboard. Then lean against the wall, your palms flat against it."

Joseph looked at him with contempt. Max leveled the gun, saying. "So I have to smash your knee, Joe."

Joseph lumbered over to the wall. Max went up behind them. Swinging the automatic in a horizontal arc, he chopped the barrel and trigger guard heavily against Joseph's head, just above the right ear. Joseph's face hit the hardwood floor with a damp, meaty smack. Then keeping the muzzle a few inches from the small of Ledecker's back, he patted the man in all places where a small gun could be concealed.

Ledecker said, "Whatever you're planning, Raffidy, it won't work. I have fifteen employees in this place. Half of them are armed."

Max said mildly, "If you were me, friend, wouldn't you at least give it a whirl? Come on now. Turn around slow. The gun is in my pocket. I'm going to be a half step behind you. Anything I don't care for—and one goes right through you."

He could see the sheen of sweat on the man's face. "Where to?" Ledecker asked.

"Right out the door and down the hall to the stairs. Slowly down the stairs and across the club room and out to the drive. Then into the car. And then to town."

"Anything you suggest, Raffidy."

"And all the time you're walking, you'll be talking to me. Not too loud and not too soft. You'll be explaining some of your equipment. Understand?"

"Perfectly."

"Start talking now."

"One of . . . ah . . . the items we've had the most luck with this year has been a specialty item used in chuckaluck where the operator by merely putting his hand in a certain position to spin the cage, can make the dice . . ."

His voice droned on. The hallway was empty. They met a man on the stairs carrying a tray of drinks. The man backed into the corner of the landing to let them by. The door at the foot of the stairway opened near the bar. Two couples sat at the far end of the club room. Ledecker walked with his back rigid. Max kept what he hoped was an amiable smile on his face. Then out the side door to the parking lot.

Ledecker stopped and said, "The car will be brought over."

The attendant brought the car over, jumped out, left the motor running. A small cement mixer chattered busily at the far end of the parking lot. Several workmen were moving about in a leisurely fashion.

The impact of the slug seemed to come before the brittle sound of the shot. To Max it was as though someone standing behind him had whammed him on the shoulder with a hand sledge. It spun him around so that he faced the door, and he went down the two steps to the gravel, stumbling and falling, rolling onto his back.

His left arm was dead. He couldn't haul the gun out of his right pocket from that position. Ledecker came down the two steps toward him, frantic in his haste to get hold of the gun arm. At the second shot, Ledecker sprawled loosely across Max's thighs. Max looked up, saw Joseph at the upstairs window, revolver aimed, a look of intense dismay on his wide face.

Max immediately realized that Ledecker had, in his eagerness, moved directly into the line of fire. He wiggled out from under Ledecker, scrambled around the car, driving his shoulder into the openmouthed attendant, staggering him off balance. He jumped in behind the wheel, dropped the big car into gear and spun the wheels on the gravel as he heard the faint sound of another shot, heard the thunk of lead against the metal side.

The attendant was racing beside the window, reaching in for the keys. Max swerved the heavy car toward the man, knocking him off his feet. Then he skidded out onto the driveway, turning toward town.

He was dizzy and faint with the shock of the wound. Pain was just beginning. He was grateful for the automatic shift on the car. He steered with his right hand at the top of the wheel, his left hand in his lap.

Captain Lowery said, "Lucky the bones in your shoulder are as thick as the ones in your head. What the hell are you doing? Leaving?"

"If it's okay with the doc, why should you mind? Thanks, nurse. Just hang the coat over my shoulder." The night lights were on in the corridor of the emergency ward.

"We went out there, as you know," Lowery said.

"Thanks."

"Skip the sarcasm. We went out and put the clamp on Joseph. There's a charge against you for trying to kidnap Ledecker, and for stealing the car. They wanted to make it murder, but we found the slug and shot it down to the lab along with Joseph's gun. It matched. But, genius, no girl. No girl at all. Was there ever a girl, or were you just wishing hard?"

"Check with Dr. Morrison, who has his office across the street from where I live. He saw her. Check with Gruber, my building superintendent."

"So there was a girl. I yanked in Walch and Antonelli

and told them some hunks of your story. They laughed until they held on to their sides. Jerry Norma is on a business trip, they think. Ledecker would know, and he's dead. They told me I was getting soft in the head listening to newspaper people. So what do we do now, genius?''

"Can I go along for the ride?"

"To where?"

"We go to the warehouse and we take some lab boys along. Suppose it turns out that there was a girl and that something has happened to her? How about Walch and Antonelli and the rest of the organization?"

Lowery gave the impression of wanting to spit on his hands. "Brother, we get our chance to smack down on the whole outfit. But good."

They parked the two police sedans outside the warehouse. The warrant was in order. The lights were clicked on. Bright lights.

Max said to the lab men, "This grease spot looks like the car was parked here. Norma drove it right in. He got out. He was probably headed that way. See if you can find out if he was shot down."

In a few moments one man reported a well-scrubbed place on the floor. They unstrapped the chemical kit and went to work, testing reagents. Finally one of them said, "Captain, there was blood here. Not too long ago. Maybe human. Can't tell yet."

Lowery himself found a bullet scar on the concrete. By lining it up with the scrubbed place, estimating the degree of ricochet, searching for fifteen laborious minutes, they found the slug half buried in the edge of a two-by-four that supported one shelf of a supply bin.

Lowery said, with a shade less contempt, "Now, genius, you're beginning to click. We'll accept the assumption that Norma was gunned right here and the girl saw it happen. Where to now?"

"They got her out of Valley Farms fast. With the big mess over Ledecker, and with my getting away, they'd be stupid to kill her. They'd hold her for a while to see what happens."

327

"And where would they do that?"

"Ledecker mentioned an apartment on Primrose."

"Nice neighborhood," Lowery said dryly. "Let's roll. This one is legwork."

It was ten o'clock before they had the right building, the right apartment. Lowery dispersed his men to cover all possible means of exit, including two in the courtyard manning the portable spotlight, armed with gas grenades.

At the end of the stairs, Lowery whispered, "Stay right here, Raffidy. This is business."

Max shrugged. It was good to lean against the wall. His shoulder throbbed heavily and incessantly. But when Lowery and his two men went down the hallway to the door, he moved up into the corridor and inched his way down toward the door.

"Open up," Lowery called.

"Who's out there?"

"Police. Open wide and come out with your hands in the air," Lowery ordered.

A different voice, a soft mild voice, said, "Thank you. No."

Lowery let go with the whistle and Max saw the bright thread of light under the edge of the door as the men out in the court turned the spotlight on the window.

Lowery said, "You're covered all the way around. Better come out the easy way or we get you the hard way."

Again the soft voice. "There's a girl in here, Officer."

"That we know!"

"I'm coming out with the girl in front of me. What then?" Max saw Lowery wipe his forehead with the back of his hand. There was a long period of silence.

Lowery said, "You won't make it."

The voice said, "I'll take my chance. Order your men to stand back."

Lowery moved away from the door. He lifted the .38 special in his hands, looked hard at it as though he'd never seen it before. He whispered to the two men with him. They walked heavily down to the end of the hall. Lowery motioned to Max. Max went with them.

Lowery said, "Okay. You're holding the cards. We'll be out of your way. But the moment you get two feet away from that girl—"

"Stop talking," the voice said.

Lowery went twenty feet from the doorway, flattened with his back against the wall, his right arm extended, the special aimed down at the doorway.

The hallway was still. Max heard the creak as the door opened inward. More silence. Then he saw her white face, the long, blond hair, the lightweight suit. She came out, one dragging step after another. He saw the fat pink hand that held her arm, the muzzle of the gun aimed at her head, the other fat hand holding the gun. Then the cheery, round, rosy-cheeked face of the fat little man. As the man's small bright eyes swiveled toward Lowery, Lowery's gun spoke with heavy authority.

The fat little man did not waver. He dropped as suddenly and completely and thoroughly as though he had fallen from a ten-foot height.

Marylen swayed. She turned, like a sleepwalker, and she saw Max. She came down toward him, walking slowly at first, and then running into Max's open arms.

Lowery leaned against the wall. The other man, a replica of Joseph, came out with his hands in the air. Lowery said, half to himself, "It had to be just right. A head shot and the reflex makes him pull the trigger. I had to get him in one spot the size of a dime, where the slug would sever the spinal column."

Max said angrily, "Why not let him go? Why take the chance?"

"Why, you poor damn fool, he'd have killed the girl as soon as he got clear."

Marylen, her face against Max's lapel, said, "I saw him kill Jerry. I remember."

Lowery, his temporary reaction over, said, "And now, Mr. Raffidy, where do we find Jerry Norma's body?"

"They're doing a hell of a lot of cement work at Valley Farms, Captain . . ."

*　　　*　　　*

It was pale, gray dawn and the sounds of the city hadn't yet begun. Lowery, his well-fed face showing the dragging lines of weariness, hung up the phone. He said, "They got him. They'd slapped him in the face with a spadeful of concrete."

"How about Antonelli and Walch?"

"Walch is beginning to crack. When he does, we can use the stuff he gives us to crack Antonelli. The little fat man's name was Stan Norton, Ledecker's blackmailer."

Max said slowly, "And now, Captain, may I phone in everything I know?"

"Hell, are you working?"

"With an exclusive like this? I've been working ever since I phoned in the eyewitness description of Ledecker's death from the hospital."

Lowery sighed. "Can I stop you? I'm going home and get some sleep."

"So am I. I'm going to stop in at Memorial on the way and check on the girl. As soon as she's well, I'll ship her home."

Lowery stood heavily at the doorway. "In some things, Raffidy," he said, "you almost achieve brilliance. However, with women, you're on the dull side."

Max said angrily, "What should I do? Keep her as a good-luck charm?"

But he was talking to the closed door. He managed the difficult feat of lighting a cigarette. He laid the receiver down and started to dial the newspaper number. By now the waiting wolves from the other papers would be plaguing Lowery.

Halfway through the number he stopped dialing, said softly, "Good-luck charm. Hmmm."

He hung up and started dialing again.

You Remember Jeanie

FOR MANY YEARS Bay Street was the place. Bar whiskey for thirty cents a shot, or a double slug for fifty. A waterfront street, where dirty waves slapped at the crushed pilings behind the saloons. A street to forget with. A street which would close in on you, day to day, night to night, until the wrong person saw some pitying old friend slip you a five. They would find you at dawn, and an intern from City General would push your eyelid up with a clean pink thumb and say, "More meat for the morgue."

Maybe, as he stood up, he would look down at your hollow gray face and the sharp bones of your wrists and wonder how you'd kept alive this long. So very long.

But something happened to Bay Street. The smart developers saw what was happening elsewhere, and they conned the city, county and federal government into a glamorous redevelopment project. A huge mall. Parking garages. Waterfront restaurants on new piers, out over the water. A marina. Smaller shopping malls with quaint stores selling antiques, paintings, custom jewelry, Irish weed.

So the old saloons were uprooted, and for a time there was no place at all for the Bay Street bums. Then some of the old places started up again on Dorrity Street, four blocks inland, and soon it was all the same as before, with the stale smell of spilled beer, the steamy chant of

331

the jukes, hoarse laughter, the scuff of broken shoes, the wet sound of fist against flesh.

Frank Bard sat on the stone step of an abandoned warehouse and stared down along Dorrity Street through the misty rain. Across the street the rain made a pink cloud around the red neon of Allison's Grill.

Bard thought vaguely that if the rain increased, he'd have to get under shelter. He didn't want to go inside; he had come out because he had been sick. The muscles of his diaphragm still ached with the violence of his retching. He turned the ragged collar of his dark blue suit coat up around his neck. He wondered if he ought to walk down the alley and see if anybody had tried to move in on him. Two weeks before, he had found a sturdy packing case and, at dawn, had dragged it down the alley and put it under a fire escape. The effort had left him weak and panting. He had filled it with clean burlap and it made a snug bed. The fall rain was chill; the packing case wouldn't be any good in the winter. He forced that thought out of his mind.

He was a dark man, with a sullen face. Once he had been solid, almost stocky, but the flesh had melted off him during the past year. He was still capable of sudden, explosive bursts of energy. His hair was long and his square jaw was dark with several days' beard. His cheeks were hollow and there was a dark wildness in his puffy eyes that the shadows concealed.

Across the street an old man with matted white hair lurched out of Allison's and fell on one knee. He got up and went on, limping and cursing in a thin, high voice, watered down by age.

Frank Bard heard the slow tock, tock of heels, heavy heels, coming down the sidewalk on his side. He knew who it was without looking. He scowled down at the sidewalk. The slow steps stopped.

He looked up. Patrolman Clarence Flynn, tall and solid, stood looking down at him. Flynn's raincoat had a cape effect across the shoulders that made him look larger than life.

He said softly, "You okay, Frankie?"

"Give me a cigarette, Flynn," Bard said hoarsely.

Flynn handed him one, lit it. Over the match flame the two men glanced briefly into each other's eyes—and looked quickly away.

In the same gentle tone, Flynn said, "When are you going to straighten out, Frankie?"

"I like it this way."

"You were a good cop, Frankie. You straighten out and you could come back in; your record's good."

"I like it this way."

"You look sick, Frankie."

"I'm fine. You got a beat to cover."

Flynn shrugged. He handed the half pack of cigarettes to Bard and walked toward his prowl car. He stopped ten feet away and said, "She wasn't worth this, Frankie; no woman was worth this."

Bard called him a foul word and snapped the half-smoked cigarette into the street. After he could no longer hear the sound of Flynn's heels, he tried to light another one. His hands shook so badly that he couldn't do it. The matches were damp. They sputtered and went out quickly.

He felt in his side pocket to make certain that the five quarters were still there. They were cool against his fingertips. He stood up, swaying slightly, and then walked across the street, pushed his way into the heat and smell of Allison's.

The bar was of plywood laid over some heavier substance. Naked bulbs were laid behind the bottles on the back bar, and the light glowed through—amber. The place was narrow and rectangular—with the bar on the left and booths on the right. An ancient jukebox sat against the far wall, bubbles rising endlessly up through the colored tubes. Arthur Allison, a small trim man with truman glasses and a gray mustache, in a spotless white shirt, waited on bar, his quick eyes flickering ceaselessly from face to face. Allison was a watchful, careful man. Jader waited on the booths and, on occasion, acted as bouncer. Jader was tall and heavy with weak eyes that watered constantly. He too was watchful. Underneath

the bar, to the left of the beer taps, was a small drawer
There were usually a few small packages in that drawer
Summer and winter a small hot coal fire burned in the
basement. In the winter, the fire heated the building; in
the summer, the radiators were turned off. On the under
edge of the drawer containing the packages was a small
loop of wire. Either Jader or Allison could, by yanking
on the loop of wire, drop the bottom of the drawer. The
little packages would then drop down a chute into the
fire. It was safer that way. For every package held and
relayed to the proper pickup men, there was a fee of one
hundred dollars. Thirty for Jader and seventy for Allison
On some days as many as eight packages spent varying
lengths of time in the drawer.

Allison and Jader were very watchful and cautious
men.

When Frank Bard walked in, there were four men at
the bar. He knew three of them by sight; the fourth was
a stranger. Two of the booths were occupied. In one
were two Swedish merchant seamen and a thin painted
girl with hair the color of ripe tomatoes and a wet
smeared mouth. In the second booth were two quiet
men wearing dark topcoats. Bard glanced at them and
guessed that they were waiting for one of the packages
to arrive.

Bard did a curious thing. He held the door wide, and
as he walked over to the bar, he smiled down over his
right shoulder. He said something in a low voice.

He stepped up beside the stranger, still smiling down
at a point about six inches from his right shoulder.
Allison moved over toward him and said, "You got the
money, Frank?"

He took the dollar in quarters from his pocket and
said, "The usual for me and Jeanie, Arthur." Allison
poured two straight ryes and smiled tiredly as he put one
in front of Bard and one in front of the empty space
Bard said, "You wouldn't rather sit in a booth, would
you, Jeanie?"

"What the hell do you keep asking her that for?

Arthur said. "She never wants to sit in a booth; she always stands up here at the bar with you."

Bard looked vaguely indignant. "It's polite to ask her, Arthur."

The stranger, a lean man in work clothes with a pinched, bitter mouth, looked with pained disgust at Frank Bard and then at Allison. "What the hell goes on?" he asked.

Allison looked amused. "Oh, Frank comes in here all the time with Jeanie."

Frank Bard turned and looked at the stranger. "Jeanie and me, we like this place. She likes to come here even if she did have a little bad luck here a little over a year ago."

The stranger looked into Bard's eyes and moved back a few inches. "Bad luck?" he inquired politely.

"Yeah. Jeanie was in here late one night and some lush hit her with a bottle. Hit her right over the left ear. I guess my Jeanie hasn't got such a tough skull. Funny how it didn't break the bottle, hey, Arthur?"

Jader came over, his pale eyes watering. He said, "Damn it, Arthur, why do you let this nut come in here?"

Arthur grinned. "Nervous?"

"No, the guy drives away trade." He turned to the stranger. "Mister, a drunk bashed her head in with a bottle and got clean away. We give the cops a description but they never found the guy." He paused and glanced at Bard, who was talking to Jeanie in a low voice, almost a whisper. He continued. "And this thing used to be a cop. Jeanie was his girl. He's been on the skids for a year, and every time he comes in here he's got that damn imaginary woman with him. I tell you, it's enough to drive me nuts."

Arthur grinned tightly. "Where's your sense of humor, Jader?"

Jader looked again at Bard, cursed and wandered off. The Swedes were pounding on the table.

Frank Bard bent low over his glass of rye. He lifted it with a quick motion, and downed it. It caught in his throat. He gagged, but it stayed down. He stood for a moment, savoring the glow of it, feeling immediately stronger, more confident. He glanced at the wall above the back bar, whistling softly. His lean hand, dirt stained into the knuckles, reached slowly out, shoving the empty glass over toward Jeanie. The hand hooked around her full glass and brought it back. He glanced down, as though surprised to see the full drink in front of him. He drank it with a steadier hand and smiled at Jeanie.

"Taste good to you, honey? If I had the dough, I'd buy you another." He took out his last quarter. He glanced over and said, "What was that, honey?"

He beckoned to Arthur. "Arthur, Jeanie says . . ."

"Yeah, I know. She wants a beer chaser." He picked up the coin, drew one beer and set it in front of Jeanie. Bard whistled again, while his right hand stole out and slid it over. He drank it quickly and, again looking at the wall, shoved the glass over in front of Jeanie.

The stranger said, "You were a cop?"

Bard looked at him and drew himself up, looking for a fraction of a second out of the wise, confident policeman's eyes. The expression faded and his eyes once more looked hot and wild. "What's it to you!" he demanded hoarsely. "I don't see you buying me and Jeanie no drinks; buy 'em and we'll talk to you, mister."

The man took hold of Bard's shoulder with what was almost gentleness. He turned him so that he faced him directly. The work-hardened hand came across, smacking solidly, fingers open, across Bard's jaw, knocking him against the bar. The hand came back in a backhand blow that straightened him up again, splitting his under-lip at the corner.

Frank Bard stood unsteadily, his hands at his side, grinning foolishly at the stranger, his eyes filling with tears from the burning pain in his lip.

Arthur said, "Take it easy!"

The stranger said, "That's for being a lousy cop; that's for nothing. You there, set up drinks for Prince Charming and his lady."

"Thanks," Bard said humbly.

"Think nothing of it, Prince." The man turned his back.

Bard drank the two drinks and stood holding on to the edge of the bar. His face grayed and he said, "Excuse me, honey."

He lurched off to the men's room and was ill. He came out in a few minutes, still shaking, his clothes soiled, and stopped by the bar. He said, "Come on, Jeanie." He walked toward the door. Jader crossed close beside him. With wild fury, Bard grabbed Jader's arm and spun him around. He said, "Why the hell don't you watch where you're going?"

He bent over suddenly, as though helping someone up from the floor. He snarled at Jader, "Okay. Okay. Go around knocking women down and don't apologize. You all right, honey?" he said softly, making brushing motions in the air. Jader grunted, balled a large white fist and slowly drew it back, his wet eyes narrowed.

Arthur snapped, "Jader! Hold it!"

The big hand unclenched and Bard walked to the door, held it open with a small bow and then walked out.

Jader said, "Arthur, I'm not going to stand for . . ."

"Shut up!" The gray eyes were cold behind the lenses, the mouth a thin tight line under the mustache. The girl with the Swedes giggled. Jader turned and walked toward the back of the place.

In the alley Frank Bard stood, his hand on the corner of the packing case, looking up at the night sky. The rain had stopped and small clouds scudded across the moon. Bard dropped to his knees and crawled into the box. He lay with his face against the damp wood and tears ran down through the thick stubble on his cheeks. He reached awkwardly into his side pocket and pulled out a small package. He unwrapped the paper. It contained a small cool metal tube that still contained lipstick. Her lipstick. He held it close to his nose. It held the elusive scent of her. His fingertips touched the little skein of hair. Her hair. Long and pale and delicate—amazingly golden. He wrapped the package and replaced it in his pocket. After a long time, he slept.

Jader was in a good mood. The drawer was almost full of packages and the first pickup was due in an hour. Arthur Allison had gone to the races. It was the first time Jader had been alone in the place in many months. He liked the feeling of being trusted. The sun was hot on Dorrity Street. It slanted through the smeared front window, lighting the dim interior. One old man was asleep, his head on the booth table. Jader planned to wake him up and get him out soon.

He glanced across the street and his cheerful smile faded. He saw Frank Bard coming diagonally across the street in the sun, looking down at a spot six inches from his right shoulder. Jader could see his lips moving. Jader's lip curled as he saw Bard's gray, shapeless shoes, the tired scuff of his walk, the stained, baggy trousers.

He stepped over into the doorway as Bard opened the door. Jader didn't move. Bard said, "Hey! Let us in!" He took a dollar out of his side pocket and held it up.

"I don't want no screwballs in here," Jader said sullenly.

"Where's Arthur? Arthur lets us come in. Get out of Jeanie's way, Jader."

"You're not coming in."

Bard stared at him for a few seconds. "Arthur won't like to hear about this. You got a public place here."

"You stand up to the bar and talk to the other customers. The hell with that noise. You drive away business."

Frank Bard considered that statement solemnly. "Okay. So Jeanie and me, we'll take the back booth in the end and we won't talk to anybody, will we, Jeanie?"

Jader glanced down the street, saw a familiar sedan coming. It would be best not to delay pickup. He moved aside. "Okay, come on in and take the end booth. I'll be with you in a minute."

Bard stood aside as though to let someone come in, and then followed. Jader waited until Bard was out of

338

sight in the booth before slipping the package across to the slim, dark man who had ordered the beer. The man drank up and left.

Jader poured two ryes and walked back to the booth with them. Frank Bard smiled up at him. "No, she's sitting right there across from me, Jader. Maybe we should take a booth oftener. It's nice and private back here in the end. Jeanie says it's nice and clean. Clean ashtray and everything. She don't mind being in the booth where she got hit. Do you, Jeanie?"

Jader scowled. "The place is good and clean because I clean it. Stop the chatter and give me the buck."

He went behind the bar, rang up the dollar and stood with his fat arms on the bar, looking gloomily across at the old man sleeping. Some of the flavor had gone out of the day with Frank Bard's arrival. He seldom showed up in the afternoon. It was just damn bad luck that he had to pick that afternoon, Jader thought.

He scowled as he heard the low sound of Bard's voice. Jader couldn't imagine why Arthur permitted Bard to come around—in fact, why he seemed amused to have Bard around. It was the type of wry joke that Jader couldn't savor.

When he heard Bard call hoarsely for another round, he pushed away from the bar, drew two more ryes and walked slowly back to the booth.

He stood in front of the booth and reached out to set one rye down across from Bard. The big white hand stopped in midair and Jader stared at the ashtray. There were two butts in the ashtray. The tip of one was crimsoned with lipstick. For a moment he thought wildly that he hadn't cleaned it. And he suddenly remembered Bard's saying it was clean. The shot glass slipped out of his white fingers and dropped, overturning on the table.

"Where'd that come from?" he said in a thin voice.

"The cigarette butt? Jeanie smoked it."

"Don't say that!" Jader said wildly.

"Don't you like women smoking? That's old-fashioned," Bard said severely.

"Where'd it come from?" Jader demanded again.

"I told you, from Jeanie." Bard suddenly leaned his dark head over and looked at his shoulder. He chuckled mildly. "She was sitting right beside me here with her head on my shoulder when she smoked it. Look here." From the surface of the dark blue coat he plucked two long strands of shining gold—held them up.

Jader's mouth worked and the other glass dropped at his feet.

Bard said, "You see, Jader, you only thought you killed her." His tone was quiet, as though explaining to a child.

Jader made a strangled sound. His wet eyes widened. "I killed her. She couldn't . . . She couldn't . . ."

He turned then and looked into Frank Bard's eyes. His underlip hung away from his teeth and he took a slow step away from the booth. Somehow Bard was in front of him. Jader clenched his white fists and struck blindly. He missed and went off balance as Frank Bard's thin, dirty fist smashed his mouth. He fell heavily to his hands and knees, going over onto his side as one of the gray, broken shoes landed against the side of his head. One of the white hands lay, as still as lard, against the floor. Frank Bard set his heel on the fingers and swiveled his entire weight, slowly.

He walked quickly to the front door and locked it. The old man still slept. He went behind the bar and carefully opened the drawer. Allison and Jader were cautious, watchful men—but who suspicions or fears a mad alcoholic? He set six neat packages on the top of the bar, opened the cash register and took a dime for the pay phone.

"Sergeant Sullivan, Police Headquarters."

"Sully, this is Frank Bard . . . Don't interrupt me . . . I'm at Allison's Grill on Dorrity Street. I've just taken over the joint. Jader confessed to killing Jean Palmray. The angle is that she was trying to do some independent spying to help me along and they got wise and Jader killed her; I think he only meant to stun her. I've got a bunch of junk here. Six small packages. Send the boys.

340

And have Arthur Allison picked up out at the track. Yeah.''

He hung up, walked back and looked at Jader. The man was beginning to stir. Bard kicked him in the head again and walked back to the bar. He was suddenly enormously tired. He still held the small golden tube of lipstick in his fist. He slipped it into his pocket.

They wouldn't take a lush back on the force, even if he had done what he'd set out to do one year before.

Too late.

He took a bottle off the back bar and pulled the patent gimmick out of the top of it and tilted it up to his lips. Drunk or sober, he had remembered to pretend that Jeanie had been with him. That was what had counted. The buildup. And after a year of buildup, Jader had cracked wide open. It had been tough, pretending that she was always beside him, looking at him.

He tilted the bottle, and as the sharp liquor filled his mouth, he felt a soft touch on his arm. He spun quickly, spraying liquor onto the bar.

The old man was still asleep in the booth and Jader was still silent on the floor. The door was locked. In the distance an approaching siren moaned softly. The bottle slipped from his hand and shattered on the floor.

ABOUT THE AUTHOR

JOHN D. MACDONALD'S career as a writer began in 1946, when his first work of fiction appeared in *Story Magazine*. Since then he has published sixty-nine novels (including the twenty about Travis McGee), two works of nonfiction, and more than five hundred magazine stories. His books have sold more than seventy million copies worldwide. Mr. MacDonald and his wife make their home in Sarasota, Florida.